South University Library
Richmond Campus
2151 Old Brick Road
Glen Allen, Va 23060

Darkly Perfect World

DARKLY PERFECT WORLD

COLONIAL ADVENTURE, POSTMODERNISM, AND AMERICAN NOIR

STANLEY ORR

THE OHIO STATE UNIVERSITY PRESS / *COLUMBUS*

Copyright © 2010 by The Ohio State University.
All rights reserved.

Library of Congress Cataloging-in-Publication Data
Orr, Stanley, 1967–
  Darkly perfect world : colonial adventure, postmodernism, and American noir / Stanley Orr.
    p. cm.
  Includes bibliographical references and index.
  ISBN-13: 978-0-8142-1125-0 (cloth : alk. paper)
  ISBN-10: 0-8142-1125-9 (cloth : alk. paper)
  ISBN-13: 978-0-8142-9223-5 (cd-rom)
  1. Detective and mystery stories, American—History and criticism. 2. Noir fiction, American—History and criticism. 3. American fiction—19th century—History and criticism. 4. American fiction—20th century—History and criticism. 5. Film noir—United States—History and criticism. I. Title.
  PS374.D4077 2010
  813'.087209—dc22
                                  2009041921
This book is available in the following editions:
Cloth (ISBN 978-0-8142-1125-0)
CD-ROM (ISBN 978-0-8142-9223-5)

Cover design by Laurence J. Nozik
Type set in Adobe Minion Pro
Text design by Juliet Williams
Printed by Thomson-Shore, Inc.

∞ The paper used in this publication meets the minimum requirements of the American National Standard for Information Sciences—Permanence of Paper for Printed Library Materials. ANSI Z39.48-1992.

9 8 7 6 5 4 3 2 1

For Cheryl, Hazel, and the Fellers

CONTENTS

ACKNOWLEDGMENTS ix

INTRODUCTION Ties Are Out 1

CHAPTER ONE The Continental Operations of Dashiell Hammett 14

CHAPTER TWO Raymond Chandler's Semi-tropical Romance 53

CHAPTER THREE Dark Places: Late-Victorian Adventure and Film Noir 88

CHAPTER FOUR Veterans of Noir: Rewriting the Good War
with Chester Himes, Dorothy B. Hughes, and John Okada 106

CHAPTER FIVE Noir and the Postmodern Novel 133

CHAPTER SIX To Look at Him or Read Him:
The Confidence Man in Postmodernist Film Noir 166

CONCLUSION Connected Guys:
The Reconstructed Subject of 1990s Film Noir 198

NOTES 211
WORKS CITED 219
INDEX 235

ACKNOWLEDGMENTS

Unlike a noir protagonist, I had a great deal of help in completing this project.

My wife Cheryl Edelson screened films, discussed ideas, read drafts, and provided unlimited encouragement. Our daughter Hazel radiated good cheer during the final and most arduous stages of the process; and she enjoined me to read something other than crime fiction.

I would also like to thank my parents Kay Eaves and Chuck ("Wrap it up, bud") Orr for boundless confidence and support, including cable and video rental subscriptions in the early years.

I am deeply grateful to staff at The Ohio State University Press—most particularly Sandy Crooms, Eugene O'Connor, and Juliet Williams—for their patience and consideration at every turn. Heartfelt thanks to Martin Kevorkian for invaluable reviews of the manuscript; his contribution cannot be overstated. I am also indebted to Sean McCann, whose keen insights led me to sharpen the focus of *Darkly Perfect World*.

Throughout the years, James Goodwin, of the English Department at UCLA, reviewed various stages of the project and offered sage council; thanks also to UCLA's Richard Lehan, N. Katherine Hayles, and Steve Mamber. One chapter emerged from a paper delivered at the 1998 MLA Convention in San Francisco; I have valued E. Ann Kaplan's response to that talk. And I would like to acknowledge Prof. Steven G. Axelrod for kindling my obsession with film noir—in a poetry class. Thank you!

I received a sabbatical leave at California Baptist University; this release was granted at just the right time. I would also recognize California Baptist University and the University of Hawai'i, West O'ahu, for enabling conference presentations relevant to this study.

Two portions of the book began as journal articles. An earlier version of chapter 3 was published in *Dark Alleys of Noir,* PARADOXA, no. 16 (2002)—www.paradoxa.com—and is reprinted with permission. Part of chapter 6 appeared as "Postmodernism, *Noir,* and *The Usual Suspects,*" reprinted with permission of *Literature/Film Quarterly* @ Salisbury University, Salisbury, MD, 21801. I appreciate the opportunities afforded by these journals.

Many friends and colleagues have provided advice, conversation, and moral support: special thanks to David L. G. Arnold, Jac Asher, Jeremiah Axelrod, Mack Brandon, Brian Carver, Melissa Conway, John Dalton, Curtis Gruenler, Lezlie Gruenler, Mark Hanson, James Lu, Tim Luther, Jed Nesmith, Tanya Paull, and Rob Perrin.

INTRODUCTION

TIES ARE OUT

In 1995, First Brands Corp., the manufacturer of GLAD® bags and plastic wrap, introduced a trash bag with built-in "Quick-Tie™ Flaps": doubling as fastener and handle, the innovative flaps allow consumers to dispense with inconvenient twist ties. As part of its multimillion dollar investment in the tieless bag, First Brands hired the Chicago-based Leo Burnett Agency which in turn embarked upon a "Ties Are Out, Flaps Are In" publicity campaign. Working with famed portrait photographer Annie Leibovitz and legendary actor Robert Mitchum, the Burnett Agency came up with an unusual image with which to market the new bag.[1] Appearing in magazines such as *Better Homes and Gardens,* this uncropped two-page color photograph features trench-coated Robert Mitchum standing in a rain-swept alley, fixing the camera with his impassive gaze. In the background to Mitchum's right, we see a pile of bagged garbage. Mitchum isn't wearing a tie, and the caption to our left, printed over another photograph of a garbage bag, reads "Ties Are Out. Flaps Are In." The ad seems to suggest that until the day that "a real rain will come and wash all the scum off the streets," as Travis Bickle (Robert de Niro) hopes in Martin Scorsese's *Taxi Driver* (1976), GLAD makes it a little easier for the consumer to manage the detritus of the modern wasteland. However successful at publicizing the tieless bag, Leibovitz's photograph also tells us a number of things about the status of the noir ethos at the end of the twentieth century. An optimist might celebrate the apotheosis of noir: no longer banished to the margins of mainstream culture, the noir hero embodied by Mitchum has

1

joined the ranks of the classical detective and the cowboy in western cultural iconography. The purist, on the other hand, may inversely see "Ties are out" as an instance of unqualified commodification, the final concession of an aesthetic and philosophical position that long enjoyed an agonistic relationship with the mass-cultural mainstream. The noir ethos that once delivered relentless jeremiads within and against the culture industries of pulp fiction and the Hollywood studio system has been recruited to sell garbage bags as well as Victoria's Secret lingerie and auto insurance, to mention just a few commercial applications.[2] But whether we applaud or derogate the mass-cultural assimilation of noir, we cannot deny that this distinctive vision of self and world has for over a century performed a powerful and manifold cultural work.

In *Darkly Perfect World* I assess this work by charting a trajectory of noir from immediate pretexts in the late nineteenth-century through twentieth- and twenty-first century transformations. I offer a critique of noir epistemology and discuss at length a series of texts that represent the postmodernist reception of hard-boiled detective fiction and film noir. We begin with a location of literary and cinematic noir within the context of western colonialism. My central contention is that noir entertains a recuperative relationship with its primary "host genres." Whereas the dialogue between late-Victorian fictions of mystery and adventure reveals an identity crisis immediately exacerbated by the colonial encounter, noir arrives at its subject through a constructive strategy of "authenticating alienation"—a radical polarization of western self and colonial other. For the noir imagination, "ties are out" in that its subject comes into being not through networks of relationship but rather in sharp contrast to the darkening modern metropolis. The majority of this study, however, is devoted to what Linda Hutcheon[3] terms "postmodernist parody"—novelists and cineastes who recast noir, variously subverting and revising its fundamental discursive formations. Though by no means exhaustive, *Darkly Perfect World* treats a broad spectrum of primary fictional and cinematic texts, offering a flexible paradigm for reading noir into the twenty-first century.

Before embarking on any journey "down these mean streets," we must run a gauntlet all but peculiar to the study of noir. On one side, there are the dictates of scholarship which demand a rigorous situation of the very term "noir." As James Naremore has pointed out, early theorists were unclear about the appellation in the 1940s and '50s, and the ambiguity persists. Rather like a noir protagonist, the scholar falls into a Sisyphean task of identifying this elusive and unwieldy cultural phenomenon.[4] Naremore offers what is perhaps the most sensible response when he suggests that the "baggy concept" of noir "functions rather like big words such as *romantic* or *classic*": "An ideological concept with a history all its own, it can be used to describe a period, a movement, or a recurrent style. Like all critical terminology, it tends to be reductive, and it sometimes works on behalf of unstated agendas. For these reasons and because the meaning changes over time, it ought to be examined as a discursive construct. It nevertheless has heuristic value, mobilizing specific themes that are worth further consideration" (6). In a similarly provisional spirit, I would maintain that terms such as noir remain useful as long as they are subject to critique and revision. Slavoj Žižek suggests one of the most enabling labels for noir contending that the phenomenon is not a genre, as such, but rather a "logic" which pervades other genres:

> From the very beginning *film noir* was not limited to hard-boiled detective stories: reverberations of *film noir* motifs are easily discernable in comedies (*Arsenic and Old Lace*), in westerns (*Pursued*), in political (*All the King's Men*) and social dramas (*Weekend's End*), etcetera. Do we have here the secondary impact of something that originally constitutes a genre of its own (the *noir* crime universe), or is the crime film only one of the possible fields of application of the *noir* logic, that is, is '*noir*' a predicate that entertains towards the crime universe the same relationship as towards a comedy or western, a kind of logical operator introducing the same anamorphic distortion in every genre it is applied to, so that the fact that it found its strongest application in the crime film is ultimately a historical contingency? . . . My thesis is that the 'proper,' detective *film noir* as it were *arrives at its truth*—in Hegelese: realizes its notion only by way of its fusion with another genre. . . . (200; emphasis in original)[5]

Whatever its shortcomings,[6] Žižek's transgeneric theory is compelling because it allows us to understand the dialogues that arise between noir and its "host-genres." As Žižek points out, the detective story is the most prominent host-genre for noir; and while the other genres that Žižek mentions are quite relevant, the list excludes a prominent generic intertext that has largely escaped critical attention: the colonial adventure story.[7] Indeed, noir represents a continuation and recuperation of the colonial discourses immanent in both the late-Victorian adventure and detective genres.

In *Dreams of Adventure, Deeds of Empire,* Martin Green argues for adventure tales as "the energizing myth of British imperialism [,] . . . the story England told itself as it went to sleep at night; and, in the form of dreams, they charged England's will with the energy to go out into the world and explore, conquer, and rule" (3). Green here suggests the first phase in a conventional three-stage scheme of generic transformation.

In texts ranging from Shakespeare's *The Tempest* (1611) through Daniel Defoe's *Robinson Crusoe* (1719) to the Victorian boys' books of G. A. Henty, the British imperial adventure formula turns upon a routine of travel, conquest, and return. As Patrick Brantlinger's has it, "the 'benighted' regions of the world, occupied by mere natives, offer brilliantly charismatic realms of adventure for white heroes, usually free from the complexities of relations with white women. Afterward, however, like Ulysses the heroes sail home, bank their treasures or invest their profits . . . and settle into patriarchal, domestic routines" (12). Following Green, Brantlinger implies the oppositions essential to imperial adventure—white/black, dark/light—unproblematically aligned with issues of race, morality, and spirituality.

But such categories become somewhat more problematic in what Brantlinger terms the "dusk" of imperial adventure. Throughout this second phase, which corresponds to the late-Victorian waning of British imperial confidence, there arises a species of adventure tale gripped by anxieties of metropolitan decay and colonial dissolution: "After the mid-Victorian years the British found it increasingly difficult to think of themselves as inevitably progressive; they began worrying instead about the degeneration of their institutions, their culture, their racial 'stock.'" The central themes Brantlinger discerns in "imperial Gothic" may be applied to late-Victorian adventure as a whole: "individual regression or going native; an invasion of civilization by the forces of barbarism or demonism; and the diminution of opportunities for adventure in the modern world" (230). This is the world of Rudyard Kipling, Robert Louis Stevenson, Louis Becke, and Joseph Conrad: a universe in which the evangelical project of adventure has devolved into crass commercialism and in which the European adventurers themselves devolve into savagery through miscegenation and hyperbolic violence. Brantlinger concludes with this terminal point of adventure, identifying Conrad's vision as the "darkness" which ensues after the "dusk" of the genre. Following Chinua Achebe, however, Brantlinger finds Conrad's indictment of imperialism in *Heart of Darkness* superficial and ambivalent: "He paints Kurtz and Africa with the same tar-brush. His version of evil—the form taken by Kurtz's Satanic behavior—is going native. Evil, in short, *is* African in Conrad's story; if it is also European, that is because some white men in the heart of darkness behave like Africans" (262).

Foregrounding Anglo-Australian literature, Robert Dixon elaborates Brantlinger's scheme of the diurnal exhaustion of the adventure story. According to Dixon, the imperial adventure story, "an archive of all that seemed already known about race, gender, nation, and empire" (200), bottoms in the "ripping yarns" of Stevenson and Australian writer/adventurer

Louis Becke. Formally dispersed into novella and short story, *fin-de-siècle* stories such as Stevenson's "The Beach of Falesá" (1892–93), alongside Becke's *By Reef and Palm* (1894) and *The Ebbing of the Tide* (1896), "strip the discourse of adventure of any semblance of moral justification, exposing its sordid economy of 'trade' and its connection with masculine violence" (180). For Dixon, however, Brantlinger underestimates the masculine adventure's potential for renewal: "At the very moment when adventure stories seemed to express the decline of the imperial ideal and a revision of its code of aggressive, militant manliness, they also sought to overcome that *fin-de-siècle* mood, not by rejecting masculine adventure, but by investment in a process of regeneration through violence." Dixon then turns to Becke's *The Pearl Divers of Roncador Reef* (1908), in which a group of entrepreneurs "go to the realm of adventure, the Pacific, find loot, and use semilegal violence to destroy a villain who personifies the dangerous form of manliness they themselves require for renewal" (190–91). He sees a refreshed adventure form carry on the twentieth century through popular writers such as Ion Idriess and Frank Clune, who, throughout the 1940s and '50s, represent a third, "regenerative" phase of the adventure formula.

Late-Victorian adventure stories reflect and reinscribe profound anxieties within the western cultural imagination, doubts not only about the failure of the colonial enterprise but also about the integrity of the metropolis. It is hardly surprising that the detective story emerges throughout the nineteenth century as a counterpoint to imperial/colonial declension. Within conventional literary historiographies, the Victorian detective embodies Enlightenment rationalism and empiricism. In William Spanos's phrase, the genre projects "the comforting certainty that an acute 'eye,' private or otherwise, can solve the crime with resounding finality by inferring causal relationships between clues which point to it" (150). Under the influence of Michel Foucault, discussions of the "detecting eye" turn from homologies about intellectual history to investigations of the disciplinary power of vision; as D. A. Miller suggests, "Detective fiction is . . . always implicitly punning on the detective's brilliant *super-vision* and the police supervision that it embodies. His intervention marks an explicit bringing-under surveillance of the entire world of the narrative" (35). In his seminal detective fictions, Edgar Allan Poe recognizes the regulatory forces at work within a disciplinary society, but seeks to reassign panoptic power from the faceless machine of the prison to the aristocratic sleuth Chevalier Auguste Dupin.[8] An emphasis on the disciplinary subtext of detective fiction also broaches colonial discourse. A species of "imperial Gothic," Victorian detective fiction often treats "exotic invasions." Interpreted against the prototypical plantation fiction "The Gold Bug" (1843), which conflates detective ratiocination, aristocratic empowerment, and slavery, "The Murders in the Rue Morgue" (1841) reads as a tale of metropolitan corruption: a weak and irresponsible colonial adventurer introduces an exotic and savage menace into the heart of Europe and the mayhem that ensues is curbed only by the *noblesse oblige* intervention of the detective.[9] Common throughout the Victorian detective stories of Wilkie Collins and Charles Dickens, such Orientalism dominates the fictions of Arthur Conan Doyle: many Sherlock Holmes stories, among them the inaugural novellas *A Study in Scarlet* (1887) and *The Sign of Four* (1890), emphasize threats of colonial enervation and invasion. As Laura Otis points out, Holmes's "calling consists largely of detecting foreign blackmailers, thieves, tyrants, intelligence agents, counterfeiters, women, drugs, and diseases that have worked their way into British society" (91).

Victorian adventure and detection therefore entertain a contrapuntal relationship; what the "defective" colonial adventurer and the metropolitan sleuth have in common, however, is a permeability, an atavism, realized or potential, which calls into question the binary categories of imperial Self and colonial Other. Against the ideal of "inner directed" imperialists, such fictions present the colonial enterprise as a threat not only to life but to identity itself. Just as Dupin corrects the Maltese sailor in "The Murders in the Rue Morgue" and Sherlock Holmes apprehends the likes of Jonathan Small in *The Sign of Four,* the detective genre as a whole very generally works to suggest some possibility of containing "defective" colonials and transgressive indigenes alike. But the sleuth capable of accomplishing this police-work is also a strangely permeable figure. The staid and portly Dr. Watson, Otis contends, embodies an empire "in decline, under siege, and dubious in its capacity to reproduce and renew itself" (99). Holmes is even more suspicious as he wanders incognito throughout colonial and "endo-colonial" worlds and is, moreover, addicted to a "seven-percent solution" of cocaine that stimulates the intellect between cases. For Christopher Keep and Don Randall, this eccentric habit gives rise to "an implicit homology between the punctured body of the great detective and the body politic of England itself": "Just as the nation struggles with a foreign conspiracy that has been released into its blood stream by the events of [the Indian Mutiny of] 1857, so too Holmes is represented as dangerously 'occupied' by a drug with distinct Orientalist overtones, one which threatens his physical health as surely as the Mutiny threatened the health of the empire" (207). The colonial adventurer who "crosses the beach" is often tinctured with indigenous tattoos; Holmes likewise becomes "all dotted and scarred with innumerable puncture marks" (5). Contrary to the rational/empirical Holmes metonymically associated with the magnifying glass is the Holmes of the syringe: an addicted and perforated figure no less compromised than the defective colonial.

As Leibovitz's portrait of Robert Mitchum attests, the noir protagonist is most often associated not with the magnifying glass, but rather the trenchcoat, a garment that symbolizes the hard-boiled detective's alienated disposition. For John Cawelti, "the hard-boiled detective is a traditional man of virtue in an amoral and corrupt world. His toughness and cynicism form a protective coloration forming the essence of his character, which is honorable and noble" (*Adventure, Mystery, and Romance* 152). Read in terms of colonial discourse, however, the noir ethos appears not so much a modernist exposure of the classical detective story as a recuperative response to the defective tendencies that literally "mark" both the late-Victorian detective and adventurer. Unlike these porous subjects, the noir protagonist enjoys a discrete identity: the hermetic trenchcoat coheres as much as it protects. In *Gunfighter Nation,* Richard Slotkin describes the hard-boiled detective as a rejuvenated figure, "a recrudescence of the frontier hero [and] an agent of regenerative violence through whom we imaginatively recover the ideological values, if not the material reality, of the mythic Frontier" (228). The cornerstone of this study is the notion that the noir subject is not only regenerated through violence, but also authenticated through alienation. Whether triumphant or defeated, the noir protagonist follows the late imperial adventurer in that he owns nothing of the confidence and integration of his Victorian predecessors. And yet this sense of estrangement enables a recuperated, alienated subjectivity. I derive the phrase "authenticating alienation" from Terry Eagleton, who argues that postmodernism dismisses even the degree-zero realities of modernity: "[T]he very concept of alienation must secretly posit a dream of authenticity which postmodernism finds quite unintelligible. Those flattened surfaces and hollowed interiors are not 'alienated' because there is no longer any subject to be alienated and nothing to be alienated from, 'authenticity' having been less rejected than merely forgotten" (132). In "The Ecstacy of Communication" (1987), Jean Baudrillard similarly clarifies alienation as a means of self-fashioning when he writes, "Certainly, this private universe was alienating to the extent that it separated you from others—or from the world, where it was invested as a protective enclosure, an imaginary protector, a defense system. But it also reaped the symbolic benefits of alienation, which is that the Other exists, and that otherness can fool you for the better or the worse" (130). In a bold response to its Victorian pretexts, the noir ethos transforms a metrocolonial identity crisis into an unlikely guarantor of identity: savage otherness creates a "protective enclosure" of alienated, authenticated subjectivity. Like the plastic garbage-bag, the hard-boiled detective's trenchcoat may ultimately retain as much as it excludes.

The first chapters of *Darkly Perfect World* address ways in which noir alienation "fools us for better or worse": I investigate a series of noir writers and filmmakers who recuperate the tradition of late-Victorian adventure by exploiting cultural memories of California as a fantastic and dangerous colonial frontier. While Dashiell Hammett evokes the ripping yarns of Louis Becke, steering exotic adventure into the urban jungle of his San Francisco detective stories, Raymond Chandler recalls in *The Big Sleep* (1939) a nonfiction adventure pretext: Benjamin Truman's 1874 promotional tract *Semi-tropical California*. In contrast to Truman's utopian Los Angeles, which yields to Angloamerican colonization, Chandler's L.A. is a wasteland that consumes adventurers such as General Sternwood and Rusty Regan. The section concludes with a treatment of the centrality of adventure motifs within "canonical" film noir. Drawing upon films by Josef von Sternberg, Orson Welles, Billy Wilder, and Rudolph Maté, I argue that film noir rehearses and yet ironically reverses the metrocolonial voyage, maintaining throughout the constructive strategy of authenticating alienation.

Given its centrality to the modernist imagination, it's no wonder that noir figures prominently in discussions of postmodernist culture. Generally speaking, critics have found in post-1970s "neo-noir" a nihilistic corruption of noir's aesthetic and philosophical authenticity. While midcentury noir shares what Jameson terms "the pain of a properly modernist nostalgia with a past beyond all but aesthetic retrieval" (19), neo-noir betrays a nostalgia for the alienated polarities of modernism itself. Alain Silver distinguishes in the "'Neo-*Noir*' period," effective since the 1970s, a moment in which many directors "recreate the *noir* mood, whether in remakes or in new narratives, . . . cognizant of a heritage and intent on their own interpretation on it." David Mamet captures the neo-noir spirit in his remarks on *House of Games* (1987), suggesting, "I am very well acquainted with the genre in print and on film, and I love it. I tried to be true."[10] What accounts for this durable loyalty to noir, and for the appearance neo-noir films such as *Chinatown* (Roman Polanski, 1974), *Body Heat* (Lawrence Kasdan, 1981), *Stormy Monday* (Mike Figgis, 1988), *The Hot Spot* (Dennis Hopper, 1990), *Red Rock West* (John Dahl, 1993), and *Palmetto* (Volker Schlöndorf, 1998)? How explain Carly Simon's album *Film Noir* (2007) or Ayala Moriel's 2007 fragrance of the same name? Erik Dussere observes that even as midcentury noirs accomplished a deliberate rejection of commercial culture, the harsh realism of these movies has become a sign of authenticity, a "marker of seriousness": "Through streetwise attitude, moral ambiguity, and existential reflections on crime and death, they posit for themselves a world that is less prettied-up than other popular film and ostensibly less commodified" (16–17). But resistance to commercial fantasy ironically renders noir attractive to the very culture industries that it seems to reject. Perhaps the driving force behind late capitalism's subsumption of noir is what Baudrillard describes as the "panic-stricken production of the real" that accompanies postmodernism:

> When the real is no longer what it used to be, nostalgia assumes its full meaning. There is a proliferation of myths of origin and signs of reality; second-hand truth, objectivity, and authenticity. There is an escalation of the true, of the lived experience; a resurrection of the figurative where the object and substance have disappeared. And there is a panic-stricken production of the real and referential, above and parallel to the panic of material production. . . .[11]

As reality itself becomes exposed as simulacrum, noir occurs to the postmodern cultural imagination as a "sign of reality," "an escalation of the true, of lived experience." This is the world of the "nostalgia film" described by Fredric Jameson in *Postmodernism, or, the Cultural Logic of Late Capitalism* (1991). For Jameson, neo-noirs such as *Chinatown* and *Body Heat* exemplify the "mesmerizing new aesthetic mode" of postmodernism. In their "conveying of 'pastness' by the glossy qualities of the image, and '1930s-ness' or '1950s-ness' by the attributes of fashion," these neo-noirs promise a return to the real; but they paradoxically contribute to "the waning of our historicity, of our lived possibility of experiencing history in some active way." In his remake of Billy Wilder's *Double Indemnity* (1944), argues Jameson, Kasdan participates in "the insensible colonization of the present by the nostalgia mode": "Everything in the film . . . conspires to blur its official contemporaneity and make it possible for the viewer to receive the narrative as though it were set in some eternal thirties, beyond real historical time" (19–21). Nor is this commodification of the noir past confined to the '70s and '80s; castigating Joel and Ethan Coen's *Miller's Crossing* (1990), Lee Tamahori's *Mulholland Falls* (1996), and Curtis Hanson's *LA Confidential* (1997), Naremore observes, "A good deal of postmodernist noir involves a conservative, ahistorical regression to the pop culture of the 1950s, or to a glamorous world before that, where people dressed well and smoked cigarettes."[12] Taken together, these critics help us to discern in neo-noir (especially the period films) not an appeal for wholeness and unity, but rather a nostalgia for the real itself. Although hard-boiled fiction and film noir may have posited an alienated world, this very alienation becomes a haven against the liquidation of self and world into commodified signs.

If nostalgia films represent a mass cultural assimilation of modernist noir, then avant-garde reiterations of film noir have also been received as a dangerous disengagement with reality. David Lynch's *Blue Velvet* (1986) furnishes a chief example of this phenomenon. For Norman Denzin, Lynch's innovative juxtapositions of genres and orders of representation are undercut by its political quietism: "postmodern individuals want films like *Blue Velvet*," he concludes, "for in them they can have their sex, their myths, their violence, and their politics, all at the same time" (472). Indeed, *Blue Velvet* recurs throughout discussions of postmodernism as sign of the movement's potential for nihilism. In *Detours and Lost Highways: A Map of Neo-Noir* (1999), Foster Hirsch reads the film as an exemplum of postmodernist corruption of the noir ethos. Heralded by French New Wave filmmakers who playfully approach noir in films like Jean-Pierre Melville's *Le Samurai* (1967)—which Hirsch terms "cool in excelsis" (98)—"*Blue Velvet* is noir conceived as pictures at an exhibition. . . . Lynch's primary interest is in making a spectacle out of bizarre behavior" (177). These receptions of *Blue Velvet* set the tone for commentaries on more recent films noirs. In an early critique of *Pulp Fiction* (1995), for example, Tom Whalen contends that Tarantino leaves us only with "the flattened corpses of the Aristotelian virtues of complexity, dimensionality, and truth":

> I'm not sure what *Pulp Fiction* is about except for its own artificiality. Its flashiness masks Tarantino's disinterest in (or ignorance of) how the camera and compositions can be made to mean, unlike most of the films he references. The violence of the film for me isn't found in having a mostly sympathetic character's head blown off, but in the director's turning this into a (approximately) twenty-minute comedy routine on how to dispose of the body and clean the blood out of the car. In the postmodernist world of *Pulp Fiction,* violence takes the place of feeling; its radical juxtapositions (of the artificial to the real, of event to response) have the effect of short-circuiting sense and effect—it flatlines us. (2–4)

Naremore finds such films part of a larger "noir mediascape"; with particular attention to *Lost Highway* (1997), he acknowledges Lynch's artistry, but finds this director's intertextual play limited and limiting: "For all its horror, sexiness, and formal brilliance *Lost Highway* ultimately resembles all the other retro noirs and nostalgia films of the late twentieth century: it remains frozen in a kind of cinématheque and is just another movie about movies" (275). Literally "drawn" from the graphic novel, *Sin City* (Frank Miller and Robert Rodriguez, 2004) is perhaps the most flamboyant contribution to this strain of postmodern noir. For reviewer Morton Marcus, the innovative crime movie, alongside Rodriguez's *El Mariachi* (1992) and *Desperado* (1995), lapses into the regressive "style without meaning, style for its own sake"; the director's "box office success," laments Marcus, "points to the decadence and waste that has come to characterize this country in its social, economic and political life, and in its foreign policy as well—a decadence and waste Rodriguez's films exemplify." Such language echoes throughout the reviews of Rian Johnson's debut *Brick* (2005), which transposes midcentury hardboiled conventions into the setting of an Orange County high school. While Stephen Holden deems *Brick* "a flashy cinematic stunt," Kristi Mitsuda tempers her praise of the film by suggesting that it skirts "a narcissistic exercise in generic cross-pollination conducted purely for its own sake."

It is not my intention to contest the broad critical reception of directors such as Lynch, Tarantino, and Rodriguez, but rather to narrate a heretofore unrecognized postmodernist reception and revision of noir. Even as noir elaborates itself in the 1940s and '50s, there arises a postmodernist aesthetic that appropriates, undermines, and ultimately transforms the noir vision of authenticating alienation. Following critics such as Woody Haut and Paula Rabinowitz, I describe the ways in which marginalized novelists reverse the alienated polarities of noir. After a prefatory reading of Chandler's *The Blue Dahlia* (George Marshall, 1946), I discuss three texts which variously critique, appropriate, and transform the noir returning veteran's formula: Chester Himes's *If He Hollers Let Him Go* (1945), Dorothy B. Hughes's *In A Lonely Place* (1946), and John Okada's *No-No Boy* (1957). These books reassign authenticating alienation to marginalized figures conventionally "othered" under high noir.

The subversions implicit in these revisionist texts become more apparent under what Linda Hutcheon articulates as "postmodernist parody." For Hutcheon, the neo-Marxist jeremiad of Eagleton and Jameson is itself inimical to activism in that it fails to recognize the subversive potential of postmodernism: "While the postmodern has no effective theory of agency that enables a move into political *action,* it does work to turn its inevitable ideological grounding into a site of de-naturalizing critique. To adapt Barthes's general notion of the 'doxa' as public opinion or the 'Voice of Nature' and consensus . . . , postmodernism works to 'de-doxify' our cultural representations and their undeniable political import." Hutcheon's theories about postmodernist parody enable us to discern a historiography of noir that negotiates a path between nostalgia and pastiche. Chapter

5 accordingly treats "anti-noir" thematics in four postmodernist novels: Thomas Pynchon's *The Crying of Lot 49* (1966), Ishmael Reed's *Mumbo Jumbo* (1972), Paul Auster's *Ghosts* (1986), and K.W. Jeter's *Noir* (1998). In the figure of Oedipa Mass, Pynchon dramatizes a collapse of the noir subject maintained through authenticating alienation. Reed's and Auster's respective novels, on the other hand, recall specific pretexts: while *Mumbo Jumbo* "signifies" on *Panic in the Streets* (Elia Kazan, 1950), *Ghosts* alludes to Jacques Tourneur's *Out of the Past* (1947) and other 1940s films, exposing noir as what Michel Foucault terms a "technology of the self." I conclude this chapter with a commentary on K. W. Jeter's science-fiction novel *Noir*. One of the most aggressive and deliberate fictional commentaries on noir extant, this book gathers the developments of literary and cinematic postmodernism to envision the "darkly perfect world" of film noir as a cybernetic retreat from the erasures of postmodernism. Though distinctive, each text under consideration relentlessly exposes the constructive mechanisms of hard-boiled detective fiction and film noir. Whereas high-noir normalizes self and world by positing an heroically alienated imperial subject, postmodernist parodies of noir collapse the distinction between Self and Other, leaving the protagonist in a terrifying epistemological crisis, and often, as in Jeter's novel, nostalgic for the alienated polarities of noir.

As suggested above, many critics decry what they see as a paralyzing negation in postmodernism. In the final chapters of this study, I read a series of contemporary films that revise the noir subject so vehemently attacked through postmodernist parody. Chapter 6 concerns the interplay within noir between the familiar figures of the existential quester and the confidence man: while the former posits an authentic subject beyond the freeplay of language, the latter conjures the specter of unchecked signification. Midcentury noir texts, such as William Lindsay Gresham's novel *Nightmare Alley* (1946), limit the deconstructive implications of the confidence man by converting this character into a variation on the existential quester. In many contemporary crime films, however, the confidence man is recast as a bricoleur who embodies the process of signification and who eclipses the modernist figure of the noir protagonist. I trace the emergence of the confidence-man-as-bricoleur in five films: Martin Scorsese's *Cape Fear* (1991), Bryan Singer's *The Usual Suspects* (1995), David Fincher's *Seven* (1995), and Christopher Nolan's *Memento* (2000). In each instance, some "bibliomancer" deftly manipulates noir conventions as well as broader western discourses such as Realism and Orientalism. *Memento*, however, represents the apotheosis of this revisionist movement within noir—the reintegration of the existential quester and the postmodernist bricoleur. Noir therefore reveals itself at the end of the twentieth century not so much a reflection of grim reality as an ideologically charged technology for the generation of reality itself.

The concluding chapter of the study suggests what is in some ways an even more substantial departure. Grounding the discussion in theorists of postmodern identity such as Calvin O. Schrag, I encounter films noirs which posit a subject derived not through authenticating alienation, but rather through openly acknowledged networks of relationships. I initially return to the 1940s and '50s, treating two directors who distinguished themselves from the comparatively reductive, constructive vision of their contemporaries. In *Stray Dog* (1949), Akira Kurosawa problematizes the noir strategy of authenticating alienation by constructing plots that probe the complexities of relational identity. Kurosawa was joined by his American colleague Samuel Fuller, whose films *House of Bamboo* (1955), *China Gate* (1957), and *The Crimson Kimono* (1959) work within the western formula of adventure noir to destabilize its racist polarization of Self and Other. More recent film makers of noir are indebted to Kurosawa and Fuller as they pervasively reconstruct the noir subject. While Carl Franklin's *One False Move* (1992), Quentin Tarantino's *Reservoir Dogs* (1992), and Mike Newell's *Donnie Brasco* (1997) continue the argument for the inevitability of the relational self, films such as *Bad Lieutenant* (Abel Ferrara, 1992), *Things to Do in Denver When You're Dead* (Gary Fleder, 1995), and *Hard Eight* (Paul Thomas Anderson, 1996) adopt diverse noir formulae in order to move away from authenticating alienation and toward a more frankly constructed human subjectivity. In each case a familiar noir protagonist journeys from hard-boiled alienation to open relationship with the Other. As the heroic isolato becomes an inextricably "connected guy" (to borrow a phrase from *Donnie Brasco*), a dramatic ideological revision is accomplished: racist/imperialist construction, relentless deconstruction, and ludic signification give way to what Schrag terms "the self in community." Whether genre, movement, cycle, or style, noir has coalesced into a site of contest between contending voices and ideologies. Though by no means exhaustive, this study offers a flexible paradigm for reading noir from its late-Victorian roots through twenty-first century permutations and transformations. My hope is that the reader will not only find here interesting reading, but also resources for understanding future encounters with noir's "darkly perfect world."

CHAPTER ONE

THE CONTINENTAL OPERATIONS OF DASHIELL HAMMETT

> *I knew a fellow once in Onehunga . . . who thought he owned all the Pacific south of the Tropic of Capricorn—had the papers to prove it. He'd been that way ever since a Maori bashed in his head with a stone* mele.
> —Steve Threefall, "Nightmare Town" (Dashiell Hammett, 1926)

It is tempting to read in the life of Dashiell Hammett a modernist conversion narrative. Often considered the father of noir, Hammett began his career as an agent for the Pinkerton Agency, where he gained the practical knowledge of detective work that would impart such realism to his later crime stories. During his time with the Pinkertons, Hammett worked as a strikebreaker for Anaconda Copper in 1920; in a famous apocryphal story, Hammett describes a pivotal encounter with an Anaconda official, in which the detective was offered $5,000 to assassinate a union organizer in Butte, Montana. Activist Frank Little was indeed killed, but not by Hammett, for whom this incident became, as Lillian Hellman recalls, "an abiding horror": "I think I can date Hammett's belief that he was living in a corrupt society from Little's murder. . . . I do not mean to suggest that his radical conversion was based on one experience, but sometimes in complex minds it is the plainest experience that speeds the wheels that have already begun to move" (48). Disgusted with the abuses of corporations like Anaconda, he quit the Pinkertons and turned to detective fiction. Like a left-wing apostle Paul, Hammett forsook persecuting the proletarian in order to become a prophet bent on exposing the underside of American capitalism.

Such a narrative serves our vision of Hammett as a modernist author, but this literary biography elides the writer's com-

plex dialogue with the adventure story. As Richard Slotkin has shown, the American proletariat was often conflated throughout the turn of-the twentieth century with "savages" such as Indians and Filipinos: "By representing politically active or 'radical' representatives of labor as instigators of 'savage' and anarchistic social strife, the exponents of managerial ideology vindicated their military metaphor as an essential component of 'Americanism'" (91). It is therefore perhaps strange that the radical Hammett began his literary career with adventure stories informed by colonialist anxieties over savage regression.

Writing both "ripping yarns" and hard-boiled detective fiction, Hammett inaugurates noir's reconstitution of fin-de-siècle adventure and detective fiction. Hammett's first *Black Mask* story, "The Road Home" (1922), is an exotic adventure story about a New York City detective who pursues a fugitive murderer into the jungles of Burma; as such, the tale anticipates the generic fusions apparent throughout his later work. Hammett further explores the colonial adventure proper in "Ber-Bulu" (1925) and "Ruffian's Wife" (1925). The former story reads like one of Louis Becke's South Sea tales; indeed, as the somewhat unusual name "Levison" occurs in Becke's 1897 tale "The Arm of Luno Capál," one wonders whether Hammett was directly inspired by the Australian writer. "Ruffian's Wife" is a supremely cynical tale about a young wife's disillusionment with her adventuring husband. In what appears almost a counterpoint to Marlow's "white lie" to the Intended in *Heart of Darkness,* Margaret Tharp cannot, at the end of the story, look her husband in the eye.

With "Nightmare Town" (1926), Hammett translates the adventurer into the domestic setting. Clad in "bleached khaki" and spinning his own ripping yarns, Steve Threefall proves that colonial wandering has not corrupted, but rather fortified the adventure protagonist. Like the Continental Op in *Red Harvest* (1929), Threefall stumbles into and ultimately devastates a Nevada town run entirely by criminals. As Robert Dixon suggests, "Civilization requires savagery to police itself because it contains savagery within itself" (183). Throughout Hammett's Continental Op stories and *The Maltese Falcon* (1929), San Francisco becomes an arena for dramas of colonial struggle and competition. Like Auguste Dupin and Sherlock Holmes, the Hammett detective confronts unruly exotics and corrupted colonials who threaten the integrity of the metropolis. In "The House in Turk Street" (1924), the Op wanders into a den of criminals at the suggestively named locale: he faces down an Anglicized Chinese mastermind who ultimately hangs for murder. Similarly, in "Dead Yellow Women" (1925), the Op imagines himself as an explorer navigating Chinatown in order to eradicate a Chinese kingpin.[1] "The Whosis

Kid" (1925), "The Creeping Siamese" (1926), and "The Farewell Murder" (1930) also concern transgressive boundary crossing, but here in the form of defective European adventurers: in the latter text, the criminal concern is a band of white mercenaries, including a former British Army officer, whose sojourns in far-flung posts like Cairo have resulted in savage regression. Such motifs are also clearly visible in Hammett's most celebrated work, *The Maltese Falcon* (1929): adventure has been exposed as "largely a matter of loot" (128) and adventurers like Floyd Thursby, Brigid O'Shaughnessy, and Caspar Gutman are variously "othered" as exotics, their collusion with figures such as Joel Cairo an index of moral turpitude. Invasion/repulsion scenarios would seem to be nothing new for detective fiction; after all, this "police work" is precisely what drives the Victorian detective fictions of Poe and Doyle. At issue here, however, is the "subject-position" of the detective. Unlike the permeable and perforated figure of Sherlock Holmes, Hammett's protagonists are indeed "hard-boiled" and "hard-bodied": insulated from otherness by the "protective enclosure" of authenticating alienation.[2]

REPLETE WITH ALLUSIONS to Pacific locales such as Onehunga (in Aotearoa) and the Sulu Archipelago, as well as scenarios of miscegenation and defection, Hammett's early adventure stories most immediately recall the fiction of Australian writer Louis Becke. Like Hammett, Becke was intimately involved in the milieu that he would represent in fiction: between 1872 and 1892, Becke traveled the Pacific, working as trader, supercargo, and labor recruiter. After serving in 1874 under the notorious "blackbirder" Bully Hayes, Becke was even charged with piracy (the charges were later dropped). While working as a journalist in Sydney, he published his first short story, "Bully Hayes: Pirate of the Pacific" in 1893, and his first collection, *By Reef and Palm,* in 1894. Becke would go on to write thirty-four books gathering dozens of colonial adventure stories; these include the anthologies *The Ebbing of the Tide* (1896), *Under Tropic Skies* (1901), and *The Pearl Divers of Roncador Reef* (1908). As this biographical sketch suggests, Becke was employed in several capacities throughout the colonial enterprise, and his letters and stories at once reflect and reinscribe the assumptions of western imperialism. At the same time, however, Becke exemplifies the contrast between *imperial* and *colonial* writers: while the former often work to quietly normalize what Edward Said terms "an imperial structure of attitude and reference,"[3] the latter tend to expose the tensions and contradictions of empire building. As Nicholas Thomas and Richard Evers point out, Becke's writings are deeply ambivalent, reiterating the racism of colonialism while exposing its brutality and "the incompleteness that is almost intrinsic to settler identity" (5). For our purposes, it is important to note the overlapping themes of failure, regression, and transgression in Becke's fiction.

As the title of the 1894 story "A Dead Loss" suggests, Becke is concerned to narrate the manifold failure of colonial ventures in the Pacific. While stories like "A Dead Loss" and "A Bar of Common Soap" (1913) conclude with a grim acknowledgment of financial catastrophe, "Saunderson and the Dynamite" (1904) speaks to the dangerous incompetence of Europeans in Oceania. "Dr. Ludwig Schwalbe, South Sea Savant" (1897) sees the failure of the ethnographic project, as the titular protagonist spends years collecting shrunken heads only to drown in a shipwreck. Colonial discourse invariably justifies itself through evangelism: whether trader, soldier, or missionary, the western adventurer purports to visit the blessings of European civilization upon infantilized and "arrested" native peoples. Though Becke does little to disturb European notions of the "intractable, bawling, and poverty stricken peoples of the equatorial Pacific,"[4] he does persistently undermine the evangelical pretenses of colonialism. Becke's missionaries are at best ineffectual, as with the unfortunate Rev. Hosea Parker in *His Native Wife* (1895), who gets himself murdered early in the novella. More often, however, these evangelists, like all of Becke's colonizers, jeopardize their native charges, as does the Rev. Gilead Bawl of "In the Old Beach-Combing Days" (1897).

Becke does not merely question the efficacy of colonialism; like Stevenson, Conrad, and Kipling, Becke describes the erosive effects of the tropics upon the colonizers themselves. In his letters and in autobiographical characters such as the trader Watson, Walker and Evers observe, Becke "fashions a particular self through the process of writing: a plucky hero struggling against the environment and peoples of the Pacific" (85). His "respectable" colonists notwithstanding, Becke is most remembered for portraits of those traders, beachcombers, castaways, and escaped convicts incapable of maintaining their European orientations—figures who call into question the notion of fixed and stable identity. "In Teaké, the bronzed, half-naked savage chief of Maiana, or Mési, the desperate leader of the natives that cut off the barque *Addie Passmore* at Marakei," Becke writes in "Deschard of Oneaka" (1895), "the identity of such men as 'Nuggety' Jack West and Macy O'Shea, once of Van Diemen's Land or Norfolk Island, was lost forever":

> [T]here were many white men scattered throughout the various islands of the Ellice, Gilbert, and Marshall groups. Men, these, with a past that they cared not to speak of to the few strangers that they might chance to meet in their savage retreats. Many were escaped convicts from Van Diemen's

Land and New South Wales, living not in dread of their wild native associates, but in secret terror of recapture by a man-of-war and return to the horrors that dreadful past. Casting away the garb of civilization and tying around their loins the *airiri* or grass girdle of the Gilbert Islanders, they soon became in appearance, manners, language, and thoughts pure natives. For them the outside world meant a life of degradation, possibly a shameful death. (291–92)

Stories such as "Deschard of Oneaka," whose very titles suggest the reassignment of European identity to the colonial periphery, perhaps most obviously illustrate Becke's pervasive attention to colonial dissolution. "Deschard of Oneaka," "Prescott of Naura" (1897), "Martin of Nitendi" (1901), and "The Methodical Mr. Burr of Maduro" (1894) are united in their treatment of white men who leave western civilization to assume sexual, cultural, and political alliances with Pacific Islanders, usually exceeding their indigenous associates in hyperbolic violence. Locating Becke within literary naturalism, we often gravitate toward terms such as "regression," "atavism" and "devolution" to describe the process of "going native" that recurs throughout Becke's work. We should also remain sensitive, however, to the ways in which this rational/empirical discourse of linear movement presages the postmodernist critique of a subject constructed and therefore susceptible to deconstruction and/or revision. Becke does maintain many essentialist assumptions about race, class, and gender; describing his castaways as "dissolute" and "renegade"; however, he also suggests the malleability of a subject that might reinvent itself by "reneging" on the social contract. When asked whether he is a white man, the titular antihero of "Prescott of Naura" confides, "No . . . I am not a white man. The cat took all the white man out of me at Port Arthur; and for fifty years I have lived with kanakas, and I am a kanaka now—backbone and soul" (85). With this grim utterance, Prescott disappears into the Auckland night: "For a moment or two he stood under the glare of the gas-lamp, then, with a quick, active step, he strode across the street and was lost to view" (86). As in Stevenson's *The Strange Case of Dr. Jekyll and Mr. Hyde* (1886) and Conrad's *Heart of Darkness,* the modern city is revealed as "one of the dark places of the earth," a caliginous world within which the colonial wanderer becomes "lost from view." As Prescott's remark suggests, the slippages of the self are commensurate with reconfigurations of the body: if the "white man" might disappear under "the cat at Port Arthur," then he might also be reinscribed as an indigene through the bodily transformations such as tattooing, like the titular beachcomber "English Bob" (1897), the sailors of "Chester's Cross" (1897), and the fugitive Henry Deschard, who is "more terrifying and savage in appearance than any of his ruffianly partners in crime, tattooed as he was from the back of his neck to his heels in broad, perpendicular lines" (310).

Scarred, tattooed, burned, and often clothed in native garb, the body of the adventurer becomes a palimpsest indicative of the general compromise of boundaries that recurs throughout Becke's universe. In many stories, such as "The Revenge of Macy O'Shea" (1897) and "The Methodical Mr. Burr of Maduro," the renegade's adoption of hyperbolic violence coincides with miscegenation. While Macy O'Shea punishes his Marquesan wife's infidelity by severing her hand, Ned Burr coldly shoots his wife's lover, then forces her to parade the head of the victim about her village, a gory spectacle which only amplifies Burr's prestige with the natives. In these tales, as in "An Honour to the Service" (1895), "The Arm of Luno Capal," and "Collier: the 'Blackbirder'" (1897), Oceania is peopled with fragile bodies, ever susceptible to mutilation. The implications of such fragmentation are especially clear in "Deschard of Oneaka." Anna Deschard brings her teenage son and daughters to the Pacific in search of her fugitive husband. In what reads almost as a pretext for Camus's play *Le Malentendu* (1944), Deschard mistakenly murders his son and then proceeds to lead his natives to "cut off" the ship bearing his wife and daughters. When the captain of the ship barricades himself and the women against the marauders, Deschard simply fires a cannon at the captain's cabin, with a grisly result that shocks even the murderers themselves. Upon learning of the identity of his victims, Deschard "sitting in the captain's chair, and leaning back, . . . placed the muzzle [of a musket] to his throat, and touched the trigger with his naked foot."[5] No "ripping yarn" more strikingly captures the apocalyptic mood of Becke's fiction: not only has Deschard himself been "dissevered" from the "outer world" of western civilization, but the domestic and exotic collide with an explosion that obliterates bodies and selves.

IMPERIAL/COLONIAL DISCOURSE in the United States has historically turned upon Manifest Destiny and exceptionalism: unlike worldly European empires, this doctrine suggests, America enjoys a divine commission to settle the continent. Against European and Asian imperial designs, American Manifest Destiny emerges an evangelical campaign to disseminate not only the message of Christianity, but also the gospel of democratic ideals. Throughout the late nineteenth century, the ideology of Manifest Destiny gains momentum with the advent of the eugenicist and social Darwinist theories endemic to Anglo-Saxonism. For Slotkin, "figures as diverse as the expansionist promoter and politician William Gilpin, the abolitionist and anti-Mexican War activist Theodore Parker, the pro-slavery expansionists George Fitzhugh and William Walker used Anglo-Saxonist concepts to justify American expansion into Mexican and Latin American territory" (45). Theodore Roosevelt is perhaps the most celebrated exponent of Anglo-Saxonism at the turn-of-the century. For Roosevelt, American conquest of the "red wastes where the barbarian peoples of the world hold sway" would involve a beneficial economy—in combat with his savage enemies on the American continent, Cuba, and the Philippines, the Anglo-Saxon would imbibe the spiritual (though not the biological) essences of a savagery that would reinvigorate his own racial vitality; the colonized savage would, on the other hand, be granted the blessings of western civilization (51–53). But while the Spanish American War serves for Roosevelt as a means of recapturing the regenerative violence of the old west, the Rough Riders providing a model for hierarchical Anglo-Saxonist society, then the ensuing Philippine-American War (1899–1902) elicits anxieties familiar to European colonial discourse. Americans such as Roosevelt had vilified the Spanish for their cruel and sadistic treatment of their colonized peoples. Faced with government of the Filipinos, however, American mass culture and foreign policy alike adopted the logic of the "savage war": the insurrectos were collapsed in the popular imagination with Indians and African-Americans, and legally accounted for under General Orders No. 11 and No. 100, "which declared the guerillas in violation of the laws of civilized warfare and licensed extraordinary measures against them."[6] Such policies reflect the tandem colonial anxiety that the adventurer will either be annihilated by or transmuted into his savage opponent. No single incident dramatized these fears more than the Balangiga "massacre" of 1901. Filipino guerrillas disguised as women infiltrated the fortified town of Balangiga and killed all but a few of the American soldiers garrisoned there. Army propagandists exploited reports of mutilated bodies to assert that the Filipinos tortured and castrated their prisoners. Such atrocities, Slotkin argues, parallel the mythology of rape in the captivity narrative: "In these acts the White victim is held powerless, while his/her body is cruelly manipulated, invaded and destroyed by a race that—according to 'natural law'—ought to be subordinate to the white" (113). Within the American cultural imagination, as with that of the British Empire, the colonial periphery is marked by corporeal ruptures which portend a threat to identity itself. Phantasms of an unbounded body coincide with and give rise to the possibility that the colonial soldier-adventurer will "go native." Following the Balangiga incident, which was compared in the popular press to Custer's Last Stand, vengeful American troops began killing their prisoners, and the Army command used the massacre as a pretext for more extreme measures of violence and terror. "I want no prisoners," General Jacob Smith is reported to have said, "I wish you to kill and burn; the more you kill and burn the better you please me" (119). However effective, the adoption of "savage tactics" evoked the familiar colonial specter of regression—U.S. commanders were not only concerned that their African-American troops would defect to the Filipinos, but feared that the conflict itself would devolve into savagery. Narrating his experience in the Philippines under General Franklin Bell, Pvt. James H. Blount described the "American soldier in officially sanctioned wrath" as "a thing so ugly and dangerous that it would take a Kipling to describe him."[7]

Blount's comment ill comports with an exceptionalism that would distinguish American imperialism from its European cousins: the veteran cites Kipling because "regenerate" America seems neither to have nor need late imperial doomsayers such as Kipling, Conrad, Stevenson, and Becke. At the risk of over-simplification, we might recognize American adventure stories of the early twentieth century as anxious responses to the colonial problem of defection more explicitly encountered in fictions of the British Empire. O. Henry's short-story "The Head-Hunter" (1908), for example, provides a tongue-in-cheek treatment of an American reporter feverishly seduced by fantasies of savagery. But for the most part, the American experience in the Philippines seems to have been elided—fictional and cinematic treatments of Filipino-American encounters concentrate on World War II rather the turn of the century. The paucity of Spanish-American War fictions and films is ironic, given Charles Musser's argument that the reporting of the war enabled the development of story film.[8] Analyzing one early film about the Spanish-American War, Billy Bitzer's *The American Soldier in Love and War* (1899), Amy Kaplan discerns a tripartite rescue-plot within which the salvific American soldier in the Philippines must himself be rescued from a savage menace by a Filipino Pocahontas, and then saved, in turn, from this figure by a white woman who intervenes to set up housekeeping abroad. In contrast to a story such as Becke's "Deschard of Oneaka," the categories of domestic and exotic may be triumphantly integrated against what Kaplan describes as the "implicit danger . . . that the American soldier will 'go native' by taking a local concubine, a situation that was both a reality and a fear in colonial administration" (1072).

Other early-twentieth-century American adventure fictions similarly address the problem of the colonial adventurer "gone native." Despite many failed attempts to serve as a soldier in Cuba, the Philippines, and China, Edgar Rice Burroughs ultimately made the even more strategic contribution to U.S. colonial culture by popularizing the racist ideologies of Roosevelt, Madison Grant, and Theodore Lothrop Stoddard. In *Tarzan of the Apes* (1912) as well as in his science fiction novels set on Mars, Venus, and "at the earth's core," Burroughs wove fantastic tales of adventure and conquest within which the white protagonist might fully immerse himself in savagery without imperiling his essential Anglo-Saxon identity. *Tarzan* is a direct counterpoint to Conrad's African fictions: while late-Victorian adventure antiheroes such as Kurtz lose their European cultural identity in the "heart of darkness," Tarzan works his way up the evolutionary ladder, conquering developmentally arrested anthropoid apes and African natives along the way. "An extended Darwinian parable," as Slotkin suggests, *Tarzan* asserts "the absolute primacy of heredity over environment in shaping individual and racial development" (207). Throughout the 1920s, the now forgotten adventure writer John Russell engaged in an even more obvious dialogue with the adventure tradition, publishing three collections of exotic adventure stories—*Where the Pavement Ends* (1921), *In Dark Places* (1923), and *Far Wandering Men* (1930)—whose colorful titles uncannily suggest the contiguity of adventure fiction and noir. Explicitly quoting Louis Becke in "The Fire Walker" (1930), Russell evokes the obliterated antiheroes of his Australian predecessor, especially in "The Fourth Man," and "Gun Metal." As in "The Price of His Head," and "The Knife," however, "The Fire Walker" features a protagonist that undergoes colonial dissolution only to experience existential regeneration: although the Australian fugitive Jamison hopes to "abolish himself" in Fiji, he undergoes a fire-walking ritual that enables him to recover his masculinity. Though sometimes singed, like Jamison, or beaten, lacerated, and exposed, Russell's heroes rarely suffer the puncturings or dismemberments visited upon the bodies of Becke's hapless colonial figures. Adopting the mode of Conrad's *Lord Jim* (1900) rather than *Heart of Darkness,* Russell most often meliorates imperial failure by dramatizing the white adventurer's redemption of the colonial experience as a means of retaining and strengthening corporeal and psychic integrity. Russell's fictions appeared in books and on the screen, but American adventure tales also filled the pages of pulp magazines such as *Black Mask* and *Sunset,* where Hammett would publish his first stories. As Sean McCann argues, the celebrated pulp *Black Mask* not only provided a forum for explicit debate about the Ku Klux Klan, but became an arena in which exotic adventure fictions contended with the emergent hard-boiled detective story.

While *Black Mask* stories such as Herman Peterson's "Call Out the Klan" forthrightly valorize the "invisible empire's" nativist crusade, his tale "One Dried Head"—along with Ivan Ignatieff's "Jungle Shadows," Phillip Fisher's "Fungus Isle," and John Ayotte's "White Tents" (all published in 1923)— perpetuates the Klannish phantasm of miscegenation that also haunts the popular imagination of the Spanish American War and the Philippine-

American War. Emphasizing motifs of infection and regression, these texts present for McCann the dangers of colonial border crossing and the consequent "yearning to re-establish crumbling cultural barriers and a longing to return from tainted lands to hermetic local community" (64). Hard-boiled detective stories, he asserts, conversely rejected Klan racism in favor of a modernist ethic of individualism: "In particular, the generic protagonist fashioned by Daly and Hammett defined himself in opposition to the emotional core of Klan rhetoric—the ideal of community. The heroes of the hard-boiled genre are notoriously far from communally minded, and they are rarely—to use a phrase crucial to Klan rhetoric of the twenties—good citizens" (46). In "Knights of the Open Palm" (1923), for example, Carroll John Daly inaugurates hard-boiled fiction with a hero who represents the multi-ethnic world of the American city as opposed to the racially homogenous communal ideals of the KKK, which Daly exposes as "narrow forms of self-interest and foolish longings for outmoded kinds of social control" (59). The more sophisticated Dashiell Hammett, on the other hand, uses figures such as the Continental Op and Sam Spade to argue for "the fictive stature and basic unreliability of the social demarcations upon which the Klan and foreign-adventure intuitively relied" (69). Though quite persuasive in his contentions that Hammett countered the triumphalist racism found in *Black Mask*, McCann elides Hammett's own forays into adventure fiction and his dialogue with the late-Victorian adventure ethos at large. Moving from exotic adventure fiction into noir, Hammett replaced the permeable subject of Victorian mystery and adventure with the hermetically alienated self embodied in the hard-boiled detective. Indeed, Hammett's detectives return to and recuperate the "border-patrolling" anxieties from which Victorian adventure emerged.

Hammett's first short story, "The Road Home," adumbrates the generic transformations that would recur throughout his fiction. Published in *Black Mask* under the pen-name Peter Collinson (underworld slang for a nonexistent person), this early tale immediately suggests the fictiveness of identity. The story accordingly begins with the entreaty of a fugitive gone native in the jungles of Burma: "'You're a fool to pass it up! You'll get just as much credit and reward for taking back proof of my death as you will for taking me back. And I got papers and stuff buried back near the Yunnan border that you can have to back up your story; and you needn't be afraid that I'll show up to spoil your play'" (31). As if resuming the questions of colonialism and subjectivity pursued by Becke, Hammett begins his literary career with an utterance that declares the contextuality and mutability of the colonial adventurer. Fleeing from a murder rap in New York City, the white fugitive Barnes has adopted local habits and sought to completely abnegate western identity. Along with Hammett's intriguing sobriquet, Barnes's suggestion that experience and subjectivity may be rendered up to shifting narrative reiterates the ideological crises of late-Victorian adventure and detection. But while Hammett might, as McCann argues, recognize race as "an empty but potent social fiction" (70), he begins in "The Road Home" a series of fictions that arrest and cohere the protean colonial self.

Barnes and his opponent Hagedorn are pivotal characters within the noir imagination: these figures constitute the most discernable link between late-Victorian adventure and hard-boiled detective fiction. In the tradition of Stevenson, Conrad, and Becke, Hammett inscribes Barnes as a "defective" whose metropolitan crimes propel him into the colonial periphery. And yet the murder that Barnes commits in New York City is neither accident nor the rebellion against society that characterizes many colonial adventurers; it is rather an example of existentialist "bad faith": "I didn't mean to kill that guy anyway. You know how it is; I was a kid and wild and foolish—but I wasn't mean—and I got in with a bad bunch" (33). This renegade has found a haven in the Orient because it lies outside western notions of law, order, and justice; it is a place, as Kipling has it in "Mandalay" (1890), "where there aren't no Ten Commandments" (1043). Having placed himself beyond the pale of western society, Barnes immerses himself in the native community: "The dark man in the garb of a native smiled an oily, ingratiating smile and brushed away his captor's words with a wave of his hand. . . . He spat over the side insultingly—native-like—and settled back on his corner of the split-bamboo mat" (32). There is even the suggestion of miscegenation, as Barnes is accused of beating the Burmese woman he has "been living with" (33). Moreover, Barnes has not only "reneged" on the social contract, but attempts to seduce his pursuer Hagedorn into defection: "I ain't offering you a dinky coupla thousand dollars; I'm offering you your pick out of one of the richest gem beds in Asia—a bed that was hidden by the *Mran-ma* when the British jumped the country. Come back up there with me and I'll show you rubies and sapphires and topazes that'll knock your eye out" (32). The dreams of white homogeneity and supremacy that pervade the adventures of writers such as G. A. Henty, as well as the Klannish pulps of *Black Mask,* are all but absent from Hammett's fiction—empire building is little more than opportunistic "jumping" of power and resources. The question in Hammett, as in Becke, is not whether the evangelical project of colonialism will succeed or fail, but whether the white adventurer will be able to remain bounded and coherent amidst ethical temptations and bodily transformations "that'll knock your eye out."

Barnes in every sense opposes Hagedorn, a "gaunt man in faded khaki" who reads as yet another avatar of imperialist adventurer or "troubleshooter" dispatched from the metropolis to colony in order to secure "law and order." And, unlike Barnes, Hagedorn is possessed of an indefatigable work ethic, an "inner directedness"[9] discrete from shifting cultural contexts:

> "I left New York two years ago to get you, and for two years I've been in this damn country—here and in Yunnan—hunting you. I promised my people I'd stay until I found you, and I kept my word . . . " Two years through unknown country, pursuing what until the very day of capture had never been more than a vague shadow. Through Yunnan and Burma, combing wilderness with microscopic thoroughness—a game of hide-and-seek up the rivers, over the hills and through the jungles . . . (32)

Along with positivist predecessors such as Sherlock Holmes, Hagedorn subjects this site of mystery, anarchy, and pathology to "microscopic thoroughness." In contrast to the classical detective story, however, Hammett's first tale features a hero dependent upon the agonistic confrontation of rational consciousness and an irrational world distilled in the colonial periphery. Whereas the classical or ratiocinative sleuth would surely get his man, Hagedorn allows Barnes to escape; the fugitive jumps ship and swims for the bank: "Barnes's head showed for a moment and then went down again, to appear twenty feet nearer shore. Upstream the man in the boat saw the blunt, wrinkled noses of three *muggars,* moving toward the shore at a tangent that would intercept the fugitive" (33). As in Conrad's *The Secret Sharer* (1910), the renegade's immersion suggests his rejection of rational consciousness; the encroaching *muggars,* on the other hand, pose the threat of obliteration, a fate conjured throughout late-Victorian adventure in the form of cannibalism and shark attack (as in Becke's "The Rangers of the Tia Kau" [1894]). Hagedorn debates whether to shoot Barnes or leave him to the reptiles, but "the sudden but logical instinct to side with the member of his own species against enemies from another wiped out all other considerations, and sent his rifle to his shoulder to throw a shower of bullets into the *muggars.* Barnes clambered up the bank of the river, waved his hand over his head without looking back, and plunged into the jungle" (33). Although this intervention on one hand emphasizes the hard-boiled detective's adherence to personal ethics, it also illuminates the primary epistemological concern of the noir ethos at large: the policing of boundaries between subject and object. Hagedorn may not return Barnes to the judicial and penal institutions of the west, but he does manage, if even for a moment, to retard the colonial adventurer's dissolution into nonbeing.

In what will become a characteristically open-ended conclusion, Hammett maintains the subjectivity of his hero by leaving him in a tableau of modernist alienation. The Sisyphean character of his task is summed up by the native captain of the *jahaz*: "*Mahok!* In the jungle here, *sahib* a man is as a leaf. Twenty men might find him in a week, or a month. It may take five years. I cannot wait that long" (34). Barnes has collapsed into nature, after all, and the object of the pursuit is reiterated as not only a quest for justice but an attempt to restore to the fugitive a western identity that he has foregone. Opposed by an unyielding natural world, on one hand, Hagedorn must finally countenance the prospect of his own defection: "'two years,' he said aloud to himself, 'it took to find him when he didn't know I was hunting for him. Now—Oh hell! It may take five years. I wonder about them jewel-beds of his.'" With this grim reflection, Hagedorn disappears into a jungle in which "a man is as a leaf"; we are left uncertain as to whether Hagedorn maintains his quest for Barnes or has himself gone native, rejected the work ethic to pursue "the richest gem beds in Asia." "The Road Home" thus endows the detective with a positivist impulse, but leaves him frustrated by a resistant world that includes the prospect of his own corruptibility. And yet this is not simply a generic fusion of late-Victorian adventure, with its emphasis upon failure and regression, and the pursuit formula of detective fiction. In his first *Black Mask* tale, Hammett writes an epigraph for his own fiction and for the noir ethos at large. In contrast to the compromised figures of *fin-de-siècle* adventure and detection, Hagedorn remains frozen in an attitude of alienation against a hostile world, a polarization that renders him all the more distinct, coherent, and "authentic."

"The Road Home" prefigures Hammett's continued negotiation of adventure and detection. With little emendation to the chronology, we might discern in Hammett's fiction a geographical progression that begins in Borneo with "The Road Home," and moves eastward across the Pacific, toward California and the American West. But this trajectory does not read as a retreat from some corrosive exotic, as in the Klannish *Black Mask* adventures treated by McCann; inaugurating a pervasive noir convention, Hammett ultimately renders "settled" California an exotic island of racial and sexual otherness that threatens to devour the white male adventurer.[10] With the 1925 story "Ber-Bulu," however, Hammett turns his attention from the detective story to adventure proper and from Burma to the Sulu Archipelago, the southernmost islands of the Philippines. Given the Moros' historical defiance of both Spanish and American incursions, the region might be taken as a synecdoche for colonial resistance in general. And, indeed, the first lines of the tale not only recall the world-weary retrospective of Becke's tales, but declare the text a parable of colonial exhaustion:

> Say it happened on one of the Tawi Tawis. That would make Jeffol a Moro. It doesn't really matter what he was. If he had been a Maya or a Ghurka he would have laid Levison's arm open with a machete or a kukri instead of a kris, but that would have made no difference in the end. Dinihari's race matters as little. She was woman, complaisant woman, of the sort whose no always becomes yes between the throat and teeth. You can find her in Nome, in Cape Town, and in Durham, and in skin of any shade; but, since the Tawi Tawis are the lower end of the Sulu Archipelago, she was brown this time. (17)

Hammett at one point confided that he intended in the story a contemporary adaptation of the Biblical story of Samson[11]; but this introduction limits the archetypal significance of "Ber-Bulu" to the world of modern empire-building—the paradigm of the story is aboriginal and colonial, rather than universal. Moreover, the basic elements of "Ber-Bulu" further situate the tale within the immediate context of late-Victorian adventure. Like many late-Victorian adventure tales, "Ber-Bulu" is a first-person retrospective: the narrator Peters implies that the story takes place at the turn-of-the-century, a few years after "the late 90s," when "the government had eased up a bit." The setting not only recalls a time when the Pacific fictions of Stevenson, Conrad, and Becke dominated the adventure genre, but it is also the precise moment of American interventions in the Philippines, including bloody contests in the Tawi Tawis. "Ber-Bulu" is oddly silent about these looming events; and yet the story explicitly treats thematics of colonial exhaustion and regression, which dogged the American experience in the Philippines. Rather like Melville's reluctant Ishmael, Peters avoids any direct treatment of self-dissolution; this fate here remains an all but unsignifyable "it" repressed and immediately returned in suggestions of miscegenation and bodily mutilation—Levison's arm "laid open" by the native *kris*. As if performing his own assessment of late-Victorian adventure, and Becke's fictions in particular, Hammett rehearses a tale of colonial obliteration mitigated only by the coherent efforts of an alienated narrator.

The longish introduction of "Ber-Bulu" implies at once Peters's evasion of Levison's disturbing experience and his ambivalent desire to simultaneously implicate and insulate himself. Despite his suggestive name, Peters is no "rock" of Christian faith; to the contrary, he describes at length his antipathy for Langworthy, a pugnacious local missionary who embodies the "muscular Christianity" of western imperialism: "He and I didn't hit it off very well from the first. I had reasons for not telling him where I had come from, and when he found I intended staying a while he got a notion that I wasn't going to do his people—he called them that in spite of the little attention they paid him—any good. Later, he used to send messages to Bangao, complaining that I was corrupting the natives and lowering the prestige of the white man" (17). Like "The Road Home," "Ber-Bulu" is a cynical adventure in which imperial idealism has given way to the brutality and manipulation of the colonial enterprise; while Langworthy boxes the Moros into Christianity ("He was wise enough to know that he could make better progress by cracking their heads together than by arguing finer theological points with them . . . "[18]), Peters takes them at blackjack. "As for this white man's prestige," Peters recommends, "maybe I didn't insist on being *tuaned* with every third word, but neither did I hesitate to knock the brown brothers round whenever they needed it; and that's all there is to this keeping up the white man's prestige at best" (18). In the wake of evangelism, maintenance of personal identity becomes the central problem of the story. More akin to Barnes than Hagedorn in "The Road Home," Peters might well terminate his adventurous career by disappearing into the world of the Moros.

Peters reads in the Moro Jeffol and his slave Dinihari distilled stereotypes of savage violence and sexuality: "Jeffol was a good Moro—a good companion in a fight or across a table. Tall for a Moro, nearly as tall as I am, he had a deceptive slimness that left you unprepared for the power in his snake-smooth muscles. . . . His hands went easily to the knives at his waist, and against his hide—sleeping or waking—he wore a sleeveless fighting-jacket with verses from the Koran on it." Committed to the "loose form of Mohammedanism [which] suited the Moros," and inheriting "his father's taste for deviltry," Jeffol "ran as wild and loose as his pirate ancestors" (17). Although Langworthy manipulates Jeffol into a tenuous Christianity, the Moro remains one of Hammett's most Orientalist portraits, a "simple son of nature" (20) associated with animality, extravagant violence, and irrationality. Dinihari, on the other hand, becomes a sign of the Orient in all of its "feminine penetrability, its supine malleability"[12]: "She was a sleek brown woman with the knack of twisting a sarong around her hips so that it became part of her. . . . She was small and trimly fleshed, with proper pride in her flesh. She wasn't exactly beautiful, but if you were alone with her you kept looking at her, and you wished she didn't belong to a man you were afraid of. That was when she was Levison's" (17).

Possessed of an irresistible magnetism, Dinihari cannot help but seduce every man she encounters, and this consuming sexual desire catalyzes the escalating violence of the story. Dinihari is, in short, an early example of the femme fatale. But this rather obvious conclusion holds more serious implications: the largely overlooked character of Dinihari, clearly derived from figures such as Kurtz's savage mistress in *Heart of Darkness,* is an explicit link between late-Victorian adventure and noir. As we shall see, Hammett would resituate the exotic femme fatale as a locus of violence and sexuality within urban California. In keeping with E. Ann Kaplan's suggestion that film noir ultimately transposes the colonialist trope of the "the dark continent" onto the female psyche, the "dangerous woman" of hard-boiled detective fiction and film noir may be generally understood as a paranoid conflation of the "savage mistress" of the colonies and the metropolitan "angel in the house," a figure set in agonistic tension against the white male protagonist.[13]

Looking forward to the threats posed by the femme fatale, Dinihari does indeed have a corrosive effect upon Levison, the titular "Ber-Bulu," or, "hairy one." In this character, Hammett presents a dense and perplexing array of signs. As suggested above, Levison might provide one of the most compelling bits of evidence that Hammett read Becke—"Levison" is a minor character in Becke's "The Arm of Luno Capal," a "ripping yarn" which, as its title implies, captures the fascination with bodily fragmentation that runs throughout the genre. Moreover, Hammett's Levison recalls the atavistic beachcombers and renegades that roam Becke's Pacific. Sarcastically acknowledging his "sweet reputation" in the region, and drawn to his copious supply of gin, Peters describes Levison as a "monster, in size and appearance":

> Below his half-hidden dark eyes, black hair bearded his face with a ten-inch tangle, furred his body like a bear's, padded his shoulders and arms and legs, and lay in thick patches on fingers and toes. He hadn't many clothes on . . . and what he had were too small for him. His shirt was split open in a dozen places and the sleeves were gone. His pant legs were worn off at the knees. He looked a like a hair-mattress coming apart—only there was nothing limp or loose about the body inside of the hair. (18)

Evoking the biblical figure of Samson, Levison also summons the Becke castaway whose retrograde tendencies surpass those of the indigenous peoples with whom he consorts. Accordingly, Levison gains ascendancy in the Darwinian struggle of savage life—he establishes his reputation among the islanders by mangling a harmless old man: "The Moros called Levison the

Hairy One (*Ber-Bulu*), and, because he was big and strong and rough, they were afraid of him and admired him tremendously" (18). This reputation for brutality enables Levison to attract Dinihari, and the hirsute adventurer hereby enters into the miscegenous relationship which is, along with hyperbolic violence, the other great marker of transgression within the colonial imagination. Much to the chagrin of Jeffol, the pair begin a "honeymoon." And yet, however deviant, Levison is also associated with the larger western presence in the Pacific; like many of the American enlisted men serving in the Philippines, Levison viciously refers to the Moros as "niggers" (20); and, as if participating in a succession of imperial power, he builds a home "beside the ruins of the old Spanish block-house" (18). Hammett may conserve essentialist categories of savagery and civilization, but he also subscribes to a cynical, entropic vision that sees colonizer and colonized alike capable of savage violence and regression.

Peters characterizes Levison as "a hair-mattress coming apart," and this bizarre image suggests the fears of dissolution which pervade the conclusion of "Ber-Bulu." Swinging the childlike Dinihari from his beard, Levison appears to Peters "a real giant"; but the "wild magnificence" (20) of this spectacle belies Levison's ultimate fate. "It's hard for me to remember him that way," Peters confesses, "my last picture of him is the one that sticks" (20). When Jeffol and his confederates ambush Levison, Peters imagines the worst:

> I suspected that Levison, gagged, was being cut, in the Moro fashion, into very small bits. . . . I had a gun under my shirt. If I could snake it out and pot Unga, then I had a chance of shooting it out with Jeffol and Jokanain. If I wasn't fast enough, Unga would turn loose the blunderbuss and blow me and the wall behind me out into the Celebes Sea, all mixed up so you couldn't say which was which. But even that was better than passing out without trying to take anybody with me. (20)

Here and throughout, Peters's phraseology betrays a preoccupation with bodily fragmentation and the loss of identity that it implies. In recounting his own experience with Levison, he has continual recourse to phrases such as "laid open," "coming apart," "ripped," "bleeding slit," and "cut . . . into very small bits"; this sequence culminates with Peters's imagination of himself blown "out into the Celebes Sea, all mixed up so you couldn't say which was which."

Such images are wholly consistent with western adventure fictions in general, which obsessively treat the disappearance, in life or in death, of the adventuring western subject. Hammett does conclude his ripping yarn with an image of body modification, albeit a bathetic one. Jeffol and his mother Ca'bi bind and shave Levison:

> My gaze went up to his head and I got another shock. Every hair had been scraped off or plucked out, even to his eyebrows, and his naked head sat upon his immense body like a pimple. There wasn't a quart of it. There was just enough to hold his big beaked nose and his ears, which stood out like palm leaves now that they weren't supported by hair. . . . No wonder he had hidden himself behind whiskers.(20)

Perhaps more than any other of Hammett's fictions, "Ber-Bulu" approaches the postmodernist, postcolonial vision attributed to Hammett by critics such as Sean McCann and John Walker Lindh.[14] Nature becomes culture as the Moros expose Levison's primordial strength as nothing but rhetoric—thus denuded, Levison cannot marshal the physical strength to resist. The semiotic dimensions of the assault deepen when we learn that Langworthy has primed Jeffol's revenge by sharing with his vengeful convert the story of Samson; we do not see here a "frontier" of contending monolithic forces—savagery and civilization—, but rather what Mary Louise Pratt terms a "contact zone" of heterogenous subjects and cultures engaged in struggles of textual production and reception (4). In this reflexive moment, Hammett refuses to naturalize the colonial discourse in which he generally participates: the helpless Levison disappears, not because he has physically devolved or dissolved, but rather because his discursive bluff has been called. Although Peters joins in laughter at Levison, the narrator yet adheres to his phantasms of corporeal disintegration: "You could almost see it—metal lashes of laughter coiled round his naked body, cut him into raw strips, paralyzed his muscles" (58). Peters is determined to inscribe the story of Levison with the violent images of bodily disruption that pervade late-Victorian adventure. Having witnessed Levison's defeat and disappearance, Peters retreats "with the pick of his goods"—"I had more right to his stuff than the Moros—hadn't I been his friend?" (58). As in "The Road Home," "Ber-Bulu" concludes with the protagonist's location of himself as an alienated spectator of entropic colonial decline. In his most pronounced foray into the genre of exotic adventure, Hammett therefore evokes a complex of ideas central to his collective oeuvre. Far from validating the essential superiority of western self and civilization, these colonial adventurers reveal a plastic subject that might be exposed as a construct and/or mutate with its context. Although he would, as McCann suggests, continue to explore such disturbing implications, Hammett also directed his talents and energies toward the recuperation of this jeopardized self.

IF STORIES such as "The Road Home" prove a counterpoint to the confident tenor of *Black Mask* adventure tales, then "Ber-Bulu" must have likewise sounded a dissonant note in its original context of *Sunset Magazine*. From the significant year of 1898, *Sunset* has served as an organ of western American boosterism, featuring articles about western living, colorful adventure fictions, editorials on western politics and even pieces on colonial management. In the June 1925 issue of *Sunset*, for example, travel-writer Nancy Barr Mavity contributed a travelogue/editorial entitled "Seeing Singapore After Dark" ("An American Girl Gets a Close-Up of Race Mixtures in the 'City of Transients'"). During the 1920s, *Sunset* is also replete with advertisements for Orientalized products such as Fatima cigarettes (the favorite brand of Hammett's Continental Op). As Rachel Lee suggests in her analysis of Sax Rohmer's serialized Fu Manchu stories, such advertisements locate the white reader as the consumer of a safe and yielding Oriental world (253). Although Hammett's modernist vision runs counter to the general optimism of *Sunset*, "Ber-Bulu" conserves the Orientalism of the magazine and of western culture at large. In October of 1925, Hammett had already published "Ruffian's Wife" in *Sunset Magazine*; it is another ambivalent adventure story that helps us to trace his literary return to the compromised American metropolis.

Domestic rather than exotic, and centered upon a female protagonist, Hammett's first *Sunset* tale in some ways presents a striking contrast with his celebrated fictions of masculine adventure. Often considered the "father of hard-boiled fiction," Hammett generally receives and amplifies the Victorian construction of woman as either domestic angel or femme fatale, a patriarchal binary that drives hard-boiled detective fiction and film noir. While metropolitan women are, in Anne McClintock's phrase, conventionally "represented as the atavistic and authentic body of national tradition (inert, backward-looking and natural)" (359), the femme fatale of noir, as suggested above, is a conflation of women with the savage and exotic. In contrast to "Ber-Bulu," however, which sees the beginnings of the racialized femme fatale, "Ruffian's Wife" treats the disillusionment of the metropolitan "angel in the house" and the compromise of the hygienic domestic space vital to preservation of boundaries within the imperial/colonial imagination. Even as, in the first lines of the story, "Margaret Tharp passed habitually from slumber to clear-eyed liveliness without intermediate languor" (55), this unlikely Hammett protagonist experiences a sudden and profound alienation from her adventuring husband.

"Ruffian's Wife" exaggerates the imperial/colonial gendered division of labor: bored with the tedium of housework and suburban society, housewife Margaret Tharp dreams of the return of her husband Guy from exotic adventures. While Margaret's neighbors reprovingly pity "'poor little Mrs. Tharp,' whose husband was notoriously a ruffian always off some distant where, up to any sort of scoundrelism," she secretly delights in the fact that "her man was a raging beast who could not be penned, because he did not wear the dull uniform of respectability, did not walk along smooth, safe ways" (58). Even as he offered a counterpoint to the racism of *Black Mask* adventure, Hammett here parodies the contemporary cult of masculinity which had, with Roosevelt's advocacy of "the strenuous life," celebrated adventure heroes like Tarzan and Zorro against their depleted middle-class counterparts. If Guy Tharp cannot be "penned" in one sense, he is *only* "penned" in another. Though Margaret "clung hard to him who alone was firmly planted in a whirling universe" (59), she seems to know her husband only through stories: "She made proud sentences for herself while she spoke other sentences, or listened to them. *Guy moves among continents as easily as Tom Milner from drug counter to soda fountain,* she thought while Dora talked of guest room linen" (58). These fantasies do not merely imply the falsity of Margaret's assumptions, but open an avenue for an even more thorough critique.

As she attends to household chores, in anticipation of her husband's return, "repolishing already glowing fixtures, laundering some thing slightly soiled by yesterday's use, fussing through her rooms, ceaselessly, meticulously, happily," Margaret rehearses Guy's tales of foreign exploit: "Guy was coming home to fill the house with boisterous laughter, shouted blasphemies, tales of lawlessness in strangely named places; . . . perhaps tell of the month he had shared a Rat Island hut with two vermin-live Siwashes, sleeping three abed because their blankets were too few for division" (57). On one hand, Guy's stories, like those published in *Sunset,* provide an escapism that mitigates the routine of domestic labor. Seemingly opposed, the categories of exotic adventure and housework enjoy a deeply symbiotic relationship. As we shall see, Margaret's "dainty nest" exists by virtue of Guy's ill-gotten wealth; but Margaret also creates in the metropolitan home a clean, well-lighted place of order and hygiene that both justifies and purifies contagious colonial filth. Upon Guy's return, the home will be contaminated "with the odors of tobacco, with odds and ends of rover's equipment that never could be confined to closet or room, but overflowed to litter the house from roof to cellar. Cartridges would roll underfoot; boots and belts would turn up in unexpected places; cigars, cigar ends, cigar ashes would be everywhere; empty bottles, like as not, would get to the front porch to scandalize the neighbors" (57). "Ruffian's Wife," is, in short, a text preoccupied with what McClintock terms "a semiotics of boundary maintenance" (170): "As colonials traveled back and forth across the thresholds of their known world, crisis and boundary confusion were warded off and contained by fetishes, absolution rituals and liminal scenes. Soap and cleaning rituals became central to the demarcation of body boundaries and the policing of social hierarchies" (33). McClintock goes on to explain that such rituals are often centered upon attention to "boundary objects": "Servants spent much of their time cleaning . . . doorknobs, windowsills, steps, pathways, flagstones, curtains and banisters, not because these objects were especially dirty, but because scrubbing and polishing them ritually maintained the boundaries between public and private and gave these objects exhibition value as class markers" (170). Anticipating Guy's return from sharing, perhaps, "a Rat Island hut with two vermin-live Siwashes," Margaret devotes manic attention to the cleaning of boundary objects that demarcate the borders between domestic and exotic: "Guy was coming home and there were so many things to be done in so small a house; windows and pictures and woodwork to be washed, furniture and floors to be polished, curtains to be hung, rugs to be cleaned" (57).

Throughout "Ruffian's Wife," Margaret's effort at boundary maintenance suffers a twofold rupture. At the outset of the narrative, Margaret is startled one morning to find a "fat man in black . . . on the point of leaving the kitchen": "He was a man past forty, with opaquely glistening eyes whose blackness was repeated with a variety of finish in mustache and hair, freshly ironed suit, and enameled shoes. The dark skin of his face—ball round over tight collar—was peculiarly coarse, fine-grained, as if it had been baked. Against this background his tie was half a foot of scarlet flame" (55–56). Conspicuously "black" and abjectly inhuman, the Greek Leonidas Ducas clearly adumbrates both "the fat man" Caspar Gutman and "the Levantine" Joel Cairo in *The Maltese Falcon* (he even exudes "the warmly sweet fragrance of magnolia" [56]). Like Cairo, he seems an exaggerated sign of the exotic geographies with which he is associated: "He turned slowly, with the smooth precision of a globe revolving on a fixed axis" (55). Although, as we shall see, Hammett accomplishes in "Ruffian's Wife" a demythologizing critique of the adventure genre, he yet engages in rather conventional representations of racial otherness. Margaret immediately realizes that Doucas not only trespasses, invading her kitchen and bedroom, but in doing so profoundly disturbs household boundaries. Ostensibly motivated by Guy's return, Margaret's cleaning rituals are also undoubtedly driven by Doucas's incursion: pursuing Guy in connection with one of the adventurer's schemes, the Greek imports the violence and strangeness of the colonial periphery into the heart of the domestic. As Margaret realizes that the intruder had been looking for Guy, she imagines, "Doucas bending over the bed, his head held stiffly upright, a bright blade in his jeweled fist.

She shivered" (56). This phantasm hyperbolically suggests Margaret's latent fears about the extent of Guy's own sexual transgressions; and, indeed, Guy's return ironically brings about Margaret's ultimate disillusionment.

Margaret immediately dismisses any notion that "a perfumed asthmatic fat man" could harm "her hard-bodied, hard-nerved Guy, to whom violence was no more than addition to a bookkeeper" (57). On one hand, this "ruddy viking in beggar's misfits" fulfills Margaret's romantic fantasies: "The odors of sweat, brine, tobacco cut her nostrils. Bearded flesh scrubbed her cheek. She lost foothold, breath, was folded into him, crushed, bruised, bludgeoned by hard lips. . . . Foul endearments, profane love names, rumbled in her ear. Another sound was even nearer—a throaty cooing. She was laughing. Guy was home" (59). This homecoming, described in terms of both pleasure and pain, captures Margaret's sense of ambivalence about Guy. In addition to the violent undertones, suggestions of septic contamination persist. Though immediately "bathed, shaved, and all in fresh white," Guy disgorges the "Ceylonese spoils" of his colonial adventures: ornaments that appear "heavy gold incongruities above the starched primness of her housedress" and a money belt that "came sluggishly away from his body, thudded on the table, and lay there thick and apathetic as an overfed snake" (59). Aside from the rather obvious sexual connotations, the money belt represents another penetration of the exotic into the home—the jungle denizens that threaten the metropolis in Poe's "The Murders in the Rue Morgue" and Doyle's "The Speckled Band" (1892) here emerge as the dividends of colonial enterprise. The stories "of a brawl in a Madras street or . . . in a gaming house in Saigon" (60), fodder for Margaret's fantasies, paradoxically underscore colonial filth and abjection—bills apparently "cool and green" "cost a pint of somebody's pink blood": "We dyed the Yoda-ela red that one night," Guy reminisces, "Mud under, darkness over, rain everywhere, with a brown devil for every raindrop. A pith helmet hunting for us with a flashlight that never found anything but a stiff-necked Buddha up on a rock before we put it out of business" (60). Images of blood, mud, racial otherness, and criminality merge here in a vision that can hardly be expunged by ritual attention to boundary objects. Guy's allusion to the "stiff-necked Buddha" reminds Margaret of Doucas, and, indeed, the conflict between Guy and his Greek partner decisively "brings home" the dirty violence of his trade. Before meeting with Doucas, Guy warns, "If you hear a racket, . . . you'd better stick your head under the covers and think up the best way to get blood out of rugs" (63). And while Guy finally strangles Doucas, traces of messy fluidity remain—Guy suffers a bloody "nick," and "Blood trickled down his cheek, hung momentarily in fattening drops, dripped down on the dead man's coat" (67). Even as Guy's hand is "dyed red" from his wounded cheek, the domestic itself becomes collapsed with the exotic "Yoda-ela" which the adventurer and his accomplices had "dyed red" during his last exploit. No amount of good housekeeping may repress the disturbing origins and implications of Guy's adventures.

Guy is troubled neither by ethics nor by the suggestive contamination of his metropolitan home; having killed Doucas over a failed Ceylonese sugar heist, he needs the wound to "show self-defense" (67). As in "The Road Home" and "Ber-Bulu," empire building is, to borrow a phrase from Caspar Gutman, "largely a matter of loot" legitimized by the alibis of romantic adventure narratives. This is the realization that visits Margaret throughout the course of "Ruffian's Wife." During his confrontation with Doucas, Guy gradually appears to Margaret less impressive. As he seems to age and diminish,

> Out of the night questions came to torment her, shadowy questions, tangling, knotting, raveling in too swiftly shifting a profusion for any to be clearly seen, but all having something to do with a pride that in eight years had become a very dear thing. They had to do with a pride in a man's courage and hardihood, courage and hardihood that could make of thefts, of murder, of crimes dimly guessed, wrongs no more reprehensible than a boy's apple-stealing. They had to do with the existence or nonexistence of this gliding courage, without which a rover might be no more than a shoplifter on a geographically larger scale, a sneak thief who crept into stranger's lands instead of houses, a furtive, skulking figure with an aptitude for glamorous autobiography. Then pride would be silliness. (63)

This exposé represents the ultimate collapse of the boundaries by which Margaret constructs her world. Recalling the conventional denigrations of the adventure-fiction savage, Hammett also calls into question the constructive distinctions by which the "glamorous autobiographies" of western colonial discourse arrive at self and world. Margaret does finally intervene on Guy's behalf, dousing the lights so that her husband might gain the advantage of his enemy. But even as Guy concocts his alibi and plots his next move—a dash to La Paz for Doucas's pearl concession—, Margaret struggles to keep the disillusionment, "that thing," out of her voice, and her "gaze faltered away from him" (68). Unlike Conrad's Marlow, Hammett refuses to protect the metropolitan angel-in-the-house from the dirty secrets of the colonial enterprise; nor does he attempt to narrate Guy's dissolution as a spectacular Faustian drama—regression is here business as usual. "Ruffian's Wife" may therefore be read as the third in a triptych of early stories in which Hammett explores the implications of exotic adventure. Along with "The Road Home" and "Ber-Bulu," the tale represents Hammett's recognition and continuation of the revisionist project most strikingly undertaken by Louis Becke. "Ruffian's Wife" should also be located as a story that not only treats the failure of metropolitan boundary-maintenance, but also as a liminal text that marks the shift between Hammett's exotic and domestic fictions.

McClintock argues that the exotic landscapes of colonial adventure fiction were themselves influenced by Victorian representations of urban slums, which "were depicted as epistemological problems—as anachronistic worlds of deprivation and unreality, zones without language, history or reason.... The strangeness and density of the urban spectacle resisted penetration by the intruder's empirical eye as an enigma resists knowledge." Within the analogy between slum and colony, journalists, social workers, and novelists inscribed themselves as imperial adventurers exploring distant lands (121). This "endo-Orientalism" persists into crime fictions, as detective and criminal protagonists alike compete in the "asphalt jungle" of the American city.[15] By 1925, Hammett had already begun to suggest the permeability of metro-colonial borders in "Nightmare Town," which appeared in *Argosy All Story Weekly* in 1924. If "Ruffian's Wife" looks forward to *The Maltese Falcon*, then "Nightmare Town" even more clearly adumbrates Hammett's first novel, *Red Harvest* (1929). Both texts see the lone hard-boiled protagonist take on an entire criminal community ensconced in a "grimy factory town" out west. Given their respective settings, "Nightmare Town" and *Red Harvest*, as well as the early short-story "The Man Who Killed Dan Odams" (1924), reveal Hammett as an interpreter of the American Western, a conclusion supported by influential readings of critics such as Philip Durham and Richard Slotkin. The first of these tales, however, explicitly evokes not the Western, but rather the exotic adventure genre with which Hammett had begun his literary career. Like "Ruffian's Wife," "Nightmare Town" is pivotal in that it not only translates the exotic adventurer into the American setting, which itself becomes a violent and unstable contact zone, but also describes that figure's "regeneration through violence."

"Nightmare Town" begins with an episode that reads more like a John Russell adventure tale than a hard-boiled crime story. Just as tales such as "The Fire Walker" and "The Price of his Head" are concerned with Pacific rovers in the final stages of alcoholic dissolution, "Nightmare Town" sees its protagonist Steve Threefall arrested for drunk-driving in a lonely Nevada town. As he awakens in jail, the "large man in bleached khaki" recalls the details of his binge:

> The two days of steady drinking in Whitetufts on the other side of the Nevada-California line with Harris, the hotel-proprietor, and Whiting, an irrigation engineer. The boisterous arguing over desert travel, with his own Gobi experiences matched against the American experiences of the others. The bet that he could drive from Whitetufts to Izzard in daylight with nothing to drink but the especially bitter white liquor they were drinking at the time. The start in the grayness of imminent dawn, in Whiting's Ford, with their drunken shouts and roared-out mocking advice, until he had reached the desert's edge. (4–5)

Hammett recognizes and rejects two distinct narrative possibilities. After the fashion of Conrad and Becke, Hammett might consign the tale to disturbing recollections of the erstwhile adventurers, an avenue which suggests the fragmentation of imperial epic into what Robert Dixon describes as "moments of gossip, or the telling of secrets or shameful anecdotes" (185). "Nightmare Town" might also elaborate the antihero's downward spiral, forestalling utter moral and physical dissolution by some unexpected regeneration, as in the aforementioned John Russell tales. Hammett evokes these alternatives only to proceed with a contrapuntal narrative that inaugurates his own hard-boiled vision. Unlike the compromised adventurers of Becke and Russell, or those of "The Road Home," "Ber-Bulu," and "Ruffian's Wife," Steve Threefall neither reveals a shameful past nor salvages a corrupted masculinity; to the contrary, this hard-boiled traveler demonstrates an alienated insular identity which remains whole in spite of savage environments domestic and exotic.

With the setting of "Nightmare Town," Hammett pursues his collapse of metro-colonial oppositions—while "Ruffian's Wife" asserts the vulnerability of the domestic to colonial "filth," "Nightmare Town" suggests that the settled American continent may not only have been, but remains "one of the dark places of the earth" comparable to exotic locales such as the Gobi desert. Izzard is ostensibly an "outpost of progress" (to borrow another phrase from Conrad)—centered around a soda-niter factory, the town boasts doctors, bankers, ministers, judges, and all the trappings of incipient civilization, right down to the steel engraving of Daniel Webster that adorns the Sheriff's desk. In a movement that will become characteristic of noir, however, the story rapidly exchanges diurnal respectability for a nocturnal world of chaotic violence. The niter operation is revealed as a front for bootlegging and insurance fraud conducted on a massive scale; Izzard is in fact largely populated with criminals. As in *Red Harvest*, big business and crime are for Hammett barely distinguishable twins. And yet, in an almost Melvillean fashion, Hammett ambiguously implies that this "endo-colonial" heart of darkness is also somehow a seat of disturbing whiteness: swilling "bitter white liquor," Threefall drives Whiting's Ford, itself "whitened by desert travel" (3), from Whitetufts to Izzard, where he almost runs down the young woman who will become the heroine of the story. Given the association of the corrupt boom-town with urban poly-ethnicity—"The slums of all the cities of America, and half of 'em out of it, emptied themselves here" (33)—, it is difficult to entirely dismiss the suggestion that Threefall represents a force of apocalyptic white violence, bent upon purging Izzard of the likes of "Gyp," the "bullet-headed Italian" (14). In Hammett's universe, conventional polarities of adventure—exotic/domestic, black/white, nature/culture, savagery/civilization—become difficult to discern; the only entity which emerges intact and coherent is the adventurous masculine subject itself.

Allusions to colonial adventure persist throughout "Nightmare Town." Attracted to the telegraph operator Nova Vallance, Threefall decides to remain in Izzard, initializing a captivity motif familiar to the adventure genre. As her name implies, Nova is the sole exception to the town's corruptions; like Threefall, she has also naively wandered into the criminal haven and is therefore exempt from its depredations: "Her face was an oval of skin whose fine whiteness had thus far withstood the grimy winds of Izzard" (9). Threefall's desire to rescue Nova from savage criminals becomes the driving force of the story. In his awkward demeanor toward Nova, Steve reveals "that for all his thirty-three years of life and his eighteen years of rubbing shoulders with the world—its rough corners as well as its polished—he was still a green boy underneath—a big kid" (10). If Nova fulfills the role of the white captive of frontier adventure, then Roy Kamp obviously, if briefly, serves as Threefall's sidekick, a sign of the homosocial world of "the camp." After a night of gambling, "Not a thousand words had passed between the two men, but they had as surely become brothers-in-arms as if they had tracked a continent together" (15). Throughout the first movements of the story, then, Hammett deploys a series of discernable characters—fraternal male travelers, hostile savages, and the white female captive— as well as continual allusions to the exotic, toward a translation of adventure into the crime story. In doing so, he sets the stage for the fundamental drama of the story, the tension between "psycho-corporeal" wholeness and dissolution.

Threefall at one point confides to Larry Ormsby, his rival for Nova's affections, "I knew a fellow once in Onehunga . . . who thought he owned all the Pacific south of the Tropic of Capricorn—had the papers to prove it. He'd been that way ever since a Maori bashed in his head with a stone *mele*" (25). Threefall's explicit point is the theme of possession; but here is yet another allusion to the Pacific adventure fictions exemplified by Becke and Russell, one which both situates Threefall as a seasoned rover and evokes the adventure genre's anxieties about threats to the embodied self. This "striking" reminiscence for a moment excites fears that exotic adventures might result in violent abrogations of corporeal and psychic boundaries. "Nightmare Town" conjures each of these fearful possibilities, but counters them in the manifold integrity of Steve Threefall. As Steve and Roy Kamp leave the saloon, they are set upon by attackers. While Steve feels "the burning edge of a knife blade [run] down his left arm," Roy suffers a much more horrific injury: "Kamp's thin body was ripped open from throat to waistline . . . the slit in his chest gaped open and he died" (16–17). Hammett's only real pretextual source for such violent images is the adventure story, more particularly the gory tales of Louis Becke. Kamp's evisceration reiterates the corporeal threats to the embodied subject that haunt western colonialism; significantly, the wound accompanies a loss of speech—uttering only the truncated phrase "Get–word–to–" (17), Kamp is finally incapable of even the most minimal gesture of self-representation. A variation on this theme of self-loss occurs later in the fate of Larry Ormsby, a professional gunman posing as the playboy heir to the soda-niter works. As "Nightmare Town" accelerates toward its apocalyptic climax, Larry's ruse is exposed, along with that of the entire operation; and while the killer in some measure redeems himself, becoming "a good guy" in Steve's estimation, he is ultimately done in by "the heavy bullets that literally tore him apart" (39), doomed to a physical dismemberment that parallels his unstable identity. Here is an early example of noir's fundamental suspicion of the confidence man: as I shall argue at length in ensuing chapters, this protean figure celebrates the unstable, textualized subject countered by the alienated authenticity of the noir hero.

And, indeed, Steve Threefall himself stands in dramatic opposition to the fragmented bodies and compromised identities of Roy Kamp and Larry Ormsby. Anticipating the "blood simple" frenzy of the Continental Op in *Red Harvest,* Steve "tore pieces . . . tore hair and flesh" (41) from his enemies in Izzard; but the adventurer himself remains whole in body and spirit. While Kamp gets ripped open in the initial fight, Steve suffers only a superficial laceration and "blows that shook, staggered him" (16): in contrast to Victorian adventurers, the "hard-bodied" and hard-boiled hero of noir is a mythologically bruised, contused figure, one largely exempt from penetrations, perforations, and dismemberments that imply subverted identity.[16] Steve's muscled body is in fact wholly consistent with the metonymic walking-stick that is his primary weapon: "It was thick and of ebony, but heavy even for that wood, with a balanced weight that hinted at loaded ferrule and knob. Except for a space the breadth of a man's hand in its middle, the stick was roughened, cut and notched with the marks of hard use—marks that careful polishing had failed to remove or conceal" (6). Though an almost hyperbolic phallus, the ebony stick is also a souvenir and sign of Steve's exotic adventures. But here is no index into corruption or regression, as with drug paraphernalia or tattoo; the staff suggests rather a subjectivity fortified by "eighteen years of rubbing shoulders with the world—its rough corners as well as its polished." Unlike the poor fellow in Onehunga, who was "bashed" body and mind by a stone *mele,* Steve comes to be identified with an exotic weapon that signifies his integrity. Thus, at the conclusion of "Nightmare Town," Steve proves himself impervious to the dangers of Izzard; there is never any suggestion of the corruption that marks Larry Ormsby (and, by extension, that which pervades Hammett's earlier adventurers); nor is there any sense in which Steve suffers the corporeal ruptures visited upon Ormsby and Roy Kamp. In the final moments of the story, Steve drives away from the devastated Izzard and into the desert with Nova Vallance, thereby completing the circuit of the captivity narrative; he dreams of returning with the girl to his mother's home in Delaware, the settled world of the east. Although the wounded hero feels "that if she tried to patch him up he would fall apart in her hands"—a harbinger, perhaps, of noir paranoia about female threats to subjectivity— he muses on the glories of the fight and assures Nova that he is "all in one piece" (41).

THE ROMANTIC denouement of "Nightmare Town" is the exception rather than the rule of Hammett's fiction—his adventure tales and crime stories alike often splinter fantasies of the nuclear family against what Fredric Jameson has termed the "great modernist thematics of alienation, anomie, solitude, and social fragmentation and isolation."[17] The roving manhunter Hagedorn, the beachcomber Peters, and even the unlikely Margaret Tharp adumbrate alienated detectives such as the Continental Op and Sam Spade. And yet this alienation becomes its own kind of reassuring fantasy: a counter not only to the implausible optimism of conventional romance, but also to the disturbing threats elicited by late-Victorian colonial adventure. Hammett recognizes the shifting identities and exploded bodies of colonial adventure only to posit a hard-boiled hero cohered—"all in one piece"—and coherent; a figure devoted, like his Victorian predecessors, to the task of policing boundaries disrupted throughout the colonial enterprise. Unlike Steve Threefall, Hammett's most celebrated detectives are not explicitly identified as exotic adventurers. I would maintain, however, that Threefall, along with Hagedorn, Peters, and Margaret Tharp, are ideological cousins of the hard-boiled detective. These protagonists must in some way traverse endo-colonial spaces, such as the liminal city of San Francisco, confronting criminals who, whatever their other crimes, have violated geographical, cultural, and corporeal boundaries. As Paul Skenazy suggests, Hammett's detectives are given to the "almost janitorial" task of descending into and sanitizing the abysmal world of the modern city (14). Having rehearsed Hammett's adventure stories in something of a "syntagmatic" fashion, I would now turn to a "paradigmatic" discussion of his Continental Op stories and *The Maltese Falcon*, encountering throughout the ways in which these texts evoke and manage a series of "adventurous" elements: the "endo-Orient," the savage Other, metrocolonial transgressors, and, finally, the detective himself, who significantly "takes blows" in pursuit of boundary maintenance.

Like the Victorian slums described by McClintock, Hammett's San Francisco often appears a nether-world that defies the detective's incursions. The Op and Sam Spade must negotiate at street level a dark and claustrophobic world: approaching "a dark block on the edge of Chinatown," in "The Whosis Kid" (1925), the Op admits: "Peering through the rain and darkness, I tried to pick out a detail or so as I approached, but I could see little" (320–21).[18] Similarly, in "Dead Yellow Women" (1925), the Op explores the labyrinths of Chinatown only to become hopelessly lost: "For a while, I amused myself by trying to map the route in my head as he went along, but it was too complicated, so I gave up" (425). Negotiating exoticized spaces like Chinatown and the suggestively named "House in Turk Street" (1924), the Op and Sam Spade find a metropolis at once developed and regressed where, as Sam Spade assures us, "Most things . . . can be bought or taken" (36). Hammett's San Francisco is pervaded by explosive crime and violence. In "The Big Knock-Over" (1927), for example, a tandem bank-heist involving dozens of criminals renders the streets a battle zone, the interiors the site of bloody massacres and melees more appropriate to colonial adventure than the mystery story.

Hammett exoticizes San Francisco by peopling this fictional world with all manner of racial and sexual others. In "Dead Yellow Women," the Op makes two stops that encapsulate Hammett's approach to endo-colonial San Francisco. He devotes the first paragraph of this section to his visit to Lilian Shan's home in San Mateo County: "full of hangings and pictures and so on—a mixture of things American, European and Asiatic" (399), the house is not only the scene of the titular double murder, but also a synecdoche for the manifold transgressions that characterize Hammett's universe. As I have suggested throughout, the Op is "Continental" in more ways than one—even as he is employed by the Continental Detective Agency, the Op's ultimate purpose is itself "continental," that is, to reassert containing borders of all kinds. As if disturbed by the boundary crossings represented in the Shan home, the Op returns to the city, where he immediately seeks out an assistant:

> I found the lad I wanted in his cubby-hole room, getting his small body into a cerise shirt that was something to look at. Cipriano was the bright-faced Filipino boy who looked after the building's front door in the daytime. At night, like all the Filipinos in San Francisco, he could be found down on Kearney Street, just below Chinatown, except when he was in a Chinese gambling-house passing his money over to the yellow brothers. (400)

Here is another of Hammett's suggestive asides; the Op describes a figure that, while symptomatic of polyglot San Francisco, yet provides a momentary return to the certainties of colonial administration. Cipriano is stereotypical and predictable: a knowable Other who resides within finite geographical boundaries and is therefore available, in his "cubby-hole," for deployment. Like Sherlock Holmes's "Baker Street Irregulars" or the Native Hawaiian "Barefoot Boys" in William Campbell Gault's "Hibiscus and Homicide" (1947), Cipriano becomes the "good native" that might be instrumentalized in the struggle against the recalcitrant savage.[19] These suggestions of administrative certainty amplify in the Op's exchange with Cipriano. "Come in, sir!" Cipriano announces, prompting the Op to confide, "He was dragging a chair out of a corner for me, bowing and smiling. Whatever else the Spaniards do for the people they rule, they make them polite" (400). With this remark, the Op utters Hammett's counterpoint to his contemporary Filipino character, Jeffol, the volatile Moro of "Ber-Bulu." For Hammett, as for the U.S. colonial imagination as a whole, Filipinos might be inscribed as either phantasm of savagery or fantasy of control; both figures, however, speak to the anxieties centered, at the turn of the century, upon the American experience in the Philippines. Recruited by the Op as an informant about criminal activities in Chinatown, Cipriano replies, "Chinaboy don't talk much about things like that. Not like us Americans" (400). An idealized colonial subject, Cipriano belies the savage others and border-crossers against which the Op must contend.

In "The Big Knock-over," the Op shadows a dapper "Armenian boy," "the Motsa Kid," only to find his surveillance complicated by the intrusion of another, more menacing figure. Even as two assailants close in on the Armenian,

> another reached them—a broad-backed, long-armed ape-built man I had not seen before. His gorilla's paws went out together. Each caught a man. By

the napes of their necks he yanked them away from the boy's back, shook them till their hats fell off, smacked their skulls together with a crack that was like a broom-handle breaking, and dragged their limp bodies out of sight up the alley. . . . When the skull-cracker came out of the alley I saw his face in the light—a dark-skinned, heavily lined face, broad and flat, with jaw-muscles bulging like abscesses under his ears. (550)

Known only as "Pogy," this unpredictable figure almost immediately turns upon his ward, slitting his throat in a seedy rooming-house. Though not so obviously racialized as some of Hammett's characters, Pogy is perhaps the most regressed and savage antagonist of the Op stories. At once "dark-skinned," simian, and altogether violent, Pogy embodies the primitive dangers lurking in the anachronistic urban jungle of San Francisco. Following Julia Kristeva, David Spurr suggests that colonial discourse persistently ascribes violation onto the indigenous body itself: "The defilement of the self's clean and proper body, here explicitly characterized as monstrous and inhuman, marks the transgression of a crucial boundary between inside and out, between the self and that which it literally must exclude in order to maintain its difference from the Other" (81).[20] Not content with describing Pogy's bestial atavism (he is in this respect reminiscent of Poe's Ourang-Outang in "The Murders in the Rue Morgue" as well as Doyle's Tonga in *The Sign of Four*), the Op goes further to compare his abnormally "bulging" body with abscesses that violate "clean and proper" body boundaries. Pogy is therefore the epicenter of a disturbing savagery that permeates "The Big Knock-Over" and Hammett's detective fiction at large. Even as he encounters the inhuman Pogy, the Op also confronts "a pock-marked mulatto" during the melee at Larrouy's (570); at another the scarred body of "Spider Girrucci" and "Nigger Vojan," who had "*Abacadabra* tattooed on him in three places" (555). There is also the Irishman Red O'Leary, a "fire-haired young rowdy" (569) whose propensity for explosive violence catalyzes the Larrouy's riot and much of the succeeding action in the story. Prowling the dark interiors of the rooming-house, Big Flora represents another variation on the endo-colonial savage: "Her head was down like an animal's coming to a fight," the Op observes, "If I live to a million I'll never forget the picture this handsome brutal woman made coming down those unplaned cellar stairs. She was a beautiful fight-bred animal going to a fight" (588). Wearing "beaded moccasins" (585) and a "green kimono affair, which gaped here and there to show a lot of orchid-colored underthings" (579), Big Flora exemplifies another recurrent Hammett figure—the exotic femme fatale.

Questioned in "The Whosis Kid" about whether he is "enamored of one yellow and white lady somewhere," the Op laconically replies that "all women are dark" (332); with characteristic cynicism, the Op collapses the distinction between the metropolitan angel and savage seductress, a misogynistic vision that will persist throughout the noir imagination, intersecting at many points with colonial discourse. As Spurr argues, colonialist rhetoric routinely indulges in a lustful drive to "unveil" and penetrate landscapes at once geographical and corporeal:

> Within a tradition that opposes sexual excess to the rationally ordered subject, the role of colonialist writing has been to project this opposition onto the arena of the confrontation between cultures. The nature of this projection . . . accounts for the peculiar double-sidedness of the discourse, by which the non-Western world stands for sexual debasement and death as well as sexual adventure. Both of these representations may be traced to the destruction of barriers—to the transgression of human borders common to eroticism and colonization. (182–83)

Hammett's detective stories are replete with dangerous, atavistic women such as Big Flora and Elvira, in "The House in Turk Street" and "The Girl With the Silver Eyes" (1924), who sports "a bobbed mass of flame-colored hair" and "little animal teeth" (130). With the exception of Dinihari in "Ber-Bulu," however, Hammett's most frankly Orientalist female character is Inés Almad in "The Whosis Kid." Speculating about the foreign origins of this temptress, the Op describes her in terms that suggest violence, sexuality, deception, and exoticism:

> She was dark as an Indian, with bare brown shoulders round and sloping, tiny feet and hands, her fingers heavy with rings. Her nose was thin and curved, her mouth full-lipped and red, her eyes—long and thickly lashed—were of an extraordinary narrowness. They were dark eyes, but nothing of their color could be seen through the thin slits that separated the lids. Two dark gleams through veiling lashes. Her black hair was disarranged just now in fluffy silk puffs. A rope of pearls hung down her dark chest. Earrings of black iron—in a peculiar club-like design—swung beside her cheeks. Altogether, she was an odd trick. But I wouldn't want to be quoted as saying she wasn't beautiful—in a wild way. (325)

Like the dark urban landscape, Inés in some measure resists the penetrating gaze of the detective, an obscurity which in itself represents a threat of castration[21]; although he cannot fully read her narrow, veiled eyes, the Op does manage to survey the body at large, in which he discerns not only a sexual object, but signs of violence—a "rope of pearls" and iron, club-like earrings. Even as she is driven by a primal desire for self-preservation, "everything else about this brown woman was all wrong": "She wasn't hampered by any pruderies or puritanisms at all" (328). Whether plying the Op with Hindu incense-tobacco, which "smelt and scorched like gunpowder" (327) or seducing her accomplices into a fatal free-for-all, Inés proves a dire threat to the urban adventurer. She certainly anticipates Hammett's most prominent femme fatale, Brigid O'Shaughnessy. Though a practiced liar, Inés Almad presents an exotic threat registered through racial markings; Brigid, on the other hand, is a femme fatale in whom Hammett conflates savagery and unchecked signification. Introducing herself as "Miss Wonderly" and, later, "Miss LeBlanc," monikers which almost parodically evoke the white metropolitan angel, Brigid initially attempts to write herself into a kind of captivity narrative: "I met him [Thursby] in the Orient. . . . We came here from Hongkong last week. He was—he promised to help me. He took advantage of my helplessness and dependence on him to betray me" (45). Beneath this appealing front, however, lies the savage predator of the colonial periphery: recalling Elvira and Red O'Leary, Brigid is a murderous Irish woman with "dark red hair" (4); like these more obviously menacing characters, she easily resorts to violence, murdering Archer and Thursby. "I couldn't be sure you wouldn't decide to shoot a hole in *me* some day" (263), Spade concludes. But self-preservation is only the most apparent motive for Spade's betrayal of Brigid at the conclusion of the novel; against Effie Perrine's assurances, Spade ultimately decides, "She's got too many names" (43). Brigid's duplicity alerts Spade to a deeper threat, but her propensity to narrate and reinvent herself also constitutes a profound threat in and of itself. Brigid is only the most prominent of many Hammett characters whose border crossings evoke the most disturbing implication of adventure fiction: that self and world are fluid cultural constructs.

When a "swarthy" hard-case introduces himself as "Tom-Tom Carey," "Paddy the Mex's brother," at the outset of "$106,000 Blood Money," the Op replies, "That would make your real name Carrera": the Op then carefully records his visitor's "real name"—"Alfredo Estanislao Cristobal Carrera"—against the alias and dispatches a file clerk to "see if we had anything on it" (592). The story's inaugural drama captures what is perhaps the central preoccupation of Hammett's detective fiction—the struggle to reinscribe borders that have been compromised within the modern metropolis. As his alias implies, Tom-Tom is one of the many savage miscreants that plague the Op's San Francisco. Pursuing his brother's killer, for the titular reward, Tom-Tom not only violates geographical borders (he is in fact a "gun-runner, seal-poacher, smuggler and pirate" who moves at will "to and fro across the line" between Mexico and the United States [594–96]), but he tortures Hank Barrows in a way that recalls the disruptions of body-boundaries familiar to late-Victorian adventure: "From his bare chest and sides and back, little ribbons of flesh hung down, dripping blood. His left arm was broken in two places. The left side of his bald head was smashed in" (605). Tom-Tom joins Brigid O'Shaughnessy in posing the added threat of unchecked signification: many of Hammett's antagonists are in effect con artists who somehow assume multiple identities and therefore call into question the notion of stable, essential selfhood. Such figures will become central to postmodernist parodies of noir. With his "cultured British drawl" and "fashionable British clothes" (133), the "anglicized oriental" Tai Choon Tau, in "The House in Turk Street," is one such figure; another is *The Maltese Falcon*'s Joel Cairo, an invasive alien who reads as an almost allegorical sign of the "Levant." Each of these dangerous criminals combines the threat of criminal violence with a transgression of geographical and cultural boundaries, the adoption of western names and/or clothing. It is the Op's task to "arrest" and/or contain such violators, if only through documenting the "real name" and identity in a Continental Detective Agency file.

Though replete with savage antagonists, the Continental Op stories and *The Maltese Falcon* follow the Victorian detective story by pitting the metropolitan sleuth against corrupted colonials whose adventures have compromised western virtues of morality and rationality. Perhaps the most prominent of these figures is Caspar Gutman in *The Maltese Falcon*, an adventurer who not only colludes with exotics Joel Cairo and Brigid O'Shaughnessy, but one who narrates a cynical historiography of colonial corruption: "For years they [the Knights of Rhodes] preyed on the Saracens, had taken nobody knows what spoils of gems, precious metals, silks, ivories—the cream of the cream of the East. That is history, sir. We all know that the Holy Wars to them, as to the Templars, were largely a matter of loot." Such a conviction might serve as a gloss on "The Road Home" and "Ruffian's Wife"; indeed, Gutman's assurance that the falcon is encrusted with the "finest [jewels] out of Asia" (128) hearkens back to Hammett's first *Black Mask* story in which Barnes tempts the detective Hagedorn with "the richest gem beds in Asia." In "The Farewell Murder" (1930), however, Hammett presents an even more striking portrait of colonial contagion. In this tale, invasion emerges in the form of a band of European mercenaries: a Russian arms dealer, an American opportunist, and a former British Army officer who commands a murderous "black devil." Recently posted in Cairo, these adventurers converge in California, where they begin to murder each other in a spree that includes throat-slashing and canine mutilation. Hammett derives such figures directly from the literature of late-Victorian adventure; colonial experience at once seduces, callouses, and enervates, rendering the prodigal extremely dangerous and amoral. The cashiered British officer Hugh Sherry, late of "Udja, a stinking Moroccan town close to the Algerian frontier" (761), exemplifies Hammett's treatment of the colonial adventurer. Noticing his "languid drawl," the Op observes Sherry: "He was one hard sane-looking scoundrel. And I didn't believe he was the sort of man who'd be worried much over any disgrace that came his way" (316).

Sherry and Ringgo, the culprits of "The Farewell Murder," devise an elaborate scheme in order to cover their conspiracy against the arms-dealer Kavalov; but other Continental Op stories feature corrupted adventurers even more closely associated with the confidence-game. Hints of such manipulations appear in the early Op stories "Arson Plus" and "Slippery Fingers," both of which appeared in *Black Mask* in 1923. The former tale concerns a career seaman returned from travels in "Rio de Janeiro, Madagascar, Tobago, Christiania" (12) only to fake his own death in an insurance fraud scheme. The murder-victim Henry Grover in "Slippery Fingers" is likewise the veteran of travels through "Yunnan, Peru, Mexico, and Central America" (23)—it turns out that the wealthy mining magnate had gotten his start by murdering a rival in the Canadian gold fields. He is himself done in by a blackmailer who witnessed the murder and who conceals his part in the crime by masking his own finger prints. Perhaps the most telling of these stories, however, is "The Creeping Siamese," a 1926 *Black Mask* tale which gathers many of the principal themes and motifs evident throughout Hammett's adventure and mystery fictions. As its title implies, the story appears at first blush a straightforward exercise in Orientalism. Looking forward to the death of Captain Jacobi in *The Maltese Falcon*, "The Creeping Siamese" begins with a murder-victim falling dead in the Op's office—a silk sarong found on the body, along with the testimony of a witness, point to a Siamese culprit. Pursuing a search for "brown men" (531), the Op and Sgt. O'Gar (a veteran of "soldiering on the islands"[525]) come to suspect the Richters, a couple acquainted with the victim through adventures in Mexico. Like Tom-Tom Carey, "Molloy," as he is momentarily known, "was running guns over the border" (529). The Op ultimately finds that each of the principals in the case is a colonial adventurer with multiple aliases. The victim Rounds/Molloy/Dawson/Lange is murdered by Richter/Holley and his own estranged wife (Mrs. Lange/Richter) over a Burmese caper that clearly derives from "The Road Home." After "drifting . . . mostly around Asia," the Langes meet Holley in Singapore in 1919:

> He knew of a gem-bed in upper Burma, one of many that were hidden from the British when they took the country. He knew the natives who were working it, knew where they were hiding their gems. My husband went in with him, with two other men that were killed. They looted the natives' cache, and got away with a whole sackful of sapphires, topazes and even a few rubies. The two men were killed by the natives and my husband was badly wounded.

"Hiding in a hut near the Yunnan border" (535), Holley and Mrs. Lange abscond with the loot, eventually migrating to San Francisco, where they operate a movie-house. When Lange shows up, they struggle, and the woman kills her husband with a handy *kris* (the weapon, we might recall, with which Jeffol attacks Levison in "Ber-Bulu"). For McCann, this text "almost polemically . . . uncovers the scapegoating fantasies of foreign adventure fiction and its Klannish analogues. Race, the story implies, is an empty but potent social fiction" (69–70). While offering a constructivist counterpoint to the essentialist racism of the Ku Klux Klan, "The Creeping Siamese" also reiterates Hammett's nomination of the colonial adventurer as a sign of the destabilized self. Even as the story turns upon the murderous desires surrounding Burmese gem-beds, the tale recalls thematic tensions that inform Hammett's fictions as early as the "The Road Home." Hammett's rovers do not simply succumb to the savage regressions implied by amoral and criminal behavior; moving at will across borders, and adopting multiple aliases, these figures lose any notion of stable identity.

Like his predecessor Louis Becke, Hammett recognizes human subjectivity as a fluid construct that might "go native" or mutate with a change in geographical and/or cultural context. Though interested in fashioning an ideal of metropolitan fidelity in figures such as the trader Watson, Becke appears yet more fascinated and preoccupied with protean characters such as Deschard of Oneaka and Martin of Nitendi. Hammett, on the other hand, foregrounds his detective heroes against savage others and mutable adventurers—the Op is "continental" not only by virtue of professional affiliation, but also in that he and his colleagues work to arrest and generally "contain" compromised spaces and subjectivities. When the Op offhandedly suggests in "The Big Knock-Over" that Dick Foley "could have shadowed a drop of water from the Golden Gate to Hongkong without ever losing sight of it" (560), he describes an ideal of metrocolonial surveillance to which he himself aspires. Whether halting the cultural confusions of Tai Choon Tau, carefully documenting Tom-Tom Carey's "real name," or discovering the confidence games of a plethora of colonial adventurers, the Op and Sam Spade faithfully discharge a mission of manifold containment. As we have seen, this "continental operation" informs Hammett's inaugural detective story, "The Road Home," and persists through the more celebrated hard-boiled fictions of the late 1920s.

One might reasonably point out that such a reading hardly distinguishes Hammett from his Victorian forbearers: does not Sherlock Holmes likewise confute lapsed colonials in tales such as *A Study in Scarlet*, *The Sign of Four*, "The Adventure of the Dying Detective" (1913), and many others? But Holmes is himself a site of conflict and instability; "The Adventure of the Empty House" (1903) is in this respect paradigmatic. The problem of the story is the threat posed by Colonel Moran, a veteran of Indian and Afghan campaigns, the author of *Three Months in the Jungle*: seasoned by combat and big-game hunting, this sometime confederate of Professor Moriarty ingeniously shoots his victims with an ingenious air-rifle. But this is also the story in which Holmes miraculously returns from the dead after supposedly perishing in his struggle with Moriarty at the Reichenbach Falls. We learn that Holmes has escaped death at the hands of Moriarty's minions (actually, Col. Moran himself) by wandering incognito throughout the reaches of the empire: "I traveled for two years in Tibet . . . and amused myself by visiting Lhassa and spending some days with the head Llama. . . . I then passed through Persia, looked in at Mecca, and paid a short but interesting visit to the Khalifia at Khartoum, the results of which I have communicated to the foreign office." Holmes returns from his tour to best the "old shikari" Moran by setting his own hunter's trap in the Baker Street apartments. What we see then in "The Adventure of the Empty House," and in Doyle's fiction at large, is an affinity between the protagonist and antagonist that is endemic to Victorian detection.[22] Holmes may police the "dark jungle of criminal London" (488)[23] precisely because he has undergone the same exotic crucible as atavistic characters such as Col. Moran. Traversing class, cultural, geographical boundaries, assuming disguises, smoking opium and injecting cocaine, however, Holmes threatens to collapse into the very otherness that he opposes. Hard-boiled writers depart from classical mystery fictions not simply because of a modernist crisis of faith in the detective's superhuman rationality, but also because this eccentric character literally embodies the subjective slippage of the protean colonial adventurer.

The Continental Op at one point worries about whether he will be able to "out-Indian" Hugh Sherry's black servant Marcus. Such a euphemism reveals a great deal about the Hammett hero. As Richard Slotkin suggests, he is "the man who knows Indians": "a recrudescence of the frontier-hero . . . an agent of regenerative violence through whom we recover the ideological values, if not the material reality, of the mythic Frontier."[24] Challenged by intrusive exotics and corrupted colonials, the hard-boiled detective is "acquainted with the night" (to borrow a phrase from Robert Frost) and yet equipped to resist its otherness. As he wanders hostile asphalt jungles, the Hammett hero insinuates himself into criminal enclaves, "out-Indianing" the opposition through detachment and ruthlessness. In "The Whosis Kid," the Op admits, "I'm no Galahad . . . the idea in this detective business is to catch crooks, not to put on heroics" (344, 347); it is an ideal realized not only in the Op's stoicism but also in Sam Spade's cold rejection of Brigid O'Shaugnessy at the conclusion of *The Maltese Falcon*. Hammett's hard-boiled detective may have forfeited chivalric ideals, rendering himself capable of expedient brutality, without abnegating his ethical center. As Angel Grace suggests in "The Big Knock-Over," the Op remains "one white dick" (562). It is this very alienated authenticity that literally sets this figure apart from his corrupted milieu. In Baudrillard's phrase, this isolation is "invested as a protective enclosure, an imaginary protector, a defense system."

"I've got horny skin all over what's left of my soul" (551), the Op assures us in "The Big Knock-Over," a corporeal trope altogether suggestive of the ways in which the alienated subjectivity of the hard-boiled detective is reiterated by a body contused but discrete and coherent. In a world of violated bodies and fluid selves, the Continental Op and Sam Spade, along with Steve Threefall in "Nightmare Town," count on "coming through all in one piece" (339). Like all noir protagonists, the Op is by no means physically invincible; he repeatedly describes himself as "pushing forty, and . . . twenty pounds overweight (569). Distinguished in part by physical vulnerability, this hero emerges a bruised and battered body. "I got a split lip and a kicked shoulder in the scuffle," the Op notes in "Slippery Fingers," "but I felt pretty chirp in spite of my bruises" (30). In "The Whosis Kid," the Op gets "clipped" twice: "Once on the shoulder. A big fist spun me half around. . . . The other time he caught me on the forehead. . . . The smack hurt me. It must have hurt him more. A skull is tougher than a knuckle" (334). Only rarely is the Hammett hero lacerated (as in "106,000 Blood Money") or punctured (the dramatic exception being *Red Harvest*). Whereas violent openings of the body—slashing, stabbing, shooting, amputation, tattooing, hypodermic injection—call into question the boundaries of the subject, contusions reaffirm a self heroically isolated from a world of compromised borders. Peopling his novels and short-stories with violent racial Others and protean con-men, Hammett opened the body of his fiction to the manifold explosions of late-Victorian adventure and detective fiction. He then countered the subversive implications of these texts by positing in the hard-boiled detective an adventurer inured to and polarized against the dark places of the metropolis. Hammett's most famous successor, Raymond Chandler, projected his own vision of alienated selfhood, engaging in an elegiac dialogue with the "tropical romance."

CHAPTER TWO

RAYMOND CHANDLER'S SEMI-TROPICAL ROMANCE

> *Even in death a man has a right to his own identity.*
> —Raymond Chandler, "The Simple Art of Murder" (1950)

The opening sequence of *The Big Sleep* finds detective Philip Marlowe in the atrium of the Sternwood mansion, reflecting on a stained-glass scene drawn from medieval romance:

> Over the entrance doors, which would have let in a troop of Indian elephants, there was a broad stained-glass panel showing a knight in dark armor rescuing a lady who was tied to a tree and didn't have any clothes on but some long and very convenient hair. The knight had pushed the vizor of his helmet back to be sociable, and he was fiddling with the knots on the ropes that tied the lady to the tree and not getting anywhere. I stood there and thought that if I lived in the house, I would sooner or later have to climb up there and help him. He didn't seem to be really trying. (3)

Looking forward to Marlowe's later pronouncement that "Knights had no meaning in this game" (95), this moment inaugurates a strain of medievalism that runs throughout *The Big Sleep* and the Chandler oeuvre at large. Indeed, as Charles J. Rzepka suggests, Chandler's casting of the detective as "ideal knight" "has become "something of a touchstone of evaluation both to Chandler's most fervent admirers and to his most derisory critics" (720). Whether explicitly evoking Mallory in *The Lady in the Lake* (1943) or giving his characters allusive names

53

such as Quest, Grayle, and Kingsley,[1] Chandler renders in Marlowe a "detective-knight," as Ernest Fontana has it, vainly struggling in "an ironic or failed romance . . . [which] establishes a mystery whose solution does not liberate or energize a diseased and entropic world" (185). Such a reading illuminates Chandler's own vision of authenticating alienation—Marlowe emerges in heroic relief against a universe hostile to his chivalric code. At the same time, however, attention to Chandler's modernist medievalism has to some extent obscured critical recognition of the novelist's Orientalism. After all, Marlowe prefaces his reading of the stained-glass romance with an observation that the image frames "entrance doors, which would have let in a troop of Indian elephants"—an offhand remark that recalls the foreign invasions pervasive to "imperial gothic" detective fiction. As we shall see, the Sternwood mansion becomes a synecdoche for Chandler's California—a world of breached borders and compromised identities countered only by the "continental" operations of the alienated hard-boiled detective. Like Hammett, Chandler achieved this vision of authenticating alienation by means of a sustained dialogue with colonial adventure.

Chandler introduces his *The Simple Art of Murder* (1950) with the line, "Some literary antiquarian of a rather special type may one day think it worthwhile to run through the files of the pulp magazines which flourished during the late twenties and early thirties, and determine just how and when and by what steps the popular mystery story shed its refined good manners and went native" (1016). Anticipating the essay's celebration of the rough-hewn pulps, this overture also hints at Chandler's own sense of the complex entanglements between hard-boiled fiction and colonial adventure—a relationship which Chandler himself nurtured and sustained. Megan Abbott notes, "It is no accident that Chandler's language is infused with a vague late-imperialist sentiment ('went native,' 'dark with something more than night'). Such heart-of-darkness rhetoric discloses the tough guy's connection to America's own racial history." Abbott finds in this passage a pretext for discussion of "American frontier and Western literature" (12–13), which trumps the classical mystery story as a primary influence upon hard-boiled fiction. As we see in Hammett's fiction, however, the Victorian detective story exemplified by Poe and Doyle shares with its cynical twentieth-century descendant an anxious preoccupation with fin-de-siècle adventure fiction. In a much earlier and lesser-known critical work, "The Tropical Romance" (1912), Chandler takes this literary form as his subject, elegizing a genre that "appears to be doomed":

> No longer does it glide majestically by glorious palm-fringed islands bathed in opalescent light, pant over burning ageless deserts, insinuate

itself through the tangled mysterious bazaars of the Orient, or have strange dealings with grave Arabs, smiling Kanakas, inscrutable Chinamen, wily Japanese. Gone too are its heroes, the strong men who looked unmoved on death and horror, picturesque, hard-living cynics of the high-seas and barbaric lands, lean as tigers, weather-beaten as figure-heads, clad in weird garments, smoking eternal cheroots. (68)

Though he mentions no specific writers, Chandler might well be describing the fictions of Stevenson, Becke, and Russell, which most conspicuously foreground "palm-fringed islands" and "smiling Kanakas," as a setting for the adventures of "hard-living cynics." Chandler goes on to elaborate the modern fate of the tropical romance—victim of a world in which "[t]he touch of strangeness, the sense of exploration, has vanished from those far-off, dangerous, inaccessible regions once loved by violent adventure" (69). In terms that look forward to the advent of the *Black Mask* school, Chandler laments the passing of adventure: "It was apt to display the raw edge of things, and to provide murderous-minded authors with a great many opportunities to enlarge on the surgical aspect of sudden death." But the real focus of the essay is the "adventurer, artless and incorrigible": "He is driven from his kingdom and has no land to call his own.... A few of his kind only, and those degenerate ones, have not scorned to set foot in cities, where they bow and strut in Brummagem-made clockwork detective stories, and may possibly appear heroic to errand boys" (68–69). It is easy to discern in "The Tropical Romance" a glimmer of Chandler's later work; the essay's argument for a populist "raw-edged" aesthetic prefigures "The Simple Art of Murder" (1934), in which Chandler describes how "Hammett took murder out of the Venetian vase and dropped it into the alley" (16). Moreover, Chandler's valorization of adventurers as "shop-soiled heroes with tarnished morals and unflinching courage" (69) holds the germs of his later characterization of the hard-boiled detective as a "shop-soiled Galahad ...," though one "who is neither tarnished nor afraid."[2] That Chandler knew and was influenced by late-Victorian adventure is indisputable; but while it would be tempting to simply recognize the genre as a source of energy and vitality for Chandler's own fiction, such a reading cannot account for the ways in which Chandler admits colonial adventure motifs into his detective stories, investigating and responding to their ideological implications.

Matthew Bruccoli imagines Chandler himself as a protagonist of exotic adventure, "one of those Englishmen who went out to settle Africa and dressed for dinner every night in the jungle."[3] This is an apt tableau, for Chandler, like Hammett and Hemingway, inherited from Conrad the agonism of the western sojourner striving to retain his "civilization" in a savage wilderness. Herein lies the fundamental drama of Chandler's crime fiction: the Sisyphean task of arresting the plastic selves of adventurers gone native in California's urban jungles. If Marlowe is a knight-errant, then he is a lonely Crusader seeking to rescue not damsels in distress so much as comrades-in-arms victimized by distressing damsels. As McCann has it, "Chandler returned time and again to a vision of male fellowship and showed the way it was undermined by the various evils of the modern world.... [E]ach of the novels for which Chandler is best remembered ... depicts the deep feeling between Phillip Marlowe and some idealized brother figure; and each shows that brotherhood falling prey to corruption and exploitation" (140–41). I pursue Chandler's dialogue with the adventure story throughout three representative texts: the early short story "Mandarin's Jade" (1937), the inaugural novel *The Big Sleep* (1939), and the later Marlowe novel *The Long Goodbye* (1953), in which Chandler most explicitly evokes and treats the epistemological problems elicited by the "tropical romance." While it is important to keep in mind the pretext of the cynical fin-de-siècle adventure story, we should also consider Chandler's response to the triumphalist spirit of Manifest Destiny, which perhaps found its highest expression in the "California adventure." I therefore read Chandler's fictions as literary responses not only to late-Victorian adventures, but also to a specific adventurous mid-Victorian text, Benjamin Cummings Truman's 1874 promotional tract *Semi-tropical California*. In *The Big Sleep*, Chandler recasts Major Truman's Utopian Anglo-American colony as the savage colonial periphery of late-Victorian adventure; following Hammett, however, Chandler then delimits the confusions of that milieu via the person of the alienated hard-boiled detective.

OFTEN EXPLOITED as a fictional setting, California in a real sense *emerges* from fiction; the region is named for a fabulous island in Garci Rodríguez de Montalvo's 1508 novel *Las Sergas de Esplandián*, "the strangest thing that could ever be found in literature, or in any case the memory of people": "Know that to the right-hand of the Indies was an island called California, very near the region of the Terrestrial Paradise, which was populated by black women, without there being any men among them, that almost like the Amazons was their style of living. ... Any male that entered the island was killed and eaten by them. ... "[4] Montalvo's seminal tropical romance proved enormously influential, guiding western cartographic representations of California until well into the seventeenth century. California has persisted as a world of contrary polarities, at once a utopian field of adventure, wealth, and pleasure and a dystopia in which the western adventurer might be wholly subsumed into savage otherness. Obvious in Montalvo's foundational myth, such ambivalence also clearly informs later texts such as Richard Henry Dana's *Two Years before the Mast* (1840), not to mention L.A. noir as a whole. Fears of white enervation are suspended in Anglo-Californian writing surrounding the U.S.-Mexican War, when such misgivings might impede Yankee conquest and settlement. Travel writers like Edwin Bryant and Frederick William Beechey continue to emphasize the entrepreneurial possibilities of California, a trend that reaches its apex in Truman's *Semi-tropical California,* a book calculated to celebrate the "climate, healthfulness, productiveness, and scenery" of Los Angeles and to thereby attract settlers from the eastern United States to the newly acquired territory.

Truman assures the reader that, "Having traveled largely in Semi-tropical California, having examined closely and carefully its agricultural and pomological limits and advantages," he has "written faithfully and elaborately of this land flowing with milk and honey . . . where every man may sit under his own vine and fig tree" (61). The biblical allusion is telling, for Truman persistently returns to the "Pisgah view" of Los Angeles. Unlike his Israelite predecessor, however, Truman has gained admission into a Promised Land that he continually surveys from above. To "the traveler inspecting this region from the deck of a steamer," who "can form but a poor idea of its wonderfully attractive features" (13), Truman recommends the "matchless panorama" that may be had from the heights:

> A stroll up Buena Vista street, on one of the matchless mornings which are the pride and boast of Los Angeles, will serve a double purpose to either resident or tourist. It will furnish him with an opportunity to look over and upon a panorama of "sea and sky, and field," which, whenever we look upon it, and we have seen it from almost every available point, seems to reveal some new and still more ravishing charm. . . . [T]he denizen of Los Angeles, or the stranger within her gates, need only ascend the first eminence to the north of its business streets, to look out upon a scene which rivals in picturesque variety any vision which ever inspired the poet's pen, or fascinated the beholder's eye.
>
> Her vineyards and orange and lemon groves, and orchards of almost every known fruit, make Los Angeles the garden spot of Semi-tropical California. It is a collection of gardens six miles square, producing, at all times of the year, almost everything that grows under the sun.
>
> But it is not alone the aesthetic taste of the rambler which is gratified. He sees everywhere around him the evidences of a constantly increasing prosperity, of the steady development of the boundless natural resources with which he is surrounded. He sees it in the comfortable and tasteful

buildings which have lately been constructed, and are in the process of construction, a sort of dim faint prophecy of what will be a very few years hence, multiplied a thousand fold, and beautified in proportion, by the constantly increasing wealth of the inhabitants. Elegant residences and villas will adorn the hill-sides, and every available building site will be considered a prize, which good taste and abundant means will struggle for the possession of. (48–49)

Truman begins with the aesthetic pleasures of the view—its "ravishing charm" and "picturesque variety." Stopping short of the sublime, however, Truman proceeds immediately to entrepreneurial possibilities. Gaining "Buena Vista street," the "gazer from the hill-tops" (48) enjoys the sense of empowerment that comes with the panoramic view; remarking at another such moment that "the greater part of the city lies stretched out before you like a map" (61), Truman assumes the voice of the Enlightenment surveyor coolly rehearsing a catalogue of natural resources and commercial prospects. Underlying and supplementing both Romantic and Enlightenment ways of seeing are the not-too-distant scriptural allusions: as suggested above, Truman imagines himself an Adamic proprietor of this new Eden (the "garden-spot of Semi-tropical California") who completes Moses's forestalled journey into Canaan. Each of these discourses, then, subserves the colonizing mission of Manifest Destiny—Anglo-American conquest and occupation of California emerges as natural, inevitable, and wholly ordained. The "good view" that Truman shares throughout his tract is a Los Angeles yielded to Anglo-American management and development. I would enlarge upon this aspect of *Semi-tropical California* by encountering Truman's visions of history and social hierarchy.

Truman's description of L.A. exemplifies what Albert Boime has described as the "magisterial gaze"; whether registered in painting or literature, this elevated perspective "represents not only a visual line of sight but an ideological one as well. . . . [T]he view from the summit metaphorically undercut the past and blazed a trail into the wilderness for 'the abodes of commerce and the seats of manufacture.'"[5] Throughout the tract, Truman indeed claims a vantage point that embraces past and present. Adumbrating the later rhetoric of Mission Revival boosters such as Charles Fletcher Lummis, Frank A. Miller, and John S. McGroarty, Truman styles the California Missions as evidences of prior European settlement that might charm the inheritors of the Golden State: "A romantic glamour hangs over the region. Before the Declaration of Independence was framed, this portion of California had been settled by Spanish missionaries; the missions and churches which they founded remain, many of them intact, and are still places of worship; others have yielded to the touch of 'time's effacing finger,' and are but piles of ruins." Truman assures us that "[w]herever the sites of these churches and missions are found, they present objects of profound interest; not only because of their venerable antiquity, but as indicating the intelligent foresight of their founders" (14). However propitious, these earlier settlements are valuable only as "the development of the resources of the locality increases among the present occupants, and as the necessity of utilizing all these elements becomes daily more and more apparent" (15). John-the-Baptist like, the Franciscans prepared the way for what Truman terms "the real march of improvement" (17), which began with the U.S. victory over Mexico.

"In 1846 Los Angeles was captured from the Mexicans after two sharply contested battles," writes Truman, a "movement . . . handsomely conceived and executed" that introduced Los Angeles not only into "the great Yankee nation," but into history itself: the war puts an end to the "'primitive' times" of the inefficient whip-saws and "slovenly" zanjas (112), inaugurating rather an era of rapid growth and improvement (26). In a particularly telling passage, Truman contrasts contemporary L.A. to the Mexican pueblo of 1867:

> Crooked, ungraded, unpaved streets; low, lean, rickety, adobe houses, with flat asphaltum roofs, and here and there an indolent native, hugging the inside of a blanket, or burying his head in a gigantic watermelon, were the, then, most notable features of this quondam Mexican town. But a wonderful change has come over the spirit of its dream, and Los Angeles is at present—at least to a great extent—an American city. Adobes have given way to elegant and substantial dwellings and stores; the customs of well-regulated society have proved to be destructive elements in opposition to lawlessness and crime; industry and enterprise have now usurped the place of indolence and unproductiveness; and places of public worship, institutions of learning, newspapers, hotels, banks, manufactories, etc., produce ornamental dottings throughout a city, the site of which might have been dedicated by nature as a second Eden. . . . (27)

Truman's portrait of "an indolent native" recalls the racist stereotypes of African-Americans in the plantation fictions of Joel Chandler Harris and Thomas Nelson Page; and, indeed, the Anglo-American vision of the "quondam Mexican town" of L.A. has much in common with the paternalist ideologies that pervade the Reconstruction era. As in colonial discourse at large, the lazy native figure here signifies an arrested culture that fails to properly develop the advantages of this "second Eden." Yankee intervention becomes therefore a salvific force capable of delivering California into history: indolence gives way to industry, stasis to progress, anarchy to order, ugliness to beauty. From atop the heights, Truman sees that his Los Angeles is the fulfillment of the promise of Manifest Destiny; Montalvo's savage island has been transmuted into the Yankee "city on a hill."

IN A SEMINAL interpretation of L.A. noir, David Fine argues that hard-boiled writers sought to counter the myth of El Dorado: "they transformed it into its antithesis; that of the dream of running out along the California shore," and thereby founded "a regional fiction obsessively concerned with puncturing the bloated image of Southern California as the golden land of opportunity and the fresh start" (7). I read in hard-boiled virtuosi such as Hammett and Chandler not so much an unalloyed counterpoint to the myth of El Dorado, but rather a return to another Spanish myth, Montalvo's terrifying and alluring island: "the strangest thing ever found anywhere in written texts or in human memory," a land of black Amazons who sexually exploit and/or cannibalize captive white men. Teeming with predatory savages and corrupted adventurers, Chandler's L.A., like Montalvo's island of California, seems the reverse of the "second Eden" purported by Truman and other boosters. On one hand, Chandler's fictions may be aligned with the "counter-discursive practices" of California narratives such as John Rollin Ridge's *Life and Adventures of Joaquin Murieta* (1854)—texts that unsettle the linear teleology of Manifest Destiny.[6] Nominating Chandler "the first uncle of western American history," Patricia Nelson Limerick lauds the novelist's attention to consequences of the exercise of power: "Raymond Chandler did not fall into the western historian's trap of acting as if the American conquest of the Southwest put the cultural, social, and economic conflicts of the region to rest" (33). Like Ridge, however, Chandler mitigates the radicality of his historiographical critique; detectives such as John Dalmas and Philip Marlowe illuminate the violent legacies of colonialism in California, but they also restrict the subversive implications of life in the contact zone.

Before turning to Marlowe, Chandler experimented with several prototypical detectives, including Ted Carmody, Steve Grayce, Mallory, and John Dalmas. The latter appeared in four *Dime Detective* stories between 1937 and 1939. My initial response to stories like "Mandarin's Jade" and "Red Wind" was that the tales turn upon a simple Orientalism, pitting the rational consciousness of the western detective against an irrational world suffused with signs of the exotic. While this Orientalist semiotic is certainly operative within Chandler, as within the noir ethos at large, it forms part of a larger anxiety about stable meanings and identities and part of larger generic dialogue with late-Victorian adventure. Along with Hammett, Chandler writes California as an exotic frontier in which the metropolitan understanding of self and world might mutate and deform. In other words, Chandler's Los Angeles, in contrast to Truman's, is the colonial periphery of late Victorian adventure, a dangerous region whose geological and climatic uncertainties (recall the Santa Anas treated in "Red Wind") find resonance in savage criminals, femmes fatales, protean confidence men, and defective adventurers.

As its title implies, "Mandarin's Jade" is a story deeply invested in the Orientalist motifs endemic to detective fiction: the mystery and mayhem incited by the introduction of some exotic object into the domestic west. Like Wilkie Collins's Moonstone, Doyle's blue carbuncle, and Hammett's Maltese falcon, the titular jade necklace, "300 carats of Fei-Tsui," is an exotic artifact of great value that generates about itself a series of thefts and murders. From the outset of the story, however, we see Dalmas "err" into a world of compromised subjectivities, a "paradise of fakers" (211). Dalmas has been summoned by Lindley Paul, a wealthy socialite who hires him as a bodyguard to guarantee the ransom of the jade necklace from thieves; endowing Paul with a "soft brown neck, like the neck of a very strong woman" and a "white flannel suit with a violet scarf inside the collar" (183), Dalmas calls into question the masculinity of this effete character—it is a homophobic subtext that would declare itself more fully in *The Big Sleep*. Indeed, Lindley Paul prefigures Chandler's portrait of Arthur Geiger: Dalmas's remark that Paul's beach-house is decorated with "peach-colored Chinese rug a gopher could have spent a week in without showing his nose above the nap" (184) is repeated verbatim in Marlowe's description of Geiger's "neat, fussy, womanish" home (25). Recalling late-Victorian Orientalists such as Gustave Flaubert, Lindley Paul and Arthur Geiger appropriate and decontextualize exotic artifacts; as Ali Behdad suggests, this species of Orientalism erases the connections between the artifact and its culture, inscribing rather "the modern traveler's nostalgic narrative of an imaginary Orient" (63). In a characteristic gesture, Chandler ironizes the Orientalist only to write him into a recuperative "tropical romance"; as we see in the next chapter of "Mandarin's Jade," the "belated traveler," to return to Behdad's idiom, becomes a reiteration of the defective colonial adventurer.

Paul's home proves a threshold into a violent Los Angeles far removed from Truman's "second Eden." After his client is murdered in an attempt to buy the stolen necklace from thieves, Dalmas embarks on a quest to apprehend the murderer, recover the necklace, and, in doing so, fulfill his ethic of professionalism. Throughout his investigation, Dalmas encounters not only the resistant environment of the hard-boiled formula, but one reminiscent of the exotic and threatening world of the colonial adventure. The murder episode proper inaugurates this trend. Having been sapped by one of the thieves (themselves racial others—Dalmas notes "a high, niggerish voice" [189] and the hold-up man turns out to be a "tough dinge gunman" [190]), Dalmas finds himself unarmed but for a "fountainpen flash" (191), and we are treated once more to an iconic noir tableau—the lone detective probing about a nocturnal murder-site, not with the exaggerated magnifying glass of the classical detective, but rather a tiny penlight. The archetypal noir scenario is underscored by thematics of corporeal coherence and compromise which Bethany Ogdon has identified as a central tenet of "hard-boiled ideology" (76). Dalmas becomes a reiteration of the bounded noir protagonist, contused but intact: though painfully sapped, the back of his head feeling "soft and pulpy, like a bruised peach," Dalmas "gathered [his] insides together again" to pursue the alienated professionalism that parallels this bodily integrity. But while Dalmas recalls the monadic alienation of Hammett's heroes (who are likewise "all in one piece"), then Lindley Paul suffers a fate consistent with cultural defection: Dalmas finds Paul "smeared to the ground," "[h]is thick blond hair . . . matted with blood, black as shoe polish under the moon, and there was more of it on his face and there was gray ooze mixed in with the blood" (193). Here is a "smearing" of body-boundaries recollective of Becke's violent adventure stories, an abjection that portends the colonial threat to identity. This grim fate becomes even more explicit in Chandler's revision of the murder episode in *Farewell, My Lovely* (1940): "His face was a face I had never seen before. His hair was dark with blood, the beautiful blond ledges were tangled with blood and some thick grayish ooze, like primeval slime" (60).[7] Paul's counterpart Lindsay Marriott has not only perished but become unrecognizable; his battered body now devolves toward a primitive and undifferentiated state of existence.

As Dalmas proceeds to investigate the murder, he encounters a number of other characters that amplify Chandler's evocation of the colonial adventure. The most significant "clue" revealed under Dalmas's light is a "cigarette case, with tortoise-shell frame and embroidered silk sides, each side a writhing dragon" (194). Found on Paul's corpse, this "Chinese box" holds a series of clues-within-clues that introduce Dalmas to the story's central characters; as in Hammett's fictions, these antagonists are slippery figures who call into question stable and essential subjectivity. The case contains Russian cigarettes which turn out to be marijuana "jujus" (194): a rather offhand and stereotypic conflation of the exotic with the irrational. The plastic mouthpieces of these cigarettes disclose a calling card which reads, "SOUKESIAN THE PSYCHIC." Dalmas imagines a figure who twists women "like silk thread around an Asiatic figure" (203), and his introductions to the Armenian psychic fulfill these Orientalist preconceptions. Soukesian summons Dalmas through his Native American medium Second Harvest, an aboriginal who in a sense recalls the dangerous cultural transgressions of Hammett's Anglicized Tai Choon Tau. Labeling himself a "Hollywood Indian," Second Harvest adopts western attire that only amplifies his alterity: his suit and hat are ill-fitting and unkempt, concealing neither his stereotypical pidgin nor what Dalmas discerns as a tell-tale odor—"His smell was the earthy smell of the primitive man, dirty, but not the dirt of the cities" (206). Dismissing Soukesian's assertion of Second Harvest as a psychic, Dalmas yet reads the Indian in terms of the mythology of the noble savage: he becomes for the detective a massive, purely physical figure who looks "as if he had been cast in bronze" and resembles a "Roman senator" (205–6). Even after he is forced to shoot the Indian, Dalmas eulogizes him as a "poor simple dead guy who didn't know what it was all about" (216).

Chandler's "Hollywood Indian" reassuringly suggests that identity is essential, unchanging, and legible beneath the superficial trappings of culture. With "sleek, black, coiled hair, a dark Asiatic face," and a smile "older than Egypt" (209), Soukesian's exotic receptionist similarly yields to Dalmas's ethnographic gaze. Dalmas expects to find in Soukesian himself "something furtive and dark and greasy that rubbed its hands," but he is greeted instead by "a matinee idol": "He didn't look any more Armenian than I did. His hair was brushed straight back from as good a profile as John Barrymore had at twenty-eight" (210). Soukesian is a dangerous cipher for illegibility itself: "His eyes were as shallow as a cafeteria tray or as deep as a hole to China—whichever you like. They didn't say anything either way.... The hands moved in a swift, graceful, intricate pattern that meant anything or nothing ... whatever you liked" (211–13). The repetition of this latter phrase suggests that Soukesian does not simply register as a discernable racial other, but rather calls into question the validity of reading such signs. This moment is therefore a rare instance of reflexivity in a noir ethos overwhelmingly devoted to the work of realism. Chandler does not, however, exploit Dalmas's unreliability, proceeding instead with the thematic tension between subjective mutation and arrest.

In the climactic chapter of "Mandarin's Jade," "I CROSS THE BAR," Dalmas leaves the affluent coastal neighborhoods of Santa Monica and pursues his investigation into the industrial wastelands of Los Angeles. Interestingly, the seedy environs of the Hotel Tremaine and Moose Magoon's beer parlor are not only dangerous and run-down, but are also characterized by geographical and corporeal liminality: each end of the bar itself is adorned with "an old frontier .44 in a flimsy cheap holster no gunfighter would ever have worn" (226); the neighborhood is peopled with "pin-jabbers" and figures such as the bartender, who wears "a thick white scar on his throat" where "a knife had gone in once" (226). But just as porous compromise threatens to overwhelm the detective's sense of self, he locates in Moose Magoon an essential otherness: "The man was very broad and swarthy. He had a build like a wrestler. He looked plenty tough. He didn't look as if his real name was Magoon" (227). If Chandler's portrait of Lindley Paul hints at that of Geiger in *The Big Sleep,* then Magoon's beer parlor looks forward to the notorious episode in *Farewell, My Lovely,* in which Marlowe enters Florian's to find "the dead alien silence of another race" (4). In the ensuing combat, Dalmas almost suffers absorption into the Armenian exotic; "The crooks had you all wrapped up in a carpet," Carol Pride informs him, "for shipment in a truck out back" (229). But, here again, the hard-boiled hero eludes any bodily penetrations or metamorphoses that might undermine his identity; he suffers rather a concussion which affirms the boundaries of the embodied self.

Chandler would later develop "Mandarin's Jade" and other short stories in the direction of the 1940 novel *Farewell, My Lovely;* but this *Dime Detective* tale is more forthrightly inflected with adventure motifs and, as such, prefigures those in *The Big Sleep* and *The Long Goodbye.* As in all of his detective fictions, Chandler here boldly reinscribes Los Angeles as an unsettled territory. In doing so, he evokes a central ideological question of imperial/colonial discourse: is human identity essential, as the normalizing rhetoric of western culture insists, or socially constructed, as suggested by the transformations of the self that recur throughout the colonial periphery? John Dalmas on one hand encounters corrupted Anglos like Lindley Paul and Mrs. Prendergast, and seemingly assimilated aliens such as Soukesian—subversive characters who frustrate the detective's analytic gaze. Reassured, however, by dangerous but discernable racial others—Lou Lid and Second Harvest—Dalmas pushes deeper into "endo-colonial" geographies of Los Angeles. Even as Dalmas finds in the Hollywood Indian a vision of essential racial identity beneath the ill-fitting constructs of western culture, he ultimately locates an "Oriental" exotic at the dark heart of the mystery surrounding the savage murder of Lindley Paul. In the midst of his encounter with the slippery Soukesian, Dalmas assures us, "I'm no schoolmarm at the snakedances" (206); as Richard Slotkin might suggest, he is a reinscription of the western "man who knows Indians." Within the context of noir, such a moniker not only denotes a savvy frontiersman well acquainted with the ways of his savage adversary, but connotes a colonial border-patrolman capable of recognizing and establishing fixed and stable selves in a shifting carnivalesque.[8] Intuiting, therefore, that Moose "didn't look as if his real name was Magoon" (we might recall the Continental Op's initial questioning of Tom-Tom Carey), Dalmas ultimately determines a bedrock of racial otherness beneath the "paradise of fakers": "Moose Magoon, who turned out to be Armenian; Soukesian, who used his connections to find out who had the right kind of jewels; and Lindley Paul, who fingered the jobs and tipped the gang off when to strike" (232). Racialized identity therefore becomes the unquestionable referent which circumscribes and contains the fluid subjectivities of Lindley Paul and Mrs. Prendergast (who manipulates the gang in order to have Paul murdered). Not surprisingly, Dalmas himself remains as the most coherent figure in the text.[9] Although Dalmas fulfills his professional obligations by unraveling the mystery of Paul's death, he concludes his narrative with an admission of failure; unable to apprehend Mrs. Prendergast, Dalmas confides to Carol Pride, "I didn't get the big warm feeling . . . I didn't get to slap anybody down. I didn't get to make it stick" (238). Contrary to the positivism of the classical detective story, this bathetic conclusion contributes in a central way to the constructive strategy of authenticating alienation. The hard-boiled protagonist experiences the absurd confrontation of the rational consciousness with the irrational world; cloaked in pessimistic realism, figures such as Dalmas reside in the "protective enclosure" of alienation, insulated from the mutability of the adventurer gone native.

IN "MANDARIN'S JADE," Chandler broadly counters the utopian mythology of California; with his first and most famous novel, however, Chandler would explicitly evoke and subvert Truman's *Semi-tropical California*. From its first pages, *The Big Sleep* conjures Truman's ideal Anglo settler, recasting that figure as the corrupted fin-de-siècle adventurer. Although they have realized Truman's dream of conquest and exploitation, the Sternwoods have also fallen prey to the atavistic dangers of the colonial periphery: Truman's Edenic garden is hereby transmuted into Montalvo's savage island of California. Throughout his promotional tract, Truman elaborates upon several settlers that exemplify the Anglo-American development of semi-tropical California, the most prominent of which is a former U.S. army officer who is "the owner of the most beautiful property . . . in Los Angeles county":

> Twenty-eight years ago, General George Stoneman, then a lieutenant in the United States army, camped with his command, after a day's march, upon the spot which he is now converting into one of the most beautiful estates in California. . . . The four hundred acres . . . he has named "Los Robles,"

the generic Spanish for "The Oaks," a beautiful natural park of which skirts the southern boundary of his lands, which form a portion of the old Gallardo grant, formerly known as "Pasqualitos."

This representative passage captures Truman's reading of Yankee conquest as a teleological force that ushers California into history; the soldier-cum-entrepreneur Stoneman first accomplishes the military occupation of Los Angeles, then acquires, renames, and refashions the "old Gallardo grant." Truman later dismisses the "interminable labyrinths" of legal disputes between the Mexican landowners and Yankee squatters; in his account of Stoneman's estate, he altogether elides the legalized dispossession of Californios in the nineteenth century, presenting instead an idyllic vision of the American Adam entering into a new Eden, "finding fresh miracles of loveliness unfolding themselves in ever varying forms at every step he takes" (120). Whether stocking his streams with trout and bass, cultivating a profusion of tropical fruits, or making "steam power and the power of gravitation do all that could be done on the premises," Stoneman indeed appears divinely appointed to manage natural resources untapped by improvident Indians and Mexicans. "The interior of the General's homestead," Truman assures us, "are in keeping with the beauty and wealth of the exterior": "Books, new and old; pictures and engravings, rare and elegant, in endless profusion; music; a hospitable and charming hostess, healthy and smiling and happy children; in short, all that can be desired to make a pleasant home, ought to make the possessor of 'The Oaks' a charming and contented man" (122–23).

The uncharacteristic qualification with which Truman concludes his remarks on General Stoneman strangely prefigures Chandler's dystopian recasting of *Semi-tropical California* in *The Big Sleep*. "Calling on four million dollars" at the outset of the novel, Marlowe encounters not General Stoneman, but General Sternwood, a fictional counterpart of Truman's historical figure. As he enters the atrium of the Sternwood mansion, Marlowe finds the alluring "stained-glass romance" together with a painting that reads as a clear allusion to Truman:

> Above the mantel there was a large oil portrait, and above the portrait two bullet-torn or moth-eaten cavalry pennants crossed in a glass frame. The portrait was a stiffly posed job of an officer in full regimentals of about the time of the Mexican war. The officer had a neat black imperial, black mustachios, hot hard coal-black eyes, and the general look of a man it would pay to get along with. I thought this might be General Sternwood's grandfather. It could hardly be the General himself, even though I had

heard he was pretty far gone in years to have a couple of daughters still in the dangerous twenties.

Marlowe's offhand suggestion that this mid-Victorian officer might be the General himself perhaps lends credence to Sean McCann's reading of the Sternwoods as a family of vampires. Less speculative is the notion that this is the General's grandfather—like General George Stoneman, the patriarchal Sternwood seems to have settled in Los Angeles following action in the U.S.-Mexican War, founding a dynasty based on rational exploitation of natural resources and transmission of wealth along familial lines of descent. For critics such as Limerick, McCann, and Blake Allmendinger,[10] Marlowe's investigation of the corruptions surrounding the Sternwood household should be recognized as Chandler's own disturbance of the Edenic mythology by which Anglo-American boosters repress the arbitrary violence of colonial contest. At the same time, however, the reverence with which Marlowe approaches the portrait implies his nostalgia for the adventurous world of empire. Even as he works to recognize and recuperate the identities of fallen adventurers such as Sternwood and Rusty Regan, Marlowe himself emerges as the authentically alienated noir protagonist, a hero rendered more coherent and distinct by virtue of his suspension between Victorian certitudes and modern fragmentations.

As the suggestive introductory sequence continues, Chandler persists in his evocation of Truman, if in a negative way. While the "stiffly-posed" portrait might hint at the artificiality of imperial ideals, the Sternwoods themselves immediately betray the horrific legacy of this colonial plantation—contrary to Truman's prophecy, there is here no "hospitable and charming hostess, healthy and smiling and happy children . . . all that can be desired to make a pleasant home"; nor is Sternwood "a charming and contented man." We might recall McClintock's reading of the Victorian home as an exercise in "the semiotics of boundary maintenance"—"As colonials traveled back and forth across the thresholds of their known world, crisis and boundary confusion were warded off and contained by fetishes, absolution rituals and liminal scenes." Like Hammett, Chandler generates narrative and thematic energy by presenting the decay of this central space of imperial/colonial signification: whereas Hammett's Margaret Tharp is a Sisyphean housekeeper incapable of purging her home of colonial filth, Sternwood's wife is nowhere to be found, and the vacuum left by this absent "angel in the house" has permitted the household itself to go native. Marlowe is therefore greeted by a perverse recasting of General Stoneman's "smiling and happy children"; his revery over the portrait ends when Carmen Sternwood emerges like the return-of-the-repressed via "a door far back under the stairs." Marked by "little sharp predatory teeth" and a "curiously shaped thumb, thin and narrow like an extra finger, with no curve in the first joint," Carmen appears a truly atavistic figure. Like the "uncanny" and "primitive" aura of Second Harvest in "Mandarin's Jade," these animalistic regressions steer colonial defection toward essentialism rather than constructivism: as the narrative proceeds, Carmen will form a central part of an entropically darkening world, a collective Other against which the white protagonist might distinguish himself. Approaching reflexivity, however, Chandler moves beyond this naturalization of alienated selfhood to dramatize the quest for identity. As he enters into the service of the Sternwood household, he encounters a spectrum of corrupted selves whose lapses he must somehow recuperate or contain.

McCann argues for *The Big Sleep* as a pseudo-Marxist Gothic tale in which "Chandler paints capital as a vampiric force driven to steal the labor power of honest workingmen" (167). Carmen Sternwood, McCann contends, "is a classic and ludicrously exaggerated example of the female vampire" whose predatory qualities are also evident in her sister and father. Reflecting that no Sternwood ever had "any more moral sense than a cat" (9), the General himself reads as a succubus who "resembles the predatory beasts of turn-of-the century fantasy" and who "needs to lure guileless young men like Regan and Marlowe to join him in corruption." Therefore, despite its ostensible thematics of male fraternity, the novel betrays "a subtle antagonism running between the detective and his client . . . an undercurrent of hostility [that] runs deeper than personal feeling to reflect the brute facts of economic exploitation." Although Marlowe, unlike Regan, "refuses to trade his body for money," he commits himself to the elegiac task of "remembering the decent and rapidly disappearing men everyone else is determined to exploit and forget."[11] Such a reading is wholly consistent with Chandler's insistence in "The Simple Art of Murder" that "even in death a man has a right to his own identity."

Whether filial or hostile, Marlowe's initial encounter with General Sternwood resembles a tableau from a captivity narrative as much as an episode from Gothic horror. If the Sternwood home is a Gothic mansion,[12] it appears so in part because of a disturbing collision between culture and nature. Under the careful supervision of the domestic angel, Victorian households might reify the geographical boundaries of empire: exotic elements such as Persian rugs and potted palms may therefore be read as signs of savagery contained and exploited. In Sternwood's mansion, however, the Edenically managed natural world represented in the hothouse becomes an endo-colonial jungle: "The air was thick, wet, steamy and larded with the cloying smell of tropical orchids in bloom. . . . The light had an unreal greenish color, like the light filtered through an aquarium tank. The plants filled the place, a forest of them, with nasty meaty leaves and stalks like the newly washed fingers of dead men" (5). This moment recalls not only Henry Morton Stanley's famous historical encounter with Dr. Livingstone in the African jungle, but, more tellingly, the search-and-rescue operation of Conrad's Marlow for the lost and corrupted Kurtz. What the detective finds in "a clearing in the middle of the jungle" (6) is neither simply a Gothic vampire nor, as Fontana has it, a "sick and dying lord" (163), but a lost adventurer. Wheelchair-bound on a Turkish rug (like the one that almost subsumes John Dalmas in "Mandarin's Jade"), the General appears to Marlowe "dying," "leaden," and "sunken," with "claw-like," "purple-nailed" hands and "the outward-turning earlobes of approaching dissolution." Often applied to castaways in late-Victorian adventure fictions, the term "dissolution" is particularly descriptive, suggesting not merely the imminent death of Sternwood, but his entropic commingling with the savage environment. And what is true of the body is here true of the psyche; the General admits that he has no more sense than his wild, bestial daughters. But while the General's eyes have lost their fire, they retain "the coal black directness of the eyes in the portrait that hung above the mantel in the hall." Marlowe significantly restores the connections between the deformed and corrupted jungle castaway and the bold, self-possessed adventurer of the atrium, the space which opposes the exotic hothouse in its relations to Victorian domesticity and U.S. imperial conquest in California. Successful or failed, this is precisely the task of the hard-boiled detective: to seek out lost and captured adventurers, to assess the degrees to which they have succumbed to native turpitude, and to somehow counter the ravages of the colonial periphery.

Sternwood's hothouse is another of the almost reflexively exaggerated signs that recur throughout both Hammett and Chandler. Though obviously arbitrary and "constructed," the endo-colonial space does, within the larger context of the novel, signify the tropical decay that has overspread the model Yankee colony of Los Angeles. Chandler evokes and inverts Truman's imagination of the victorious yet "toilsome struggles with savage nature, and still more savage tribes" (139) that have characterized the Euro-American experience in Los Angeles. The rank jungle growing within the very heart of the Sternwood mansion diametrically opposes the ideal "semi-tropical" environment fantasized by Truman. "Purity of atmosphere is another great desideratum," writes Truman, as he favorably contrasts the climate of Los Angeles against those of "Florida, Cuba, and most of the Italian landscapes, [which] are covered with a rank, rich growth of tropical vegetation, saturated always with moisture, and undergoing a constant and rapid decomposition": "The purity of Los Angeles is remarkable. Vegetation dries up before it dies, and hardly ever seems to decay. Meat suspended in the air dries up, but never rots. The air, when inhaled, gives to the individual a stimulus and vital force which only an atmosphere so pure can ever communicate" (33–34). Mild and temperate, this "sanitarium of the Union" (35) does not enervate, as do the other tropical climes: "The *dolce far niente* has not yet, in the slightest degree, weighed down the wings of American energy. This may be abundantly seen in their railroad building and other costly enterprises, and the indications of an extraordinary degree of public spirit that may be observed at every turn, and felt in the very atmosphere" (80). As its title implies, *The Big Sleep* is a text that discerns torpor in the midst of the "energetic" Anglo-American civilization in California. The crippled body of General Sternwood represents an exhaustion that pervades the community at large; suggesting tropical rot rather than semi-tropical abundance, the hothouse becomes an important symbol of the backslidden "outpost of progress" that Marlowe must negotiate throughout the course of the narrative.

Reminiscent of the nostalgic storytellers of Conrad, Stevenson, and Becke, General Sternwood would sit for hours in his greenhouse swapping yarns with his son-in-law Sean "Rusty" Regan, the Irish rover who has gone missing prior to Marlowe's arrival. The subtle contrast between Regan's and Marlowe's respective conversations with the General is telling, for while Regan's bull sessions are consistent with the nostalgic recollections of late-Victorian adventure, Marlowe speaks with Sternwood about immediately pressing "family secrets." Embarking upon a tandem investigation of Carmen's indiscretions and Regan's disappearance, this archetypal hard-boiled detective assumes the role of colonial administrator/trouble-shooter, after the fashion of Edgar Wallace's Commissioner Sanders, but tempers the cynicism of such a figure with the elegiac voice of Conrad's Marlow. Even as the novel's recurrent allusions to medieval romance encourage us to read Marlowe's investigations in terms of an alienated ethic of comitatus,[13] attention to the adjacent intertext of colonial adventure proves no less relevant, illuminating the former quest as a suppression of the insurgent racial Other, and the latter as the search-and-rescue mission for the lost adventurer. Both inquiries take Marlowe from the wilds of the greenhouse through similarly dangerous endo-colonial spaces, and into confrontation with a host of beleaguered and corrupted whites, who, like General Sternwood, have fallen prey to the "island of California."

As he surveils Arthur Geiger's bookstore, Marlowe notes that the humid "air was as still as the air in General Sternwood's orchid house" (17); the simile signals not only the tropical decay that pervades the city at large, but also the collapse of fundamental borders between inside/outside, nature/culture, East/West. Geiger is himself a prominent casualty and sign of this compromised world. For Rzepka, the pornographer-cum-blackmailer reads, along with Eddie Mars and Lash Canino, as a grotesque parody of chivalric virtue: though evocative of Arthurian romance, Geiger's first names—Arthur and Gwyn—also call into question his masculinity. Moreover, "Geiger's 'Chinese robe and farcical Charlie Chan mustache' suggest his Oriental or, in Gothic terms, 'Saracenic' tendencies, a constant temptation to crusaders-gone-wrong such as the renegade Templar, Brian de Bois-Guilbert, in *Ivanhoe,* or the brothers Sans Foy, Sans Joy, and Sans Loy, in *The Faerie Queen*" (Rzepka 710). To be sure, such renegades are variations upon the theme of going native, which drives later colonial adventures; and Geiger even more strikingly recalls the defective Orientalist, which Chandler had treated via the character of Lindley Paul in "Mandarin's Jade." Geiger's shop reflects his fin-de-siècle decadence: here is "oriental junk" and "Chinese screens" which obstruct Marlowe's penetrating gaze, not to mention a femme-fatale receptionist whose "black dress ... didn't reflect any light" (14–15). These conflations of exoticism and "indescribable filth," as Marlowe terms Geiger's pornographic tome, persist into Marlowe's description of the blackmailer's Laurel Canyon home.

"Far more interesting than the Oriental landscapes in detective novels," writes Walter Benjamin in "One Way Street" (1928),

> is that rank Orient inhabiting their interiors: the Persian carpet and the ottoman, the hanging lamp and the genuine Caucasian dagger. Behind the heavy, gathered Khilim tapestries the master of the house has orgies with his share certificates, feels himself the Eastern merchant, the indolent pasha in the caravanserai of otiose enchantment, until that dagger in its silver sling above the divan puts an end, one fine afternoon, to his siesta and himself. (64–65)

Explicitly addressing mystery writers such as Poe, Doyle, and Gaston Leroux, Benjamin might well have been describing Geiger's death-room in *The Big Sleep*. Like his precursor John Dalmas, Marlowe finds here "brown plaster walls decked out with strips of Chinese embroidery and Chinese and Japanese prints in grained wood frames ... [T]here was a thick pinkish Chinese rug in which a gopher could have spent a week without showing his nose above the nap." The pornographer's camera is concealed, suggestively, in a totem pole (conspicuously replaced by a Buddha's head in Hawks's film adaptation). If Marlowe encounters the natural rot of the jungle in Sternwood's hothouse, then he finds in the "Geiger menage" (23) a cultural decay that likewise threatens coherent boundaries, most especially those of the white male adventurer. Amidst the exotica, Marlowe discerns "an odd assortment of odors" (22) and a "sticky riot of colors" (39) which, true to Benjamin's analysis, presage the horrible spectacle of Geiger's corpse: "Geiger was wearing Chinese slippers with thick felt soles, and his legs were in black satin pajamas and the upper part of him wore a Chinese embroidered coat, the front of which was mostly blood" (23). For Marlowe, Geiger was already deformed by a missing eye; besides, as he suggests after taking Carol Lundgren's punch, gay men are inherently characterized by a plasticity at odds with the hard-boiled ideal: "a pansy has no iron in his bones, whatever he looks like" (61). It is therefore appropriate that Geiger dies with a "soft messy thump" (21)—like Lindley Paul, who was "smeared to the ground," Geiger perishes in a physical abjection that underscores his cultural defection. As if to generically locate this fate, Chandler places the oozing corpse at the feet of "an Egyptian goddess": clothed only in "long jade earrings" and drugged with ether, Miss Carmen Sternwood stares at the prone figure with "mad eyes" (22), as if she has herself wrought the destruction. The tableau is indeed Gothic, but it is the "imperial Gothic" characterized for Brantlinger by thematics of "individual regression or going native; an invasion of civilization by the forces of barbarism or demonism." Cynically adopting the title "Miss," which conjures Victorian proprieties, Marlowe recognizes the failure of imperial/colonial evangelism. The island of California has not been conquered by adventurous men and civilized by angelic metropolitan women, as Truman had predicted; conversely, these figures have been assimilated into savagery.

Marlowe's response to this scene of abject confusion and inversion may be read as a synecdoche for noir ideology. He sets about the "janitorial" work of the hard-boiled detective, retrieving documents that might implicate the Sternwoods: "I put the notebook in my pocket, wiped the steel box where I had touched it, locked the desk up, pocketed the keys, turned the gas logs off in the fireplace, wrapped myself in my coat and tried to rouse Miss Sternwood. It couldn't be done. I crammed her vagabond hat on her head and swathed her in her coat and carried her out to her car. I went back and put all the lights out and shut the front door . . . " (24). Like Hammett's Margaret Tharp, Marlowe must perform the "semiotics of boundary maintenance" central to imperial/colonial housework. More importantly, he engages in prophylactic gestures that lie at the heart of noir subjectivity: he *wraps himself* in the archetypal trenchcoat and similarly *swathes* the toxic Carmen (she is "breathing ether" [24]). As best he can, Marlowe restores the corporeal boundaries compromised by Geiger's decadent spectacle. Fittingly, Marlowe delivers his dangerous package to

Sternwood's domestics, recommending, "The job needs a woman's touch" (25). Marlowe has no illusions about the continued efficacy of an imperial ideal that would, as Victorian soap advertisements insist, spread sanitation throughout a septic colonial world.[14] Along with the General's butler, however, who intones that "We all try to do right" (25) by the contaminated Sternwood household, the detective persists with his arduous task of boundary-maintenance. Wrapped as much in distancing irony as in the cohering trenchcoat, Marlowe concludes the chapter with a vision of alienation: "I went to bed full of whiskey and frustration and dreamed about a man in a bloody Chinese coat who chased a naked girl with long jade earrings while I ran after them and tried to take a photograph with an empty camera" (26). Marlowe is deeply anxious about his ability to contain the boundless horrors of semi-tropical California[15]; but whether or not he succeeds in his janitorial mission, the distinct figure of the noir hero becomes a last bastion against self-loss in the "sticky riot" of California.

Many episodes of *The Big Sleep* find Marlowe suspended between savagery and the lost adventurer: to the opening sequence of the novel and the lurid scene at Geiger's home, we might add the moment in which Lash Canino murders Harry Jones in the dilapidated Fulwider Building (perhaps one of the "comfortable and tasteful buildings" noted by Truman). Rzepka counts Canino, along with Geiger, as one of the "Knights of Mars"; I would suggest, however, that this "brown man" (113)[16] joins the hissing, murderous Carmen as a savage predator of the urban jungle. The animalistic Canino coldly poisons Harry, who conversely emerges as one of the lost white men eulogized by Marlowe: "You died like a poisoned rat, Harry, but you're no rat to me" (108). However noble, Harry is yet linked in death and abjection to General Sternwood and Arthur Geiger; the "funny little hard guy" (102) vomits on himself as he dies, an unsettling fact that Marlowe mentions twice. This episode recalls not only the first sequence of the novel, in which Marlowe mediates between Carmen, with her "little sharp predatory teeth," and the decrepit General, but also with the bloody murder scene in Geiger's home. *The Big Sleep* reaches a narrative climax with a similar tripartite composition, Marlowe's "shooting-lesson" with Carmen in the Sternwood oil fields.

Marlowe initially notes that he "could barely see some of the old wooden derricks of the oilfield from which the Sternwoods had made their money": "The Sternwoods, having moved up the hill, could no longer smell the stale sump water or the oil, but they could still look out of their front windows and see what had made them rich" (14). Chandler replaces the forward-looking expansionist gaze with closed and circular vistas that reveal exploitations of the past, rather than possibilities of the future. Not so with Truman, whose entrepreneurs, "with an eye always open for big things," discern in the landscape signs of "vast pools of petroleum which exist in many places in Southern California" (100–1). A little more than a half-century after Truman surveyed the oil-rich possibilities of semi-tropical California, Chandler found himself enmeshed in the heart of the Los Angeles petroleum industry: before turning to the pulps, Chandler worked his way from accountant to vice-president of a number of L.A. oil companies, only to be fired in the midst of the Depression in 1932. Whether Chandler was fired because of alcoholism, business scandal, insubordination, or the collapse of the oil markets,[17] his own story reads as an intertext for *The Big Sleep*. Critics agree that the wizened General stands as some kind of objective correlative for the exhaustion of the natural resources in Southern California and, as Fontana observes, for the diminishing "world of the courageous entrepreneur who develops socially beneficial, primary raw materials," the "early capitalist ethic of the heroic, individualistic production of empowering energy" (163).[18] In other words, General Sternwood represents the withering of Truman's adventurous colonizer, General George Stoneman.

It is therefore fitting that the novel peaks in the dilapidated oil field that the Sternwoods might wish to ignore. As with the bizarre juxtapositions of the Sternwood mansion, the slowly disintegrating site of modern production assumes an aspect of natural decay. There is plenty of industrial "junk"—the rotting derrick, rusting pipes, cables, and oil drums—but there is also the "stagnant, oil-scummed water of an old sump iridescent in the sunlight," the smell of which "would poison a herd of goats," and "dusty" eucalyptus trees with "flat leathery leaves" (132). In short, the climactic setting of the oil field joins Sternwood's orchid house and Geiger's Orientalist interiors to suggest that the pliant environment of semi-tropical California, which yields to the hand of the colonizer, has in fact become the savage milieu of the tropical romance; indeed, these locales are linked not only by death and exoticism, but also by poisonous odors which threaten the protagonist. Unlike its utopian counterpart, this is a hostile world which wreaks insidious transformations upon the body and spirit of the adventurer: hence, the deformed Sternwood, the bloody Geiger, and the poisoned, vomit-soiled Harry Jones. So when Marlowe, having placed Carmen's target, turns to face the shooter, he emerges as the "cornered" adventure hero: "When I was about ten feet from her, at the edge of the sump, she showed me all her sharp little teeth and brought the gun up and started to hiss. I stopped dead, the sump water stagnant and stinking at my back.... The gun pointed at my chest.... The hissing sound grew louder and her face had the scraped bone look. Aged, deteriorated, become animal, and not a nice animal" (133). The "sump" might as well be the "swamp" of tropical adventure, and, indeed, Marlowe suggests that the "empty and sunny" spot seems as though it were "not in the city at all, but far away in a daydream land" (132). Although the reader does not know it yet, this episode reiterates the tripartite composition of the earlier moments: Marlowe is confronted by an essentialized savage, who oscillates between bestial predation and infantile regression (after her animalistic fit has passed, Carmen giggles and wets herself). Behind him, in the sump, however, lies Rusty Regan (the nickname is surely a perverse, foreshadowing joke): once a "weather beaten," "hard-living cynic" of the tropical romance, he is now "a horrible decayed thing" (138).

Here again recalling Hammett's detectives, Marlowe must work to quarantine the devastations wrought by the literally incontinent Carmen. Marlowe's relationship with Carmen might indeed be read as a drama of containment. In addition to jeopardizing the hierarchical structures and coherent bodies of semi-tropical California, this femme fatale also menaces the strategies by which Marlowe maintains his own moral and epistemological integrity. Turning up naked in his bed, Carmen penetrates the monastic cell that reflects Marlowe's own chaste individualism; moreover, her invasion, coded by Marlowe as a breach of racial and geographical boundaries (he dubs her "Cute as a Filipino on Saturday night" [93]), provokes in the detective a momentary regression: with the affront of Carmen's "small corrupt body" in "the room [he] had to live in" (96), Marlowe "tore the bed to pieces savagely" (97).[19] Recognizing her manifold threat to the subjectivity of the adventurer, Marlowe punctuates his dealings with Carmen by consigning her to an asylum, "Somewhere far off from here where they can handle her type, where they will keep guns and knives and fancy drinks away from her" (138). What we have witnessed throughout the novel is an escalation of the "continental ops" directed toward Carmen. Marlowe's initial response of literally keeping Carmen at arm's length gives way to his prophylactic gestures at Geiger's death-house, and, finally, to this decisive recourse of institutionalization.

Like Melville's Ishmael and Conrad's narrators, Marlowe is "alone returned" to relate a story of catastrophic colonial adventure; *The Big Sleep* is, in McCann phrase, a "survivor's tale" in which Marlowe, "[h]aving escaped the parasitic Sternwoods, . . . can only look back with sorrow and longing on the fraternal figure who failed to resist so assiduously and who paid for his weakness with his life" (170). The elegiac conclusion of the novel therefore represents Marlowe's attempt at damage control, at somehow halting the metamorphic forces unleashed by Carmen. Whatever antagonisms Marlowe might feel for General Sternwood, he persists in his mission "to protect what little pride a broken and sick old man has left in his blood, in the thought that his blood is not poison, and that although his two little girls are a trifle wild, as many nice girls are these days, they are not perverts or killers" (138). Excepting Geiger, a lapsed adventurer for whom Marlowe has little sympathy, the detective's investigation is aimed at re-humanizing the victims of "entropical" California. Thus, Harry Jones, who "died like a poisoned rat," may be remembered as a continent "hard guy"; Sternwood and General and Rusty Regan, both in a sense "horrible, decayed things," might also be given humanizing eulogies:

> What did it matter where you lay once you were dead? In a dirty sump or in a marble tower on top of a high hill? . . . You just slept the big sleep, not caring about the nastiness of how you died or where you fell. Me, I was part of the nastiness now. Far more part of it than Rusty Regan was. But the old man didn't have to be. He could lie quiet in his canopied bed, with his bloodless hands folded on the sheet, waiting. . . . And in a little while he too, like Rusty Regan, would be sleeping the big sleep. (139)

Fulfilling Chandler's dictum that "Even in death, a man has a right to his own identity," Marlowe seeks to segregate Sternwood and Regan from abject "nastiness" and to thereby restore to these disfigured men discrete and coherent identities. Although he admits himself "part of the nastiness," Marlowe yet enjoys the alienated authenticity that is noir's response to late-Victorian adventure. "Outside the gardens had a haunted look," Marlowe warily notes as he leaves the Sternwood mansion, "as though small wild eyes were watching me from behind the bushes, as though the sunshine itself had a mysterious something in its light" (139). Semi-tropical California becomes an entropical heart of darkness, and, like his Conradian namesake, Marlowe might yet stand in stark relief against the savage nature/native that he has failed to subdue.

AS A RETORT to one of Carmen's many advances, Marlowe at one point replies, "What you see is nothing . . . "I've got a Bali dancing girl tattooed on my right thigh" (54). The crack is on one hand an unremarkable instance of Marlowe's signature sarcasm, part of the irony which, like the iconic trenchcoat, bounds the alienated detective. Keeping in mind the generic pretext of colonial adventure, however, we might note that such a badge of exotic travel distantly recalls the elaborately tattooed defectors of the nineteenth century. As I argue at greater length in chapter 6, tattooed bodies persist in noir, but usually in the form of antagonists opposed to the sealed body/self of the hard-boiled hero. A tattoo of a Bali dancing girl, in short, is precisely something that Marlowe would never have: neither tattoos nor the more radical bodily mutations that befall characters such as General Sternwood and Rusty Regan in *The Big Sleep*, or the horribly crushed John Degarmo in *The Lady in the Lake*, will be visited upon Marlowe.[20] As we have seen, gruesome physical transformations are central to Chandler's fictions, underscoring the self-abnegation that constitutes the principal danger of the colonial periphery. No one of Chandler's novels stages the drama of the embodied self more forcefully than *The Long Goodbye*. Often considered Chandler's magnum opus, this novel continually evokes themes and motifs of colonial adventure, offers an interpretation of their ideological significances, and places these elements in a contrapuntal relationship against the "janitorial" work of the hard-boiled detective. In the person of Terry Lennox/Paul Marston/Cisco Maioranos, Marlowe encounters a lapsed adventurer who, more than any Chandler character, captures the nexus of exotic sojourn, body modification, and (de)constructed identity. In other words, Lennox is not only a compromised white man beset by another savage femme fatale, but a confidence man whose transformations threaten the very notion of an essential self. Along with the roving con artists of Dashiell Hammett, Lennox sees the incipience of a dynamic figure that will haunt noir throughout the twentieth century.

In the first paragraphs of *The Long Goodbye*, Terry Lennox falls out of a Rolls Royce, a British automobile which, as Marlowe observes, possesses an indelible aura. Lennox's spill into the gutters of Los Angeles is not only a fall from socioeconomic grace and propriety, but descent from a superior metropolitan culture into the tumult of an unsettled territory. On one hand, Lennox suffers the manifold signs of decay that represent western culture in decline: he is drunk (connoting moral and rational compromise) and broke (forced to sell his roadster for "eating money" [2]). Upon their second meeting, Marlowe finds a disheveled and haggard figure bereft of the "energy" that would, for boosters like Truman and Teddy Roosevelt, revitalize exhausted empires: "He was leaning against a store front. He had to lean against something. His shirt was dirty and open at the neck and partly outside his jacket and partly not. He hadn't shaved for four or five days. His nose was pinched. His skin was so pale that the long thin scars hardly showed. And his eyes were like holes poked in a snowbank" (6). Scarred, sick, poor, and alone, Lennox might well remind us of Hemingway characters such as Nick Adams and Jake Barnes, traumatized anti-heroes who embody a western world devastated by two world wars. And yet this very comparison implies an important counterpoint to regression. Recognizing Chandler's admiration of Hemingway, Frank MacShane argues that while Chandler would parody and significantly depart from Hemingway's formal style, he would retain the modernist devotion to "divided individuals who are trying to come to terms with their surroundings . . . to give themselves some stability [and] evolve patterns of behavior that permit them to cope" (42, 207). Deeming Lennox "the politest drunk I ever met," Marlowe is captivated by his dogged self-possession: "Whatever he didn't have he had manners . . . I'm supposed to be tough but there was something about the guy that got me. I didn't know what it was unless it was the white hair and the scarred face and the clear voice and the politeness" (5). Like the old man in Hemingway's story "A Clean, Well-Lighted Place," Terry Lennox impresses Marlowe as a clean and dignified drunk capable of self-possession amidst dissolution.

It is possible to chart a literary genealogy that works backward from Lennox through Hemingway and into the milieu of colonial adventure. Possessed of a certain "grace under pressure," Lennox resembles not only Hemingway's "old men," generally, but also figures like Francis Macomber and Harry (in "The Snows of Kilimanjaro" [1936]): in essence, African adventurers for whom the exotic becomes a stage for self-realization. This motif may also be found within the canonical modernist adventure stories of Conrad—in an existential hero such as Lord Jim—and throughout western fictions about the Pacific. While Stevenson's and Becke's unkempt beachcombers and castaways rarely return, "in one piece," to western civilization, the "prodigals" of Charles Warren Stoddard and John Russell experience in the exotic a baptismal regeneration, an identity "neatly recovered, renewed, refurbished, reanimated, and restored," as the narrator suggests in Russell's "The Price of His Head."[21] Like the colonial periphery of these tales, Chandler's Los Angeles may be read as an all-or-nothing existential proposition for the adventuring anti-hero. The disheveled drunk who falls out of the Rolls-Royce at the outset of *The Long Goodbye*, is, in short, a figure drawn immediately from the prodigals of late-Victorian adventure.

"Down and out, starving, dirty, without a bean," and a yet possessed of "the pride of a man who has nothing else," Lennox fascinates and vexes Marlowe: "I didn't know why . . . a man would starve and walk the streets rather than pawn his wardrobe. Whatever his rules were he played by them" (9–10). Here again, body modification reflexively underscores the mutative potential of the self: "The right side of my new friend's face was frozen and whitish and seamed with thin fine scars. The skin had a glossy look along the scars. A plastic job and a pretty drastic one" (3). Lennox's reconstructive surgeries become an outright statement of the "plastic" identity implied by the various bodily transformations that pervade Chandler's fictions. Even as he braces up Lennox in the first two chapters of the novel, Marlowe will make it his business to arrest this plastic subjectivity, to render Lennox "human again" (7). In other words, throughout the course of their relationship, Marlowe hopes to steer his friend and alter-ego into the subject-position of the existential hero and away from the slippages of the itinerant confidence man, both of which are discernable trajectories of modern colonial discourse. Along with Hammett's fictions, as well as later romans noirs such as William Linsday Gresham's *Nightmare Alley* (to which I return in chapter 7), *The Long Goodbye* reflexively demonstrates the noir commitment to authenticating alienation.

Taking place through the Christmas holidays, the first phases of Marlowe's encounter with Lennox create an aura of heroic alienation via another modernist ethos: the economy of gift exchange. Marlowe's personal economy is a subject worthy of study in its own right. Here is a small businessman curiously loathe to accept payment: in *The Big Sleep;* for example, Marlowe refuses not only General Sternwood's initial offer of retainer but final payment as well. While this reluctance may on one hand be attributed to his professional ethics—he cannot accept compensation for anything but a job well done—it also reveals Marlowe's commitment to a mode of exchange that predates the accumulative philosophy of capitalism.[22] Marlowe's second meeting with Lennox accordingly takes place "the week after Thanksgiving" as the "stores along Hollywood Boulevard were already beginning to fill up with overpriced Christmas junk, and the daily papers were beginning to scream about how terrible it would be if you didn't get your Christmas shopping done early." As he laments, "It would be terrible; it always is" (5), Marlowe does not merely decry the season's inconveniences, but rather seconds Marcel Mauss's complaint that ancient gifting practices once central to a society have been supplanted by corrupt rituals of accumulation. These anxieties deeply inform Marlowe's relations with Lennox, which are characterized by "expensive" tensions. The fact that Lennox sends Marlowe a cashier's check for $100, "three days before Christmas" (12), anticipates the compromises that will recur throughout the novel. Whereas Lennox tends to compensate his friend with cash, Marlowe himself encourages a personal economy oriented toward objects and rituals that symbolize their relationship: traditions such as the shared gimlets at Victor's and the circulation of the pigskin suitcase. Indeed, the pair's attraction to the "quiet bar," with its ceremonially prepared cocktails and reverent atmosphere, might be read as another allusion to Hemingway.[23] Here as elsewhere, Lennox emerges an ambivalent figure caught between contrapuntal modes of conduct: although he recognizes the communal potential of personal exchange, he also falls into the corrupted economies of his marriage to the wealthy Sylvia Lennox and his wartime camaraderie with Randy Starr and Mendy Menendez. The obligatory principles of exchange are at work here, but, for Chandler and Marlowe alike, these are inverted and inappropriate relationships that reflect and lead to the ultimate dissolution of the white adventurer. In the former instance, Lennox does not appear a human self bound in expensive obligation to a person or community so much as a man transmuted by the femme fatale into a "thing" alongside other pricey objects. As suggested above, Marlowe is himself impressed with high-end commodities such as the Rolls-Royce, the Jupiter-Jowitt roadster, and the gold-fitted English pigskin valise; his approach to these items parallels his take on Lennox, in that he strives to emphasize the craftsmanship of objects that lie somewhere between art and mass-culture.

The murder plot of the novel amplifies Marlowe's quest for aesthetic aura, expensive exchange, and alienated humanism. Her face "beat to pieces with a bronze statuette of a monkey" (31), Sylvia Lennox is not simply murdered but obliterated: more than any other bodily trauma, "losing face" means losing identity, and the brutal killing therefore refracts Terry's own jeopardized identity. In this savage and violent milieu, the besieged fraternity of Marlowe and Lennox stands forth in stark relief. This tradition of bonding exchange culminates as Marlowe aids Terry in his flight to Mexico, a gift compromised only by Lennox's continual attempts at monetary compensation—the "five Cs" about which Marlowe remains "sore." Marlowe therefore envisions himself and Lennox as Orwellian, world-weary British colonials, solemnly and ritualistically sipping their Gimlets—which Marlowe assumes "a tropical drink, hot weather stuff. Malaya or some place like that" (131)—as they contemplate the decaying social order of California. We might imagine Marlowe strangely reassured, when he receives the lonely missive from Lennox, a note which momentarily ties up three thematic loose-ends. Although Lennox has feinted toward ethnic defection—not only removing to Mexico but adopting the guise of a Latino—he seems to reinscribe himself into a harshly realistic narrative of authenticating alienation:

> I'm sitting beside a second-floor window in a room in a not too clean hotel in a town called Otatoclán. . . . There's a swarthy character with pointed shoes and a dirty shirt outside the door watching it. He's waiting for something, I don't know what, but he won't let me out. It doesn't matter too much as long as the letter gets posted. . . . I feel a little sick and more than a little scared. You read about these situations in books, but you don't read the truth. When it happens to you, when all you have left is the gun in your pocket, when you are cornered in a dirty little hotel in a strange country, and the only way out—believe me, pal, there is nothing elevating

or dramatic about it. It is just plain nasty and sordid and gray and grim." (67–68)

With a vignette worthy of Marlowe himself, Lennox staves off the mutations of "going na(rra)tive" by writing himself into the "last stand" scenario common to colonial adventure. The "not too clean" hotel room suggests a monadic self besieged by dark and hostile forces—the "swarthy character" and the "strange country" without. In addition to the inadequate handgun, Lennox is also possessed of a rational consciousness capable of lucid reflection and self-expression. In good existentialist fashion, he unflinchingly assesses his situation and, against the romantic mythos of adventure, pronounces it "just plain nasty and sordid and gray and grim." Against Lennox's protestations, however, we might recognize in his bleak outlook something that is indeed "elevating and dramatic." His calm reflections and his refusal to somehow save himself by adapting to the surrounding otherness create the conditions for authenticating alienation.

These reassuring "situations" are underscored by Lennox's statements about Sylvia's murder and by his treatment of the gift economy. "I might have killed her and perhaps I did," Lennox insists, "but I never could have done the other thing. That kind of brutality is not in my line" (67). Though marked by his own disturbing facial "plastic job," Lennox could have no hand in these kinds of mutilations, which call into question the integrity of the self. However "sore," Marlowe is also assuaged by the way in which Lennox narrates his gift of the five-thousand-dollar bill, the "portrait of Madison" prominent throughout the novel. In his letter, Lennox insists that "it isn't meant to buy anything"; he encourages Marlowe to accept the gift as an apology and a "token of esteem for a pretty decent guy" (67). As McCann observes, the bill is "on one hand, . . . a mark of Lennox's central qualities—his 'manners,' 'breeding,' and generosity. On the other, its extraordinary denomination sums up Lennox's own decadent wealth and the dangerous abundance of the postwar world" (180). Like Terry Lennox himself, the bill reads for Marlowe as a site of disturbing contradictions and possibilities; he therefore persistently sacralizes this object, emphasizing its rarity and referring to it as a "portrait," a work of art. Endowing Marlowe with this aesthetic impulse, McCann claims, Chandler "stumbles into a tenet of the Klannish thinking that Hammett and Daly worked so diligently to undermine thirty years before" (181). But this tendency does not represent a clean break with Chandler's early fiction. Even as he aligns the bill with other rescued mass cultural objects, Marlowe tries to maintain Lennox as a white adventurer safely ensconced in protective alienation, a "continental" operation central to Hammett, Chandler, and the noir ethos at large. One of the characteristics that distinguishes *The Long Goodbye*, however, is the complicated reflexivity with which Chandler treats these problems. Marlowe might wish that Lennox had met his end in a heroic last stand in a dirty Mexican hotel room; but this conclusion occurs rather too early in the narrative trajectory.

The first twelve chapters of *The Long Goodbye* certainly satisfy Marlowe's desire for isolated fraternity in a "world gone wrong." Terry's lonely pitched battle in Mexico is complemented by Marlowe's conclusive gift, his dogged protection of Lennox's secrets against the threats and intimidations of the police. With the introduction of the Wades, however, the novel replicates Marlowe's relationship with Terry Lennox, prefiguring its ultimate demise. As we have seen in *The Big Sleep*, Chandler writes Marlowe as a mediator between a helpless adventurer and a threat to masculine identity, often the femme fatale. This is certainly the case with the dissolute Lennox, who is menaced by his wife Sylvia, even in death, and with Roger Wade, who faces a series of threats to selfhood. A purveyor of hackneyed historical romances (a species of debased adventure, perhaps), Wade has already conceded artistic integrity, and is therefore vulnerable to predators such as Dr. Verringer, Candy, and his wife Eileen. Characterized by Australian eucalyptus trees, aloha shirts, and especially the solipsistic "play world" of the cinematic cowboy Earl, Dr. Verringer's remote compound represents the constructivist threat of exotic adventure, the possibility that the subject might forego any sense of reality, agency, and identity. Verringer readily attributes his lack of professional ethics to the fact that he is "a mixed character, like most people" (117); it is an admission that, for Marlowe, suggests the abnegation of an essential self—the central problem of the novel. In keeping with his holistic function as custodian of white male subjectivity, Marlowe "finds [Wade] when [he is] lost in the savage splendor of Sepulveda Canyon," physically and emotionally bracing the writer just as he had supported Terry Lennox (151). But while Verringer and Earl recede into the exotic (the doctor purports a connection in Cuba), even more explicitly savage predators confront Wade in his own home.

Having rescued Wade from Verringer, Marlowe returns to the Idle Valley mansion to find Candy, the houseboy, who "looked like a Mexican who was getting fifty a week and not killing himself with hard work" (140). "I didn't think I was going to like Candy," Marlowe admits, inaugurating a rhetorical struggle that persists throughout the novel. Slinging epithets such as "cholo," "pachuco," and "greaseball," Marlowe doggedly attempts to locate Candy as a member of the Mexican underclass identified by Anglo-American boosters like Truman as a potential, if problematic, labor pool in Southern California (158, 176). Against Marlowe's assignments, Candy insists, "Don't call me cholo. I'm no wetback. My name is Juan Garcia de Soto yo Soto-mayor. I am Chileno . . . from Viña del Mar near Valparaiso" (159, 258). Candy refuses Marlowe's "lazy Mexican" stereotype to assume an even more aggressive, subversive role. Though Wade had imagined his houseboy an easily instrumentalized "cockroach in a white jacket," and "a helpful little guy—in spots" (168, 194), Candy becomes a threatening presence in the Wade household. "I gave Candy too much money," Wade laments, "Mistake. Should have started him with a bag of peanuts and worked up to a banana" (167). Wade has not only lost the baronial prestige and authority of Truman's California nobility, but he suffers phantasmic racist visions of "a dark animal underneath the bed" (165) and a figure "with a knife . . . leaning over the bed. . . . Looked a little like Candy. Couldn't of been Candy" (169). Here is another opportunity for Marlowe to exercise his housekeeping proclivities; he intervenes to discipline Candy through a program that includes verbal reprimands and even corporal punishment. Going so far as to slap Candy for calling him a "son of a whore," Marlowe continually reminds the houseboy of "his place": "Just don't get out of line around here. Keep your nose and mouth clean when you talk about the people you work for" (159). By the conclusion of the novel, Marlowe has accomplished what Wade could not—absolute control of the knife-wielding insurgent: "'Give me the knife, Candy. You're just a nice Mexican houseboy. . . . You're free. You've got money saved. You've probably got eight brothers and sisters back home. Be smart and go back where you came from. This job is dead.' Then he reached out and dropped the knife into my hand. 'For you I do this'" (260). Marlowe is so confident in his management of Candy that he returns his switchblade a few moments later; "Nobody trusts me, but I trust you, Candy," he intones. Chandler's climactic moments often take place in and around the homes of the decadent elite who, contrary to Truman's colonialist fantasy, have failed in their *noblesse oblige* to govern semi-tropical California. Marlowe must therefore intervene to at least partially recuperate the domestic "semiotics of boundary maintenance." He is here interested in "personnel" rather than sanitation: in addition to disciplining and "deporting" Candy, the detective-cum-major domo criticizes the insolence of the "Jap gardener," dubbed "Hardhearted Harry" (261), and tacitly approves the educated deference and distance of the Lorings' black chauffeur, Amos (293–94). As McCann observes, Amos, like the disciplined Candy, "knows enough to know his place and accept it graciously" (196).

With Verringer "gone to Cuba or . . . dead" and Candy sent packing to Chile, Marlowe has yet another continental operation to perform. Upon seeing the lovely Eileen Wade for the first time, her hair "the pale gold of a fairy princess" (71), Marlowe reflects, "There are blondes and blondes and it is almost a joke word nowadays. . . . All blondes have their points except perhaps the metallic ones who are as blonde as a Zulu under the bleach and as to disposition as soft as a sidewalk" (72). Nominating Eileen "unclassifiable, as remote and clear as mountain water, as elusive as its color" (73), Marlowe initially exempts her from noir misogyny, which collapses two polar patriarchal stereotypes—the metropolitan wife/mother and the savage temptress of the colonial periphery. He even at one point imagines Eileen the heroine of a conventional captivity narrative—"she was behind a locked door and somebody was howling outside and trying to break it in, she was running down a moonlit road barefoot and a big buck Negro with a meat cleaver was chasing her" (154). Concurring with the Continental Op's generalization that "all women are dark," however, Marlowe also imagines that there might lurk "a Zulu under the bleach." As in "Mandarin's Jade" and *The Big Sleep,* the compromised boundaries of the Wade household and of society at large may be traced back to the corruption of the metropolitan angel—the perfidious Eileen proves the chief culprit of the novel. She encompasses the manifold threats to subjectivity that confront latter-day adventurers such as Terry Lennox and Roger Wade. On one hand, Eileen, along with Carmen Sternwood, practices a savage violence upon the body—her murder and mutilation of Sylvia Lennox "defaces" that form in such a way as to undermine its suggestion of discrete and coherent identity. At the same time, however, Chandler associates Eileen with a rampant constructivism that is just as threatening to notions of essential reality and selfhood. Using props such as the replicated British military badge, she has "tried to build another kind of memory—[if] even a false one" (248). As with Verringer's "hyperreal" universe, in which Earl plays at being a screen cowboy—, Eileen's fantasy world subsumes authentic subjectivity. Roger warns Marlowe that he might go missing, along with Eileen's "first love," who "got so lost a man sometimes wonders if he ever existed. You figure she could have maybe just invented him to have a toy to play with?" (151). Similarly, Bernie Ohls assures Marlowe that Eileen had regarded him as just another pliable text—"She wanted to milk you, and she had the charm to use, and a situation ready- made for an excuse to get next to you. And if she needed a fall guy, you were it. You might say she was collecting fall guys" (267). In McCann's reading, Eileen Wade "inverts Marlowe's homosocial romance," thereby raising the "disturbing possibility that all ideal bonds are but masturbatory fantasies" (182). She also exploits the most unsettling implication of the "tropical romance"—the possibility that empirical reality, history, and subjectivity are mutable, porous, and therefore subject to infinite manipulations.

Circe-like, Eileen deforms adventurers on the colonial periphery of Los Angeles. But while the mythological seductress transforms men into animals, Eileen reveals and exploits their ultimate insubstantiality—she characterizes Roger as a "mercenary hack . . . a weak man, unreconciled, frustrated," and Paul Marston as "less than nothing" (251). Despite all his efforts to authenticate Lennox/Marston, Marlowe must ultimately concur—as his multiple aliases imply, Marston/Lennox/Maioranos is ultimately nothing more than a "plastic job," a con-man who shifts with his many changes in context. Marlowe's investigations never in fact yield Terry's "true" identity. Paul Marston promises to be the primary self antecedent to Terry Lennox—it is the name that Eileen associates with the man she married in London. In a climactic moment, however, Marlowe reveals that "There was no such person as Paul Edward Marston. It was a fake name because in the army you have to get permission to get married. The man faked an identity. In the army he had another name. I have his whole army history" (246–47). In an effort, perhaps, to retain some sense of his friend's authentic self, Marlowe does not divulge this name. Whether due to his foxhole camaraderie with Mendy Menendez and Randy Starr or his traumatic experience with Nazi surgeons, Marston/Lennox emerges from the war, as Eileen suggests, "an empty shell," "the friend of gamblers, the husband of a rich whore, a spoiled and ruined man, and probably some kind of crook in his past life" (271). Sylvia's murder initiates another transformation, as Terry flees to Mexico, undergoes a false (though symbolic) death, and is resuscitated as Señor Cisco Maioranos. The product, Marlowe suggests, of Mexican "doctors, technicians, hospitals, painters, [and] architects," not to mention the machinations of Menendez and Starr, Maioranos seems more construct than authentic human subject: "They couldn't make Terry's face perfect, but they had done plenty. They had even changed his nose, taken out some bone and made it look flatter, less Nordic. They couldn't eliminate every trace of a scar, so they had put a couple on the other side of his face too. Knife scars are not uncommon in Latin countries" (308). Perhaps more than any noir character, Marston/Lennox/Maioranos evokes the protean tendencies of the late-Victorian adventure, in which metrocolonial travels broach the possibility of a radical cultural relativism and reassignment—as with Becke's "Martin of Nitendi" and "Deschard of Oneaka," Lennox might become Maioranos, "permanently in Mexico" (309). Chandler hereby literalizes the implications of such itinerant shape-shifters—as he debarks down an "imitation marble corridor," Maioranos wholly abnegates any possibility for authentic subjectivity: "an act is all there is," he remarks "There isn't anything else" (311).

Chandler does not merely anticipate the critique of the western subject that would dominate contemporary postmodernism; he responds rather to anxieties forthrightly encountered under modern colonial discourse. Marston/Lennox/Maioranos represents for Chandler, as McCann points out, "moral decline as a kind of corruption in national, and, implicitly, racial identity" (178); but the figure also conjures anxieties about whether identity is real enough to become corrupted. In a gesture redolent of noir ideology, Marlowe attempts a modernist intervention into a postmodernist/postcolonial problem. As he returns Terry's iconic portrait of Madison, Marlowe frankly explains his intentions:

> For a long time I couldn't figure you at all. You had nice ways and nice qualities, but there was something wrong. You had standards and you lived up to them, but they were personal. They had no relation to any kind of ethics or scruples. You were a nice guy because you had a nice nature. But you were just as happy with mugs or hoodlums as with honest men. Provided the hoodlums spoke fairly good English and had fairly acceptable table manners. You're a moral defeatist. I think maybe the war did it and again I think maybe you were born that way. (310)

Persisting with the search-and-rescue mission evident in earlier texts, Marlowe recognizes in Terry Lennox a mutable adventurer whose fluctuations might be arrested via the recuperative mechanism of authenticating alienation. He therefore attempts to narrate Terry as an isolato who derives himself from the opposition between peculiar personal values and a hostile world. Terry's initial defection, then, does not conclusively signal racial corruption; indeed, the "sad and lonely and final" last stand that Terry stages in his letter amplifies the noir strategy for alienated selfhood—hence its appeal for Marlowe. The final and fundamental conflict of the novel occurs when Terry returns as Maioranos, not only contradicting his drama of white alienation, but reflexively exposing that narrative as a recuperative mechanism. In the last paragraphs of *The Long Goodbye*, Marlowe must abandon his rescue mission and look to himself. By returning the $5000 bill and refusing a last gimlet, Marlowe formally dissolves the gift economy and the homosocial bond that had existed between "those two other fellows": "It's just that you're not here anymore. You're long gone" (309, 311).[24] Having cited what is, in a sense, a more successful candidate for his elegies—Roger Wade, "[j]ust a human being with blood and a brain and emotion" (309)—Marlowe retreats into his own "protective enclosure" of alienation: "I never saw any of them again—except the cops. No way yet has been invented to say goodbye to them" (312).

In order to demonstrate the centrality of late-Victorian adventure to the noir ethos, I have directed my attention to the two most celebrated practitioners of hard-boiled detective fiction. Hammett and Chandler aggressively pursue the interceptive mission inaugurated by Poe and Doyle, admitting the colonial adventure story, with all its disturbing possibilities, into their own tales of crime and detection. But while the classical detective admits otherness into his own person, the hard-boiled detective lives up to his moniker by maintaining an ethic of alienated heroism that might guarantee the borders between white domestic subjectivity and exotic otherness. "One white dick," as he is labeled in Hammett, the noir detective seeks to perform a "continental operation" upon the breached households and embodied selves of the colonial adventurer: figures such as the Continental Op and Philip Marlowe are devoted to the task of cleaning up abjection and arresting the ever shifting mutations of the confidence man "gone na(rra)tive." The last stand of the hard-boiled hero, however, is his own contused, coherent body, a form commensurate with his isolated ethical core. This vision of protective alienation is not peculiar to Hammett and Chandler; as I shall argue throughout the course of this study, such recuperative humanism may be found in noir novelists as diverse as William Lindsay Gresham, Frederic Brown, John D. MacDonald, and Jim Thompson. Thematics of authenticating alienation also govern film noir, where its constructive polarities would be strikingly depicted in Expressionistic mise-en-scène, as well as in narratives of beleaguered adventure.

CHAPTER THREE

DARK PLACES

LATE-VICTORIAN ADVENTURE AND FILM NOIR

> *"'And this also,' said Marlow suddenly, 'has been one of the dark places of the earth.'"*
> —Joseph Conrad, *Heart of Darkness* (1899)

In their seminal study, Borde and Chaumeton find in early film noir "a total submission of cinema to literature": "The immediate source of film noir is obviously the hard-boiled detective novel of American or English origin. . . . [T]he fact that the first great film noir is *The Maltese Falcon,* adapted from one of his finest tales, underlines Dashiell Hammett's importance" (16–17). While film scholars such as David Bordwell marginalize film noir's fictional pretexts, most agree that hard-boiled fiction plays a decisive role in the emergence of the bleak crime movies that began to appear in the early 1940s.[1] Whether attributable to influence or affinity, hard-boiled fiction and film noir unite in a preoccupation with colonial adventure and its attendant racial ideologies. Eric Lott accordingly contends that "'[b]lack film' is the refuge of whiteness": " . . . the troping of white darkness in noir has a racial source that is all the more insistent for seeming off to the side. . . . Noir may have pioneered Hollywood's merciless exposure of white pathology, but by relying on race to convey that pathology, it in effect erected a cordon sanitaire around the circle of corruption it sought to penetrate" (85). Pointing out "white critics' blindness to the importance of blackness in a racial sense to film noir" (183), E. Ann Kaplan pursues the implications of Lott's analysis. In *Looking for the Other,* Kaplan argues that for directors such as Jacques Tourneur and Orson

Welles, "the idea of the dark continent moves from literal travelling to lands dubbed by the west 'dark' because unknown and mysterious to the West, into the dark continent of the psyche and especially the female psyche." Julian Murphet treats such anxieties as the "racial unconscious" of film noir, the residue of ideological tensions in the U.S., and an emergent French existentialism itself preoccupied with the problematics of empire and decolonization. Film noir "seeks to produce a new subjectivity, a new white man, able to withstand the shocks of . . . urban transformation. In order to do so, however, it exploits the figurative and narrative resources of misogyny—not only to dramatize a tension between traditional and consumer society—but also to displace a more profound racial antagonism from conscious expression" (30). Naremore similarly acknowledges the racial dynamics of film noir, "the other side of the street." He points out that the Continental recognition of film noir emerged from a "European male fascination with the instinctive" and was characterized by an attraction to crime films about "white characters who cross borders to visit Latin America, Chinatown, or the 'wrong' parts of the city" (12–13). But Naremore is reluctant to theorize noir racism, gravitating instead toward a discussion of the progressive potential of mainstream noir films: "Although my remarks emphasize the racism and national insularity of Hollywood, my chief purpose is to show that noir, like the popular cinema in general, has a potential for hybridity or 'crossing over'" (224). However impressive, these readings allow noir colonial discourse to hide in plain sight. Noir ideology is neither simply "off to the side" nor wholly "unconscious"; indeed, though possessed of the subtle machinations identified by these scholars, film noir is quite obviously inflected with both the form and ideology of colonial adventure.

In keeping with the preoccupation of hard-boiled fiction, many prominent films noirs foreground the white adventurer against a dark canvas of racial otherness. Focusing upon Welles's *The Lady from Shanghai,* I argue that *film noir,* as a whole, rehearses and yet revises metrocolonial circulation between exotic[2] and domestic. While films such as Josef von Sternberg's *The Shanghai Gesture* (1941) and *Macao* (1950) cast the protagonist as a cynical imperial adventurer who wanders exotic lands, Rudolph Maté's *D.O.A.* (1947) and Billy Wilder's *Sunset Boulevard* (1950) envision the noir antihero embattled within the "endo-Orient" of urban California. Almost epic in scope, Welles's *The Lady from Shanghai* embraces both of these geographical movements. Like Conrad's Marlowe, Michael O'Hara (Orson Welles) leaves the metropolis, adventures through terra incognita, and returns to a compromised, endo-colonial San Francisco. As in the colonial adventure, such passages open the noir protagonist to a panoply of disturbing transgressions and dissolutions. As Kelly Oliver and Benigno Trigo point out, this "noir anxiety" may be warded off by "the polarization of ambiguity into extremes that can easily be located and can help reestablish lost boundaries: black or white, masculine or feminine, familiar or foreign" (xxx). True to its hard-boiled origins, film noir dampens the triumphalism of Enlightenment and Romantic imperial narratives, but only in a way that preserves the constructive alienation of rational westerner against an irrational exotic.

NO SINGLE DIRECTOR of films noirs is more preoccupied with imperial adventure motifs than Josef von Sternberg, whose films *The Shanghai Gesture* and *Macao* together comprise point and counterpoint within the colonial discourse of noir. Like Hammett, Sternberg rehearses the trajectory of noir from late imperial adventure to the hardboiled detective formula. A seminal film noir, *The Shanghai Gesture* bares the late imperial roots of the noir logic as a whole: the western rational consciousness, embodied in Sir Guy Charteris (Walter Huston), fails to contain the seductive irrational metonymically posited in Shanghai. From the outset of the film, Sternberg suggests Shanghai as metonymy for both the Orient and the irrational; the film's epigraph reads: "Years ago a speck was torn away from the mystery of China and became Shanghai. A distorted mirror of the problems that beset the world today, it grew into a refuge for people who wished to live between the lines of laws and customs—a modern Tower of Babel." Shanghai becomes in the film a microcosmic reflection of late imperial disorder that threatens to engulf the world. The opening sequence of the narrative clearly argues for imperial decay as the cause of "the problems of the world"; we initially find a foggy Shanghai street where a Ghurka policeman calmly gives traffic directions ignored by the milling crowd. This opening image recalls that of Hammett's *Red Harvest*, in which the Continental Op observes a disheveled traffic-cop who represents the entropic corruption of "Poisonville." Sternberg racializes this tableau, presenting a happily ineffectual Indian policeman, a turbaned and uniformed remnant of empire, who embodies disorder at once metaphysical and local. When the Ghurka accepts a "squeeze" on behalf of Dixie Pomeroy (Phyllis Brooks), he confirms Shanghai as a liminal zone beyond imperial control and therefore "between the lines of laws and customs." Sternberg hereby complies with paternalist arguments for the incapability of colonized peoples to govern themselves and the consequent "white man's burden" of colonial management.

The Shanghai Gesture explicitly arises from anxieties about the experience of white adventurers in exotic locales. Mother Gin Sling's casino reads as the dark locus of Shanghai: with its circular tiers, the casino resembles a Dantean inferno where diverse gamblers torment themselves. As Victoria's escort remarks, "Look at those faces. Half of them are Eurasians. Who said never the twain shall meet? Java, Sumatra, Hindu, Chinese, Portuguese, Filipino, Russians, Malaya. What a witch's Sabbath." As the initial casino sequence proceeds, we become further acquainted with the denizens of Shanghai: the narrative momentarily dwells upon Boris, a Russian gambler of aristocratic bearing who, after great losses, attempts suicide. Mother Gin Sling (Ona Munson) appears to calm the gambler, giving him an extended line of credit and advising him to kill himself at home. Boris suggests of the film's primary movements: Shanghai is a chaotic Babel where once powerful westerners are seduced and ultimately destroyed. As Said puts it in *Orientalism*, this is a Far East in which "[r]ationality is undermined by eastern excesses, those mysteriously attractive opposites to what seem to be normal values" (57).

Opening sequences point to the central plot involving Mother Gin Sling, Victoria Charteris/"Poppy Smith" (Gene Tierney), and the antiheroic protagonist Sir Guy Charteris (Walter Huston). This core narrative certainly bears out the connection between late-Victorian adventure and noir. Like many imperial protagonists, Sir Guy Charteris has reinvented himself on edges of empire and changed his name in order to evade familial attachments. The narrative finds Sir Guy poised at the apex of imperial strength, head of a syndicate of western entrepreneurs bent upon redeveloping Shanghai by evicting "undesirables" like Mother Gin Sling. This is the Sir Guy we continually find in the imperial postures of mapping Shanghai redevelopments, enjoying rickshaw rides, barking pidgin at coolies, and lecturing his unruly daughter. But the noir vision of the film arises from its harsh qualification of the Enlightenment imperial project: Sir Guy is incapable of executing imperial designs public or private. Adventure has occasioned moral lapses that recur to spoil Sir Guy's paternalist schemes. Mother Gin Sling turns out to be his abandoned wife, Victoria/Poppy their daughter. When Mother Gin Sling learns of Sir Guy's true identity, she conspires to publicly expose him, ruin his credibility, and save her thriving business. Mother Gin Sling uses Victoria/Poppy as a pawn, captivating her with gambling and the charms of the lascivious Dr. Omar (Victor Mature). But when Mother Gin Sling unveils the corrupted Victoria to her father, she also learns the girl's true paternity. After a bitter quarrel with her estranged daughter, Mother Gin Sling shoots Victoria and resigns herself to the law. In the powerful final shot of the film, the character known only as "the Coolie" (Mike Mazurki) reiterates Sir Guy's condescending question to the helpless father: "You likee Chinee New Year?" We leave Sir Guy unable to respond, paralyzed before the Eurasian giant who represents the dangers of border crossing and the impossibility of colonial control.

On one hand, *The Shanghai Gesture* seems to enact a critique of empire building. Most of the turmoil and anguish in the film has, after all, been caused by Sir Guy, whose abandonment of Mother Gin Sling catalyzes the problems of the narrative. Mother Gin Sling herself has been given voice and agency: she eloquently denounces Sir Guy and western racism in general, at one point sarcastically warning the drunken Victoria: "You're in China and you're white. It's not good for us to see you like this. You'll bring discredit to your race." Mother Gin Sling even implicitly indicts the viewer eager for Orientalist spectacle, as she confides to her dinner-guests that lurid exhibitions like the white-slave auction are faked for tourists. Indeed, the subaltern gets the last word as the Coolie reproves Sir Guy.

Such a reading, however, seems tortured when laid alongside Sternberg's thoroughgoing collusion with imperial/colonial discourse. Given the almost constant reminders of Shanghai's turpitude, the Orient of the film remains true to western expectations. As with exotic settings throughout late-Victorian adventure, Shanghai becomes prime cause and refraction of the westerner's corruption. Moreover, imperial/patriarchal constructions dominate both central women characters in the film. Mother Gin Sling fulfills at once Orientalist and misogynist expectations as she destroys herself through an act of explosive, unpremeditated violence inconsistent with her otherwise calculating demeanor. As her names imply, Victoria/Poppy also embodies "Victorian" fantasies of white womanhood and anxieties about dark women who might exert some "narcotic" effect upon the white rational consciousness. In other words, she is both metropolitan angel and femme fatale. In the end, *The Shanghai Gesture* is perhaps most preoccupied with fears of the miscegenous compromises that occur throughout the contact zone. The film virtually begins with lines which label polyglot Shanghai a "witch's Sabbath" and concludes with the eradication of Victoria/Poppy, the conflicted product of a miscegenous relationship. As a seminal film noir (one labeled as such by Borde and Chaumeton[3]), *The Shanghai Gesture* illustrates the centrality of colonial adventure within the noir logic of authenticating alienation. Sir Guy Charteris might fail to realize Victorian dreams of empire, but he does emerge a coherent white subject, ensconced within the "protective enclosure" of alienation from the exotic.

As Hammett's work attests, the noir imagination is replete with motifs of colonial competition: the anxiety of influence so often attributed to Angloamerican artists plays itself out in scenarios within which the American protagonist variously defeats or rescues some exhausted "Old World" figure, most often the British imperial adventurer. In *The Shanghai Gesture,* Sir Guy Charteris takes his place among the frustrated colonizers of late Victorian adventure. Though suffused with noir cynicism, *Macao* sounds a triumphalist strain as Nick Cochran (Robert Mitchum) assuages postwar angst with an assertion of Angloamerican superiority. Mitchum had already played a hard-boiled returning veteran in *Till The End of Time* (1946): seasoned in (Orientalist) noir endeavors such as *Murder, My Sweet* (1944), Edward Dmytryk casts Mitchum here as a Marine veteran traumatized by island-hopping campaigns in the Pacific Theater and alienated by the painful return to civilian life. Sternberg perhaps remembers Mitchum's performance in *Till the End of Time* when he directs Mitchum as a Pacific veteran who aimlessly wanders the Orient, unable to return stateside because of his complicity in a New York City murder. Throughout the course of the film, Macao provides Cochran with an opportunity for regeneration: like many noir protagonists, the ex-G.I. stumbles into a criminal milieu, in this case a lapsed European colony that evokes, tests, and ultimately validates his sense of self.

As in *The Shanghai Gesture,* Sternberg deploys in *Macao* the *mise-en-scène noir* within the formula of colonial adventure. The opening credits of the film mimic travelogue as "Oriental" characters appear over serial shots of sunny Macao. But these benign images, promising an Orient which yields to the western gaze, are succeeded by a conventional noir sequence: shadowy figures chase a lone white man, clad in a white suit, through a dark underworld of docks, nets, and obstructive stacked crates. One of the Asians, (Itzumi [Philip Ahn]), throws a well-aimed knife into the back of the white man, who plunges into dark waters of the harbor. Here again, the visual polarities of noir concur with the larger color-codings of western imperial/colonial discourse. Just before his death, the white figure, climbing towards escape, is foregrounded against a darkness both racial and metaphysical. These visual and thematic binaries translate quickly into narrative particulars: the murdered man is a New York police detective sent to Macao in order to apprehend Halloran (Brad Dexter), an American fugitive operating in the colony under the protection of corrupt Portuguese officials. In a sense, *Macao* begins where *The Shanghai Gesture* concludes: the dark Orient not only refuses western colonization and civilization, but seduces "defective" westerners—criminals and exhausted colonials. Westerners are incapable of subduing the chaotic Orient, and, as in the confrontation between Sir Guy Charteris and the Coolie, East and Westerner remain frozen in an attitude of authenticating alienation.

The second major sequence of *Macao,* however, promises a resolution to this dilemma: the frame is filled by a great white passenger ship sailing into the harbor. In a conspicuous conflation of the tropics with mysterious danger, the ship's barometer reads "Healthy for Plants/Unhealthy for Humans"; this ironic punctuation of the previous sequence declares that only westerners are human, while the inhabitants of Macao are more like rank vegetation. The establishing long-shot gives way to vignettes that introduce the principal characters of the film. Julie Benson (Jane Russell) appears initially as a stock femme fatale: clad in a dark, form-fitting dress, she negotiates a questionable relationship with a lascivious fellow-passenger. As with Dixie Pomeroy and Poppy Smith in *The Shanghai Gesture*, Julie Benson's Eastern travels concur with moral turpitude. In a moment of foreshadowing, Benson is rescued by passerby Nick Cochran, who intervenes to save her from the masher. After a predictable exchange full of wisecracks and sexual tension, Nick and Julie part. Lawrence Trumble (William Bendix) obtrudes to flirt with Benson and to establish himself as a central and yet comic figure, subordinate to Cochran's prestige. Posing as a traveling-salesman, Trumble is actually another NYPD detective, sent to retrieve Halloran. The successive "Customs" sequence cements the implicit hierarchy of *Macao*. At the bottom of the structure is a nameless Chinese photographer (George Chan), an innocuous ancient who takes souvenir photos of the tourists. Next comes the Portuguese officer Lt. Sebastian (Thomas Gomez); fat and slovenly, he reads as a symbol of colonial mismanagement. Our three principals are photographed in characteristic attitudes: Julie appears exotic and seductive; Trumble appears avuncular and comic; and Nick Cochran wears Mitchum's signature mask of stoic indifference. Macao here literally forms the background against which the principals emerge, another "speck of mystery" which suggests a world beyond colonial government and imperial control.

Macao proceeds by sorting Nick Cochran's relationship with Julie Benson and Trumble; and each resolution suggests the imperial/colonial investments of noir. Cochran pursues Julie, at one point proposing that they run away to Melanesia where Cochran hopes to work as the manager of a friend's plantation. Nick's proposal is fraught with heavy-handed ideological implications: his very desire to rescue the "fallen" Julie from Oriental turpitude reads almost as the resolution of a captivity narrative. Such race-and-gender-political implications amplify with Nick's escapist fantasy. Julie's ultimate refusal is based not upon aversion to plantation-life, but rather upon her doubts about Nick's faithfulness. Cynicism, rather than social conscience, is also what drives the film's rejection of colonial nostalgia: "it would be pretty to think" that one could return to the certainties of Victorian colonial life, but Macao itself exemplifies the dangerous fruits of such an enterprise.

Trumble resolves Nick and Julie's dilemma by drawing Nick into the case against Halloran. In one of two counterpoints to the opening sequence, Cochran and Trumble pursue Itzumi through the dark labyrinth of the docks. Trumble suffers the same fate as his predecessor; before expiring, however, he secures Nick's redemption: he has cleared the charges so that Nick might return stateside. Trumble's recommendation provides an existentially authentic alternative to plantation fantasies. Nick must clear his name before he can "make an honest woman" of Julie. This multivalent resolution, in turn, may only occur when Nick completes Trumble's mission, a show of "good faith" which expunges the uncomfortably defective westerner. In the climactic sequence, Nick and Halloran struggle on the deck of Halloran's yacht; clad alike in white suits, the combatants merge. Nick triumphs by throwing Halloran overboard and then diving into the dark water after him. The gymnastic suggests a second counterpoint to the opening sequence in which the murdered detective was submerged. Nick hereby rescues Halloran from a fate worse than prosecution: he redeems the colonial defector from the regression which haunts the antihero of late-Victorian adventure. With his last line to Julie—"You've got to get used to me fresh out of the shower"—Nick implies not only the fulfilment of the classical Hollywood love-story, but also colonial regeneration through violence. Both *The Shanghai Gesture* and *Macao* sound an elegiac note for the passing of the evangelical project of western empire: the colonist is no longer capable of changing the world. But the passing of these halcyon days does not mean that the Orient is useless. To the contrary, the category of the Orient yet provides throughout noir the dark opposing term within and against which the "white noir" hero comes into being.

NICK COCHRAN reads as a variation of the hapless protagonist that had already come to pervade films noirs of the '40s. Frank Krutnik describes this central noir formula as "male suspense thriller," a subgenre in which "the hero is in a position of marked inferiority, in regard both to the criminal conspirators and to the police, and seeks to restore himself to a position of security by eradicating the enigma."[4] Krutnik's description assuredly emerges from films such as *The Lady from Shanghai,* in which Michael O'Hara must steer a course through the criminal machinations of the Bannisters and Grisby, on one hand, and the penalty of the law, on the other. *The Lady from Shanghai* is regarded as one of the most celebrated films noirs of the 1940s, a film that fully realizes subjectivity through authenticating alienation. Welles inherits and masterfully transforms the imperial adventure formula without disturbing its fundamental ideological assumptions. Recalling Welles's 1938 radio adaptation of *Heart of Darkness,* and his proposed screen version, Andrew Britton points out the plausibility of reading *The Lady from Shanghai,* along with *Touch of* Evil (1958), "as a clandestine variation on the theme of Conrad's novella" (221). James Naremore deems *Heart of Darkness* "a kind of *roman noir,*" which "served as the inspiration for Graham Greene's thrillers, especially *The Third Man,*" and further suggests that Welles's proposed film adaptation for 1940 "would probably be regarded today as the first example of the American film noir" (237). Naremore's analyses of the 1939 screenplay reveal the ways in which Welles sought to cast himself as a Marlow whose identity is derived through frightening encounters with black otherness:

> Welles's screen version would have updated the African materials in the original text, placing the opening narration against the background of a sound montage and a series of dissolves that took the viewer through contemporary Manhattan at night, ending with a Harlem jazz club. When the action moved to the Congo, the exploitation and murder of the black population would have been carried out by modern-day fascists. . . . The camera he describes is impressionistic and subjective in a more complete sense, often showing us what Marlow thinks and feels. . . . Ultimately it creates a kind of white dream or hallucination about blackness . . . [h]e gives us an eerie narrative presence who stands by and watches, occasionally being confronted by grotesque sights and sounds. (237–39)

Naremore's and Britton's respective comments remind us that Conrad's Marlow is perhaps the most enabling pretext for the noir subject, that most evocative of the amalgam of subversive and conservative tendencies found in modernism as a whole. I argue that *The Lady from Shanghai* reads as Welles's elaboration of the imperial adventure trajectory of the journey into, through, and back from an exotic heart of darkness. Like Conrad, however, Welles ironizes the protagonist's return to the western metropolis. For both Conrad and Welles, the alienated protagonist-subject arises from the collision of light and dark, east and west, rational and irrational.

From the outset of the film, Welles literally foreshadows the compromised metropolis with which the film concludes. E. Ann Kaplan suggests racial overtones of the dark *mise en scène* in the initial New York sequence:

> . . . the deliberate, even heavy-handed, ways in which whiteness and blackness are contrasted in the visual style of the film references suppressed knowledge of racial blackness versus the whiteness of the majority of Americans at the time. The film opens in darkness: the titles appear across images of black water accompanied by gloomy musical tones. This is

followed by a very black silhouette of a Brooklyn skyline split between a light band at the top, and a black band at the bottom of the shot.[5]

This collusion of visual style with race-politics becomes even more dramatic within the context of the adventure formula. Like late-Victorian adventure writers and the innovators of American hard-boiled detection, Welles associates modernity with imperial decay, with the compromise of the metropolis. Indeed, Welles's handling of New York City in *The Lady from Shanghai* strongly recalls the way in which Marlow describes London in *Heart of Darkness*:

> The air was dark above Gravesend, and farther back still seemed condensed into a mournful gloom, brooding motionless over the biggest, and the greatest, town on earth. . . . The water shone pacifically; the sky, without a speck, was a benign immensity of unstained light; the very mist of the Essex marshes was like a gauzy and radiant fabric, hung from the wooded rises inland, and draping the low shores in diaphanous folds. Only the gloom to the west, brooding over the upper reaches, became more somber every minute, as if angered by the approach of the sun.
>
> And at last, in its curved and imperceptible fall, the sun sank low, and from glowing white changed to dull red without rays and without heat, as if about to go out suddenly, stricken to death by the touch of that gloom brooding over a crowd of men.

Conrad of course adumbrates the trajectory of his novella: Europe's entropic civilizing mission cannot hope to eradicate savagery either at home or abroad. After relating the story of Kurtz's fall, Marlow concludes that the western metropolis "has been one of the dark places of the earth" (18). With the somber opening shot of the Manhattan skyline, Welles was able to at least partially realize his adaptation of *Heart of Darkness*. And this darkness is illuminating; the "dark city" of noir derives from the corrupted metropolis of imperial Gothic, its visual darkness always racial as well as metaphysical.

Welles assures us that the city's darkness is not merely visual; our chivalric hero does not have to travel very far into the "asphalt jungle" to encounter a figure who is both metropolitan angel and savage mistress. Conrad had hinted at such a collapse with the dark shadows which cloud the brow of the Intended at the conclusion of *Heart of Darkness;* Welles amplifies the conflation by juxtaposing in Elsa Bannister (Rita Hayworth) a series of oppositions endemic to western culture: masculine/feminine, West/East, light/dark, rational/irrational, good/evil. Venturing into the endo-colonial jungle of Central Park, O'Hara finds a conventional motif: the rescue of a white captive. But after repelling the attackers, Michael finds Elsa a sign of Oriental contagion. Elsa initially confides that she was raised in China, in Chi Fu, which Michael pronounces "the second wickedest city in the world" ("the first is Macao"), and has been living in Shanghai (we might recall Brigid O'Shaughnessy, who has come to San Francisco from Hong Kong). In keeping with her exotic origins, Elsa not only seduces and manipulates Michael, in the fashion of the femme fatale, but does so in a way that harnesses anxieties about a threatening Orient. She becomes not the sign of imperial domesticity (as in the conventional adventure), but rather a portal into exotic danger.

Christening the Bannister's yacht *Circe,* Welles evokes *The Odyssey* (the Ur-text of imperial adventure[6]), casting Michael as Odysseus and Elsa as the misandrous sorceress. Elsa is identified throughout the film with animality—verbally, as in Michael's anecdote about the frenzied sharks off Brazil, and visually, in the aquarium scene in which Elsa and Michael tryst against a backdrop of predatory sea creatures.[7] As she lures Michael aboard the *Circe,* and into the conspiracy, Elsa indeed threatens to transform Michael into a beast, a "shark" like Bannister or Grisby. Throughout the course of the narrative, Elsa persistently attempts to seduce Michael to compromise with the irrational that she represents: "Everything's bad, Michael, everything. You can't escape it or fight it, you've got to get along with it, deal with it, make terms." Far from offering a floating sanctuary, the yacht itself is the locus of danger and intrigue. But for this fact, the cruise becomes the most formulaic phase of Michael's own "odyssey"—the underworld journey of the epic. From the moment he signs on as mate of the *Circe,* Michael finds himself baffled by a series of exotic spaces that underscore his consuming desires for Elsa and his inability to read and control the deepening mystery. As he attempts to win Elsa away from Bannister, Michael proposes that the couple fly to "some one of the far places." Elsa's ironic reply—"We're in one of them now"—replaces one form of Orientalism, Michael's romantic escapism, with another: the late-Victorian vision of the exotic as intractably savage. The *Circe*'s cruise appears a succession of strange and foreign tableaux: the dark, labyrinthine streets of Acapulco; the predatory animals of the picnic expedition; the torchlit, infernal beach scene—all accompanied by Heinz Roemheld's exotic score (perhaps Welles here realizes his design to film Marlow's surreal perceptions). As in late-Victorian adventures, exotic settings enable and refract the savage degeneration of white colonials.

Welles punctuates this string of exotic locales with a more elaborate reinscription of endo-colonial San Francisco. Having escaped from the authorities in the midst of his trial, Michael is returned to the unchartable (and uncharitable) spaces of Chinatown, which represent Elsa's malign influence. Like Hammett's Op, the drugged Michael remains bewildered by the strange environs of Chinatown, with its indecipherable characters and baffling sounds (this latter especially apparent in Welles's rendition of the Chinese theater). Having "made terms" with the "badness" of the world, Elsa conversely moves with ease through the urban jungle, speaking Chinese and tracking Michael through a network of Chinese operatives.[8] For Oliver and Trigo, this "Asian femme fatale" (53) embodies a threatening polyphony that connotes "fluid identity" (70). Even the climactic "funhouse" sequence of the film conflates Oriental and irrational, as a Chinese dragon swallows up a helpless O'Hara. With this final location, Welles problematizes the conventional structure of the imperial adventure, which dictates a return to the domestic space of settlement or metropolis. Michael neither embarks from nor returns to an incorruptible American "city on a hill." He might have been able to elide the implications of compromise in New York City; but he returns to the U.S. to find San Francisco a backslidden metropolis that has lost its feeble grasp of western civilization. In developing the noir visual style, Welles seems to echo and revise Marlow's lament: "This also *is* one of the dark places."

Michael O'Hara is in many ways as ironic a figure as the American city itself. As E. Ann Kaplan points out, Michael's "Black Irish" identity connotes darkness and "savagery."[9] That said, Michael inherits the tarnished chivalric ideal epitomized by Chandler's Philip Marlowe; he is, as Elsa Bannister at one point suggests, a "foolish knight errant." Despite his protestations that he is "no hero," Michael initiates his narrative with a recount of his gallant rescue of Elsa. Michael has indeed killed a man, but the murder is explained as an act of war, the execution of a Franco spy during the Spanish Civil War. Michael also inherits the hard-boiled characteristics of lucidity and insularity. Even as O'Hara confides to Grisby his recognition of the essential "guilt" and "hunger" that lie beneath the "fair face" of the land, he seeks to remain aloof from the naturalistic "hunger" about him: "I'm independent . . . I've always found it very sanitary to be broke." As J. P. Telotte suggests, the very act of O'Hara's voice-over represents his resistance to naturalistic disorder: "In effect it emphasizes O'Hara's desire to arrange these strange events into a story for himself, to make a narrative of the jumble of his past, especially his obsession with Elsa, in order to render it all meaningful in some way" (*Voices in the Dark* 63). As in the conclusive high-angle shot, Michael appears juxtaposed against a darkness at once visual, metaphysical, and racial. Therefore, while Welles may appear to amplify the problematic transgressions of late-Victorian adventure, he counters these possibilities with a coherent protagonist lodged once more in the "protective enclosure" of alienation.

THE FILMS of Sternberg and Welles obviously exploit and conserve the Orientalisms of colonial adventure, and, in doing so, point to similar motifs in "domestic" noir narratives. Both Rudolph Maté's *D.O.A.* and Billy Wilder's *Sunset Boulevard* participate in this tradition as they reinscribe coastal California as an exotic contact zone. In *D.O.A.*, Frank Bigelow epitomizes what Silver and Ward term "the truly noir figure [who] represents the perspective of normality assailed by the twists of fate of an irrational universe" (2), a characterization perhaps offhandedly implied in Bigelow's name ("big-and-low"). Chafing under the prospect of married life, Bigelow, a notary public in the small inland town of Banning, California, makes a pleasure trip to San Francisco. Bigelow awakens from a night of hard drinking with a persistent stomach ache; doctors tell him he has been poisoned with iridium, a radioactive substance that will kill him within a week. Given only days to live, he embarks on an investigation of his own murder. And although Bigelow finds and kills his poisoner, he dies unappeased, his "need to know" frustrated by the arbitrariness of his fate (he has been murdered for unwittingly notarizing a bill of sale for the stolen Iridium).

As Macek notes, *D.O.A.* assumes an "existential outlook" (77); Bigelow's narrative recounts his attempts to wrest meaning from "an ever-darkening nightmare world filled with grotesque and crazed people" (77). Like Camus's Meursault, Bigelow is faced with the problem of finding a basis for action in the face of annihilation. After learning of his imminent death Bigelow runs in desperation through the streets of San Francisco, as if to escape his fate. Witnessing scenes of the domestic life now denied him—an embracing couple, a little girl playing—Bigelow resolves to find his killer, a resolution suggested both in his determined expression and in the shift in the tenor of the score. With all gestures leveled before the prospect of death, Bigelow embraces what Robert Porfirio identifies as one of the central existential motifs of film noir—the quest for sanctity, ritual, and order in an irrational universe (92–93). *D.O.A.* also resembles Camus's work in its exploitation of Orientalism; as in *The Stranger*, Bigelow confronts an irrational world metonymically posited by the Oriental. Though already in a sense living on the colonial frontier (Banning is ground-zero for the "last great Indian manhunt in the Western tradition"[10]), Bigelow rehearses the last phases of Manifest Destiny as he travels from inland to coast. His very decision to visit San Francisco depends upon broadly Orientalist suppositions. As with Dashiell Hammett's fiction, *D.O.A.* presents San Francisco as a liminal zone infused with the excesses conventionally ascribed to the Orient; as the bellboy of Bigelow's hotel wonders, "Why does everybody go to San Francisco to tear loose?" These rather vague suggestions of excess coalesce with Bigelow's visit to "The Fisherman," a waterfront nightclub. For Macek, this becomes an episode in which the atmosphere of the film is significantly reversed": "The intense use of jazz music, interpreted through the tight close-ups of sweating musicians caught up in the fury of their music combines with images of patrons lost in the pounding jazz rhythms and approaches a chaotic climax" (77). With its tropical decor and African American jazzmen, The Fisherman is inscribed as a distilled version of the endo-colonial San Francisco, an urban jungle that seduces white westerners to the irrational. The Fisherman's bartender remarks of one patron, "He's flipped. The music's drivin' him crazy"; of another, "She's jive crazy." Even as Halliday (William Ching) exploits this frenetic scene to poison Bigelow's drink, The Fisherman reads as the threshold of the irrational. The clues which Bigelow derives at The Fisherman lead him south to another liminal space, the city of Los Angeles.

True to its Victorian origins, *D.O.A.* casts women in conventional, polarized roles.[11] In the tradition of the metropolitan angel, Bigelow's blonde secretary/fiancee Paula Gibson (Pamela Britton) spends the bulk of the narrative confined to rural, domestic space and consigned to ignorance and ineffectuality; at the conclusion of the film she has not yet been told the truth about Bigelow's plight. In contrast, most of the women treated in the latter sequences of the film are "dark" Angelinas—brunettes who function as agents of mystery from whom Bigelow forcibly and violently extracts information.[12] The most prominent of these women, Marla Rakubian (Laurette Luez) reifies the Orientalized femme fatale. Like so many noir women, she reads as a sign of the exotic (she is Armenian) and dangerous gender transgression: she seduces one man into the fatal plot and likewise threatens Bigelow, "If I were a man I'd punch your face in."

Marla draws Bigelow into the heart of a mystery clothed in Oriental signifiers. Bigelow's interrogation of Marla attracts the attention of Majak (Luther Adler), Raymond Rakubian's uncle and co-conspirator in the iridium scheme. A trio of heavies, including the psychopathic killer Chester (Neville Brand), who tortures Bigelow by hitting him in the stomach, return Bigelow to Majak's "lair," of which we see a sunken room furnished with exotic trappings: samovars, large pillows, curtains, and Persian rugs. These cues are accompanied by a sudden shift in the score to a rather obvious exotic leitmotif (a theme which follows Majak throughout the film). This accompaniment intensifies as Majak conducts Bigelow to a curtained alcove housing a shrine to the memory of Raymond Rakubian, an urn that contains his ashes and is inscribed with Armenian characters. *D.O.A.*

thus appears to have inherited many of the Orientalist strategies that mark Chandler's work. Majak's home, like Geiger's in *The Big Sleep*, becomes a reinscription of the endo-Orient that baffles the noir protagonist. Bigelow discovers here that Rakubian, the key figure of his investigation, is dead and beyond his reach; and it is here that Majak stoically, if redundantly, sentences Bigelow to death at the hands of Chester. Recalling Chandler's "Mandarin's Jade," *D.O.A.* is populated with Armenian hostiles—the Rakubians, the thickly accented Majak; even the two photographers Bigelow interrogates. One might argue that the Orientalism of *D.O.A.* is undercut by the fact that the Armenians are not, as in Chandler, the prime agents of crime and corruption: it is rather the Anglo businessman Halliday who has poisoned Bigelow in an attempt to conceal the iridium scheme. But here is another defective adventurer gone native through miscegenation and criminal collusion with the exotic denizens of Los Angeles. The final showdown between Bigelow and Halliday demonstrates that the film is ultimately about white adventurers who represent the alternatives of dissolution and alienated authenticity.

The films I have discussed so far recruit various adventure formulae toward the end of authenticating alienation. In doing so, such texts sensitize us to more subtle, though no less effective, deployments of colonial discourse throughout the noir canon. One such film is Billy Wilder's *Sunset Boulevard,* which demonstrates the pervasiveness of noir Orientalism and the persistence of the imperial adventure formula. *Sunset Boulevard* has attained the status of an exemplary film noir that pits the rational male consciousness against a psychotic femme fatale. The film follows canonical Modernist writers such as F. Scott Fitzgerald, Nathanael West, and Clifford Odets in its treatment of the corruption and redemption of a Midwestern artist amidst the temptations of Hollywood. Indeed, co-writer Charles Brackett was a friend of Fitzgerald and quotes both "The Crack Up" and *The Great Gatsby* in the opening swimming-pool sequence.[13] Brackett was himself an eastern émigré who sees the westward trek to Hollywood as a literally exhaustive journey for both individual and national culture. This expansionist movement joins other imperial adventure motifs that course through the film, working in tandem with its obvious misogyny. Through judicious and strategic deployments of Orientalism, Wilder reiterates the formula of white dissolution and regeneration that operates not only in late-Victorian adventure, but also in and throughout the whole corpus of noir.

Deep in the film, Joe Gillis (William Holden) playfully suggests a cinematic formula that provides a key into the film's deployment of imperial adventure:

BETTY. Are you hungry?

GILLIS. Hungry? After twelve years in the Burmese jungle, I am starving, Lady Agatha—starving for a white shoulder—

BETTY. Phillip, you're mad!

GILLIS. Thirsting for the coolness of your lips—

BETTY. No, Phillip, no. We must be strong. You're still wearing the uniform of the Coldstream Guards! Furthermore, you can have the phone now. (Wilder 67)

Poking fun at Hollywood cliché, the impromptu lines spoof the adventure formula that had become a Hollywood staple. The central movements of *Sunset Boulevard* purport something different, a "realistic" alternative to the hackneyed imperial romance. Nevertheless, Wilder's film remains dependent upon the epistemological bedrock of imperial/colonial ideologies, rehearsing an adventure narrative within which Joe Gillis wanders into the domain of Norma Desmond (Gloria Swanson). Having made the westward trek of Manifest Destiny (from Ohio to California), Joe meets in Norma Desmond not only the Gothic decadence of Dickens's Miss Havisham (to which he explicitly alludes), but also the dystopian California of Raymond Chandler. As Joe literally and figuratively moves from the daylight world of everyday problems into the twilight universe of Norma, architecture provides a powerful index into the thematics of the film. Norma's mansion becomes throughout the narrative a charged semiotic space. Set amidst the rank, exotic landscaping, Norma's mansion evokes the Spanish Revival,[14] which, in turn, often represents California as a lapsed Spanish colony in dire need of Angloamerican recuperation. Venturing into Norma's domain—with its ornate curvatures of stuccoed arches, wrought iron fixtures, and spiral staircase with drooping rope banister—Joe Gillis subtly assumes the jungle-adventurer pose which he playfully mocks later in the film.

Norma remains ensconced within this Gothic/exotic lair; surveilling Joe from the protection of bamboo-blinds and wrought-iron, Norma recalls the introduction of Phyllis Nirdlinger (Barbara Stanwick) in *Double Indemnity,* the shot in which the temptress greets Walter Neff (Fred MacMurray) from behind the elaborate iron banister of her own Mission Revival home in Pasadena. Exotic signifiers intensify as Joe proceeds into the heart of Norma's dark mansion. Conducted by Max (another lapsed adventurer) into Norma's *boudoir,* Joe finds a garish semitropical milieu: Norma's Gothic-black ensemble is crowned with a leopard-skin collar and hat which persists, later in the film, as the upholstery of her car. Norma immediately reveals to Joe another jungle denizen, the dead chimpanzee—given Norma's predatory "habit" (both sartorial and behavioral), the animal certainly appears, at the moment, a trophy of the hunt. Joe quite obviously remains oblivious of himself as a potential prey-item for Norma.

In keeping with silent film acting technique, Norma strikes poses that refract the exotic, contorted decor of her home: the curves, arches, and loops of both Norma and the house confront the tall vertical figure of Holden and the existential "uprightness" that he gradually develops and struggles to maintain, even in his death-throes. Norma's posturing reaches its apex at the conclusion of the film when she collapses into the role of Salome—an originary femme fatale—which she has, in fact, played throughout her life (Max offers a reinterpretation of the biblical story, in which Norma compels an Indian prince to strangle himself with one of her stockings). Norma here sheds black gown for the wispy veils of an Oriental dancer. The mansion becomes a near-eastern "palace" and Norma arches hands above head in an attitude concurrent with the elaborate wrought-iron sconce at her side. With her famous "close-up," Norma looms over the viewer and, through a hazy iris effect, blends indistinguishably with her weird surroundings. A similar dynamic pervades the *mise en scène* of *Sunset Boulevard:* doggedly erect as he plunges into his pool/grave, Joe Gillis embodies a beleaguered western rationalism agonistically frozen against Norma's curvaceous, Orientalized figure. The thematic achieved at the climax of *Sunset Boulevard* derives from the imperialist existentialism of writers such as Conrad and John Russell: Gillis might be read in this sense as a conflation of Lord Jim, for whom the colonial world becomes both fall and redemption, and Marlow, who returns to the metropolitan center not with spoils of empire, but only a recuperative, coherent narrative.

In an interview with Cameron Crowe, Billy Wilder suggested a strange and yet illuminating eulogy for William Holden:

> He died, unfortunately. He was a drunk. . . . He was drunk, terribly drunk, and he fell, and he hit his head on the corner of a table there. And there was nobody around, and he bled to death. When that happened, when somebody told me Holden is dead, I thought it could be only two things: either he died in a helicopter crash in Hong Kong, where he had an apartment, or he was trampled to death by a rhinoceros in Africa, where he also had a house. But that he's gonna die through a small little thing? (48)

Wilder's commentary returns us to our late-Victorian pretexts and the lament for lost opportunities for heroic adventure. It is as if Wilder has been persuaded of the late imperial persona which Holden accrued throughout his career. In films such as *The Bridges at Toko Ri* (Mark Robson, 1954),

The Bridge on the River Kwai (David Lean, 1958), and *The Wild Bunch* (Sam Peckinpah, 1969), Holden played varieties of the exhausted adventurer, disillusioned with dreams of empire and "out for number one." As in *Sunset Boulevard,* however, each narrative concludes with a sudden revival of imperial zeal whereby the Holden character performs some authentic "last stand" against a savage antagonist. Wilder seems to lament the loss of adventure as much as that of Holden himself: he should have died "with his boots on," like one of the characters in his films or, as Wilder's latter scenario suggests, like Hemingway's doomed but reinvigorated Francis Macomber. Wilder's eulogy for Holden therefore proves a fit epitaph/epigraph for a tradition which seems to die, but is written anew through the authenticating alienation of noir.

CHAPTER FOUR

VETERANS OF NOIR

REWRITING THE GOOD WAR WITH CHESTER HIMES, DOROTHY B. HUGHES, AND JOHN OKADA

It was a dirty city. Dirtier, certainly, than it had a right to be after only four years.
—John Okada, *No-No Boy* (1957)

We have seen that both fictional and cinematic noir turns upon a productive tension between an Expressionism, "edging toward nightmare," and a "straining for documentary realism"; "[s]ometimes the two modes collide within the same film," observes Foster Hirsch, "more often the divergent styles result in two distinct sub-categories within the *noir* keyboard" (53). This oft-noted duality speaks not only to the aesthetic and thematic dimensions of the noir vision, but also to its ideological foundations, for the contrast between the overt significations of Expressionism against a spare realism parallels what I have nominated the fundamental drama of noir: the struggle to limit meaning and to thereby recuperate a self in crisis. The noir hero, especially the hard-boiled detective, makes it his business to steer the subject away from unchecked semiosis (most powerfully embodied in the colonial adventurer-cum-conman) and toward an existential drama that coheres subjectivity. In keeping with the naturalizing program of realism, this continental operation is also very generally a "covert op"; we are only occasionally privy to reflexive moments in which the constructive mechanisms of noir are laid bare. Throughout the remainder of *Darkly Perfect World,* I describe the ways in which a series of novelists and cineastes exploit and amplify this reflexive potential, ultimately revising the means by which noir arrives at self and world.

Even amidst the heyday of noir, as Borde and Chaumeton describe the 1940s and '50s, the strategy of authenticating alienation was variously appropriated and subverted in a fashion that we might now describe as "postmodernist." Yet more vexed than noir itself, the term postmodernism will here be used to describe those critical and aesthetic practices that somehow denaturalize the process of meaning-making: at the risk of gross oversimplification, it might be observed that postmodernist art and theory share a hostility to the mimetic faith that is a lynchpin of noir, and an according preoccupation, whether in the form of pessimism or revolutionary celebration, with signification unleashed. This brings us to a deep fissure that runs through postmodernist culture and one that in large measure governs postmodernist receptions of noir. In an earlier draft of this book, I recognized the complicity of noir with colonial discourse and then turned immediately to an investigation of postmodernist artists who undermined noir by illuminating authenticating alienation as a fragile constructive mechanism. As I argue in later chapters, this pan-critical mode, which often leaves the hard-boiled protagonist in a terrifying identity crisis, is central to the story of noir. What I failed to acknowledge in that scheme, however, is the fact that "nihilist" postmodernism is circumscribed by more optimistic and revolutionary responses to noir. While writers such as Thomas Pynchon and Paul Auster evoke and undo noir recuperations, contributing to the postmodernist broadside against modern western subjectivity, marginalized artists, heretofore cast as one-dimensional bit-players in the noir drama, aggressively appropriated the means by which hard-boiled fictions celebrated an alienated white masculinity. A recognition of such texts offers a counterpoint to the paralytic nihilism often attributed to postmodernism. As Stanley Aronowitz and Henry Giroux point out, the postmodernist decentering of the subject occurs amidst and often runs counter to cultures of resistance. The announcement of the death of the self, they maintain, "makes it more difficult for those who have been excluded from the centers of power to name and experience themselves as individual and collective agents" (79). Before turning to the more properly deconstructive practices of the postmodernist literature and cinema, I shall analyze three novels that variously critique, appropriate, and transform the noir returning veteran's formula: Chester Himes's *If He Hollers Let Him Go* (1945), Dorothy B. Hughes's *In A Lonely Place* (1946), and John Okada's *No-No Boy* (1957). With particular attention to the returning veteran's narrative, these books reassign the strategy of authenticating alienation to protagonists conventionally "excluded from the centers of power," and in doing so inaugurate a denaturalizing critique of noir that will gain momentum throughout the twentieth century.

FOR BORDE AND CHAUMETON, World War II at once enabled and suppressed the emergence of film noir. On one hand, the fighting in Europe gave rise to a cinematic realism that, in turn, enabled film noir, along with the war film and the police documentary. At the same time, however, incipient noir was postponed by the American war effort, for the "antisocial" noir ethos was "out of place in a world under fire, in which American soldiers were defending a certain kind of order and set of values. There was an obvious discrepancy with official ideology. Whence this laying dormant for five years" (59). Sheri Chinen Biesen challenges the widespread notion of film noir as a postwar phenomenon. With attention to films such as *This Gun For Hire* (1942), *Street of Chance* (1942), and *Double Indemnity,* Biesen argues that the inchoate spirit of noir countered optimistic wartime propaganda. After the conclusion of hostilities in 1945, noir reached an apex impelled not only by the techniques of semidocumentary realism, but also by the "disturbing problems" of postwar America, including "unemployment relating to the redeployment of workers, the declassé status of certain veterans, the rise in crime. . . . As a statement on a society, the new series came just at the right time."[1] The post-WWII returning veteran's narrative is therefore another receptive host for the logic of noir; it might indeed be observed that the prominent returning veteran's films *The Best Years of Our Lives* (William Wyler, 1946) and *Till the End of Time* prefigure the apex of film noir, featuring Dana Andrews and Robert Mitchum, respectively, as veterans who negotiate the anomic world of civilian life with alternating stoicism and explosive violence. Many ensuing noirs would orchestrate stories of soldiers' painful reentry into domestic life with groundplots of crime and mystery, as in John Huston's *Key Largo* (1947), in which Humphrey Bogart plays a former infantry officer faced now with gangsters instead of fascists. For Paul Schrader, "The immediate post-war disillusionment was directly demonstrated in films like *Cornered, The Blue Dahlia, Dead Reckoning,* and *Ride the Pink Horse,* in which a serviceman returns from the war to find his sweetheart unfaithful or dead, or his business partner cheating him, or the whole society something less than worth fighting for" (55).

Schrader distinguishes George Marshall's *The Blue Dahlia* (1946) as a particularly telling example of returning veteran's noir; concurrent with more celebrated releases such as *The Best Years of Our Lives,* this film encapsulates many of the conventions that would be strategically recast by Himes, Hughes, and Okada. Post-WWII returning veteran films generally turn upon some variation of the following formula: the veteran protagonist faces an array of conflicts, including the "delayed stress" of wartime trauma and the resumption of domestic and vocational roles. Reintegration is at once eased and impeded by persistent homosocial bonding with war buddies, which tempts the protagonist to forgo the painful "return to normalcy." The veteran's narrative frequently treats a central protagonist with whom the broad viewership might identify, but whose inner conflicts are dramatized by more extremely alienated and/or alienating characters. These suggestive figures are often marked by some physical injury, such as amputation or trepanning, and by more pronounced psychological dysfunction. Returning veteran films most generally conclude with the protagonist's successful reintegration, itself punctuated by the reconciliation of the veteran hero with a lover: even in many films noirs, the classical Hollywood narrative demands a conclusive kiss, embrace, or promise of commitment to the nuclear family.

Written by Raymond Chandler, *The Blue Dahlia* distills the cultural work performed by the returning veteran's film. Alan Ladd plays Johnny Morrison, a Pacific Theater Liberator pilot who returns to Los Angeles with his two-man crew George (Hugh Beaumont) and Buzz (William Bendix). As even the opening sequence demonstrates, a tripartite characterization of the veteran's narrative is fully invoked: Ladd's trio share a parting drink in a convenient bar only to run into trouble with another serviceman. The jukebox selections of said soldier exacerbate Buzz's head-injury (a shell fragment covered by a steel plate); despite George's soothing admonitions, the "monkey music" drives Buzz to violence. He confronts the soldier and the scuffle is curtailed only by Johnny's forceful intervention. Although the veterans ultimately bond with each other against a panicky bartender, the episode immediately establishes the tense atmosphere of the film as a whole. Wartime traumas magnify the quotidian problems of urban life; in what reads as a reductive Freudian allegory, Johnny Morrison finds himself suspended between the ineffectual recommendations of the super-ego (George was a lawyer before the war; this role adumbrates Beaumont's more famous role as Ward Cleaver in *Leave It To Beaver*) and the libidinal Buzz. Throughout the film, Johnny will be faced with the potentially dehumanizing prescriptions of modern society and the visceral violence of combat.

When Johnny "comes marching home," he finds that his unfaithful wife, Helen (Doris Dowling), has not only taken up with gangster/club-owner Eddie Harwood (Howard da Silva), but that she has lost their only son in a drunk-driving accident. Though Johnny forbears shooting Helen, she soon turns up dead, murdered with his service automatic. Against George's insistence that he give himself up to the police, and Buzz's encouragements to flee, the suspect Johnny must turn detective in order to clear himself. In doing so, he must draw upon the rational tendencies embodied in George as well as Buzz's proclivities for reactionary violence. Chandler in a sense offers in Morrison another inscription of Phillip Marlowe, a hard-boiled detective stranded between reason and emotion, law and criminality. An exemplary noir hero, Johnny has withstood the crucible of the colonial periphery—the South Pacific combat zone—only to return to the violent and chaotic milieu of Los Angeles. In contrast to Buzz, whose invasive injuries coincide with his loss of rational self-control, Johnny emerges as the contused but coherent embodied self familiar to noir. But the imperatives of the classical Hollywood narrative obtrude to blunt Chandler's presentation of authenticating alienation. Johnny ultimately finds new love with Harwood's estranged wife Joyce (Veronica Lake). More strikingly, Chandler's original screenplay, which scripted Buzz as the murderer, was rewritten because of the Navy Department's objections to the criminalization of a serviceman. As Naremore concludes, "The loss of Buzz as the killer is even more significant, because it turns *The Blue Dahlia* into the sort of entertainment that Chandler spent his entire literary career attacking: a classical detective story, bringing all the suspects together in a single room and dramatically revealing one of them as the guilty party" (111).

THE BLUE DAHLIA is therefore a paradigmatic text that not only reflects the tensions surrounding Chandler's career and the genre of the returning veteran's film, but also suggests the contradictions that vex noir ideology: whatever its antipathies to Enlightenment capitalism and positivism, noir yet remains committed to the recuperation of an alienated white male subject. Even a comparatively benign film such as *The Blue Dahlia* betrays the importance of colonial discourse to the strategy of authenticating alienation—the world of savage otherness that confronted the veterans in the Pacific War also suffuses the Los Angeles "home front," echoing in the "monkey music" that pulses through Buzz's tormented psyche. Consistently exploited as some Other for the hard-boiled Self, minority and women writers have appropriated returning veteran's noir for their own purposes. Such recastings are endemic to the polyglot world of the contact zone, argues Mary Louise Pratt. When diverse cultures meet and struggle within contexts such as conquest and slavery, those subordinated inevitably contest and reclaim the colonizer's representations for "autoethnographic expression" (7). Hence, Richard Wright and Ralph Ellison, in Paula Rabinowitz's view, recruit noir to "dissect race, postwar America, and the CPUSA" (89). In the hands of these novelists, noir conventions such as the first-person "tale of descent" and the depiction of an urban jungle become part of an indictment of failed democracy: "Where the white noir hero lurks the black streets of steamy (or more often rainy and foggy) cities; the black noir figure is alone in a bleached landscape devoid of color, his body in constant contrast.... The heart of darkness for an African American is frozen—white as snow-covered pavement, as a blonde's neckline" (95). According to Rabinowitz, the angst of the returning veteran is another noir figure adopted by African American writers like Richard Wright; an early draft of *The Outsider* (1953) treats the experience of a "disillusioned veteran" languishing in a ship's brig. We shall see that returning veteran's noir was seized upon not only by other black writers, such as Chester Himes, but also by Dorothy Hughes and John Okada.

Early in the narrative of Himes's 1960 novel *All Shot Up*, Mammy Louise's bulldog obstructs Coffin Ed and Gravedigger Jones from leaving the back room of the pork store, where they have been eating "chicken feetsy." Gravedigger characteristically produces a long-barreled, nickel-plated revolver, prompting Mammy Louise to admonish the dog, "Not dem, Lawd Jim, mah god dawg . . . You can't stop dem from goin' nowhere. Them is de *mens*" (21). The regenerated paternalist hero of late Victorian adventure, "Lawd Jim," hereby makes his way into this hard-boiled detective story as the most peripheral of figures, a pet that might be incidentally swept away by the apocalyptic violence of "de mens." Formerly the adjuncts of white colonial subjectivity, these "noir" protagonists inherit the hard-boiled legacy of mobility and authenticating alienation. Published at a time when films such as *The Best Years of Our Lives* and *The Blue Dahlia* were under production, Himes's earlier novel *If He Hollers Let Him Go* similarly recasts the returning veteran's narrative; even as the novel's protagonist, Bob Jones, is wont to wear his "tin hat back at a signifying angle" (128), Himes signifies upon this genre by directing its basic conventions toward a recasting of noir authenticating alienation. For Bob Jones, as for Chandler's Johnny Morrison, the "home-front" is itself a combat zone that demands vigilance bordering on paranoia.[2] As he negotiates this tense and dangerous world, Jones confronts a series of characters that broadly reflect a panoply of available subject-positions: in keeping with the existentialist tenor of noir, however, none of these alternatives represents an adequate response to the contradictions of wartime America, and the antihero must somehow forge his own alienated identity in opposition to the encompassing threats and seductions. Himes's ultimate response to the false dichotomy of American democracy and Axis fascism is a reversal of the returning veteran's trajectory: while mainstream films about veterans see the protagonist safely pass from military to domestic life, *If He Hollers* concludes with Jones's conscription—the Army becomes a wartime equivalent of incarceration.

Cinematic returning veterans find both trauma and redemption in the realization that a fight for democracy will persist into the postwar universe.

When Major Frank McCloud battles Rocco (Edward G. Robinson) in *Key Largo* or when Rip Murdock (Humphrey Bogart) successfully deploys Pacific War tactics (including Japanese incendiary grenades) against racketeers in *Dead Reckoning,* the returning veteran comes to understand that his combat experience is vitally important in a cosmopolitan free-market society. One such pivotal moment transpires in *Till the End of Time,* when Cliff Harper (Guy Madison) and Bill Tabeshaw (Robert Mitchum) defend a black soldier insulted by racist agitators; heretofore confused and frustrated, the vets find renewed purpose in the continued fight for democracy against fascism. In this scenario, the black serviceman mutely suffers both nativist contumely and liberal intervention; as in more explicitly colonialist noir fictions, he is not autonomous agent, but rather an adjunct to white self-realization.

In *If He Hollers Let Him Go,* Himes likewise treats the home front as a combat-zone subject to tremendous ideological conflict. On one hand, wartime California lives up to its promise of hope and possibility. Having moved from Cleveland to Los Angeles, Jones finds that his wartime position as a leaderman at the Atlas Shipyard offers the means for self-realization: "Something about my working clothes made me feel rugged, bigger than the average citizen, stronger than a white-collar worker—stronger even than an executive" (8–9). At the same time, however, the onset of the war catalyzes a paralyzing angst:

> Maybe I'd been scared all my life, but I didn't know about it until Pearl Harbor. . . . Maybe it had started then, I'm not sure, or maybe it wasn't until I'd seen them send the Japanese away that I'd noticed it. Little Riki Oyana singing 'God Bless America' and going to Santa Anita with his parents next day. It was taking a man up by the roots and locking him up without a charge. Without even giving him a chance to say one word. It was thinking about if they ever did that to me, Robert Jones, Mrs. Jones's dark son, that started me to getting scared.
>
> After that, it was everything. It was the look in white people's faces when I walked down the streets. It was that crazy, wild-eyed, unleashed hatred that the first Jap bomb on Pearl Harbor let loose in a flood. All that tight, crazy feeling of race as thick in the street as gas fumes. Every time I stepped outside I saw a challenge I had to accept or ignore. Every day I had to make one decision a thousand times: *Is it now? Is now the time?*" (3–4)

America's fight for democracy has paradoxically transformed the home front into a fascist state in which racial minorities might be at any moment "taken up by the roots." With racism poisoning the air like a gas attack, the domestic becomes for Jones a battlefield zone. He intuits that the racism directed at the Japanese is part of the same complex of white supremacist hatred historically visited upon African Americans. Just as an apparently peaceful landscape might be suddenly revealed as a minefield or subjected to an ambush, an artillery barrage, or an airstrike, the seemingly prosperous and unified American metropolis may explode into incendiary race riots. Like the edgy returning veteran, who cannot easily shed his combat reflexes (as in the opening sequence of *The Blue Dahlia*), Jones moves through L.A. with the tense expectation of murderous violence.

Reading the suspicion and hatred in white faces, Jones debunks the Enlightenment fantasies inscribed onto the California dream. "The huge industrial plants flanking the ribbon of road . . . the thousands of rushing workers . . . and the snow-capped mountains in the background like picture post-cards, didn't mean a thing to me," he bitterly reflects, "I didn't even see them; all I wanted to do was push my Buick Roadmaster over some peckerwood's face" (14). Clocking in to work at the Atlas plant, Jones must shed even his cherished automobile, which he explicitly identifies as a symbol of security, agency, and mobility (31). The troopship under construction is likewise a central symbol of the novel; but we do not find in this vessel the hermetic microcosm of conventional narrative. Ostensibly the heart of western technorationality, the ship is characterized by Jones as a "littered madhouse": "It was cramped quarters aft, a labyrinth of narrow, hard-angled companionways, jammed with staging, lines, shapes, and workers who had to be contortionists first of all (20). . . . I had to pick every step to find a foot-size clearance of deck space, and at the same time to keep looking up so I wouldn't tear off an ear or knock out an eye against some overhanging shape" (16). Moreover, this suggestive space is transmogrified throughout the novel into a battlefield that justifies Jones's hostility and paranoia. Amid the "stifling heat" and the "terrific din" (21), a mundane conversation or a crap game among co-workers might devolve into vicious hand-to-hand fighting. After one such skirmish, Jones recalls, "that sick, gone feeling came in the pit of my stomach . . . [a]nd a blinding explosion went off just back of my eyes as if the nerve centres had been dynamited" (33). Such incidents are generally the result of Jones's resistance to the Jim Crow hierarchies that govern the Atlas shipyard and American society as a whole; but Jones's co-workers, Elsie and Tebbel, also routinely indulge in racist diatribes against Jews and Mexicans—though patrolled by fighter planes against enemy attack, the industrial plant has been infiltrated with the same racist dogma that is the ideology of the Axis powers. Suggesting chaos rather than reason, violent divisions rather than unity, and racism rather than democracy, the skeletal vessel represents

Himes's larger deconstructive exposure of the contradictions governing America.

As if realizing Du Bois's notion of African American "double-consciousness," Himes imbues his antihero with an ambivalent attitude toward the war-effort. Gazing at the shipyards in the "hard, bright California sunshine," Jones at one point admits that he "felt the immensity of the production" and "the importance of the whole war": "I'd never given a damn one way or the other about the war excepting wanting to keep out of it; and at first when I wanted the Japanese to win. And now I did; I was stirred as I had been when I was a little boy watching a parade, seeing the flag go by. That all filled-up feeling of my country. I felt included in it all; I had never felt included before. It was a wonderful feeling" (38). While these lines imply a resolution to Jones's conflicted psyche, his inner turmoil persists throughout the novel. If the sight of bustling industry and production inspires a fleeting sense of filial patriotism, then seeing a cruiser "silhouetted against the skyline . . . the black sailors aboard waiting on the white . . . [in the] the good old American way," rekindles Jones's feelings of alienation and antagonism:

> I wondered what would happen if all the Negroes in America would refuse to serve in the armed forces, refuse to work in the war production until the Jim Crow pattern was abolished. The white folks would no doubt go on fighting the war without us, I thought—and no doubt win it. They'd kill us maybe; but they couldn't kill us all. And if they did they'd have one hell of a job burying us. (115–16)

This imagination of a passive resistance to American apartheid gives way in other moments to violent fantasies that turn wartime propaganda back upon itself. Jones at one point finds himself in Little Tokyo "where the spooks and spills had taken over" in the wake of Japanese internment. In a seedy bar called "The Rust Room" (suggesting the decay at the heart of American industry), Jones participates in a sad drama of racial tension: a poor white woman flaunts her sexuality for both the black patrons and white servicemen, playing the two groups against one another. As the collective anxiety increases, Jones muses about a war picture, Victor Fleming's 1943 "*A Guy Named Joe;* about that cat making a last bomb-run, sinking a Nazi flat-top. Going out in a blaze of glory." Jones goes on to imagine himself as the war hero; recalling Wright's Bigger Thomas, in the opening pages of *Native Son* (1940); however, he envisions "going out blowing up the white folks like that cat did the Nazis" (74). The episode explicitly reverses the war film, but more subtly evokes and subverts noir. Whereas noir virtuosi ranging from Hammett to Maté inscribe the urban "dive" as a locus of exotic otherness, Himes finds in the Little Tokyo bar an opportunity to dramatize America's ideological contradictions. Jones predicts that "if there was any kind of a rumpus with a white chick in it, there wouldn't be any way to stop a riot—the white GI's would swarm into Little Tokyo like they did into the Mexican districts during the Zoot Suit Riots. Only in Little Tokyo they'd have to kill and be killed, for the spooks down there were some really rugged cats" (77).

Himes's portrait of "Arky jill" in The Rust Room points to his general disposition of women in *If He Hollers Let Him Go* and to another way in which he negotiates noir conventions. In films such as *The Blue Dahlia*, the protagonist is flanked not only by "typical" comrades, but also by antithetical women—the idealized "domestic angel" Joyce Harwood and the dark femme fatale Helen Morrison—types that derive, respectively, from the metropolitan and colonial women of late-Victorian adventure. Himes conserves but inverts these reductive figures; whereas Jones's black girlfriend Alice is the ineffectual bourgeoisie (in this case suggestive of the assimilationist temptation of "passing"), the white "tacker" Madge, like "Arky jill," is a white femme fatale that embodies race hatred. Though beautiful and elegant, Alice infuriates Jones with her condescending "social worker attitude" and her desire to elide the contradictions of American democracy: "I want a husband," she admits, "who is important and respected and wealthy enough so that I can avoid a major part of the discriminatory practices which I am sensible enough to know I cannot change" (96–97). Anticipating films such as *Out of the Past, Sunset Boulevard,* and *D.O.A.,* Himes presents in Alice a middle-class alternative that is unattainable and inauthentic. Not merely ineffectual, however, Alice becomes in Jones's mind a real liability to black resistance: "even though the solid logic of my hangover told me that Alice's way was my only way out, I didn't have anything for it but the same contempt a white person has for a collaborator's out in France" (152).[3] If the domestic angel reads for Himes as a collaborator, then the femme fatale emerges as another mythic WWII female figure, "Rosie the Riveter." Jones immediately discerns that his relationship with the white Texan tacker will be determined by hegemonic role-playing: "I knew the instant I recognized her that she was going to perform then—we would both perform. As soon as she saw me she went into her frightened act and began shrinking away." Despite protestations that she "ain't gonna work with no nigger" (27), Madge turns to sexuality as a means of maneuvering Jones into the stereotypical role of hypersexual Negro:

> So it wasn't that Madge was white; it was the way she used it. . . . And without having to say one word she could keep all the white men in the world feeling they had to protect her from black rapists. That made her doubly dangerous because she thought about Negro men. . . . She wanted them to run after her. She expected it, demanded it as her due. I could imagine her teasing them with her body, showing her bare thighs and breasts. Then having them lynched for looking. (125)

As the narrative proceeds, Madge at once excites the ire of the Jim Crow management at Atlas and poses a psychic threat to Jones, who feels "nailed to the bed" at the very thought of her. As McCann points out, the "antidemocratic forces" of corrupt black bourgeoisie and white supremacy are represented in "the illegitimate power of women" (268). However objectionable, these female characters are also the locus of Himes's signifyin' on returning veteran's noir; with the binary opposition between Alice and Madge, Himes inverts the racialized coding of the domestic angel and femme fatale[4] even as he dissolves the false dichotomy separating democratic America from fascist Europe. Deeming Alice a Vichy traitor, Himes casts Jones as a Resistance fighter who operates "behind the lines" to subvert enemy operations.

These diverse layers of signification come together in the climactic moments of *If He Hollers Let Him Go*. The final episode is framed by encounters with the domestic angel and the femme fatale. After conceding to Alice's vision of "separate but equal" middle-class life, Jones clocks in at Atlas only to encounter Madge asleep in a cabin: "I could hear her sighing like an animal, see the vague outline of her body as she flexed the sleep out of it" (178). Though paralyzed by the fear of being caught alone with a white woman, Jones rejects Madge's advances until they are discovered by a Navy inspector. With the cry "Some white man, help!" Madge immediately resumes her role as white rape victim, and the construction site once again explodes into violence: "The sight of one hard hating face across my vision shook loose my reason again. Now I was moved by rage, impelled by it, set into motion by it, lacerated by it. I started hitting, kicking butting, biting, pushing. I carried the mob outside the companionway, striking at faces, kicking at bodies . . . I looked up, saw a white guy wielding a sledge hammer, his face sculptured in unleashed fury. A flat cold wave of terror spread out underneath my skull, freezing the roots of my hair" (182). This riot certainly recalls the hand-to-hand combat of the military narrative as well as the melees of Hammett's fiction (particularly those of "Nightmare Town" and "The Big Knock-Over"). But whereas Hammett celebrates the insular coherence of the Op against the savage otherness of figures such as "Nigger Vojan," Himes installs a contused black body as a sign of the heroically alienated protagonist. Framed by Madge, Jones flees Atlas, his Buick Roadmaster roaring like a P-38 fighter. The climactic pattern of flight and pursuit even more closely aligns the novel with a film like *The Blue Dahlia;* unlike Johnny Morrison, however, who clears himself to resume middle-class life, Jones is apprehended by the police. Celebrating Madge's "forbearance" as "a patriotic gesture comparable only to the heroism of men in battle," the president of the Atlas Corporation condemns Jones as "an animal" possessed by "uncontrolled lust." In the final moments of the novel, Jones finds himself conscripted into the more radical Jim Crow regime of the U.S. Army:

> "Come on, boy," the cop said.
> The two Mexican youths he had with him grinned a welcome.
> "Let's go, man, the war's waiting," one of them cracked.
> "Don't rush the man," the other one said. "The man's not doing so well . . . Looks like this man has had a war. How you doing, man?"
> They were both brown-skinned, about my colour, slender and slightly stooped, with Indian features and thick curly hair. Both wore bagged drapes that looked about to fall down from their waists, and greyish dirty T shirts. They talked in the melodious Mexican lilt.
> "I'm still here," I lisped painfully. (203)

This downbeat conclusion reverses the trajectory of the returning veteran's films under production in the mid-1940s. Both classical Hollywood and noir returning veteran films envision the home front as a combative world that tests the vet's military experience; and while films noirs such as *The Blue Dahlia* and *Dead Reckoning* more cynically treat the protagonist's traumatic resumption of civilian life, they too conclude with a sense of heroic closure. In *If He Hollers Let Him Go,* the home front is the site of an ongoing race war between whites and "underclassed" peoples of color: hence, the Latinos headed for the induction center with Jones recognize that "the man looks like he's had a war." But Himes's most dramatic intervention into veteran's noir is his reversal of its narrative trajectory; this novel concludes with induction rather than demobilization. And yet the antihero Bob Jones is not defeated even by this grim prospect: with the conclusive line, "I'm still here," lisped through broken teeth, he emerges the coherent and resilient protagonist alienated from the "superstructures" of white power rather than the dark places of the American metropolis.

HIMES INVERTS the racial codings of the domestic angel and the femme fatale, but he leaves intact this fundamental noir opposition. Paula Rabinowitz identifies as a central tension of postwar noir the returning vets' displacement from the "newly scrubbed world of appliances and women's shoulder-padded assertiveness," "a new world not of their making and strangely dangerous beyond imagination" (4). The misogyny endemic to noir from the 1920s and '30s only gained momentum after the shifts in gendered divisions of labor that accompanied World War II. "Women had experienced a different kind of mobilization during the 1940s," suggests Rabinowitz, "when many left poorly paying jobs as domestics or clerks in search of more lucrative employment in factories and federal government offices." Film noir registers this transformation in women's work as a "dangerous autonomy, visualized in the snarl that comes invariably at the moment when the female takes control of the man and the situation" (27–28). In *The Blue Dahlia*, Chandler and Marshall eliminate the distance between the femme fatale and the "liberated" postwar woman as they present Helen Morrison as a sneering seductress whose transgressive sexuality explodes with the absence of her soldiering husband. For Rabinowitz, before films noirs like *The Blue Dahlia* legitimized a violent reaction to the "parallel excursion of women into the workforce and onto the dance floors" (159), the noir femme fatale was peremptorily "invented" by female artists who were later excluded from the phallocentric noir canon. Working under the auspices of the Office of War Information, photographer Esther Bubley documented the lives of working women on the home-front. Bubley centered the alienated women who would later be pushed to the edge of the cinematic frame: "Alone and mobile they are free from family scrutiny and control; yet their availability is limited by the absence of men who have deserted this and other urban spaces for war" (Rabinowitz 30). Even as Bubley "charted what happened to Mary Astor's Brigid O'Shaugnessy," Caroline Slade wrote the female social worker as a private eye, "offering tantalizing clues to unravel the larger racket of capitalism that was the subject of so many film noirs" (Rabinowitz 167).

Bubley and Slade were not the only women to question and revise noir at its very apex. Wryly suggesting that "being female in the pulp culture era was itself cause for paranoia," Woody Haut argues that novelists such as Leigh Brackett, Dolores Hitchens, and Dorothy B. Hughes "were able to undermine traditional notions of the *femme fatale*, and though they often portray women as victims, refrain from portraying them as helpless objects" (131). Hughes wrote a series of hard-boiled novels throughout the 1940s, three of which were adapted as films that are now firmly situated in the noir canon.[5] Rejecting the first-person narrative that became a hallmark of noir, Hughes writes in a third-person voice that distances and disempowers the male noir antiheroes. This narrator registers the hard-boiled monologue through which the protagonist insulates himself from compromising entanglements, but she also transcends this perspective for omniscient revelations of the characters' fears, anxieties, and motivations. "Although none of her 1940s novels is directly in first-person," writes Dana Polan, "the narration sticks very closely to the central character as he or she moves through a world of menace, reads the clues of that world and wonders about them."[6] A good example of this approach occurs early in the narrative of *Ride the Pink Horse* (1946), as Sailor Martin confronts the otherness of New Mexico: "The unease of an alien land, of darkness and silence, of strange tongues and a stranger people. . . . What sucked into his pores for that moment was panic although he could not have put a name to it. The panic of loneness; of himself the stranger although he himself was unchanged, the creeping loss of identity" (42). Hughes denies her antiheroes the agency and lucidity of the first-person, arrogating to the third-person narrator the ability to analyze their psychic responses. In other words, Hughes revisits existentialist noir with literary naturalism, and, in doing so, defamiliarizes its strategy of authenticating alienation.

Treating the experience of a vengeful Chicago enforcer in an unassimilable Southwest, *Ride the Pink Horse* reads as a subversive recasting of adventure-noir. Hughes's later novel *In A Lonely Place* is even more germane to the present discussion in that it explicitly takes on the noir returning veteran's narrative. Hughes directs her denaturalizing critique toward the returning veteran's formula in both *The Fallen Sparrow* and *In A Lonely Place,* but its consequences are more visible in the latter novel. This book explores the violent, misogynistic psyche of fighter-pilot-cum-novelist Dixon Steele. But this appellation may be too charitable, as Dix only maintains writing as a way to mooch from his rich uncle and to cover his real pursuit—serial murders of young women. For Dix, the war was not a cataclysmic event that renders civilian life impossible; to the contrary, "The war years were the first happy years he'd ever known" (109), when "the best was none too good for Colonel Steele" (157). Growing up on the edge of power and prosperity, Dix finds in the war a satisfying confluence of status and excitement that he "missed after the war had crashed to a finish and dribbled to an end" (1). Apparently grieved by the loss of his lover Brucie, an English woman who, we might presume, died in the Nazi attacks on London, Dix recaptures the thrill of air combat by stalking and killing women—"Risks were stunt flying," he reflects; and pitting his mind against another's was "breathing as a man could breathe when he was lifted into the vastness of the sky, when he knew himself to be a unit of power, complete in himself, powerful in himself" (135).

Dix's postwar experience sharply contrasts with that of Brub Nicolai, a flier with whom Dix served in England. "I don't like killing," reflects Brub, "I hated it then, the callous way we'd sit around and map out our plans to kill people. People who didn't want to die any more than we wanted to die. And we'd come back afterward and talk it over, check over how many we'd got that night. As if we'd been killing ants, not men." For Brub, modern "rational" warfare is not thrilling, but dehumanizing; he has therefore become a police detective, "To help make one little corner of the world a safer place" (89). This interesting subplot in itself represents a significant reinterpretation of the returning veteran's narrative: two ex-G.I.'s meet each other after the war, their radically divergent responses to combat translated into crime and punishment. Ironically, their camaraderie at once advances and impedes the investigation, in that Dix becomes known to the detectives, but remains free from suspicion throughout most of the narrative. Dix significantly finds this postwar reunion exciting not only because of the danger it entails but also because it reestablishes the bond with Brub: "There was something amusing about Brub Nicolai being able to lay hands on him whenever he wished. Amusing and more exciting than anything that had happened to him in a long time. The hunter and the hunted arm in arm" (15). In many returning veteran's narratives, the safe haven of the homosocial world becomes a temptation for the protagonist seeking reintegration into domestic life (Wyler dramatizes this pitfall with the aptly named bar "Butch's"). Hughes amplifies neurosis into full-blown pathology as she presents in Dix a returning veteran whose fraternity with detective war buddy Brub depends upon the murder of female victims.

Hughes therefore exaggerates certain tendencies of veteran's noir in order to reveal the formula's commitment to patriarchal values. Moving beyond parody, however, Hughes undermines the strategy of authenticating alienation only to extend its constructive possibilities to the women conventionally marginalized within the noir imagination. Anticipating postmodernist parodies of noir, Hughes writes Dix as a "floating signifier" by turns indicative of self and other. As he wanders the dark and foggy streets of L.A., Dix at least imagistically assumes his place as one of the antiheroes of noir: "[H]e walked on, down the incline to the pool of fog light at the intersection. . . . He passed [houses] slowly, as if reluctant to accept the closed gates barring the intruders of the night. He went on to the open lot, through which, in sunlight, the beach crowds passed over the broad sands to the sea beyond." Enraged by his own dislocation (especially poignant when he lurks outside the bourgeois comfort of the Bannings' beach-house), Dix moves further out onto the beach, toward a heaving ocean that might be read as an objective correlative for his tormented psyche (it is here that "the red knots tightened in his brain" [163]).

But while Dix himself may be "lost in a lonely place," he is also an embodiment of the violent nocturnal forces that confront the noir protagonist. Dix is startled out of his solipsistic grief by Betsy Banning, who "didn't know that behind that smile lay his hatred of Laurel, hatred of Brub and Sylvia, of Mel Terriss, of old Fergus Steele, of everyone in the living world..." (164). Betsy, along with Dix's other victims, appears the passive object of his hatred, lending credence to Polan's notion that "Hughes does not seem a writer much concerned to give women power in a narrative" (26). On the other hand, to Dix's dismay, both Laurel Gray and Sylvia Nicolai assume the agonistic role of the hard-boiled hero. Neither of these women conforms to the reductive polarities of noir, which are themselves registered in Dix's own assumptions about women in general. Although Dix imagines Sylvia as the "mistress of the house... beautiful in her context" (8), he cannot ultimately understand his friend's wife—"She was too many women" (43). Sylvia quickly turns detective to surpass Brub's investigative power. "I don't trust Brub's taste," she playfully remarks, "He just looks at the envelope. Now I'm a psychologist. I find out what's inside" (47). Appropriating the gaze usually ascribed to the male noir hero, Sylvia confutes Dix's presumptions about the passive domestic angel consumed by "aimless female business" (81): "Sylvia's eyes were disturbing, they were so wise. As if she could see under the covering of a man" (52).... She burrowed under words, under the way of a face and a smile for the actuality" (98). Even as Sylvia evokes and eludes the fixed subject-position of the domestic angel, Laurel excites in Dix's imagination the figure of the femme fatale. Dix conflates both women with nature; but while Sylvia "was made long and lovely like a birch tree," Laurel is "lush and warm, like a woman" (92) or "like an animal, one of the big cats, a young golden puma" (128): "she was a bitchy dame, cruel as her eyes and taloned nails. Cruel as her cat body and sullen tongue" (158). As these lines suggest, Dix casts Laurel in the feline mold of the femme fatale, a pattern so recognizable by the mid-1940s that it could be literalized in Tourneur's *Cat People* (1942). Like Sylvia, however, Laurel complicates the neat binaries of noir; while the femme fatale threatens to compromise male subjectivity, Laurel herself must assume the defensive posture of the hard-boiled hero. Recalling the insularity of Chandler's Marlowe, Laurel is "damn careful to keep men out of her apartment" (183) and she defies Dix's possessive sense that "she belonged to him" [127]), warning "If you don't take your hands off me you won't be good to any woman any more" (101).

Sylvia and Laurel, respectively, signify Hughes's revision of the angelic/demonic opposition that governs representations of women in hard-boiled fiction and film noir. At the conclusion of the novel, these conventionally segregated female characters cooperate in an unprecedented way against the threat posed by "old lady killer Steele" (36).[7] Infuriated by Laurel's prolonged absence, the murderous Dix searches her apartment only to find Sylvia waiting in the courtyard, wearing his lover's coat—a sign of the women's identification and collusion. "She isn't coming back, Dix," explains, Sylvia: "She's safe. She's going to stay safe. . . . Laurel came to Brub. Because she was afraid. Afraid of the way you looked at her. . . . It wasn't the first time she'd been afraid. But it was beginning to grow" (212). Conflating all women in his misogynistic fury, Dix attacks Sylvia; but this is a trap, and she is rescued by Brub and Lochner. Ironically, Sylvia saves Dix from the wrath of Brub, whose "face was the face of a killer" (212). As Dix finally admits, "I killed Brucie" (214), Hughes realigns the network of characters in the novel: whether fighting or cooperating, men pose a danger to themselves and others. Even as Dix and Brub unite in homicidal rage, Sylvia and Laurel—domestic angel and femme fatale—combine to protect each other and to stem this escalating violence. Like Himes, Hughes astutely revises veteran's noir, but she attends to gender rather than racial politics.

Given that *In A Lonely Place* is a title more closely associated with Nicholas Ray's 1950 film than with Hughes's novel, we might be tempted to conclude that the director restored the countercultural book "back into" the patriarchal noir imagination. The trajectory of this adaptation in some measure supports such a conclusion. As Polan points out, Dix's homicidal tendencies became more "virtual" at every stage of the process: "From Hughes's novel (where Dix kills often) to the screenplay hinted at in producer Robert Lord's censorship letter (where Dix kills, but only twice), to Solt's first screenplay (where Dix didn't kill Mildred, but does kill Laurel), to the version shot (where Dix kills no one, but comes awfully close to killing Laurel), we remain in a story of a man's culpability, of a potential (whether realized or not) for violence" (64). In the film, Dix ends up a composite of Hughes's Dix and Brub: an "innocent" man possessed by unrealized homicidal potential. Even its promotional materials, Polan observes, underscored the film's sentiment "that all men are potentially violent and should be interrogated (by themselves and those around them) for their susceptibility to violent impulses" (62–63). Though to some extent diffusing the feminist critique levied by Hughes, Ray also amplifies the novelist's rendition of Laurel as a female noir protagonist. As implied by its working title, *Behind the Mask, In A Lonely Place* casts Laurel and Sylvia as determined and frustrated investigators trying to penetrate Bogart's impassive visage for the "real" Dixon Steele. Along with King Vidor's *Gilda* (1946) and John Auer's *Hell's Half Acre* (1954), *In A Lonely Place* stands as one of the few films noirs that permits a female figure to transgress the boundaries of the angel/femme fatale binary in favor of the lonely centrality of authenticating alienation.

WRITING IN THE 1940s, Chester Himes and Dorothy Hughes accomplished daring interventions into contemporary returning veteran noirs; in doing so, they appropriated constructive strategies conventionally devoted to the maintenance of white male subjectivity. About a decade later, at the height of the Cold War, John Okada pursued a similarly dramatic revision of returning veteran's noir in his 1957 novel *No-No Boy*. Despite the many Asian characters deployed in hard-boiled fiction and film noir, Japanese Americans remain scarce, the notable exceptions being the sinister Japanese figures in von Sternberg's *The Shanghai Gesture*, Huston's *Across the Pacific* (1942),[8] and Richard Thorpe's hard-boiled WWII adventure *Malaya* (1949). These films emerge from an amalgamation of hard-boiled Orientalism and the barrage of anti-Japanese propaganda that attended the Pacific War. Indeed, all of these representational strategies stemmed from the discourses of Victorian colonialism. As John W. Dower demonstrates, the Pacific Theater in World War II was characterized in the West as a struggle between civilization and savagery. Within this national narrative, however, American soldiers fighting the Japanese, like their comrades in the Philippine-American War, risked losing their humanity via contact with so brutal an enemy. Professor E. B. Sledge, who served with the Marines at Peleliu and Okinawa, recalls, "Time had no meaning, life had no meaning.... The fierce struggle for survival... eroded the veneer of civilization and made savages of us all."[9] Films noirs such as *Dead Reckoning* (John Cromwell, 1947) and *Somewhere in the Night* (Joseph L. Mankiewicz, 1946) are gripped with the metrocolonial anxieties common to Hammett and Chandler's earlier fiction. Having faced the savage Japanese enemy, the Pacific War veteran may retain and clarify his subjectivity by disciplining and deploying his combat experience within the alienating milieu of the American city. And this was the cultural environment that Okada broached in *No-No Boy*.

From its first pages, *No-No Boy* situates itself as a returning veteran's narrative on the order of *The Blue Dahlia*, *Till the End of Time*, and *The Best Years of Our Lives*. The novel's preface briefly surveys Japanese-American experiences of World War II—discrimination, internment, "passing," and military service (recollective of Okada's own wartime experience in the Air Force)—to conclude by associating the latter with the even less publicized story of the "no-no boy": "I've got reasons [for volunteering,] said the Japanese-American soldier soberly and thought some more about his friend who was in another kind of uniform because they wouldn't let his father go to the same camp with his mother and sisters" (xi). After the Japanese-American population at large was interned under FDR's General Order 9066, all internees over the age of seventeen were posed with two questions: "Are you willing to serve in the armed forces of the United States on combat duty, wherever ordered," and "Will you swear unqualified allegiance to the United States of America and faithfully defend the United States from any or all attack by foreign or domestic forces, and forswear any form of allegiance to the Japanese emperor, or any other foreign government, power, or organization?"[10] As Stan Yogi remarks, "The government demanded either 'Yes' or 'No' answers, denying internees the opportunity to voice their complex reactions to these questions" (63). Having refused to serve in the military and to foreswear allegiance to Japan (the titular "no's"), Okada's protagonist Ichiro "Itchy" Yamada has been consigned to federal prison instead of the internment camp. As Ichiro returns to Seattle after serving in "another kind of uniform," Okada redefines the veteran's experience to encompass narratives suppressed by mainstream American historiographies. Moreover, with the first lines of chapter 1, Okada reiterates and transforms the opening sequence of *The Blue Dahlia*:

> Two weeks after his twenty-fifth birthday, Ichiro got off a bus at Second and Main in Seattle. He had been gone four years, two in camp and two in prison.
>
> Walking down the street that autumn morning with a small black suitcase, he felt like an intruder in a world to which he had no claim. . . . Christ, he thought to himself, just a goddamn kid is all I was. Didn't know enough to wipe my own nose. What the hell have I done? What am I doing back here? Best thing I can do would be to kill some son of a bitch and head back to prison.
>
> He walked toward the railroad depot where the tower with the clocks on all four sides was. It was a dirty looking tower of ancient brick. It was a dirty city. Dirtier, certainly, than it had a right to be after only four years. (1)

In terms of both form and content, this inaugural moment evokes the bathetic world of veteran's noir. Like Chandler's veterans in *The Blue Dahlia* or Dmytryk's Cliff Harper in *Till the End of Time*, Ichiro steps off the bus into an alienating postwar society, "a world to which he had no claim." Nor is this environment itself the prosperous metropolis of a triumphant world power: with clipped lines worthy of any hard-boiled voice-over, Okada describes Seattle as a noir cityscape captured in the begrimed clock tower (a symbol not only of urban decay but of the oppressive past that leans heavily upon Ichiro).[11] As if pursuing an inverted recasting of

The Blue Dahlia, Okada allows Ichiro to immediately encounter another veteran: "The fellow wore green, army-fatigue trousers and an Eisenhower jacket: Eto Minato. The name came to him at the same time as did the horrible significance of the army clothes" (2). We may recall that in *The Blue Dahlia,* Johnny, George, and Buzz find their farewell drink interrupted by a confrontation with a Marine playing "monkey music" on the jukebox—a dispute resolved as soon as the soldier realizes that Buzz, despite his civies, is likewise a former serviceman. Ichiro's reunion with Eto, by contrast, devolves from camaraderie to hostility. However tolerant of internees, Eto refuses veteran's status to a no-no boy who calls into question his own national identity. "'Rotten bastard. Shit on you,'" he intones: "'Rotten, no-good bastard . . . I'll piss on you next time'" (4). For Chandler, the traumatized vets fraternally bond against the anomie of postwar society; and race politics are sublimated into the persistent echo of "monkey music."[12] Okada conversely inscribes Itchy Yamada an unlikely and angst-ridden veteran explicitly alienated and oppressed by the racist milieu of postwar America. Dazedly retreating from Eto, "God in a pair of green fatigues, US army style," Ichiro walks down mean streets echoing with the racial slurs of a group of black soldiers—"'Jap! . . . Go back to Tokyo boy.' Persecution in the drawl of the persecuted" (5).

As in this epigraphic scene, Okada pursues in *No-No Boy* the primary conventions of the veteran's noir, but does so in order to "subjectify" a Nisei protagonist historically precluded from such texts. Films such as *The Best Years of Our Lives, Till the End of Time,* and *The Blue Dahlia* construe the veteran's dilemma in terms of the domestic melodrama, the love story, and the success story—Hollywood genres that broadly reify middle-class American social values of the nuclear family and upward mobility.[13] In the "para-noir" film *Till the End of Time,* for example, Cliff Harper must negotiate not only his changing relationships with two very different war-buddies, but also maturity beyond his parents' household, a budding romance with the war widow Pat Ruscomb (Dorothy Maguire), and vocational alternatives represented in college and factory labor. The returning veteran's narrative embraces these diverse generic strains in that Cliff's responses to bourgeois norms are registered via the experiences of his Marine buddies Bill Tabeshaw and Perry Kincheloe (Bill Williams). Not surprisingly, noir icon Mitchum plays a more radically alienated and explosive figure: like Buzz in *The Blue Dahlia,* Bill has suffered a head wound and consequent trepanning that amplifies his erratic, aggressive behavior. Dmytryk opposes Bill's libidinal impulsiveness with Perry—a double-amputee whose disabilities pose total psychological defeat. Cliff mitigates between these poles of violent impulse and rational resignation;

physically intact and "normal," Cliff represents the ideal male ego that must reconcile extremes of reactionary assertiveness and fatalistic passivity. While it may be too much to interpret *No-No Boy* as an adaptation of *Till the End of Time*, the novel does pursue an uncannily similar narrative pattern in its illumination of postwar Nisei experience.

In one of the most revealing sequences of *Till the End of Time*, a tearfully frustrated Cliff, surrounded by the icons of his childhood, kicks away the blanket that his mother had tucked around his sleeping form. Although the Pacific War hurls this adolescent into adulthood, such maturity ill comports with his mother's vision of her son as teenager. The struggle to embrace adulthood also centrally informs *No-No Boy*, in which Ichiro is welcomed home by a mother fiercely proud of her son's filial piety. But Okada elides the "universal" drama of maturation in order to emphasize the historically and culturally specific circumstances of Ichiro's dilemma. Fanatically loyal to Japan, Mrs. Yamada imagines her son a hero whose sacrifice will be honored when the American victory is debunked as propaganda and Japanese forces occupy the United States. In other words, the mother-son relationship here dramatizes Ichiro's ideological suspension between national identities: "He looked at his mother and swallowed with difficulty the bitterness that threatened the last fragment of understanding for the woman who was his mother and still a stranger because, in truth, he could not know what it was to be a Japanese who breathed the air of America and yet had never lifted a foot from the land that was Japan" (11). Whereas Ichiro's father is "okay" but ineffectual—"a fat, grinning, spineless nobody"—, "Ma is the rock that's always hammering, pounding, pounding, pounding in her unobtrusive fanatical way until there's nothing left to call one's self." As I point out below, there are only two prominent women characters in this masculinist novel—the benign war widow Emi and Mrs. Yamada, who in a sense fulfills the role of the femme fatale bent upon destroying the hapless male protagonist: "It was she who opened my mouth and made my lips move to sound the words which got me two years in prison and an emptiness that is more empty and frightening than the caverns of hell" (12). With these grim meditations, Ichiro, in a posture reminiscent of Cliff Harper, lies in bed and "wished the roof would fall in and bury forever the anguish which permeated his every pore. He lay there fighting with his burden lighting one cigarette after another and dropping the ashes and butts purposely on the floor" (12).

As the "dangerous woman" of the novel, Mrs. Yamada cannot survive; confronted with the reality of Japanese defeat, she commits suicide. Her death frees Ichiro's father, who comfortably assumes the role of widower. But for Ichiro himself, the psychic damage has been done: the failure of the domestic melodrama precludes Ichiro's realization of "dignity, respect, purpose, honor, all the things which added up to schooling and marriage and family and work and happiness" (12). Throughout the course of the novel, Ichiro explores the various dimensions of the middle-class dream of love and success. In Professor Brown, Ichiro encounters the possibility of resuming his engineering studies at the University of Washington; seemingly sympathetic, the cloistered academic shows no interest in the particulars of Ichiro's experience. His brief and superficial conversation with the professor is "like meeting someone in a revolving door . . . seeing without meeting, talking without hearing, smiling without hearing." Turning his back on "the buildings and students and curved lanes and grass which was the garden in the forsaken land" (57), Ichiro achieves a more authentic moment of connection with Mr. Carrick, the Oregon engineer who offers him a position as draftsman. Unlike Professor Brown, Carrick frankly recognizes Japanese internment as a "big black mark in the annals of American history": "I've always been a big-mouthed, loud-talking, back-slapping American but, when that happened, I lost a little of my wind." Hoping in some measure to atone for this injustice, Carrick offers Ichiro a shot at the American dream—"two-sixty a month. Three hundred after a year" (150). However tempting, the proposal leaves Ichiro unsatisfied; he feels impelled to return to Seattle: "If he was to find his way back to that point of wholeness and belonging, he must do so in the place where he had begun to lose it" (154–55). With such lines, Okada fully evokes the returning veteran's narrative as an existential parable, a story of the search for "wholeness and belonging" beyond the well-worn path of liberal capitalism. And yet Okada reminds us that any such philosophical narrative is not "timeless," but embedded in the ideologies of its historical moment.

Ichiro's vocational dilemma illuminates a contradiction at the heart of Enlightenment ideology: democracy subverted by racism. The same may be said of Okada's handling of the classical Hollywood love story. The notion that "love conquers all" pervades even a comparatively complex production like *Till the End of Time*. As compared to Helen Ingersoll (Jean Porter), the Harper's doting teenage neighbor, Pat Ruscomb appears to Cliff a lover appropriate to his emergent adulthood. "Boy loses girl," however, because of the complexities surrounding Pat's grief over her husband, a flier killed in action during Europe's air war. In the film's climactic sequence, the couple's reconciliation is folded into the larger reintegration plot as Pat enables Cliff to transcend the tragic homosocial world of the veterans. In *No-No Boy,* Okada parallels Pat Ruscomb with Emi, a young Nisei woman whose husband Ralph fought with the 442nd in Europe. "She waited four years for Ralph to come back," Kenji explains to Ichiro, "We were in the same outfit. Ralph signed up for another hitch. Don't ask me why. . . . He asked me to look her up and tell her he wasn't coming back for a while. No explanations" (89). Emi's husband is indeed a casualty of the war, but not of combat: along with his older brother Mike—an embittered WWII vet who emigrates to Japan after internment—Ralph refuses the racial tensions that dominate American society. Although Ichiro and Emi begin a passionate relationship, the love story in this instance accedes to the returning veteran's narrative. "I may not come to see you again, then I might," Ichiro assures Emi. "I'll surely love you very deeply. That mustn't happen because Ralph will probably come back" (170). Here again, Okada uses classical Hollywood formulae not to resolve ideological tensions, but rather as a means of illuminating the problems of postwar America. Wondering, "Where is that place they talk of and paint pictures of and describe in all the homey magazines?" Ichiro calls into question the efficacy and reality of bourgeois ideals:

> Where is that place with the clean, white cottages surrounding the new red-brick church with the clean, white steeple, where the families all have two children, one boy and one girl, and a shiny new car in the garage and a dog and a cat and life is like living in the land of the happily-ever-after? Surely it must be around here someplace, someplace in America. Or is it just that it's not for me? (159)

This is a characteristic moment in *No-No Boy*, for Ichiro constantly surveys the wealth and abundance of postwar America and reads in this plenty a sign of his own alienation. In stark contrast to *The Best Years of Our Lives*, *Till the End of Time*, and even films noirs like *The Blue Dahlia*, Okada decisively rejects the concomitant narratives of domestic melodrama, love, and success to concentrate instead on the existentialist potential of the returning veteran's formula.

The dominant trajectory of *No-No Boy* concerns the relationship of Ichiro with fellow veterans Freddie Akimoto and Kenji Kanno: a narrative structure derived almost explicitly from the returning veteran films of the 1940s. Just as *The Blue Dahlia* and *Till the End of Time* dramatize the plight of the protagonist through sharply polarized characters, *The Best Years of Our Lives* foregrounds a middle-class family-man Al Stephenson (Fredric March) suspended between double amputee Homer Parrish (Harold Russell) and noirish isolato Fred Derry (Dana Andrews), each of whom experiences a more acutely traumatic, painful return to the small town of Boone City. Ichiro's experience is refracted on one hand through the impulsive no-no boy Freddie Akimoto. Like Chandler's Buzz or Dmytryk's Bill

Tabeshaw, Freddie responds to his alienated condition with hedonism and violence—drinking, carousing, and fighting. Freddie thus vainly attempts to "catch up" on the life missed in prison. True to the pattern of the veteran narrative, Freddie represents an externalization of Ichiro's own resistant tendencies. When confronted with Ichiro's humiliation at the hands of Eto Minato, Freddie assures his friend, "He ever try that on me, I'll stick a knife in him. . . . Nobody's got a right to spit on you" (48). Near the conclusion of the novel, Ichiro concedes that while "Freddie was much too erratic to be trusted . . . there was a hint of logic to his stubborn defiance. It was a free world, but they would have to make peace with their own little world before they could enjoy the freedom of the larger one" (244). Okada provides a counterpoint to Freddie's libidinal defiance in Kenji, a 442nd veteran awarded the Silver Star for action in Europe. Kenji's military service has earned him a place in American society, but it has also cost him a leg, which, because of lingering infection, continually undergoes piecemeal amputation. Like the amputees in Hollywood veteran's films, Kenji suffers a psychic trauma commensurate with the physical wound. Fatalistic and suicidal, Kenji dismisses himself as "half a man, and when [his] leg starts aching, even that half is not so good" (89). Indeed, Kenji feels so emasculated that he defers to Ichiro the opportunity for a sexual relationship with Emi. Ichiro's "objective correlative" friends do refract his psychic turmoil; but Okada does not stop with the internal, "universal" conflict between libido and superego. Like Himes, Okada charges these conventional figures with heightened ideological significance. If decorated veteran Kenji represents the temptation of assimilation (70–71), then the intractable Freddie reads as an explosion of Itchy's own insurgence. Even as Kenji's slow and agonizing death illustrates the self-loss posed by American racism, Freddie's fate, unfolded in the climactic episode of *No-No Boy,* speaks to the cost of resistance.

Vivian Sobchack has helpfully identified a tension between the "idyllic" home and the "nightclubs, cocktail lounges, bars, anonymous hotel or motel rooms, boardinghouses, cheap roadhouses, and diners" that pervade film noir. Coalescing into what Sobchack terms "lounge time," such spaces "substitute impersonal, incoherent, discontinuous, and rented space for personal, intelligible, unified and generated space. They spatially rend and break up the home—and, correlatively, family contiguity and generational continuity" (158). Lounge time, Sobchack contends, is "one of the dominant—or master—chronotopes of the historical period that begins in the early 1940s with the rumblings of war and declines in the 1950s as the 'security state' becomes a generally accepted way of life" (166). Central to noir and para-noir veteran's films of the '40s, lounge time may be further delineated in terms of the nightclubs associated with the danger of the femme fatale and the bars that offer homosocial havens against the strange and unfamiliar civilian world. The telling inaugural sequence of *The Blue Dahlia* takes place in a bar, as does the pivotal sequence of *Till the End of Time*. In *The Best Years of Our Lives*, the veterans gather at Butch's, as if to underscore the centrality of the space to masculinity in crisis. Clearly important within *The Blue Dahlia* and *The Best Years of Our Lives*, the oppositional spaces of nightclub and bar are united in their function as a pathological alternative to the domestic sphere. At best, a bar like Butch's in Wyler's film may serve as a kind of "halfway house" for veterans gradually moving from the man's world of the military into the heterosexual bastion of the home. Okada similarly utilizes space in *No-No Boy* as he steers Ichiro, Kenji, and Freddie to the Club Oriental: a "bottle club" situated "halfway down an alley, among the forlorn stairways and innumerable trash cans" of downtown Seattle. With its "soft, dim lights, its long curving bar, its deep carpets, its intimate tables, and its small dance floor," the Club Oriental initially seems a refuge from the "filthy alley" of the novel's alienated milieu. "I like it here," Kenji contentedly intones, "If I didn't have to sleep or eat, I'd stay right here" (71–72).

Seemingly a haven of "quiet and decency and cleanliness and honesty" (134), the Club Oriental ultimately proves a site of intensified intra-ethnic conflict in which vets such as Bull relentlessly taunt Ichiro and Freddie ("I wasn't fightin' my friggin war for shits like you" [247]). In the novel's final episode, Bull violently expels Freddie "away from the illumination around the club's entrance": for most of the Nisei veterans in the novel (Eto, Bull, and Ichiro's newly enlisted brother Taro), the no-no boys represent the impossibility of their own assimilation and therefore undermine the significance of their sacrifice.[14] After Ichiro and Freddie resist Bull's attack, Freddie attempts a getaway and is immediately killed in the ensuing car crash, which "just about cut him in two" (249). Even as Kenji's slow demise suggests a murderous assimilation, Freddie's gruesome death allegorizes a self that might be catastrophically rent by the forces of competing national cultures and contrary alternatives of conformity and resistance.[15] This conclusive sequence on one hand appears an inversion and subversion of the "bar scenes" in conventional returning veteran's films. In the opening scene of *The Blue Dahlia*, a dangerous encounter between two combat vets is diffused over drinks; in *Till the End of Time*, the climactic bar-fight results in Tabeshaw's injury, but also in growth and regeneration for all three veterans. Against these pretexts, Okada's final episode at the Club Oriental might strike one as hyperbolically violent and tragic. And yet the novel's brief denouement suggests a resolution that mitigates such nihilism.

Consoling Bull, who ultimately sobs "not like a man in grief or a soldier in pain, but like a baby in loud, gasping beseeching howls" (250), Ichiro "gave the shoulder a tender squeeze, patted the head once tenderly, and began to walk slowly down the alley away from the brightness of the club and the morbidity of the crowd. . . . He walked along, thinking, searching, thinking and probing, and, in the darkness of the alley that was a tiny bit of America, he chased that faint and elusive insinuation of promise as it continued to take shape in mind and in heart" (251). Like his cinematic counterparts, Ichiro does gain self-confidence and resolve throughout the ordeal that culminates in the violent encounter at the Club Oriental. As Yogi recommends, the conclusion of *No-No Boy* posits "tempered hopes for the healing of the Nikkei community and America as a whole" (74). But Okada refuses his antihero the safety of the Hollywood ending: "searching and probing," Ichiro heads alone down a dark alley rather than into a suburban home with Emi. Working at the margins of the culture industries, Okada enacted a much more harshly conditioned noir returning veteran's narrative than those of his Hollywood counterparts.

Epitomizing the critical consensus on postwar film noir, Hirsch identifies the traumatized returning veteran as the sole noir figure "connected directly to the period, without any exaggeration," an antihero wholly expressive of "the country's sour postwar mood": "This darkest, most downbeat of America's film genres traces a series of metaphors for a decade of anxiety, a contemporary apocalypse bounded on the one hand by Nazi brutality and on the other by the awful knowledge of nuclear power" (21). In this respect, film noir entertained toward World War II the same critical and recuperative stance that hard-boiled fiction had assumed with regard to U.S. colonial discourse at the turn-of-the-century. Whether in the revelation of Nazi atrocities, realization that the body might be instantly vaporized in an atomic attack, or simply in stories of American soldiers "going Asiatic" amidst Pacific Theater combat,[16] the ideological "fallout" of World War II is an amplified sense of the fluidity of self and world. As Marc Vernet contends, film noir cannot be wholly or decisively attributed to postwar anxiety[17]; in keeping with the philosophical and artistic vision inaugurated by Hammett in the 1920s, however, film noir very generally maintained its "last stand" for western subjectivity. Far from "going Asiatic," protagonists like Chandler's Johnny Morrison have been inured by combat for the shifting boundaries of the postwar universe. Chester Himes, Dorothy Hughes, and John Okada contributed a second tier of critique to the conditioned humanism of noir. These marginalized artists reversed the polarities of the noir universe, placing the constructive mechanism of authenticating alienation at the disposal of figures historically inscribed as various foils of alienated white subjectivity. Such a gesture denaturalizes a noir ethos that camouflages its operations via an artful blend of Realism and Expressionism; reading *If He Hollers, Let Him Go*, *In a Lonely Place*, and *No-No Boy*, we may begin to suspect that noir is a way of making a self rather than a stark reflection of one.

CHAPTER FIVE

NOIR AND THE POSTMODERN NOVEL

He'd paid to see a world that was to his liking. Not beautiful—it was based, after all, on cultural artifacts of more than a century ago, the bleak and brooding crime and thriller movies of the 1930s and forties—but with beautiful things in it. More beautiful, actually, for being surrounded by constant threat and darkness.
—K. W. Jeter, *Noir* (1998)

The story of noir is itself something of a hard-boiled fiction. Hammett, Chandler, Welles, Wilder, and other noir virtuosi have in a sense operated as imperial troubleshooters who carried on the prophylactic work of Poe and Doyle by intervening into the chaotic world of late-Victorian adventure. Exemplified by the fictions of Louis Becke, fin-de-siècle adventure tales often envision a western subject that might psychically and bodily "explode on contact" with the colonial periphery. Hard-boiled protagonists such as the aptly named Continental Op not only engage in a "janitorial" arrest of volatile adventurers, but in themselves reify a coherent self that resides within the monad of alienation. As Himes, Hughes, and Okada demonstrate, such tactics may be appropriated and reassigned to figures conventionally othered within the noir imagination. As these novelists reverse the race and gender polarities of authenticating alienation, noir begins to appear not so much a timeless expression of the modern human condition as a vulnerable "technology of the self." With this phrase, Michel Foucault describes various historically and culturally specific means of "deciphering who one is" (223). Foucault here clarifies his life's work as an attempt to reveal the "truth games" that operate by virtue of four main constructive strategies:

1) technologies of production, which permit us to produce, transform, or manipulate things; 2) technologies of sign sys-

tems, which permit us to use signs, meanings, symbols, or signification; 3) technologies of power, which determine the conduct of individuals and submit them to certain ends or domination, an objectivizing of the subject; 4) technologies of the self, which permit individuals to effect by their own means, or with the help of others, a certain number of operations on their own bodies and souls, thoughts, conduct, and way of being, so as to transform themselves in order to attain a certain state of happiness, purity, wisdom, perfection, or immortality. (225)

These techniques interact, Foucault argues, to produce culturally and historically specific identities. As he surveys self-constructive technologies under Greco-Roman philosophy and early Christianity, Foucault encounters many classical metaphors for identity, including Seneca's representation of self-examination as "when a comptroller looks at the books or when a building inspector examines a building" (237). Indeed, with a characteristic revisionist impulse, Foucault contends that the naturalizing tendencies of modern thought have led to an emphasis of the Socratic maxim "know yourself" which was in reality a corollary of the principle "Take care of yourself": the acquisition of an "upper hand" or "*teknè*" in the pursuit of identity formation (228–30). While hard-boiled fiction and film noir may hint at this constructivism, postmodernist fictions of the later twentieth century relentlessly expose the machinations of this "darkly perfect world." Read together, Thomas Pynchon's *The Crying of Lot 49*, Ishmael Reed's *Mumbo Jumbo*, Paul Auster's *Ghosts*, and K. W. Jeter's *Noir* demonstrate a mounting awareness among postmodernist novelists of noir's constructive potential. With recourse to the respective theories of Bertolt Brecht and Roland Barthes, we may argue that these novels direct "alienation effect" against "reality effect." As implied by the titles *Mumbo Jumbo* and *Ghosts*, each book explicitly "conjures" hard-boiled conventions only to denaturalize noir's self-constructive technologies.

Critics have long recognized the noir commitment to realism. Echoing Chandler's famous tribute to Hammett, Carl Richardson contends that film noir "took the camera out of the studio and moved it through the dirty streets and commerce-ridden main thoroughfares of various localities"[1]: "*Films noirs* . . . dealt with a world that was unmovielike, where the hero didn't always wind up with the girl, and was sometimes better off if he didn't. . . . It boldly debunked pre-depression optimism and like a one-dish menu, serves up post-war doom, take it or leave it" (2). Emphasizing both literary and cinematic pretexts, Richardson sees film noir realize itself not only through the confluence of hard-boiled detective fiction and German Expressionism, but through its intersection with the emergence of the semidocumentary film. Throughout the 1930s individual filmmakers such as Robert Flaherty began to practice a form of "social realism," a shift from "Hollywood's roseate vision of contemporary life" to subjects that reminded the public of the harsh realities of social and political injustice. Such "real life drama" demanded a literal departure from the contrived scripts, acting, and, most importantly, studio sets. Pare Lorentz's semidocumentaries (re) introduced location shooting into the mainstream of commercial cinema, where it found a ready harbor in the budding film noir. And although the documentary style may be said to in some way affect noir aesthetics as a whole, certain films remain exemplary. In addition to Richardson's chief example, Jules Dassin's *The Naked City* (1948), we might also recall William Dieterle's *The Turning Point* (1952) and Stanley Kubrick's *The Killing* (1956), which represent the full convergence of the "criminal" subject matter and bleak philosophical tenor of the hard-boiled formula; the moody atmospheres created by Expressionist techniques; and the social awareness, detached narration, and location shooting of the documentary.[2]

Such conventions enable hard-boiled fiction and film noir to exert a heightened form of what Barthes articulates as "the reality effect": the tactic of deploying "concrete detail" as "a neutral, prosaic excipient which swathes the precious symbolic substance" (132). In other words, a canvas of "insignificant notation" forms the backdrop against which frank symbolism might emerge. This strategy culminates in a "referential illusion": "[j]ust when these details are reputed to *denote* the real directly, all that they do—without saying so—is *signify* it[,] . . . say nothing but this: 'we are the real.'" (148).[3] Even as the agonistic dramas of noir unfold against a canvas of insignificant notation, they elevate the human encounter with meaninglessness into an existential parable about the protagonist's frustrated attempt to read an oppressively insignificant universe. The contradiction is that extraneous details become important precisely because they do not mean anything. As we have seen, noir's authenticating alienation threatens to tip its own hand as the hard-boiled hero assumes the responsibility to locate and arrest the protean subjectivity of the adventuring con artist. Despite these reflexive tendencies, noir fictions valorize alienation without necessarily alienating the reader.[4]

With the advent of postmodernism, noir's reality effect relents to a different kind of "alienation effect," one by which the reader is jarred into recognizing the manipulations of the text. "Good or bad, a play always includes an image of the world," writes Bertolt Brecht in a seminal statement on art and ideology: "Quite apart from the fact that one can be gripped by bad art as easily as by good, even if one *isn't* gripped something happens to one. . . . [T]he spectator is encouraged to draw certain conclusions about how the world works.... He is brought to share certain feelings of the persons appearing on the stage and thereby to approve them as universally human feelings, only natural, to be taken for granted" (150). If, as Brecht suggests, "moral and aesthetic influences all radiate from the theatre" (152), then one's response to these all-encompassing pedagogies comes down to either passive manipulation or active inquiry. Brecht exhorts dramatists to displace bourgeois realism (which he deems "spiritual dope traffic ... the home of illusions" [135]) in favor of an alienation effect intended "to make the spectator adopt an attitude of inquiry and criticism in his approach to the incident" (136). Depending upon techniques such as spoken stage directions, disclosed lighting sources, and a general dissolution of the "fourth wall" separating actor from audience, the "A-effect" demands recognition of the constructed, historically contingent nature of the text-at-hand; the spectator must therefore "justify or abolish [the social conditions represented] according to what class he belongs to." Brecht mentions Peter Lorre as one of the young actors who developed methods of dramaturgical alienation. It is interesting to reflect that Lorre also figured prominently in film noir, where he was cast not only as an exotic villain, but as a reflexive figure contrary to noir's reality effect. Whether playing a conspicuously labeled murderer in Fritz Lang's *M* (1931) or the allegorical "Levantine" Joel Cairo in Huston's *The Maltese Falcon,* Lorre appears a locus of the alienation effect that encourages critical investigation of the world projected by these texts.

Brecht impels us away from what Hal Foster terms a "postmodernism of reaction" characterized by "an instrumental pastiche of pop—or pseudo—historical forms" and toward a "resistant postmodernism" that "seeks to question rather than exploit cultural codes, to explore rather than conceal social and political affiliations" (xii). While critics such as Jameson, Hirsch, and Naremore discern what the latter describes as a "noir mediascape" devoted to nostalgia and pastiche (257), I concentrate upon "critical replayings" of noir—postmodernist fictions that evoke noir in order to question its tactics of authenticating alienation. Such investigative parodies recur throughout the nebulous phenomenon of the postmodernist novel. As Hutcheon suggests, literary postmodernism "puts into question the entire series of interconnected concepts that have come to be associated with what we conveniently label as liberal humanism: autonomy, transcendence, certainty, authority, unity, totalization, system, universalization, center, continuity, teleology, closure, hierarchy, homogeneity, uniqueness, origin." This critical program is accomplished, Hutcheon argues, by postmodernist parody: "a process of installing and then withdrawing (or of using and abusing) those very contested notions."[5] Indeed, postmodernist fiction is perhaps simply an amplification of deconstructive tendencies endemic to the novelistic form itself. I am thinking here of Mikhail Bakhtin, who delineates a generic and epistemological shift consistent with the broader movement from constructive discourses (such as the Enlightenment, Romanticism, and Modernism) into postmodernism. For Bakhtin, the novel arises in opposition to the conservative epic; it is subversive and ironic, eliminating the distance and reverence installed by its counterpart. Bakhtin explains that the novel, as a form, depends upon "parodic stylizations of canonized genres and styles": "Throughout the entire history there is a consistent parodying or travestying of dominant or fashionable novels that attempt to become models for the genre. This ability of the novel to criticize itself is a remarkable feature of this ever-developing genre."[6] In contrast to "the closed and deaf monoglossia" of the epic, the novel "emerged and matured precisely when intense activization of external and internal polyglossia was at the peak of its activity."[7] The correspondence between Bakhtin's novel and the general current of postmodern theory is apparent, for both models emphasize intertextuality, self-reflexivity, and deconstructive revision. According to Bakhtin, the novel accomplishes the decentering critique often attributed to postmodernism; "plasticity itself,"[8] the novel assures that "the boundaries between fact and fiction, literature and nonliterature and so forth are not laid up in heaven."[9] Exemplifying the subversive techniques described by Brecht, Hutcheon, and Bakhtin, the respective fictions of Pynchon, Reed, Auster, and Jeter evoke hard-boiled fiction and film noir, recalling at once general motifs and specific texts. What we observe in each of the texts at hand is a sensitivity to the "constructedness" of the subject; if the noir protagonist is figured in high-contrast relief against its world, then these postmodernist texts see the loss of self that occurs with the failure of authenticating alienation.

In *Gravity's Rainbow* (1973), Pynchon at one point imagines that "Philip Marlowe will suffer a horrible migraine, and reach by reflex for the pint of rye in his suit pocket, and feel homesick for the lace balconies of the Bradbury Building" (752)[10]; the detective here joins a cavalcade of ineffectual superheroes who cannot stop Weissman's apocalyptic rocket launch. But Marlowe's headache might get even worse if he could see "the famous ironwork of the Bradbury Building" decorating a shopping mall in *Vineland* (1990): "Noir Center here had an upscale mineral-water boutique called Bubble Indemnity, plus the Lounge Good Buy patio furniture outlet, the Mall Tease Falcon, which sold perfume and cosmetics, and a New York style deli, The Lady 'n' the Lox. Security police wore brown shiny uniform suits with pointed lapels and snap-brim fedoras"

(326). Like the Marlowe of *Gravity's Rainbow*, *Vineland* protagonist Prairie Wheeler waxes nostalgic for the lost world of noir, for she "happened to like those old weird-necktie movies in black and white, her grandfolks had worked on some of them, and she personally resented this increasingly dumb attempt to cash in on the pseudoromantic mystique of those particular olden days of this town . . . " (326). As many critics have noted,[11] this moment stands as Pynchon's wry exposure of voracious culture industries that will exploit any ethos, no matter how disturbing it might seem. While *Gravity's Rainbow* and *Vineland* hold explicit allusions to hard-boiled fiction and film noir,[12] none of Pynchon's novels is more alive to the constructive power of noir than *The Crying of Lot 49*. For Tony Tanner, Pynchon's first book summons the "California detective story" epitomized by Chandler, MacDonald, and Gardner. But while these novelists proceeded from mystery to solution, argues Tanner, Pynchon takes us from "a state of degree-zero mystery—just the quotidian mixture of an average Californian day—to a condition of increasing mystery and dubiety" (56). What needs to be recognized, however, is the extent to which *The Crying of Lot 49* departs from its hard-boiled pretexts by subverting the constructive opposition between rational subject and irrational world. As Oedipa attempts to decode the mysteries of Inverarity's estate, she enters a realm of absolute textuality that jeopardizes the referential "object" against which she defines herself.

While Pynchon targets the detective story in general, the pretext of noir in a sense provides yet more insight into the novel's critique of subjectivity. Oedipa is not an amateur detective after the fashion of Dupin or Holmes, nor a professional "private eye" in the tradition of the Continental Op, Sam Spade, and Philip Marlowe. She reads quite convincingly, however, as Silver and Ward's "truly noir figure [who] represents the perspective of normality assailed by the twists of fate of an irrational universe."[13] Like Frank Bigelow in *D.O.A.*, Oedipa finds her suburban status quo disrupted by the intrusion of mystery. We may ultimately decide, however, that the intrusive Tristero enigma ironically rescues Oedipa from her "hyperbolically banalized world."[14] Oedipa is surrounded by the flattened, commodified artifacts of late capitalism: Tupperware parties, "the greenish dead eye of the TV tube" (9), housing developments ("Kinneret-Among-the-Pines"), and Muzak. This is a world in which the "only ikon in the house" is a bust of the infamous financier Jay Gould (10). Like the Rapunzel figure in the Varo painting, Oedipa initially appears an isolato who yearns to transcend these layers of "insulation." Such a predicament, however, posits a modernist binary of inside/outside which the novel ultimately questions: if the real is, as Baudrillard suggests, "the unrepresentable itself," then *The Crying of*

Lot 49 envisions rather a condition of unchecked signification and differential decay. Oedipa anticipates this postmodern dilemma as she wonders, "If the tower is everywhere and the knight of deliverance no proof against its existence, what else?" (22).

Rescue emerges not from the chivalric romance, but rather from the detective story, a form that offers a sense of purchase upon reality. Much has been made of the novel's allusive character names: Oedipa Maas suggests both that Ur-detective Oedipus and the "Maze" or mystery Oedipa must negotiate. "Pierce Inverarity" similarly reads as a challenge to the detective, a call to "seek truth," if you will. But Pynchon characteristically skews the terms of the conventional mystery story. Though perhaps the first literary detective, Oedipus is also, as Cawelti observes in *Adventure, Mystery and Romance,* arguably the first "anti-detective" figure—a sleuth implicated in the enigma he proposes to solve. Pierce's moniker similarly points to a subversion of traditional detection; like Borges's criminal mastermind Red Scarlach in "Death and the Compass" (1942), Inverarity represents a mystery deliberately threatening to the detective-subject.[15] As she sets about "sorting" Inverarity's assets, and descends into the mystery of the Tristero, Oedipa engages in an investigation that will either secure or jeopardize her sense of self. *The Crying of Lot 49* then begins to assume decidedly noir overtones with Oedipa's trip Los Angeles. The "descent" into the city is itself suggestive of the hard-boiled formula, whose protagonist leaves the cerebral sanctum to wander urban "mean streets." In fact, Pynchon's evocation/deconstruction of noir may be most readily grasped in terms of Oedipa's "error" through urban California: San Narciso, Echo Courts, The Scope, and, finally, San Francisco. The sequences that take place in these locales situate Oedipa in the noir tradition, but subtly erode its foundations.

We have seen that the California cities of Los Angeles and San Francisco loom large in the noir imagination not only as exempla of the modernist wasteland, but also as endo-colonial urban jungles that threaten to subsume the detective and other belated adventurers. Chandler's L.A. is indeed "the center of a world gone wrong"; but however Chandler may expose the fraudulence and superficiality of Southern California, he always maintains beneath the "glitz" a brutal naturalistic reality. When Pynchon consigns Oedipa to the fictional town of San Narciso, "further south, near L.A.," he critically rehearses a geographical gesture common to hard-boiled fiction and film noir:

> Like many named places in California it was less an identifiable city than a grouping of concepts—census tracts, special purpose bond-issue districts,

shopping nuclei, all over-laid with access roads to its own freeway.... If there was any difference between it and the rest of Southern California, it was invisible on first glance.... She looked down a slope, needing to squint for the sunlight, onto a vast sprawl of houses which had grown up all together, like a well-tended crop, from the dull brown earth; and she thought of the time she'd opened a transistor radio to replace a battery and seen her first printed circuit. The ordered swirl of houses and streets, from this high angle, sprang at her now with the same unexpected, astonishing clarity as the circuit card had ... [;]there were to both outward patterns a hieroglyphic sense of concealed meaning, of an intent to communicate. There'd seemed no limit to what the printed circuit could have told her (if she had tried to find out); so in her first minute of San Narciso, a revelation also trembled just past the threshold of her understanding. (24)

This oft-cited passage recalls the grim Southern California portraits of hard-boiled detective writers such as Chandler and MacDonald; San Narciso itself, perhaps a version of Santa Monica, is reminiscent of Chandler's fictional Bay City. But here again, Pynchon's purpose is not simply to rehearse the universe of noir, but rather to critique the constructive dynamics of such fictions. Pynchon rejects the opposition between nature and culture; his L.A. landscape is a "grouping of concepts" wholly subsumed by semiotics. For Maurice Courtier, "The city is not real, it is textual: everything has been meticulously planned, projected, in advance. The city existed on paper before it found its way onto a tract of land, and eventually onto a map of California" (15). In this *postmodernist* wasteland nature seems a distant memory and, as Ranjit Chatterjee and Colin Nicholson have it, the "open frontier has become 'census tracts, special purpose bond-issue districts' ... under the control of moguls like Pierce Inverarity."[16]

Immersed in a built environment rather than an unsettled frontier, Oedipa faces the problem of reading a landscape fraught with excessive meaning. We are not surprised then to find Oedipa eager to discern some pattern in the weirdly suggestive cityscape: "The ordered swirl of houses and streets, from this high angle, sprang at her now with the same unexpected, astonishing clarity as the circuit card had." Here as throughout, however, epiphany eludes Oedipa—"revelation also trembled just past the threshold of her understanding." Though troubling under the paradigms of classical detection and noir, inscrutability proves constructive for Pynchon; as long as Oedipa merely verges upon "an odd religious instant" (24) she is, like other Pynchon characters such as *V.*'s Herbert Stencil, able to maintain a sense of herself as detective-subject. We may suspect Oedipa's hermeneutic instincts, suppose that her very desire to read engenders "the hieroglyphic sense of concealed meaning." Pynchon all but names this solipsistic potential, which increases with the allusion to the Narcissus myth: Oedipa is likewise in jeopardy of unconsciously "inventing," at least modifying the supposedly independent Tristero mystery. The Narcissus allusion gains more momentum when Oedipa finds at the San Narciso motel "Echo Courts" a thirty-foot painted sheet-metal nymph: "The face of the nymph was much like Oedipa's, which didn't startle her so much as a concealed blower system that kept the nymph's gauze chiton in constant agitation, revealing enormous vermillion-tipped breasts and long tipped thighs at each flap. She was smiling a lipsticked and public smile, not quite a hooker's but nowhere near that of any nymph pining away with love either" (26–27). Echo Courts certainly evokes the seamy environs of noir—we might recall the La Baba "bungalow courts" in Chandler's *The Big Sleep,* the anonymous motels that pepper the fictions of Ross Macdonald and John D. MacDonald, or even Hitchcock's unforgettable Bates Motel in *Psycho* (1960). But Pynchon again problematizes this rather straightforward allusion—the neon nymph at Echo Courts proffers an ambiguous smile that resists interpretation. Furthermore, we are once more treated to suggestions of solipsism; the nymph resembles Oedipa and threatens to simply return mocking "echoes" of her own hermeneutic gestures. The classical Echo tried to woo Narcissus with his own words; similarly, "Oedipa's language is never her own, but consists of cultural fragments she merely reflects."[17] Appropriately inhabited by a Beatle-esque rock group called The Paranoids, Echo Courts ultimately "became impossible, either because of the stillness of the pool and the blank windows that faced in on it, or a prevalence of teenage voyeurs . . . " (47). Whereas the noir universe is defined by overwhelming diversity, the milieu of *The Crying of Lot 49* tends toward stasis, a "closed system" in which difference itself disappears.

Supposing that the Tristero mystery might "bring an end to her encapsulation in her tower" (44), Oedipa pursues the investigation into The Scope, a "strange bar" and "haunt for electronics assembly people from Yoyodine" (47):

> The green neon sign outside ingeniously depicted the face of an oscilloscope tube, over which flowed an ever-changing dance of Lissajous figures. . . . Glared at all the way, Oedipa and Metzger found a table in back. A wizened bartender wearing shades materialized and Metzger ordered bourbon Oedipa, checking the bar, grew nervous. There was this je ne sais quoi about the Scope crowd: they all wore glasses and stared at you, silent. (47–48)

Along with Echo Courts, The Scope reads on one hand as a noir staple, a dive like The Fisherman in *D.O.A.* These sordid night-spots are conventional sites for violence and alienation, sites from which viable "clues" must be bribed or extorted. The hostility of The Scope denizens reminds us of the "dead alien silence" Marlowe encounters in Florian's at the outset of Chandler's *Farewell, My Lovely*. But this initial association is misleading, as the crowd, like so many other "clues" in the novel, hovers on the edge of legibility. Oedipa once more encounters in The Scope a conspicuously constructed environment. The flashing neon sign—a shopworn noir signifier—here denotes not the unrepresentable real, but the medium of electronic representation itself. Such implications are confirmed when the "hip graybeard" explains The Scope's "strictly electronic music policy": "Come on around Saturdays, starting midnight we have your Sinewave Session, that's a live get-together.... They put it on tape here, live, fella. We got a whole backroom full of your audio oscillators, gunshot machines, contact mikes, everything man" (48). In Maté's *D.O.A.*, the black jazzmen at the Fisherman become a sign of the primitive and therefore offer Bigelow an unmediated encounter with reality. The Scope promises a similar confrontation, but does so by excising "live performance," the real itself, from the equation.

The Scope in some sense fulfills its obligation as a charged site as Oedipa meets Mike Fallopian and finds the "hieroglyphic" WASTE symbol on the bathroom wall. Though typical of the clues a hard-boiled dick might garner from a bar like The Scope, both of these disclosures serve but to propel Oedipa further into the "hypertextual" reality of the novel. For Robert M. Watson, Fallopian's name suggests female anatomical processes, perhaps pointing out the growing possibility that the mystery at hand is simply Oedipa's own creation (60). Each contact that Oedipa makes—Metzger, Driblette, Nefastis, and so on—leads not to definitive revelation, but rather deeper into seemingly endless textual "mazes." This is certainly also the case with respect to the WASTE acronym and its accompanying symbol, "multiform signifiers"[18] that constitute a questionable lead at best. N. Katherine Hayles points out that "the values assigned to the Tristero," like the fluid Lissajous figures, "keep changing—sometimes menacing, sometimes comforting; sometimes metaphysical abstraction, sometimes historical conspiracy; sometimes illusory, sometimes real."[19] I would reiterate that Oedipa's total experience of The Scope only superficially rehearses the frustration of the noir protagonist; what Oedipa finds here is not the unrepresentable, and therefore "real" otherness, but persistent echoes of self and culture.

The pattern of evocation/deconstruction witnessed in and around San Narciso amplifies with Oedipa's visit to San Francisco. Unable to locate Professor Bortz and frustrated by Nefastis, Oedipa begins what Prasanta Das calls a "night journey" through the city's streets. For Das, Oedipa's nocturnal errand inverts the conventional literary night-quest; whereas texts such as Hawthorne's "Young Goodman Brown" revolve around an expressionist journey of self-discovery, Oedipa wanders the city in hopes of confirming an external, objective reality (5): "Either Trystero did exist, in its own right, or it was being presumed, perhaps fantasied by Oedipa, so hung up on and interpenetrated with the dead man's estate. Here in San Francisco, away from all tangible assets of that estate, there might still be a chance of getting the whole thing to go away and disintegrate quietly. She had only to drift tonight, at random, and watch nothing happen, to be convinced it was purely nervous, a little something for her shrink to fix" (109). If Oedipa is, in Driblette's phrase, "projecting a world," then the mysterious object of the Tristero becomes unrealized, thus exposing the fragile constructedness of the self. As this threat emerges, Oedipa must either verify the existence of the Tristero or utterly dispel its possibility, and perhaps move on to some new means of self-construction. In a sense, the San Francisco night-journey serves a dual function—like the detective figures in *V.*, Oedipa must at once establish where the mystery is and where it is not.[20]

Wandering through the nightscape, Oedipa recalls Hammett's Continental Op and Sam Spade as well as Maté's Frank Bigelow—agonistic detectives who strive to wrest meaning from endo-colonial San Francisco. Oedipa, however, suffers an inverse problem in that she literally finds more *significant* clues than she knows what to do with:

> [Oedipa] spent the rest of the night finding the image of the Trystero post horn. In Chinatown, in the dark window of an herbalist, she thought she saw it on a sign among ideographs. But the streetlight was dim. Later, on a sidewalk, she saw two of them in chalk, 20 feet apart. Between them a complicated array of boxes, some with letters, some with numbers. A kid's game? Places on a map, dates from a secret history? She copied the diagram in her memo book. When she looked up, a man, perhaps a man, in a black suit, was standing in a doorway half a block away, watching her. She thought she saw a turned collar but took no chances; headed back the way she'd come, pulse thundering. What fragments of dreams came had to do with the post horn. Later, possibly, she would have trouble sorting the night into real and dreamed. (117)

As Oedipa comes to see the Tristero as a part of a projected world, the conventional noir setting of San Francisco's Chinatown appears wholly configured by the detective gaze. Given this predicament, the alienated universe of noir begins to assume a strangely attractive aspect. The suspicious figure Oedipa "recognizes" does not represent a genuine threat so much as a savior; she "thought she saw a turned collar but took no chances." Does not the "turned collar" connote danger and intrigue, as with Halliday in *D.O.A.*? If so, why does Pynchon's syntax imply that Oedipa runs *despite* the possibility of turned collar? Oedipa flees the scene because she doubts the efficacy of the noir narrative, its ability to "limit" signification and make clear the distinction between "real and dreamed." The conclusion of this night-journey literalizes the hard-boiled/noir pretext. "Where was the Oedipa who'd driven so bravely up here from San Narciso?," the heroine wonders after a "long dark night" throughout which "she grew to expect" the ubiquitous post horn: "That optimistic baby had come on so like the private-eye in any long-ago radio drama, believing all you needed was grit, resourcefulness, exemption from hidebound cops' rules, to solve any great mystery. But the private eye sooner or later has to get beat up on. This night's profusion of post horns, this malignant, deliberate replication, was their way of beating up" (124).[21] Pynchon hereby insightfully subverts the underpinning logic of noir. Oedipa does remind us of the hard-boiled detective who takes the investigation into the streets; but as the narrative moves through its series of suggestive locales, it turns detective-noir back upon itself. Oedipa "gets beat up on" by the very excess signification that noir attempts to suppress.

Given these developments, not to mention the fate of Pynchon detectives such as Sydney Stencil and Tyrone Slothrop, we might expect Oedipa to somehow dissolve, her differential subjectivity nullified by the revelations of the night journey. The conclusion of *The Crying of Lot 49* forestalls this eventuality, though in a way no more affirmative of human identity. Perhaps acting on Inverarity's advice to "keep it bouncing" (178), Oedipa finally returns to San Narciso to attend the auction of Pierce's assets. While cognizant of the epistemological dangers of the investigation, Oedipa "stays on the case," "trying to guess which one was her target, her enemy, possibly her proof" (183). Oedipa does not suffer self-dissolution, as do many of Pynchon's hapless protagonists; but this persistent constitution in no way signals an endorsement of the unified human subject. Although the Tristero may emerge at the conclusion of the novel a "magical Other" (180) against which Oedipa defines herself, this differential system is denaturalized and destabilized by Pynchon.

I have proposed a reading of *The Crying of Lot 49* that underscores the novel's treatment of the noir subject, its illumination of the shift from "alienation affect" to an "alienation effect" that exposes the mechanics of differential identity. Such an approach gains momentum with the strange fate of Oedipa's husband, Wendell "Mucho" Maas. As the text unfolds, Mucho undergoes a radical revision of identity, progressing from alienated subjectivity to a hardly imaginable state of nonbeing. It is a transformation interestingly signaled by the nightmare vision of the used car lot:

> " . . . In the dream I'd be going about a normal day's business and suddenly, with no warning, there'd be the sign. We were a member of the National Automobile Dealer's Association. N.A.D.A. Just this creaking metal sign that said nada, nada, against the blue sky. I used to wake up hollering."
>
> She remembered. Now he would never be spooked again, not as long as he had the pills. She could not quite get it into her head that the day she'd left him for San Narciso was the day she'd seen Mucho for the last time. So much of him already had dissipated. (144)

Pynchon here evokes Ernest Hemingway's use of the term "nada" in the short story "A Clean, Well-Lighted Place"[22] to illustrate the shift from modernist alienation to postmodern self-collapse. In Hemingway's story, the older waiter gives his own nihilistic version of the *pater noster*, substituting "nada" for most of the pronouns and verbs: "It was all a nothing and man was nothing too . . . he knew it all was nada y pues nada y nada y pues nada. Our nada who art in nada, nada be thy name . . . "[23] The older waiter and the old man in the story are exceptionally sensitive to the existential confrontation between rational consciousness and an irrational world; "cleanness and order" vs. "nada." But as we have seen, this opposition yet asserts a tactic for authentic selfhood. Pynchon identifies Mucho Maas, and his nightmare of the meaningless existence boded by "NADA," with Hemingway's alienated existential heroes. As he "wakes up hollering" from angst-ridden dreams, Mucho perhaps even distantly recalls Steve Fisher's 1941 roman noir *I Wake Up Screaming*. Mucho does indeed suffer a kind of angst: "He used to hunch his shoulders and have a rapid eyeblink rate . . . "; but "both were now gone" (141). Since beginning Dr. Hilarius's regimen of LSD pills, Mucho acquires the ability of spectrum analysis "in his head" and comes to realize, "Everybody who says the same words is the same person . . . the same voice" (142). True to Eagleton's analysis, however, Mucho's dissemination occasions the end of alienation; the spectre of "nada" troubles him no longer. But with this realization, Mucho begins to "dissipate"; Funch observes, "He's losing his identity, . . . how else can I put it? Day by day Wendell is less himself and more generic. He enters a staff meeting and the room is suddenly full of people. . . . He's a walking assembly of a man" (140). As his name implies, Mucho Maas is "much more" than he seems—he embodies the almost almost unthinkable alternative to Oedipa's obvious gambit for self construction.

LIKE THE CRYING OF LOT 49, Ishmael Reed's 1971 *Mumbo Jumbo* is a celebrated postmodernist novel that takes square aim at hard-boiled detective fiction and film noir. Perhaps the most famous commentator on the novel, Henry Louis Gates, Jr. recognizes in the book a complex response to the detective novel. For Gates, *Mumbo Jumbo* encompasses the three major strains of the detective fiction identified by Tvetzan Todorov—the "whodunit," the *serie noire* thriller, and the novel of suspense—, Signifyin(g) upon both the form and function of the manifold detective genre (227). A number of critics, including Lizabeth Paravisini, Jon Thompson, and Richard Swope, concur with Gates in his analysis of *Mumbo Jumbo*'s detective, or, more properly, anti-detective elements. Both Gates and Paravisini mention Reed's treatment of the hard-boiled detective tradition (Gates makes the most of Reed's relationship with Chester Himes); but little attention has been given to the ways in which *Mumbo Jumbo* parodies film noir. This omission is surprising, given the novel's private detective motif and its explicit allusions to crime film. In chapter 6 of *Mumbo Jumbo*, for example, the narrator describes how "Men who resemble the shadows sleuths threw against the walls of 1930s detective films have somehow managed to slip into the Mayor's private hospital room" (18). Moreover, in addition to this rather vague allusion, *Mumbo Jumbo* holds at least one explicit reference to a "canonical" film noir: "And then Musclewhite laughs, all weird and sicklike. Early Richard Widmark; *Kiss of Death* (1947)" (121). On one hand, Reed's allusion to *Kiss of Death* argues for the pervasiveness of the sadistic Atonist conspiracy, which manifests itself in both high and low cultural forms. On the other hand, however, Reed points us to another Widmark noir—Elia Kazan's *Panic in the Streets* (1950)—, a film that he critically replays throughout the basic movements of *Mumbo Jumbo*.

Panic in the Streets itself approaches reflexivity in its interpretation of the mystery story. As early as 1913, A. Conan Doyle exploited the symbiotic tropes of metropolitan crime and contagious disease. In "The Adventure of the Dying Detective," Doyle pits Sherlock Holmes against a returning colonial adventurer who wields exotic tropical diseases against his enemies. This story is one of the first literary instances of the metonymic association of the criminal, especially the exotic invader, with the infectious disease: if body boundaries are penetrated by deadly micro-organisms, then the national corpus may be breached by foreign invaders bent upon destruction. As concerns about biological warfare make horrifyingly clear, the criminal/pathological trope is deeply embedded within the western cultural imagination. I would therefore nominate both Doyle's story and Kazan's 1950 film "quasi-reflexive" texts; that is, texts that explicitly conjure the criminal/pathological metaphor in an almost exaggerated or self-parodic fashion: like many noir fictions, these texts almost threaten to bare their own constructive mechanism. Neither Doyle nor Kazan, however, proceeds with the subversive potential of their tropical play. Consistent with noir logic as a whole, Kazan balances constructive figurations, such as the criminal/pathological trope and Expressionist stylistics, against the reality effect—semidocumentary techniques that conceal the mechanics of signification.

Kazan commences with the catalytic murder that drives many mystery plots. Kochak (Lewis Charles), an ailing poker player, is killed for cheating at cards in a New Orleans waterfront dive. The autopsy reveals that the victim was already dying of pneumonic plague; the murderer, criminal kingpin Blackie (Walter Jack Palance), and his accomplices therefore become not only criminal suspects, but potential carriers of the disease. In short, containing the epidemic means solving the murder. Kazan pushes the envelope of realism with an almost allegorical cast of characters. Conducted by New Orleans police detective Tom Warren (Paul Douglass), the investigation is in fact driven by a Navy doctor, Clinton Reed (Richard Widmark), working for the U.S. Dept. of Health. The result of these narrative decisions is a composite investigative team suggestive at once of detective and clinician, civic and federal power. Hard-nosed empirical investigation joins processes of inoculation, sanitation, and quarantine. The usual suspects of the murder plot are similarly exaggerated in a way that nudges realism toward allegory. The victim turns out to be a "mixed-blood" illegal alien who has entered the country via a circuitous route from Armenia through Orans (Camus's North African plague-city) and into New Orleans on a freighter suggestively christened *Nile Queen*. If in name only, the killer "Blackie" activates the racial diversity for which New Orleans is both loved and feared. And indeed, throughout the noir ballet of realism and expressionism, Kazan renders New Orleans the dark and threatening urban jungle which forms the milieu of late-Victorian detection and noir. In *Panic in the Streets,* the western metropolis here again becomes, in Anne McClintock's phrase, "an epistemological problem," an "urban spectacle" that resists "penetration by the intruder's empirical eye as an enigma resists knowledge." Reed and Warren doggedly pursue the contagious murderer Blackie through New Orleans; the chase appropriately ends in the concentrated and labyrinthine liminal space of a dockside warehouse, where Blackie and Fitch (Zero Mostel) seek refuge among great mounds of exotic produce being imported into the U.S. Like the more infamous vermin that disseminated plague throughout Europe, Blackie attempts to climb a hawser aboard an outward bound freighter; he is stopped only by a collar-like shield intended to prevent rats from infesting the ship. What we see then in *Panic in the Streets* is another audacious film noir that risks heavy-handed coding only to contain the epidemic spread of excess signification and reflexivity through a skillful deployment of semidocumentary realism. In other words, Kazan pits reality effect against alienation effect. The result yields a world within which "clean, well-lighted places" of metropolitan order must be constantly monitored against exotic intrusion by criminal pathogens.

In chapter 50 of *Mumbo Jumbo*, Atonist conspirators speculate that an artificially created economic depression might prevent the spread of the mysterious epidemic—"put an end to Jes Grew's resiliency and if a panic occurs it will be a controlled panic. It will be our Panic" (155). These lines offer a fitting epigraph for a discussion of Ishmael Reed's own interpretation of the criminal/pathological trope: for Reed, "panics" over criminal and revolutionary "epidemics" are carefully deployed strategies on the part of the white power structure. Given *Mumbo Jumbo*'s allusions to film noir, it is tempting to read the novel's treatment of an insurgent New Orleans epidemic as a reply to Kazan's film. I would argue that Reed's critique of the detective story, and of western culture in general, is delivered through a tactical parody of *Panic in the Streets*.

As Gates suggests, the opening chapter of *Mumbo Jumbo*, preceding as it does the title page of the novel, recalls cinematic narrative syntax. The novel's prologue reads as a "false start of the action" resembling the prologue of a film punctuated by titles and credits; Reed then concludes the novel with the conspicuous phrase "Freeze frame" (218). According to Gates, Reed deliberately infuses the conventional prose narrative with a cinematic fluidity that "announces . . . an emphasis on figural multiplicity rather than single referential correspondence, an emphasis that Reed recapitulates throughout the text" (227). The "pre-credit" New Orleans sequence alerts us not only to cinematic form, but also to the specific film intertext of *Panic in the Streets*. Early in the film, clinicians headed by Clinton Reed examine diseased tissues under a microscope and begin inoculations; there follows a meeting of civic authorities—including the mayor—who discuss containment strategies against the murder-mystery/epidemic:

> REED: [T]his morning, right here in this city . . . your police found the body of a man who was infected with this disease. If the killer is

incubating pneumonic plague, he can start spreading it within forty-eight hours.... Shortly after that, you'll have the makings of an epidemic.... I may be an alarmist. I may be entirely wrong about the whole matter. But I've seen this disease work and I'm telling you if it ever gets loose, it can spread over the entire country and the result will be more horrible than any of you can imagine.
MAYOR: What can we do?
REED: Find this man.

In the prologue of *Mumbo Jumbo*, Reed evokes the early sequences of *Panic in the Streets*; but his recollection of this cinematic pretext already bears the marks of subversive revision. A doctor informs the mayor of New Orleans,

> We got reports from down here that people were doing "stupid sensual things," were in a state of "uncontrollable frenzy," were wriggling like fish, doing something called the "Eagle Rock" and the "Sassy Bump"; were cutting a mean "Mooche," and "lusting after relevance." We decoded this coon mumbo jumbo. We knew that something was Jes Grewing just like the 1890s flair-up. We thought that the local infestation area was the Place Congo so we put our antipathetic substances to work on it, to try to drive it out; but it started to play hide and seek with us, a case occurring in 1 neighborhood and picking up in another. It began to leapfrog all about us. But can't you put it under 1 of them microscopes? Lock it in? Can't you protective-reaction the dad-blamed thing?

These images of white-masked clinicians and their prognostications certainly recall early scenes in *Panic in the Streets*. Reed, however, begins an investigative parody of the criminal/pathological metaphor central to the novel. Unlike Kazan, who stops short of parodic reflexivity, Reed exposes the epidemic as a trope for black social and cultural revolution: "Don't you understand, if this Jes Grew becomes pandemic it will mean the end of Civilization As We Know It? ... This is a *psychic epidemic,* not a lesser germ like typhoid yellow fever or syphilis.... This belongs under some ancient Demonic Theory of Disease" (4–5). As the prologue continues, Reed persists in his reinterpretation of the pathological trope; the Jes Grew is not simply a figure for the blackness/blankness that western culture imposes on the Other, but rather a vital and dynamic tradition demonized by the "Atonists": "*They thought that by fumigating the Place Congo in the 1890s when people were doing the Bamboula the Chacta the Babouille the Counjaille the Juba the Congo and the VooDoo that this would put an end to it....*

But they did not understand that the Jes Grew epidemic was unlike physical plagues. Actually the Jes Grew was an anti-plague" (6). Reed exaggerates and illuminates the semiotics present in Kazan's film noir, demonstrating the way in which black artists have appropriated and recontextualized the rhetorical strategies by which western culture has sought to "protection-reaction" the peoples and traditions that threaten "Civilization As We Know It."

But Reed does not stop at a conjuration of the epidemic trope; parodying Kazan, he yokes the disaster formula of the epidemic to the hard-boiled or "noir" detective story. Here lies another important series of revisions. *Panic in the Streets* deviates slightly from noir convention by conserving the Enlightenment protagonists of the policeman and the soldier/clinician, instead of adopting the private detective who shares some superficial identification with his seedy milieu. As the narrative of *Panic in the Streets* proceeds, however, Reed and Warren must descend into the urban jungle of New Orleans in order to detect and contain the incipient plague. Like the hermetically sealed hard-boiled detective, Dr. Reed wears the iconic trenchcoat as he conducts legwork among merchant sailors—here again, the garment becomes both practical disguise as well as prophylactic against the contaminated underworld of the Big Easy. As we learn of Reed's previous battle against epidemic in another liminal city, Los Angeles, we understand him as a figure whose identity is deeply invested in the containment of the symbolic disease.

Ishmael Reed contrarily returns to a figure more recollective of the private detective; in the Harlem houngan Papa LaBas, he at once replaces the white detective with a black man and, in a counterpoint to *Panic in the Streets,* writes a detective protagonist who "carries Jes Grew in him like most other figures carry genes" (23). As I suggest above, Reed's revisions to both the "mainstream" and the African-American detective traditions have been thoroughly explicated by commentators who variously discuss the ways in which Papa LaBas departs from ratiocinative detection and its attendant epistemologies. What I would point out here is the disposition of Papa LaBas to the Jes Grew: as a "carrier" of the "anti-plague," LaBas stands in sharp contrast to detective figures such as Sherlock Holmes and Clinton Reed, "immunological" sleuths who embody the triumph of western reason over the exotic negations represented in invasive diseases.[24] Like the conventional noir detective, LaBas "falls" into a mystery that he neither fully understands nor controls; indeed, LaBas does not partake of the will-to-power that undergirds "Atonist" detection. Not only does LaBas ally himself with countercultural forces such as the museum-raiding *Mu'tafikah* and the Jes Grew itself, but his investigation refuses the certainties endemic to classical detection. In a parodic revisitation of the "cozy" mystery's revelation scene, in which the rational sleuth reconstructs the crime and names a suspect, LaBas and his partner Black Herman apprehend the Atonists Hinckle Von Vampton and Safecracker Gould at the Villa Lewaro. While this scene concedes something to the cozy's formulaic closure (as Von Vampton and Gould are to be extradited to Haiti for trail by the loas), many aspects of the mystery remain unresolved. La Bas fails to turn up the Book of Toth and the Jes Grew, the novel's real protagonist, never finds the text through which it will definitively realize itself. Against the need for closure that drives both detective fiction and the black novel, argues Gates, "Reed posits the notion of aesthetic play: the play of tradition, the play on tradition, the sheer play of indeterminacy itself" (227).

Mumbo Jumbo therefore reads as a counterpoint to *Panic in the Streets* and the noir ethos in general. Reed calls up the fundamental elements of this cinematic pretext, but refuses to be confined by them. Adopting highly suggestive, almost allegorical codings, Kazan dramatizes the efforts of Enlightenment epistemology against a criminalized, racialized natural world; he resoundingly enforces detective fiction's traditional closure as his composite police/military/clinical protagonists capture the murderous carrier Blackie and save the nation from a catastrophic epidemic. Here, in other words, is Hammett's "continental operation" writ large. Although *Mumbo Jumbo* targets many literary genres and specific pre-texts, including a number of detective formulae, this altogether novelistic novel exploits *Panic in the Streets* for its central ground-plot of a New Orleans epidemic that threatens the hegemonic social order. Like Dr. Clinton Reed and Capt. Warren, LaBas finds himself deeply involved in this all-consuming mystery. In contrast to the autonomous noir hero, however, LaBas's involvement means a radical complicity with the insurgent epidemic; he is himself a "J.G.C.," a "Jes Grew Carrier," and his investigation serves its ends. The structure of *Mumbo Jumbo* not only differs from the streamlined simplicity of *Panic in the Streets*, but its very profusion represents a kind of textual pandemic inimical to Kazan's manifest sense of containment. LaBas's explication of the mystery at the Villa Leawaro transgresses the boundaries conventionally ascribed to such moments. Asked to "rationally and soberly" explain the crimes of Von Vampton and Gould, LaBas begins, "Well, if you must know, it all began 1000s of years ago in Egypt" (160); the ensuing thirty page narrative, argues Swope, "is far from the typical, tidy summary of how clues lead to and incriminate the murderers.... LaBas offers an explanation of the crime that is actually the product of supernatural, collaborative effort, a fact that is obviously disruptive to the illusion of the detective's authority" (614). In short, Reed exchanges the white buddy cop team of *Panic in the Streets* for one in which a black detective teams with the epidemic that represents the carnivalesque traditions of black culture itself. This endorsement of ludic signification is central to postmodernist parodies of noir and will come to occupy a central place in films of the 1990s in which the figure of the confidence man rises up to subsume the coherently alienated noir protagonist.

LINKING HIS WORK to Bakhtin's theories of the novel, Paul Auster deems his prose "a chance to articulate . . . conflicts and contradictions. Like everyone else, I am a multiple being, and I embody a whole range of attitudes and responses to the world. . . . Writing prose allows me to include all of these responses."[25] Nowhere does Auster's attention to multiplicity emerge more clearly than in his handling of detective noir. Strains of crime and detection appear in many of Auster's novels: in Peter Aaron's attempt in *Leviathan* (1992) to write his friend's story before the FBI releases an "official" account; in Walter Claireborne Rawley's bizarre rehearsal of the gangster story in *Mr. Vertigo* (1994); in David Zimmer's pursuit of Hector Mann in *The Book of Illusions* (2002). Mystery intertexts persist with *Oracle Night* (2003), in which the Flitcraft episode of *The Maltese Falcon* conducts the protagonist and reader alike into a textual mise-en-abyme, one of Auster's signature gestures.[26] When questioned about being labeled a "detective writer," however, Auster replies, "I've found it rather galling at times: "[I]t's just that my work has very little to do with it. I refer to it in the three novels of the *Trilogy*, of course, but only as a means to an end, as a way to get somewhere else entirely. If a true follower of detective fiction ever tried to read one of those books, I'm sure he would be bitterly disappointed. Mystery novels always give answers; my work is about asking questions."[27] Taken as-a-whole or in parts, *The New York Trilogy* is indeed a multivocal text that deconstructively recasts the conventions of both classical detective fiction and noir. Although the *Trilogy* was nominated for the Edgar Award (best mystery of the year), the detective careers charted in *City of Glass* (1985), *Ghosts* (1986), and *The Locked Room* (1986) will, as Auster predicts, sorely disappoint the "true follower" of the mystery story.

As many commentators have recognized, various subgenres of detective fiction are central to the *Trilogy*.[28] At the outset of the inaugural *City of Glass*, Quinn greets us as a character redolent of the hard-boiled legacy: he is himself a mystery writer whose private eye Max Work comically underscores the hard-boiled detective's essential professionalism. But the irony and reflexivity do not stop here; even as the staid Quinn receives a midnight phone-call which would normally open a portal into the irrational noir universe (an event, appropriately enough, based upon a call Auster once received for a Pinkerton agent), we are reminded of the fictiveness of the whole scenario: the call is directed to author Paul Auster. Despite its title, which appears to recall the ratiocinative detective story, *The Locked Room* also conjures the noir protagonist obstructed from normality by unforeseeable circumstances. But the second novel, *Ghosts,* even more conspicuously raises the spirit of noir. Like its companion pieces, *Ghosts* calls into question the way in which noir constructs identity. As detective Blue's investigation begins to deteriorate, the noir hero suffers translation into an insubstantial "ghost" of the alienated modernist subject. I have noted that *The New York Trilogy* does not consist of discrete units, and this assumption is borne out by the introduction of *Ghosts.* In *The Locked Room,* the narrator, presumably Auster,[29] at one point describes his method of convincingly falsifying census forms. Attempting to "stay within the bounds of realism" the narrator resorts to "certain mechanical devices" such as the names of presidents, literary characters, distant relatives, and "the colors (Brown, White, Black, Green, Gray, Blue)."[30] With characteristic playfulness, Auster offers an ironic meditation on the permeable boundaries of fiction and documentation, authorship and reportage. In the attempt to provide "realistic" data that is apparently free from signification, the narrator resorts to names based on color. This should remind us of the first lines of *Ghosts:* "First of all there is Blue. Later there is White, and then there is Black, and before the beginning there is Brown" (162). Such "chromatics" underscore not only the interconnectedness of the three novels, but also the "realism" of *Ghosts:* is Auster here meditating on the mechanics of realist noir, as he experiments with the documentary census in *The Locked Room?* We are furthermore prompted to consider the allied tension in the novel between two of Auster's favorite genres—the detective story and the fairy-tale. By reducing the characters in *Ghosts* to chromatic labels, Auster tenders not a realist detective story (one which unflinchingly reports the horrors of a modernist wasteland), but rather the reflexive enactment of a highly codified genre. Even as the novel commences, we are privy to suggestions that firmly seat *Ghosts* within the mythology of noir.

Ghosts begins on February 3, 1947, a date significant not only as Auster's birthdate,[31] but also in that it reflects the heyday of noir. More than any of the novels in the trilogy, *Ghosts* evokes the hard-boiled detective formula. Protagonist Blue appears at the outset an incarnation of the down-and-out private eye who "needs work" and "doesn't ask many questions" (162). Recalling Chandler, the narrator describes Blue as a "man-of-action": "He likes to be up and about, moving from one place to another, doing things. I'm not the Sherlock Holmes type, he would say . . . " (166).[32] Such cues give way to a coherent noir philosophy. Blue "is a devoted reader of True Detective magazine and tries never to miss a month"; his fascination with a particular article, "[b]uried among the feature stories on gangsters and secret agents," gives rise to a reflection on hard-boiled ethics:

> Twenty-five years ago, it seems, in a patch of woods outside Philadelphia, a little boy was found murdered. Although the police promptly began to work on the case, they never managed to come up with any clues. Not only did they have no suspects, they could not even identify the boy. Who he was, where he had come from, why he was there—all these questions remained unanswered. Eventually, the case was dropped from the active file, and if not for the coroner who had been assigned to do the autopsy on the boy, it would have been forgotten altogether. This man, whose name was Gold, became obsessed by the murder. Before the child was buried, he made a death mask of his face, and from then on devoted whatever time he could to the mystery. After twenty years he reached retirement age, left his job, and began spending every moment on the case. But things did not go well. He made no headway, came not one step closer to solving the crime. The article in True Detective describes how he is now offering a reward of two thousand dollars to anyone who can provide information about the little boy. . . . Gold is growing old now, and he is afraid that he will die before he solves the case. Blue is deeply moved by this. If it were possible, he would like nothing better than to drop what he's doing and try to help Gold. There aren't enough men like that he thinks. . . . Gold refuses to accept a world in which the murderer of a child can go unpunished, even if the murderer himself is now dead, and he is wiling to sacrifice his own life and happiness to right the wrong. (168–70)

Blue is not simply attracted to the piece because of the affinities with the field of detection, nor only because of the heroism of Gold. Rather, these very attributes quietly harbor for Blue the authenticating alienation endemic to noir. Speaking on "the emotional basis of the hard-boiled story," Chandler suggests, "obviously it does not believe that murder will out and justice will be done—unless some very determined individual makes it his business to see that justice is done."[33] Gold seems a conspicuous avatar of the hard-boiled detective locked in absurd confrontation between human will and an irrational, indifferent world. The conclusion is obvious—like Oedipa Maas, Blue derives a sense of self against the insoluble mystery or against the succession of cases: "Blue goes to his office every day and sits at his desk, waiting for something to happen." Auster thus provides a "cut-away" view of the noir constructive mechanism "epically" (in Bakhtin's terms) consigned to a static historical nether-world: "The place is New York, the time is the present, and neither one will ever change" (161).

The circumstances of Blue's immediate case are no less important. Playing on the famous appellation of "private eye," Auster ensconces Blue within a virtual monastic cell, his task to "keep an eye" (161) on the movements of a party named Black who resides in an apartment across the street. Whether in the form of surveilling detective or simply a curious child, the voyeuristic figure recurs throughout the noir canon as an emblem for the isolated subject. Like Ishmael Reed, Auster conjures specific noir pretexts: we might immediately recall Cornell Woolrich's short-story "The Boy Cried Murder" (1947), in which an imaginative youngster witnesses a murder, only to find that no one will believe the story. Later filmed as *The Window* (Ted Tetzlaff, 1949), this text reflects a concentration on problems of perception treated throughout Woolrich's fiction and noir in general.[34] It is worthwhile to dwell for a moment upon Woolrich's "Rear Window" (1942), which Hitchcock adapted in 1954 for his renowned thriller and a tour de force in "voyeur-noir." Originally titled "It Had to Be Murder," this fiction significantly reifies the motif of the alienated spectator. A temporarily disabled man is confined to a small apartment; in his malaise, Hal Jeffries surveys his neighbors from the titular window: "Sure, I suppose it *was* a little bit like prying, could even have been mistaken for the fevered concentration of a Peeping Tom. That wasn't my fault, that wasn't the idea. The idea was, my movements were strictly limited just around this time. I could get from the window to the bed, and from the bed to the window, that was all."[35] In one sense, Jeffries's incarceration recalls the panoptic surveillance of Auguste Dupin or Sherlock Holmes, figures who enjoy the dominating vantage point suggested by their second-story apartments. Jeffries does indeed turn detective when he witnesses the evidences of a murder in the facing apartment. But Jeffries's confinement, his ultimate helplessness, as well as his lack of self-insight (he obviously attempts to rationalize his voyeurism), place him squarely in the noir tradition as a type of the modernist subject condemned to watch his world from a peculiar, restricted point-of-view. Indeed, as the narrative progresses, we almost wonder whether Jeffries's world will devolve, in true postmodernist fashion, into the multiple surfaces of electronic media: "I blew out the match, picked up the phone in the dark. It was like television. I could see to the other end of my call, only not along the wire but by a direct channel of vision from window to window" (26). Suffused with noir visual imagery (juxtapositions of light and darkness), this moment also adumbrates the mediated world of postmodernity. Like Chandler and Hammett before him, Woolrich forgoes the implications of this postmodern moment; but he does quietly unsettle the subjective boundaries established at the outset of the text. Amidst the guilty pleasures of his voyeurism, Jeffries must assume a degree of culpability while the murderer Thorwald, as he flees the police, assumes the role of Sisyphean hero. In any case, "Rear Window" remains a noir classic replete with modernist assumptions; Woolrich here as elsewhere envisions a universe peopled by tortured isolatoes whose insular worlds periodically and haphazardly collide. Auster's Blue initially appears a reinscription of the alienated modernist voyeur, as he likewise finds himself ensconced in his own monadic cell, compelled to merely observe the object of the investigation.

Ultimately, Blue has to do more than "merely watch"; he must also transcribe his observations of Black into reports forwarded to employer White. With Blue's first report, we are treated to an exposition of his hermeneutic philosophy:

> His method is to stick to outward facts, describing events as though each word tallied exactly with the thing described, and to question the matter no further. Words are transparent for him, great windows that stand between him and the world, and . . . they have never impeded his view, have never even seemed to be there. Oh, there are moments when the glass gets a trifle smudged and Blue has to polish it in one spot or another, but once he finds the right word, everything clears up. . . . No references to the weather, no mention of the traffic, no stab at trying to guess what the subject might be thinking. The report confines itself to the known and verifiable facts, and beyond this limit it does not try to go. (174–75)

In Blue's hermeneutic, Auster conjures a variety of realist pretexts—not only literary realism in general but also the "writing degree zero" delineated by Barthes: a "transparent form of speech, initiated by Camus's *The Outsider*, [that] achieves a style of absence which is almost an ideal absence of style; writing . . . reduced to a sort of negative mood in which the social or mythical characters of a language are abolished in favor of a neutral and inert state of form."[36] As in Pynchon's *The Crying of Lot 49*, excess signification poses an ultimate danger to stable subjectivity; Blue therefore aspires to a self-effacing idiom that conveys a reality without getting in the way, without exploding into an infinitude of all too *significant* details. As long as Blue maintains this voice, he is able to preserve a sense of the referential world within which he takes shape. The reference to Camus points us indirectly back to our immediate context of noir: the celebrated author was attracted and indebted to the muscular prose of writers such as James M. Cain.[37] It suffices at this point however to recognize that Blue's effort at *écriture blanche* advances the evocation of noir and offers a probing look into its epistemology.

But Blue's "window" onto the world is at best opaque, as constructive as it is conductive. Excess signification again proves the culprit, for the referential is hopelessly bound with Blue's pretextual memories and associations. According to Barthes, such a process of interpretation itself implies a radical revision of human subjectivity, for the "'I' which approaches the text is already itself a plurality of other texts, of codes which are infinite or, more precisely, lost (whose origin is lost)." For Barthes, identity is therefore "a plenary image, with which I may be thought to encumber the text, but whose deceptive plenitude is merely the wake of all the codes which constitute me, so that my subjectivity has ultimately the generality of stereotypes."[38] Even as Blue presumes the uninflected noir idiom, the voice which, in Chandler's phrase, "had no overtones, left no echo," he ironically suffers a fall into unchecked textuality, finds himself an unstable "plurality of other texts." We are therefore privy throughout the duration of the novel to a progressive textualization and concomitant unrealization of "Black and Blue."

Like Oedipa's Tristero, Black becomes a figure for the referential—an Other crucial to the formation of Blue's identity. But the autonomy of this object is immediately called into question as Blue inevitably clothes Black with his own pretexts: " . . . everything is a blank so far. Perhaps he's a madman, Blue thinks, plotting to blow up the world. Perhaps that writing has something to do with his secret formula" (164). Many more "pitches" follow: "Murder plots, for instance, and kidnapping schemes for giant ransoms. Blue realizes there is no end to the stories he can tell. For Black is no more than a kind of blankness, a hole in the texture of things, and one story can fill this hole as well as any other" (174). Such suppositions are hardly surprising, given Blue's reading habits—"newspapers and magazines, and an occasional adventure novel, when he was a boy" [194]). But the implication here exceeds an emphatic treatment of intertextuality; if Black suggests an absolute reality, Auster refuses to posit a referent separable from the inexhaustible competing narratives applied to it.

Consumer culture teaches us that the phrase most often associated with the blank space is "Your Name Here"; and this is precisely what occurs in *Ghosts*. Despite resolutions to "suspend judgements" (165), Blue is quick to write Black into one of his pulp fiction synopses, which temptation provides a segue into the ultimate collapse of Blue into Black. Moved to include these naked fictions in the report, Blue concludes, "This isn't the story of my life . . . I'm supposed to be writing about him, not myself" (175). Against the grain of conventional voyeur-noir, in which the viewing subject witnesses some alien spectacle, Blue beholds a figure uncannily similar to himself: a man of about the same age, writing in a notebook at a desk. In the following excerpt, Auster concisely forges the passage between Blue's hermeneutic and his progressive collapse into Black:

> He has moved rapidly along the surface of things for as long as he can remember, fixing his attention on these surfaces only in order to perceive them, sizing up one and then passing on to the next, and he has always taken pleasure in the world as such, asking no more of things than that they be there. And until now they have been, etched vividly against the daylight, distinctly telling him what they are, so perfectly themselves and nothing else that he has never had to pause before them or look twice. Now, suddenly, with the world as it were removed from him, with nothing to see but a vague shadow by the name of Black, he finds himself thinking about things that have never occurred to him before, and this, too, has begun to trouble him. If thinking is perhaps too strong a word at this point, a slightly more modest term—speculation, for example—would not be far from the mark. To speculate, from the Latin *speculatus,* meaning to spy out, to observe, and linked to the word speculum, meaning mirror or looking glass. For in spying out at Black across the street, it is as though Blue were looking into a mirror, and instead of merely watching another, he finds that he is also watching himself. (171–72)

As in conventional noir, Blue finds his self-constitutive routine disrupted by some intrusion of the irrational; but Auster modifies the formula by installing the hard-boiled detective as the complacent Everyman whose assumptions are challenged. Blue is initially possessed of a hermeneutic which limits meaning, "rapidly passing along the surface of things," and maintaining a stable referential. But the prolonged surveillance of Black amplifies noisy signification—in the vacuum of the monadic apartment, Blue registers "tiny events" which "persist in his mind like a nonsense phrase repeated over and over again": "The trajectory of the light that passes through the room each day, for example, . . . The beating of his heart, the sound of his breath, the blinking of his eyes" (172). The "vague shadow called Black" localizes Blue's hermeneutical dysfunction; he is the suspect against whom the detective draws being and, as such, suggests the referential as-a-whole. Black therefore operates as a mirror in which the literally "speculative" Blue reads his own projected significations.

Blue will at one point even confess an ironic "fondness" for his suspect (181), an affinity perhaps understandable given the crucial bond they share. While Blue often feels that he is able to anticipate Black's actions, "there are times when he feels totally removed from Black, cut off from him in a way that is so stark and absolute that he begins to lose sight of who he is" (186). Far from resolving the modernist dilemma of alienation, Blue's identification with Black gives rise to the deeper problem of self-dissolution. Slipping in and out of focus, as it were, with his constructive counterpart, Blue experiences a frightening encounter of the kind described by Julia Kristeva in *Strangers to Ourselves:* "Confronting the foreigner whom I reject and with whom at the same time I identify, I lose my boundaries, I no longer have a container, . . . I feel 'lost,' 'indistinct,' 'hazy.'"[39] Kristeva's optical language concurs with Auster's notion of a subject *coming into focus* against its object, establishing a perfect distance that might be regarded as a "focal length." When Blue "slips out of focus" with Black, he undergoes an identity crisis, "loses sight" of himself. We therefore find Blue throughout the latter stages of the narrative in various attitudes of dissolution: "he feels empty, the stuffing all knocked out of him" (187); "a spectre" (195); " . . . so inactive as to reduce his life to almost no life at all" (201). Even in the execution of the investigation, Blue falls victim to a fracture of identity; he assumes the "new identity" of Jimmy Rose, a relatively obscure Melville character and thus an allusion that comprises part of the densely fictive milieu of the *Trilogy*.[40]

In a climactic encounter, Blue beats Black into unconsciousness; even then he is unable to discern whether his victim is dead or alive, subject or object: "listening for Black's breath, . . . he can't tell if it's coming from Black or himself" (231). But the novel's conclusion, if it can be said to have one, consists not in some definitive climax, but in an open-ended series of *self*-recuperative gestures. Having stolen a sheaf of Black's own writings, inevitably identical to his own, Blue desperately scans his room for some recourse, and sees a series of memorabilia which comes to reflect his strategies for subjectivity: pictures of his parents, for instance, along with a portrait of the transcendentally empowered Walt Whitman. Inspired by the clipped story of Gold from *True Detective,* Blue also admires "a movie still of Robert Mitchum from one of the fan magazines: gun in hand, looking as though the world were about to cave in on him" (225). Mitchum's image ill comports with the preceding narratives, and there is certainly more to it than sympathetic identification. Noir here again emerges as one of many constructive alternatives for situating and naturalizing subjectivity. This potential undoubtedly lies behind Blue's "particular weakness for movies about detectives":

> [H]e is always gripped by these stories more than by others. During this period he sees a number of such movies and enjoys them all: Lady in the Lake, Fallen Angel, Dark Passage, Body and Soul, Ride the Pink Horse,

> Desperate, and so on. But for Blue there is one that stands out from the rest, and he likes it so much that he goes back the next night to see it again.
>
> It's called Out of the Past and it stars Robert Mitchum as an ex-private eye who is trying to build a new life for himself in a small town under an assumed name. He has a girl friend, a sweet country girl named Ann, and runs a gas station with the help of a deaf-and-dumb boy, Jimmy, who is firmly devoted to him. But the past catches up with Mitchum, and there's little he can do about it. . . .
>
> For the next few days, Blue goes over this story many times in his head. It's a good thing, he decides, that the movie ends with the deaf mute boy. The secret is buried, and Mitchum will remain an outsider, even in death. (191–92)

We have already noted Blue's attraction to the pulp magazines from which he broadly derives a sense of existential heroism. Situated as it is within Blue's crises of subjectivity, however, this moment leaves no doubt as to Auster's sensitivity to noir's constructive power. The initial filmography consists of canonical films noirs which share, among other things, the plight of an alienated male protagonist.[41] Blue's attraction to these films goes beyond the "natural connection" of vocation. The plot thickens with the more elaborate commentary on Tourneur's *Out of the Past* (1947), a film saluted as "the *ne plus ultra* of 'forties *film noir*.'"[42] The sequence forces the reader to consider the very incongruity of Blue's attraction to noir: why should Blue, a detective genuinely interested in "solution," find himself compelled by a text which concludes with the death of its protagonist and the perpetuation of mystery? Threatened by identification with Black, and convinced that "it might be better to stand alone than to depend on anyone else" (187–88), Blue retreats into noir texts primarily about alienation, and its concomitant "dream of authenticity." Though unable to contend with the forces arrayed against him, Mitchum's character is assured, in the midst of his travail, a coherent identity: "The secret is buried, and Mitchum will remain an outsider, even in death." This last phrase recalls Chandler's axiomatic statement, "Even in death, a man has a right to his own identity"[43]; in keeping with this pronouncement, Blue seeks refuge in self-stabilizing noir fictions that enable authenticating alienation.

But this strategy fails to maintain the ideal focal length between Black and Blue; nor can laconic hard-boiled syntax hide the fact of contingent identity:

> . . . I like you Blue. I always knew you were the right one for me. A man after my own heart.

> If you stopped waving that gun around, maybe I'd start feeling the same way about you.
>
> I'm sorry, I can't do that. It's too late now.
>
> Which means?
>
> I don't need you anymore, Blue. (229)

Black menaces Blue with a "thirty-eight revolver, enough to blow a man apart at such close range" (228), and the sequence reads as a classic noir confrontation in which the protagonist counters annihilation with cynical bravura. But these trappings cannot hide the real dynamics of the episode, which address the undeniable contingency of identity. Black suggests that Blue has existed as a mere foil for his own self-construction. Whatever its priority, this system of difference fails at the conclusion of the narrative when Blue pummels Black, perhaps to death, and feels "as though turned into someone else" (231). As with Oedipa in *The Crying of Lot 49*, however, this radical transformation is forestalled as the narrator conspicuously intervenes with the possibility of another situational tactic that will perhaps secure Blue another context for identity:

> I myself prefer to think that he went far away, boarding a train that morning out West to start a new life. It is even possible that America was not the end of it. In my secret dreams, I like to think of Blue booking passage on some ship and sailing to China. Let it be China, then, and we'll leave it at that. For now is the moment that Blue stands up from his chair, puts on his hat, and walks through the door. And from this moment on, we know nothing. (232)

In this final gambit, the narrator assigns Blue to another distant narrative within which his subjectivity might be retained. The narrator's choices are significant—as if returning to the roots of hard-boiled fiction and film noir, he writes Blue into a colonial adventure that takes him beyond the western frontier and into the exotic geography of the Far East. We have explored the potential of such narratives to generate and sustain the western subject; Auster certainly alludes here to the Orientalism deeply embedded in the logic of noir. As in *The Crying of Lot 49*, the novel's open-ended conclusion veers away from a catastrophic collapse of subject/object binaries; but it does so in a way that reveals the tenuous strategies by which noir envisions human identity. As the narrative trajectory of *Ghosts* bares the reality of noir, and Blue's identity along with it, the narrator resorts to an obviously recuperative strategy of deferral, placing subject Blue beyond the reach of any erosive developments.

IN RECASTING NOIR conventions, Pynchon, Reed, and Auster broach many other allied literary genres, including the detective story and Gothic horror. Even as Vivian Sobchack, alluding to James Cameron's *The Terminator* (1984), identifies the intersection of cyberpunk and hard-boiled elements "Tech Noir" (249), Claudia Springer notes, "Cyberpunk's dark, bleak surroundings and its convoluted plot twists that often involve treachery and betrayal are derived from the cynical world of film noir" (78). Philip K. Dick here comes to mind, in that this "spiritual father of cyberpunk" has been "regarded a postmodern author in his own right," as Derek Littlewood and Peter Stockton reflect (45), as well as a dedicated interrogator of the noir ethos. Moreover, *Do Androids Dream of Electric Sheep?* was adapted for the most celebrated "tech noir" achievement: Ridley Scott's 1982 film *Blade Runner*. For Žižek, *Blade Runner* exemplifies the "*noir* of the eighties in its purest form*,*" undercutting the self-affirmation that attends the amnesiac scenarios of "classical *noir*": "In the universe of *Blade Runner* . . . recollection designates something incomparably more radical: the total loss of the hero's symbolic identity. He is forced to assume that he is not what he thought himself to be, but somebody-something else" (12). I would conclude this chapter by turning to another cyberpunk novel—K. W. Jeter's 1998 novel *Noir,* a book that offers what is perhaps the most sustained and aggressive postmodernist parody of noir extant. One of Dick's close associates, Jeter is well known for his novelized sequels to *Blade Runner* (1995–2000). In *Noir,* Jeter amplifies Dick's combustible mixture of hard-boiled and cyberpunk fictional motifs, literalizing the notion of noir as a "technology of the self."

Noir projects a not-too-distant future in which borders political, geographical, and textual collapse alongside those of the embodied subject itself. The inaugural murder of this mystery story involves an executive who dies while enjoying vicarious pleasures through his "prowler" or surrogate clone; before the investigation begins, the victim's employer has his organs extracted for medical transplant. The detective-protagonist called in to investigate the murder is himself an intellectual property bountyhunter who punishes bootleggers by surgically removing cortical material that holds the perpetrator's psychic essence (we see one such unfortunate consigned to infernal torture as a speaker cable). The most striking image of corporeal disruption, however, occurs when poverty-stricken burn victims are treated with indiscriminate applications of fire-retardant gel. November, a "femme fatale" assassin engaged in obliterative attacks against male victims, finds the results profoundly unsettling:

> . . . a vision came to November unbidden, of the strictures of form and

identity dissolving, the prisoning matter of the city's heart reverting to some premammalian coitus.... The distinction between one body and another was erased, the membrane between the body's interior and the soft outside world forgotten; she almost envied them. Or it. November decided it was the oncoming tide of the future, humans finally having gotten tired of bones and jobs to do.... A generalized terror, the sense of her own boundaries melting away, the result of a horrifying *connectedness;* this was what she had run from all her life. (217–18)

Within this "soup," bodies, selves, and even the laws governing representation have dissolved. High-tech animated tattoos, ostensibly pictures which represent reality, "had been set free, achieving a new life in the habitat of the sterile nutrient medium. They swam about now like pilot fish, darting among the blind kidneys and lungs, past the loose ropes of nerve tissue" (399). In the entropic world of *Noir,* anxieties about collapse into otherness are so immediate that the word "connect" has become an obscene epithet. "In short, if you're connected you're fucked," writes Steven Shaviro of *Noir*: "Reach out and touch someone? It's the worst thing that could happen to you. Every connection has its price..." (3).

Jeter counters this "connected" universe with the essentialist humanism of noir; unlike his modernist forbears, however, he refuses to naturalize this possibility. As his name suggests, McNihil is a son of modernism who loathes the late capitalist wasteland characterized by *Lucy* reruns cut with Tarantino dialogue and Peckinpah slow-motion violence, "collect-the-set chocolate bars with ... installments of an updated Story of Job on the wrapper," and "postliterate romance novels with audio chips sighing and moaning in synch with the nearest ovulation cycle that the built-in hormone sensors could pick up" (108). Although the stage is set for a reification of alienated humanity, Jeter frustrates any such readerly desire with a device that is the centerpiece of the novel. Fearing absorption into this hypercommodified dystopia, McNihil retreats into an unlikely sanctuary: the mise-en-scène of film noir. Cashing in his (and his spouse's) retirement fund, McNihil has undergone a surgical procedure that allows him to perceive "a darkly poetic world" (320):

> He'd paid to see a world that was to his liking. Not beautiful—it was based, after all, on cultural artifacts of more than a century ago, the bleak and brooding crime and thriller movies of the 1930s and forties—but with beautiful things in it. More beautiful, actually, for being surrounded by constant threat and darkness. So that if he could sit in a shabby, too small room that smelled like dust settling on bare, flickering lightbulbs, if he

could sit across from a girl who looked—at least to him—like an actress from those ancient films that nobody watched anymore, a woman with heartbreaking eyes . . . that was all right by him. (54)

For McNihil, "Real time had ended somewhere in the early 1940s," relenting to "the cheap-'n'-nastiverse that people so foolishly believed in" (302). When he encounters a prostitute, for example, McNihil sees a "young Ida Lupino" with "a general air of brave vulnerability and period early-forties outfit from Raoul Walsh's *High Sierra*. . . . The worn-and-mended woolen skirt, the thin unbuttoned sweater with a zigzag decorative pattern around the bottom and at the cuffs showing at the tiny wrists, the plain high-collared blouse" (44). By virtue of this technology, the black-and-white polarities of noir reinscribe lost boundaries, cloaking its constructions in semidocumentary realism. Noir writers and filmmakers often gravitate toward this exposure, inscribing characters and scenarios that verged upon the "A-effect"; but they generally retreat from this metafictional terminus. Under Jeter's handling, however, the noir ethos becomes not so much an unflinching reflection of brutal reality, but rather one more narrative mechanism for generating self and world. Here, then, is a highly reflexive dramatization of Baudrillard's notion that alienation serves as a "protective enclosure, an imaginary protector": McNihil's cybercinematographic body generates an "eternal clockless night" within which the protagonist's subjectivity becomes authenticated by "being surrounded by constant threat and darkness."

Shaviro glosses McNihil's strange retreat a Nietzchean will to power, "not an effort to flee the world so much as . . . a way of acting upon it—and being acted upon in turn" (143). Even as he fails to keep the "the cheap-'n'-nastiverse" from "seeping back into [his] little private existence" (289), McNihil has embarked on a constitutive program that is doomed to failure. The reflexivity of McNihil's cybercinematographic vision is at odds with noir's reality effect: a canvas of insignificance that supports its expressionistic polarities. Moreover, in his pursuit of noir boundaries, McNihil quite obviously reveals and exploits the permeability of the body, becoming a paradoxically cyborg hard-boiled hero. As Gabriele Schwab contends, "Technology, meant to extend our organs and our senses and even top support our phantasms of immortality and transcendence, seems to threaten what we wanted to preserve by destroying us as the subjects we thought ourselves to be when we took refuge in technological projects and dreams" (209). This contradiction is in some respects meliorated by McNihil's heuristic approach to the situational noir narrative; by the conclusion of the novel, however, he accomplishes an even more radical departure from noir authenticating alienation. In an elaborate plot to foil his exploitative corporate employer (Dyna Zauber), McNihil inflicts upon himself a gaping gunshot wound, so that he might be reanimated as an undead debtor (in the world of *Noir*, outstanding debts must be expunged before the debtor can actually die). McNihil joins his undead wife in the necropolis of Los Angeles, suggesting a subject not only corporeally reconfigured, but now derived through networks and relationships rather than heroic anomie. As I argue in the final chapter of this study, the reconstruction of the alienated subject represents one of the central movements of 1990s film noir. But Jeter's primary gesture is one of subversion rather than revision—the apex of postmodernism's assault on the "darkly perfect world" of hard-boiled fiction and film noir.

Noir represents a culmination of the reflexive, investigative, and in a word, "novelistic" program pursued by Pynchon, Reed, and Auster. With both explicit and veiled allusions to a series of noir texts, each of these novelists helps us to understand authenticating alienation as a recuperative strategy, a "technology of the self." In its uninflected degree-zero idiom, hard-boiled fiction and film noir offer an apparently authentic account of modernist alienation, a record all the more compelling and "realistic" in its ostensible unattractiveness. At the same time, however, celebration of this condition establishes a sharp contrast between Self and Other. In the fictions of Pynchon and Jeter, in particular, the constructive capability of noir therefore becomes an attractive investment amidst the hyperreality of late capitalist postmodernism, which, in Baudrillard's phrase, sees "a proliferation of myths of origin and signs of reality . . . the panic-stricken production of the real and referential." It is a world in which noir shopping-malls and garbage-bag advertisements become imaginable. In such a climate, noir is also rendered up to the irreverent scrutiny of the postmodern novel. As we shall see, the triumph of reflexive alienation effect over naturalizing reality effect would also deeply inform postmodernist cinema of the later twentieth century.

CHAPTER SIX

TO LOOK AT HIM OR READ HIM

THE CONFIDENCE MAN IN POSTMODERNIST FILM NOIR

> *I don't know whether to look at him or read him.*
> —Lt. Elgart (Robert Mitchum), *Cape Fear* (Martin Scorsese, 1991)

Parodists such as K. W. Jeter denaturalize a self-fashioning technology often veiled by the representational tactics of literary realism and semidocumentary filmmaking. As Stanley Aronowitz and Henry Giroux suggest, however, such postmodernist subversions may also engender a self-defeating nihilism in which "[f]atalism replaces struggle, and irony resigns itself to a 'mediascape' that offers the opportunity for a form of refusal defined simply as play. Foundationalism is out, and language has become a signifier, floating anchorless in a terrain of images that refuse definition and spell the end of representation" (66). But this kind of "dedoxifying" program may also provide a starting point for a reconstruction of the subject attacked under postmodernism. While the present discussion treats the centrality of the confidence man within contemporary film noir, the concluding chapter addresses ways in which film noir has revised the modernist subject through community rather than through authenticating alienation. Many films noirs of the late twentieth century see the reintroduction of the confidence man, an especially charged figure attended by enormous anxiety and suspicion within the noir imagination. As we have seen, noir fictions and films of the earlier twentieth century continually draw protagonists from the ranks of private detectives, policemen, criminals (perhaps most often heist men), and the "common man" that falls into the underworld. Few noirs foreground the confidence man, the criminal who operates exclusively through narrative subterfuge. Unlike the agonistic hero of noir, the con man is not so much an alienated figure as one who blends into the surrounding milieu. When the con man does surface in noir fictions and films, he is handled in such a way as to limit his "signifying" powers. Throughout the last two decades, however, many postmodernist films noirs allow the con man to eclipse the conventional noir protagonist. Modernist humanism therefore gives way in these films to a vision of the self as protean textual construct. And yet this transformation is inflected with neither the cynicism associated with nihilist postmodernism nor the nostalgia for modernist alienation; the vision of self that emerges from these films is, in Roland Barthes's terms, a subject that is "already itself a plurality of other texts, of codes which are infinite, . . . the generality of stereotypes."[1]

The confidence man is a familiar figure in the western literary canon, recurring in texts as various as *The Odyssey* and *Adventures of Huckleberry Finn*. Herman Melville's 1857 novel *The Confidence-Man, His Masquerade* certainly represents the most radical deployment of the con man in fiction: identified only by his continual use of the word "confidence," the titular figure appears so mutable and dispersed as to reject the notion of an essential self. John G. Blair concludes that Melville "carries the confidence figure as far as it can go"—"[I]f the fiction is given over any further to the principles implicit in the con man . . . he himself would disappear out of sight behind the mechanisms of the fiction: everything inconsistent, changeable, shifting, identity-less" (139). At least part of what makes *The Confidence-Man* so challenging a novel is Melville's refusal of any privileged glimpse into the "essential" identity of the swindler; it is all but impossible to discern a figure that consists only of a series of "masquerades." Within the noir imagination, however, the excess signification posited by the confidence man becomes delimited by the reaffirmation of a "core" self.

For Blair, the confidence man erodes "the moral significance of the congruence between the inner self and outer presentation of the self—the sincerity so dear to the Romantics, or the authenticity praised by some of their twentieth century offspring" (131). Accordingly, noir virtuosi have warily handled the confidence man, seeking to maintain a subject authenticated through alienation against the threat of unchecked signification. A hard-boiled hero such as Chandler's Phillip Marlowe may misrepresent himself in the course of investigation, but he arrests this textual play by insistence upon a subjective code of conduct and by rooting out the plastic tendencies of con men like Terry Lennox. In a number of prominent noir texts, the confidence man is more centrally evoked but circumscribed within the modernist polarities of Naturalism and Existentialism; these include William Lindsay Gresham's *Nightmare Alley,* Frederic Brown's *The Fabulous Clipjoint,* Jules Dassin's film *Night and the City,* and Jim Thompson's *The Grifters.* Unlike Melville's writerly novel, these texts operate within the tradition of realism to reveal the alienated essential self beneath the shifting surfaces of the confidence man. The con man in each of these novels operates via some manipulation of available signs. But the self-as-bricoleur implied by such figures becomes obscured as the narrative focus shifts toward the alienated universe of noir: ludic signification yields to the binary struggle of the rational self against an irrational world.

NO ARTIST more fully realizes the noir ethos than William Lindsay Gresham, whose life, in a real sense, reads like one of his plots. After an eclectic career that included folk singing in Greenwich village, soldiering with the Abraham Lincoln Brigade during the Spanish Civil War, and editorial work with a crime magazine, Gresham was diagnosed with cancer. He registered at the Dixie Hotel in New York City and committed suicide with an overdose of sleeping pills. But Gresham's tragic course also holds elements that ill consist with the stark realism of noir—he experimented, for example, with religions as diverse as Presbyterianism, Zen Buddhism, and Dianetics. In retrospect, we might find in the adjacent text of Gresham's life chapters that conjure both modernism (Communist activism and fighting in the Spanish Civil War) and postmodernism (philosophies derived from pulp science-fiction). Gresham's most successful novel, *Nightmare Alley,* similarly proves a site of contest between the modernist ethos of noir and the postmodernist practices of the con man. From its outset, *Nightmare Alley* grapples with the "carnivalesque" via realism: "Stanton Carlisle stood well back from the entrance of the canvas enclosure, under the blaze of a naked light bulb, and watched the geek" (523). Even this opening line reflects Gresham's aesthetic, for just as the naked bulb (itself a noir icon) sheds harsh light upon the geek, the bottom of the carnival hierarchy and a fit subject for naturalist exposé, Gresham's minimalist prose seeks purchase upon the "carny," which is constantly broken down, moving, reassembled, and populated with grifters of all description. Gresham introduces his *dramatis personae* through a catalogue that moves freely between barkers' pitches and interior monologue: "'Here you are folks—brimful of assorted poems, dramatic readings, and witty sayings by the world's wisest men. And only a dime . . . ' Sis wrote me the kids are both down with whooping cough. I'll send them a box of paints to help keep them quiet. Kids love paints. I'll send them some crayons, too" (531). As in this introduction of Joe Plasky, "Half-Man Acrobat," the fluid discourse of the carny is hedged by the counterpoint of "realistic" interior reflections that posit a human figure behind the pitch and the quotidian world beyond the play of the carnival. This juxtaposition of ludic signification and realism governs Gresham's presentation of the protagonist Stan Carlisle. On one hand, Stan emerges from a background that collapses self and world into narrative play; Stan's father is a preacher-cum-real estate agent—"Church vestryman on Sundays, con man the rest of the week . . . the Bible-spouting bastard" (341). Resentment aside, Stan inherits his father's rhetorical skills as he works the carny as magician and apprentice mentalist: "The old gent was a great hand at quoting scripture. I guess a lot of it rubbed off on me" (605). At a pivotal moment in the novel, Stan saves the troupe from police harassment as he deftly reads and manipulates a small-town sheriff: "The face had changed. The savage lines had ironed out and now it was simply the face of an old man, weary and bewildered. Stan hurried on, panicky for fear the tenuous spell would break, but excited at his own power. If I can't read a Bible-spouting, whoremongering, big-knuckled hypocrite of a church deacon, he told himself, I'm a feeblo" (597). Stan concludes the reading by "[m]aking his face look as spiritual as possible" and by resting his hand against the carnival tent "in a gesture of peace and confidence[,] . . . a period at the end of the sentence" (599). In such moments, Stan recalls Melville's amorphous confidence man in that he becomes wholly subsumed by his own rhetoric: "Now he rambled; with a foolish drunken joy he let his tongue ride, saying whatever it wanted to say. He could sit back and rest and let his tongue do the work" (761). As the novel proceeds, Stan becomes "the Great Stanton" and eventually "the Reverend Carlisle," exploiting increasingly wealthy "chumps" through a mentalist routine and a phony religion, a "spook act"—"He read, sketchily, in Oupensky's *The Model of the Universe*, looking for tag lines he could pull out and use, jotting notes in the margin for a possible class in fourth dimensional mortality" (678). In moments such as these, Stan indeed emerges as the con man who implicitly posits a vision of the self as "a plurality of other texts."

As the novel proceeds, however, it becomes apparent that *Nightmare Alley* mounts a conservative response to the deconstructive implications of a text such as *The Confidence-Man*. Early on, Gresham seems to declare his recuperative intentions in his portrait of "Sailor Martin," the "living picture gallery":

> He was shipwrecked on a tropical island, which had only one other inhabitant—an old seafaring man, who had been there most of his life—a castaway. All he had managed to save from the wreck of his ship was a tattoo outfit. To pass the time he taught Sailor Martin the art and he practiced

on himself. Most of the patterns you see are his own work.... On his back, a replica of that world-famous painting, the Rock of Ages. On his chest ... the Battleship Maine, blowing up in Havana Harbor. (532)

Martin embodies the ludic textuality of the carnival. Although it turns out to be a ruse, his "castaway" narrative recalls the transgressive boundary crossing treated throughout late-Victorian adventure. Despite Zeena's debunking ("If he was ever in the Navy, I was born in a convent"), Sailor becomes a striking image of the self collapsed into signification. As Zeena points out, "He started by having a lot of anchors and nude women tattooed on his arms to show the girls how tough he was or something. Then he got the battleship put on his chest and he was off. He was like a funny paper, with his shirt off, and he figures he might as well make his skin work for him" (557). Sailors' body art is itself reflective; like the autonomous tattoos in Jeter's *Noir,* these images suggest the power of textuality. Both the Rock of Ages and the battleship *Maine* are common enough early- and mid-twentieth-century tattoo motifs; but while the replica painting might suggest the destruction of aesthetic aura, the latter tattoo alludes to a moment when the "real world" of history and politics becomes swallowed up by journalistic narration. At first blush this character merely underscores the carny underworld; and yet Sailor Martin proves central to Gresham's vision of meaning and identity. He symbolizes unchecked signification, concentrating the deconstructive tendencies latent within the con man. Martin and Stan Carlisle are at one point interestingly conflated under a strange image that occurs at Pete's funeral: "Sailor Martin had one eye closed.... He [Stan] had done that a hundred times himself, sitting beside his father on the hard pew.... There's a blind spot in your eye and if you shut one eye and then let the gaze of the other travel in a straight line to one side of the preacher's head there will be a point where the head seems to disappear and he seems to be standing there preaching without any head" (569). This moment not only aligns Stan with the tattooed man, but ties both these characters to the bizarre tableau of the headless preacher: an image of the confidence man as pure rhetoric, "preaching" without the rational agency and subjectivity implied by the head. In a move reminiscent of Phillip Marlowe's treatment of Terry Lennox, Gresham expels Martin from the carnival; in doing so, he jettisons the disturbing possibilities of the con man. From this point, the novel turns from the volatile significations of the grifter toward a noir drama of authenticating alienation.

After this expulsion, *Nightmare Alley* resolves itself into a recognizable noir story of frustrated desire. Like criminal protagonists of James M. Cain, William Gaddis, and W. R. Burnett, Stan attempts the Enlightenment dream of upward mobility by pitting his talents and resources against an irrational world. As he pitches his spook racket to wealthy marks, however, Stan confronts a series of obstacles. Perhaps most obviously, he finds himself caught between two destructive women, recurrent figures within the noir imagination. Stan's wife and accomplice Molly fulfills the noir stereotype of the virtuous but ineffectual "domestic angel": she constantly impedes Stan's designs, finally ruining his ghoulish scheme to use her as paranormal prostitute for the industrialist Ezra Grindle. At the other end of the spectrum is Dr. Lilith Ritter, a psychologist who, as her name suggests, proves a more dangerous, misandrous threat: "Was she an animal? . . . Was she merely a sleek golden kitten that unsheathed its claws when it had played enough and wanted solitude?" (689). Like Charlotte Manning in Mickey Spillane's *I, the Jury* (1947), this femme fatale exploits her skills as a therapist to con the con man. In addition to negotiating these hazards, Carlisle must contend with his own pathological hatred of his father and the mental exhaustion that comes with operating the racket. These combined forces continually imperil Stan's dream of wealth and power, coalescing into the terrifying image of the "nightmare alley": "Ever since he was a kid Stan had had the dream. He was running down a dark alley, the buildings vacant and black and menacing on either side. Far down the end of it a light burned; but there was something behind him, close behind him, getting closer until he woke up trembling and never reached the light" (585). Stan never does "reach the light"; he ends up on the run, ultimately falling to the nadir of the carny world. As with his treatment of Sailor Martin, Gresham here returns us to the origins of noir in Victorian adventure: donning a "Hindu outfit with dark makeup" (794), Stan for a time assumes the guise of "Allah Rahged," a traveling palmist. After learning of the marriage between Lilith Ritter and Ezra Grindle, however, Stan falls into alcoholism and the dreaded role of carny geek, a figure initially pitched in terms of exotic regression: "He was found on an uninhabited island five hundred miles off the coast of Florida. . . . Is he man or is he beast?" (524). It is therefore possible to discern in Stan's fall from "Rev. Stanton" through "Allah Rahged" to castaway geek a pattern of colonial regression. Such undertones similarly emerge from Edmund Goulding's 1947 film adaptation of *Nightmare Alley*, in which the initial exhibition of the geek is accompanied by a turbaned fire-eater act and a mural featuring the geek as a troglodyte that adumbrates the unkempt, enervated Stan (Tyrone Power). Gresham therefore enacts his own rendition of the colonial adventure motifs common to noir: far from regenerated civilization, the USA is itself an unstable contact zone where westerners might "go native."

NIGHTMARE ALLEY steers the confidence man away from intertextuality and toward a sociological and psychological vision of human atavism. The tension between naturalistic disempowerment and existentialist resolve informs other noir con-man narratives. In *The Fabulous Clipjoint*, Brown presents an investigation scenario that juxtaposes modernist and postmodernist thematics: with the help of his Uncle Ambrose, a carnival pitchman, Ed Hunter pursues his father's murderer throughout the brutal cityscape of Chicago. This routine noir groundplot conjures the disturbing implications of the confidence game when Uncle Am, himself a grifter, inducts Ed into the art of disguise and manipulation. Moreover, Ed discovers in his father an erstwhile adventurer, carny hand, and vaudevillian blackface minstrel, not to mention a master printer. Brown reasserts the noir hedge against surplus meaning, however, by concluding with psychological realism. It turns out that Ed's father suffered from a lifelong suicidal depression, ultimately arranging his own murder—a naturalistic revelation that is countered only by Ed and Am's humanistic resolve to unravel the mystery. In *Night and the City*, Jules Dassin similarly conjures and contains the grifter as he casts Richard Widmark in the role of Harry Fabian, an American hustler in postwar London who opportunistically breaks into the professional wrestling business. Exploiting the tension between the aesthetic purism of Greco-Roman wrestler Grigorius (Stanislaus Zbysko) and his racketeering son Kristo (Herbert Lom), who stages sensationalist wrestling exhibitions, Fabian engineers a match between a young Greek athlete and Kristo's wrestler "The Strangler" (Mike Mazurki). But when Grigorious preemptively defeats the Strangler, a victory that costs him his life, Fabian becomes a hunted man and climactically sacrifices himself for his fiancée Mary (Gene Tierney): this gesture sees the playful bricolage of the con-man exchanged for the existential redemption of noir.

Thompson's *The Grifters*, on the other hand, returns to the naturalistic world of *Nightmare Alley*. Like Stan Carlisle, Roy Dillon is a hustler on the verge of the big-time "long con." Thompson characteristically ups the ante of con-man noir: Roy is stymied by two femmes fatales—his lover Myra Langtree and his mother Lily Dillon (with whom he has suffered an abusive, possibly incestuous relationship). As in Thompson's short story "The Cellini Chalice" (1956), everyone in the universe of *The Grifters* is on the make. But just beneath the surface of these shifting identities is the epistemological bedrock of modernist angst and Darwinian competition. Much of the narrative is given over to treatment of the alienation and psychological trauma that Roy suffers under the strains of the short con. Myra and Lily, on the other hand, compete for Roy and his "stake," a contest eventually decided in favor of Lily, who kills both Myra and Roy. After accidentally stabbing Roy in the throat with a broken water glass, a sobbing Lily gathers up her loot and leaves town; even maternal affections yield before the predatory impulses engendered by the urban jungle. *The Grifters* exemplifies noir treatments of the confidence man in that the novel mitigates its nihilistic vision through a commitment to realism: beyond the narrative power of the grifter is a dystopian referential world that hems in signification.

Alfred Hitchcock's *Vertigo* (1958) stands as one of the first texts in which a con artist "takes" the noir subject: Gavin Elster (Tom Helmore) manipulates a series of narratives ranging from Gothic horror and mystery fiction to California historiography in order to dupe the traumatized detective Scottie Ferguson (James Stewart) into the plot to murder his wife. Elster's game is so successful that it forces Scottie himself into the role of a deceiver who aggressively participates in the construction of the fictional Madeleine (Kim Novak). While Scottie solves the crime perpetrated by Elster, he cannot deny his own complicity in the murderous scheme nor the extent to which the con man has invaded his own psyche. *Vertigo* prefigures a strain of revisionist noir that persists into the twenty-first century. Martin Scorsese's *Cape Fear*, David Fincher's *Seven*, and Bryan Singer's *The Usual Suspects* posit various noir actants that become subsumed within the boundless textuality of the confidence game. Christopher Nolan's *Memento* on the other hand represents an apotheosis of this revisionist movement within noir, as this film concludes with the reintegration of the modernist quester and the postmodernist bricoleur—a dynamic and heuristic subjectivity derived from a pastiche of fragmentary signifiers. The humanist subject implied by the noir hero is displaced by the confidence man himself, who projects what Calvin Schrag describes as "the self in discourse," a subject that emerges from "stories in the making" (26–27).

Critics almost uniformly panned director Martin Scorsese's 1991 remake of the 1962 thriller *Cape Fear* (directed by Lee J. Thompson and written by James R. Webb). Terrence Rafferty condemns the film as "a disgrace: an ugly, incoherent, dishonest piece of work."[2] And even the most enthusiastic respondent, J. Hoberman, who acclaims Scorsese a "national treasure," half-heartedly endorses the film as "more skillful than inspired."[3] Angela McRobbie offers a somewhat more helpful, though similarly ambivalent, review as she off-handedly argues for *Cape Fear* as proof of Scorsese's contention for "a postmodernist of the year award"; a film which may "claim pastiche as [its] get-out clause."[4] Considered within the broader context of 1990s noirs, however, Scorsese and screenwriter Wesley Strick's remake of *Cape Fear* lies precisely in its postmodernist revision and subversion of the first two versions of the story—John D. MacDonald's 1957 novel

The Executioners and the 1962 film adaptation. While these earlier texts interpret domestic melodrama through the suppressed signification and authenticating alienation of noir, Scorsese erodes the boundaries between text and referent as he translates Max Cady from unsignifiable menace into signifying con man. The case of the family melodrama bears out Žižek's contention for noir as a logic that exploits other "proper" genres. Melodrama is most generally considered a "low" popular form characterized by its obvious polarizations between good and evil as well as its heavy-handed "melos," which literally underscore narrative developments. Melodrama is almost invariably centered around domestic tensions within and between individual, family, and society. As in MacDonald's *The Executioners*, the nuclear family itself may often become a kind of "protagonist" that faces various external threats. *The Executioners* and *Cape Fear* (1962) are in this sense characteristic noirs that appropriate the domestic melodrama in their presentation of the beleaguered Bowden family.[5]

Perhaps most famous for his Travis McGee detective novels, John D. MacDonald cut an influential figure among those postwar crime writers moving from pulps to the incipient paperback novel. MacDonald has been described as an idiosyncratic novelist, recruiting the hard-boiled formula to "his own brand of popular philosophizing."[6] As Woody Haut explains, however, MacDonald participates in a discourse common to crime writers in the American South: "With its reputation for corruption, racism, poverty, backwardness and primitive sexuality, the South is an ideal setting for pulp culture crime fiction. . . . Manipulating specific clichés, Southern pulp culture crime writers . . . were unafraid to exploit the popular conception of a primitive, if not polymorphously perverse, South."[7] Set in the small Southern town of New Essex, *The Executioners* taps assumptions about the South and questions the efficacy of social and political institutions. Neither the law nor aristocratic *noblesse oblige*, often associated with Southern culture, are able to protect Sam Bowden and his family from Max Cady. Faithful to his modernist context, MacDonald calls into question the certainties of Enlightenment positivism. David Geherin has suggested that "[t]he frightening (albeit sometimes melodramatic) elements of [*The Executioners*] also serve to embody a kind of existential parable in which the orderly life of the average man is exposed to the sudden intrusion of the irrational and unexpected."[8] While the domestic melodrama may be said to broadly treat external threats to the family, the "existential parable" sees the human subject estranged from its world. Both of these generic forms come into play throughout *The Executioners* to render a narrative in which the Bowdens are alienated from and yet cohered by a hostile universe.

In *The Executioners,* Sam Bowden strives to preserve a haven of law, order, and community against the naturalistic forces embodied in Cady. While Sam inhabits sanctuaries such as the Bowdens' home and the "tidy little city" (12) of New Essex, Cady haunts the darkness just beyond the Bowdens' property line. Described as an "animal" at least a dozen times throughout the text, he may be read as the repressed unconscious or as a "reversion to a more primitive stage of evolution"[9] that has "come bobbing up out of ancient history" (7). Cady cannot be accounted for by the legal system, by science, or even by language: "He looks like he's got muscles they haven't named yet" (32). Although Sam fears that Cady will at best "turn their world into a jungle from which they could never escape" (185), the external threat ultimately consolidates the family. As Carol assures her husband, "They can't lick us Bowdens" (72). When Sam succeeds in killing Cady, he experiences "a feeling of strong and primitive fulfillment. All the neat and careful layers of civilized instincts and behavior were peeled back to reveal an intense exultation over the death of an enemy" (211). Throughout the novel, Sam is driven by the natural forces embodied in Cady into the ultimate refuge of his own consciousness. However Sam might desire to "submerge himself completely in the rhythms of the summer night," he cannot "halt the ticking of the clock in the back of his mind" (108). *The Executioners* conclusively endorses a subject that is isolated but protected by that alienation from unlimited textual play. As MacDonald suggests in Cady an objective, unmeaning material universe, Sam himself attempts to maintain the distinction between representation and reality, at one point warning his son, "This is for real. . . . This isn't television" (31). Expelled from meaning, Cady bounds the creeping threat of signification and emerges as referent against which the subject draws distinction.

Like its original, Thompson's 1962 *Cape Fear* has been located at the intersection of two genres; as Jenny Diski suggests, "The original version of *Cape Fear* is pure *film noir*" in which "the family—The Family—is under threat."[10] Nor is this a surprising turn, for, as Nina Leibman points out, "[*noir*] narrative is often centered around family issues, with the plot's problematics motivated or resolved by and through the family unit," which entity parallels the "existential angst of the male hero."[11] Thompson and Webb's interpretation of *The Executioners* may be inferred from the film's final sequence, in which the Bowdens stage an ambush for Cady. While MacDonald chooses the rural home for his novel's climax, Thompson and Webb set the showdown on the Bowdens' houseboat on the Cape Fear River, where marshlike environs strongly suggest an elemental opposition between humanity and nature.

Visual style plays a decisive role in this telling sequence. MacDonald frequently employs imagery that underscores the absurd dichotomy of self and world: "naked bulbs" and "dark shadows" (99), "utterly black nights" (195), and polarized imagery in general: "The dark water and sky made the white houses stand out clearly at the end of the lake" (179). MacDonald's descriptive technique lends itself to the cinematographic devices that Place and Peterson ascribe to film noir: "Small areas of light seem on the verge of being completely overwhelmed by the darkness that threatens them from all sides."[12] MacDonald's high-contrast description of the lakefront houses returns to its filmic source in the final scenes of Thompson's *Cape Fear*. The brilliant houseboat, besieged on all sides by dark water, foliage, and night sky becomes an iconic "clean, well-lighted place," bearing out Leibman's general contention that the family "remains one of the few brightly lit entities in the otherwise completely dark *noir* style, and it is constructed within a *mise-en-scène* that is far more calm than the film in which it rests."[13]

Perched on the riverbank and then crawling down into the water, Cady (Robert Mitchum) assumes the appearance of "some sort of prehistoric reptile—a cold blooded predator that we thought had disappeared from the earth a few geological ages ago."[14] The encroaching darkness moves with Cady as he gains on the houseboat and the adjacent cottage. Photographed through a darkened set of shelves, Peggy Bowden is trapped within her own kitchen. Nancy is similarly pursued into diminishing areas of light until she is overtaken. Cady's reptilian aspect persists as his serpentine gaze "mesmerizes" Nancy into dropping the poker with which she defends herself.

This sequence reifies Cady's animality; and it comes as no surprise that Thompson's version has retained Siever's (Telly Savalas) pivotal line: "A type like that is an animal. So you've got to fight him like an animal." Sam's recourse to "uncivilized" methods, including hired thugs, culminates in the final struggle with Cady, which recites a version of evolutionary history. The pair begin by fighting hand-to-hand in the waters of the river; their thrashing motion, coupled with Bernard Hermann's horrifically effective musical accompaniment, lends an unmistakable impression of two animals locked in mortal combat. As they crawl ashore, the combatants learn weapons—Sam strikes Cady with a rock, Cady conveniently finds primitive maul. When Sam regains his revolver, he forbears killing Cady, and consigns him to "a long life, in a cage. That's where you belong and that's where you're going. And this time for life." Sam's decision to spare Cady at once reflects a triumph of consciousness, a desire to repress reminiscent of Carol Bowden's attempt to "lock [Cady] in a neat little corner in the back of [her] mind." But this conclusion of *Cape Fear* manages to preserve MacDonald's essential conflict between rational mind and irrational world. Diski ultimately decides that what Cady does to the Bowdens "is literally *unspeakable*. No detail is shown or said, it is all shadow and implication . . . "[15] Taking the cue from its literary model, Thompson's *Cape Fear* invents a Cady beyond the scope of human language and culture. But in this first adaptation it is the family unit which comes to the fore. As Nina Leibman suggests, "*Film noir,* by virtue of its contrasts, centers the family as the locus of normalcy, a haven from a hateful world, and a cure for angst and alienation[;] . . . in 1950s society Americans were encouraged to see the happy family huddling together against the visceral terror of modern times."[16] Thompson leaves us with an image of the disillusioned Bowdens huddled against a threat that insures their identity.

Thompson would be succeeded by an auteur whose directorial approach is at odds with the noir realism. Robert Philip Kolker contends that Scorsese, unlike other post-New Wave directors, "always provides a commentary upon the viewer's experience, preventing him or her from easily slipping into plot. He creates an allusiveness, a celebration of cinema through references to other works. . . . "[17] None of Scorsese's films is more redolent of this reflexive tendency than *Cape Fear*. For J. Hoberman, "the new *Cape Fear* assumes that the viewer has seen the earlier one . . . [it] oscillates between a critique of the original and a variation of a common text; it's a choreographed hall-of-mirrors, an orchestrated echo-chamber."[18] The 1991 *Cape Fear* manages a critique of its predecessor *by virtue* of its status as "a variation of a common text." As McRobbie has astutely observed, "It's a film about film—about the surface of the screen, about image-making. And it's about archetypal struggles between good and evil, the outsider who invades the fragile fabric of the nuclear family with the intention of destroying it."[19] It is important to recognize, however, that Scorsese renders in Max Cady a signifying confidence man who undermines rather than coheres the Bowden's collective identity.

Assigned in a high-school English course to write a "reminiscence" "in the same style" as Wolfe's *Look Homeward Angel,* Danny Bowden (Juliette Lewis) introduces the film's narrative frame: "My reminiscence. I always thought that for such a lovely river, the name was mystifying—Cape Fear—when the only thing to fear on those enchanted summer nights was that the magic would end, and real life would come crashing in." Predicated upon the distinction between the sentimental and "real life," Danny's story recalls the earlier renditions of *Cape Fear:* she attempts her own domestic melodrama in order to shore up a splintered family. Scorsese and Strick hereby establish in *Cape Fear* a postmodernist investigation and subversion of its pre-texts.

Scorsese's favored tactics of allusion and quotation are also apparent in his evocation of literary and cinematic intertexts. Two allusive instances, in particular, foreground Scorsese's subversive program. The first occurs when the Bowdens initially encounter Cady in the darkened movie theater. The sequence on one hand evokes the family melodrama, recalling Thompson's scene in which the marauding Cady interrupts the Bowden's evening of bowling. Scorsese heightens the reflexivity of this moment by staging the encounter in a cinema—a gesture very much in keeping with the film's reflexivity. Even more interesting is the fact that the Bowdens are screening *Problem Child* (Dennis Dugan, 1990), a parodic family melodrama about a couple terrorized by their adopted seven-year-old. In the quoted sequence, the frustrated father (John Ritter) becomes a homicidal maniac who smashes through the child's door with an axe for a comic recasting of Jack Nicholson's famous role in *The Shining* (Stanley Kubrick, 1980). This *mise-en-abyme* counters the recuperative function of the family melodrama; we shall see that these Bowdens are already riddled with violent, explosive tensions. In this light, Cady may be ironically read as a kind of *deus ex machina,* the cohering Other of the first two versions. Cady quite literally steps into the frame to obstruct the Bowdens' vision of familial fragmentation that lies in their own domestic sphere.

This early sequence is seconded late in the film during the Bowdens' tense vigil with the private detective Kersek (Joe Don Baker). The later episode is of general interest, as it irreverently confuses the polarities of the family melodrama: while the invasive Cady poses as the family maid in order to murder Kersek, Danny's emblematic teddy bear is also ironically deployed as the warning-signal in Kersek's ambush. We here see the Bowdens cast once more as spectators, "huddled together" not *against* the real threat of Cady, but *around* a televised version of Douglas Sirk's *All That Heaven Allows* (1955). While the conventional polarities of the family melodrama blur, the Bowdens look to a text about a widow struggling to keep her family together as she incorporates her lover, an "outsider" beneath her social station. As she falls in love with her Thoreauvian gardener Ron (Rock Hudson), Carry (Jane Wyman) must weather the censure of her pretentious bourgeois children and social circle. The Sirk quotation in one sense counters the earlier instance of film spectatorship; if the Bowdens are rescued from a picture of their own internal tensions by the intrusion of Cady, then they look to Sirk's earlier, successful family melodrama for a model of recuperation. But despite its snug conclusion, *All That Heaven Allows* here again underscores fractures within the family: throughout the film Sirk deploys noir cinematography to render Carry a woman trapped within her own home, threatened not by an external force, but by her own repressive and conservative children. Scorsese's allusions collectively denaturalize and undermine *Cape Fear* 1962 and *The Executioners.*[20]

Cape Fear's reflexivity also emerges through the many "directoral tricks" dismissed by many reviewers of the film as "mere baroque excess."[21] We shall presently see that many of the particular effects Letts describes are used strategically, to achieve specific ends. For Stuart Klawans, *Cape Fear*'s "screen becomes almost non-representational."[22] If the "insignificant notations" of the realist text "say nothing other than 'we are reality,'" then Scorsese's special effects say, among other things, "we are not."

One such effect cues the erosion of the "othered" Max Cady. In an early scene Cady walks out of prison toward the camera until his face fills the frame. The shot recalls D. W. Griffith's close-up of the first American film gangster, the Snapper Kid (Elmer Booth), in *The Musketeers of Pig Alley* (1912). In the hands of Scorsese and cinematographer Freddie Francis, Cady becomes not so much an embodiment of "unspeakable" natural forces as a generic villain who emerges only from the "unconscious" of cinematic convention. The critical response to the revised Cady underscores its visual "unrealization." Rafferty's dismissal of De Niro's Cady typifies its reception as "a riff"[23] and a "stick figure"[24]: "De Niro's frenetic but thoroughly uninteresting performance is emblematic of the movie's inadequacy. He's covered with tattooed messages and symbols, but he doesn't seem to have a body. We could feel Mitchum's evil in all its slimy physicality; De Niro's is an evil we merely read." Mitchum's visceral performance preserves the illusion of a real threat that becomes part of a flattened "depth-model." The first scene of the narrative proper articulates the process of this collapse. Danny's introduction is immediately followed by a widening dolly-shot that reveals: 1) the collage of photographs on Cady's cell wall—comic-book characters and historical figures such as Lenin and Robert E. Lee; 2) Cady's bookshelf—the Bible sitting atop titles such as Nietzsche's *Will To Power* and *Thus Spake Zarathustra;* 3) the heavily tattooed figure of Cady itself. This sequence is punctuated by Cady's parting shot at a prison guard; when asked if he wants to take his books, Cady replies, "Already read 'em." This first sequence introduces Cady as Barthes's "I" which "is already itself a plurality of other texts." Indeed, Scorsese's Cady reads as a counterpoint to Gresham's *Nightmare Alley*: while Gresham steers the subject away from signification and into nature, announcing the gesture with the expulsion of the tattooed Sailor Martin, Scorsese isolates a noir figure that is paradoxically a sign of the referential and proceeds to elaborate its "meaning" potential. As the narrative proceeds, Cady proves himself a confidence-man who deftly manipulates the Bowdens.

Refracting the cineaste himself, Cady communicates through texts (he at one point even leaves for Danny a copy of Henry Miller's *Sexus*). Although the elaborate tattoo which covers Cady's back ostensibly installs the Bible as transcendental "Truth," his other tattoos consist largely of decontextualized and openly manipulated scriptural quotations ("Vengeance is mine," for example) which belie this assertion. MacDonald's Sam Bowden faces a Cady who "looks like he's got muscles they haven't named yet"; Scorsese's Police Chief Dutton (Robert Mitchum) says, upon beholding the "walking hieroglyph"[25] of 1991, "I don't know whether to look at him or read him." Sacred language is in fact parodied throughout the film—as Cady engages in baffling tautologies with Danielle ("Do you know what paradise is? It's salvation."); and at the film's conclusion, the drowning Cady sings hymns and "speaks in tongues." It is also helpful to note in this context the lengthy scene in the high-school theater in which Cady virtually seduces Danny. Cady here coyly suggests that he is "from the black forest," an admission that might ostensibly ally him with his naturalistic predecessors. But the "black forest" of Scorsese's film is, after all, a theater set (the sequence in this sense looks something like Little Red Riding Hood vs. the "Big Bad Wolf"). This Cady is neither "missing link" with the primordial past nor an externalization of the libidinal unconscious; he is rather a walking tissue of quotations from anterior texts.

Conversely, an "unspeakable" Cady serves as the linchpin for the first two versions; both the nuclear family unit and the alienated self depend upon an external force which will guarantee their differential identity. Danny Bowden's own attempted domestic melodrama fails precisely because Scorsese and Strick render in Cady a figure not only "unrealized" or "flattened," but also a projection of the entity which it is meant to oppose; "Whereas the 1962 evil stalked the Bowden family from without, the threat is now to be found within."[26] Sam at one point significantly complains to Kersek, "I don't know whether he's inside or outside." Such confusion readily translates into *Cape Fear*'s erosion of oppositions. Negative imaging not only implies that Scorsese's remake "contains its own negative image,"[27] but also manages to suggest a reversal of binaries. The reappearance of Mitchum and Peck, in roles contrary to their originals, likewise playfully recognizes the instability of identity. But the paramount example of self-loss in the film has to do with the central figure of Sam Bowden, who comes to resemble his nemesis, Max Cady. Despite Bowden's vehement protestations, Cady insists that they are "colleagues" in the law. Sam also exercises Cady's brand of explosive violence: on the racquetball court with Lori, whom Cady later brutally rapes[28]; against his own daughter, in reprisal for her "tryst" with Cady; and in the final sequence, against Cady himself. The film's conclusion in some sense underscores Sam's loss of alienated identity. Having failed to finish Cady, Sam finds his hands covered with blood, an effect that does not recall the "damn'd spot"of Lady Macbeth[29] so much as the stigmata of Christ. Rinsing his bloody hands, Sam is left in a yet more dejected attitude than when he discovered the stains, for he has been denied the role of alienated martyr.

The dissolution of Cady as authentic Other undoes Danny's recuperative domestic melodrama. Cady's unrealization gives way to that of Sam, whose central assignment as "father" guarantees the individual identity within the family of the melodramatic world. As Robin Wood recommends in a commentary on film melodrama, "The Father must here be understood in all senses, symbolic, literal, potential: patriarchal authority (the Law), which assigns all other elements to their correct, subordinate, allotted roles...."[30] We may locate the moment of Sam's failure as an authority figure in the argument with Leigh about his fidelity; although he tries to muster a cohesive response to Cady ("I keep feeling there's some animal out there stalking us; ... we can beat that son-of-a-bitch, the two of us together, working as a team"); his wife cynically replies, "You're really scared, aren't you? Somebody finally got through to you." We next see Sam banished to the living room couch. De Niro's diffused, "new-and-unimproved" Cady cannot, in this instance, inspire a terror commensurate with a fragmented family in which the mother believes "they switched babies on me at the hospital." Scorsese concludes with an image of the Bowdens once more "huddled together," this time on the banks of the Cape Fear River; but, as Danny's mechanical epilogue implies, theirs is a cohesion based on deliberate repression: "We never spoke about what happened, at least to each other...." Glossing the "crucial shift" accomplished in *Cape Fear*, Žižek argues that "what gets lost is precisely the remainder of an outside" (208–9)—an apt designation for the delimiting referential that noir conserves. *Cape Fear* is perhaps most obviously a characteristic Scorsese production in that it persistently references not some free-standing existential reality, but other cinematic and literary texts, traditions, and conventions—thereby eroding the possibility of the crucial "remainder of an outside."

THE CON MAN'S will to power would become even more apparent in two mid-1990s films noirs—*The Usual Suspects* and *Seven*. Working within clearly discernible noir formulae, each of these films dramatizes the shift from existential heroism to intertextual manipulation. As with Scorsese's *Cape Fear*, these films have been greeted with an ambivalent critical response—a reception typified by Foster Hirsch's remarks in *Detours and Lost Highways: A Map of Neo-Noir*. For Hirsch, *The Usual Suspects* deploys "genre conventions like voiceover, labyrinthine plotting, spatial and temporal ruptures" in the service of "a commentary on noir resources, a cunning masterful meta-noir." But Hirsch qualifies his praise by suggesting that these sophisticated devices hamstring a film which "ends up being about nothing other than its own admirable, if finally hollow, ingenuity" (287). In my view, such criticism is more suited to Lynch's films noirs than to *The Usual Suspects,* which offers an education not only in noir conventions, but also in the worldview purported by these tactics. We have seen that while many revisionist noirs target specific cinematic pretexts, others elicit memories of Hollywood genres and subgenres that proved fertile ground for the noir logic. Hirsch's dismissive comments belie the importance of the heist or "caper" formula conventionally centered on a protagonist faced with the Sisyphean task of coordinating a complicated criminal operation. As John Cawelti notes, the caper formula has its origins in the ancient tale of the Trojan Horse, which dramatizes "a very clever stratagem involving a carefully trained group of men and a major piece of equipment in a skillfully coordinated sequence of actions, subject to the dangers of discovery and mistake, but, when successful, resulting in a feat of great importance that had earlier seemed impossible."[31] Endemic to the missions, secret and otherwise, of war fiction and film, caper stories find similar application in the universe of crime. This resilient form proves constructive especially when the operation fails. But however bleak, the noir heist film endows its human subject with grandeur and authenticity. Although noir protagonists seldom "pull off" the caper, they retain the existential lucidity, determination, or, more importantly, definition which marks the noir subject. Kubrick's *The Killing* exemplifies the ways in which semidocumentary techniques—on-location shooting and voice-of-god narration—convey and normalize authenticating alienation: as Telotte points out, "They draw on our tendency to valorize the real and on the authority of the seemingly objective, detached vantage we normally associate with the scientific method to qualify their treatment of a sordid subject matter" (137).

Singer and McQuarrie repeat the noir heist motif, but they move beyond ludic reiteration for the "de-doxifying" critique that Hutcheon ascribes to revolutionary postmodernism. Beginning with an existentialist drama centered on Dean Keaton (Gabriel Byrne), *The Usual Suspects,* like its malleable narrator, metamorphoses into a reflexive meditation on the process of fiction-making itself. The first phases of the film in a sense read as a eulogy for the departed figure of the noir antihero. After an opening sequence in which Keaton is murdered aboard a San Pedro freighter, the suggestively named Verbal (Kevin Spacey), questioned by Customs Agent Dave Kujan (Charles Palminteri), enters into an elegiac narrative about the rise and fall of the titular criminals. Harassed by the police over a hijacking, Keaton, McManus (Stephen Baldwin), Todd Hockney (Kevin Pollock), Fenster (Benecio DelToro), and Verbal bond against the authorities: "And that was how it began. The five of us brought in on a trumped-up charge to be leaned on by half-wits. What the cops never figured out, and what I know now, was that these men would never break, never lie down, never bend over for anybody . . . Anybody." Among this band of outsiders, Keaton emerges as the most Satanic of the lot: this fallen cop receives the worst beating and later proves a catalyst for the gang. As we shall see, the corrupt cop formula is itself a noir fixture caught up within the larger thematics of existential regeneration. Having insulted their interrogators and, in one of the film's most celebrated scenes, mocked the ritualistic lineup, these antiheroes ultimately pull off a devastating revenge caper that exposes the corruption of the NYPD. As Ernest Larsen has it, "The suspects begin to look like the best kind of victims: the kind that courageously refuse to be victimized" (26).

This defiant spirit persists into the central plot-line of *The Usual Suspects,* in which the criminals, having bested the authorities, lock horns with the underworld of Keyser Soze. Though much more competent than the police, the shadowy Soze initially appears yet another form of institutional power that opposes our populist gang of thieves. He is after all represented by the starched and corporate Kobayashi (Pete Postlethwaite), through whom he demonstrates an omniscience worthy of a government intelligence agency. Kobayashi informs the suspects that they've been unwittingly indebted to Soze for years and that the bill has finally come due. He offers the team a chance to clear the slate by hijacking an Argentinian drug deal in San Pedro. The ensuing office-building sequence mirrors the earlier climactic episode in which the suspects rip off New York's Finest Taxi Service: posing as maintenance men, Keaton and Co. murder Kobayashi's bodyguards—a brutal refusal of Soze's coercive proposition. However promising, this gesture of humanistic resistance against the sterile world of late capitalism[32] falls flat when Kobayashi reveals that he has ensnared Edie Finneran (Suzy Amis) and may have her killed at any moment. With his lover held hostage, Keaton has no choice but to lead the gang into a pitched battle against Soze's rivals. Singer and McQuarrie hereby feint with an homage to films noirs such as *The Asphalt Jungle* and *The Killing,* in which Sterling Hayden plays a criminal suspended between the polarities of establishment and underworld. In this respect, *The Usual Suspects* entertains toward noir the same disposition that a film such as *The Wild Bunch* (Sam Peckinpah, 1969) entertains toward the western. "[F]or all its ugliness and violence," writes Cawelti, *The Wild Bunch* "is a more coherent example of the destruction and reaffirmation of myth. . . .

[T]he film leaves us with a sense that through their hopeless action these coarse and vicious outlaws have somehow transcended themselves and become embodiments of a myth of heroism that men need in spite of the realities of their world."[33]

If we take Verbal's narrative at face value, then the final conflagration sees Keaton and the gang "transcend themselves" to enter the world of mythic heroism. In the midst of this elegiac narrative, however, Singer and McQuarrie subtly transfer the emphasis from heist to confidence game and from humanistic realism to postmodernist parody. Even those elements that represent a straightforward reiteration of heist-noir are peppered with clues to the film's disturbing reflexivity. In addition to the comical lineup—undoubtedly a centerpiece of performativity—, there is a general sense of theatricality about the film as well as persistent allusions to mass and popular culture which encourage the viewer toward reflection about radically different orders of knowledge and experience. In other words, like many noirs of the 1990s, *The Usual Suspects* demands familiarity with everything from the Kennedy assassination to "Old MacDonald" and *The Incredible Hulk*. These kinds of devices undercut the gravity of noir heist films; but an even more radical alienation effect awaits the viewer at the conclusion of *The Usual Suspects*. Accomplishing one of the most notable surprise endings in film history, Singer and McQuarrie ultimately reveal in the final moments of the film the fact that Verbal has taken advantage of found materials to bamboozle the arrogant Agent Kujan. Beginning with credible facts, Verbal carefully constructs a narrative that allows him to escape Kujan's grasp. Verbal therefore reads as a reinscription of the heist mastermind more remarkable for his narrative acumen than for his organizational skill; as his nickname suggests, Verbal "talks too much" (18). Put a different way, Verbal represents the confidence man's displacement of the humanistic subject of conventional noir. As Kujan's coffee cup smashes on the floor, we are treated to a montage that reveals Verbal's artistry; but rather than simply asserting the con man's preeminence, Singer and McQuarrie take this pivotal moment as an opportunity to illuminate the ways in which representation itself may be understood as a confidence game perpetrated upon the reader/viewer.[34]

Far from naturalizing a reality, *The Usual Suspects* bares the constructive machinery by which a reality is generated. More particularly, the film exposes "insignificant notation" and Orientalism as two tactics fundamental to western modes of representation. Verbal's most dramatic strategy lies in "the reality effect" that he manages as he is questioned in the office of his colleague Sargeant Rabin (Dan Hedaya). Our first perspective of Rabin's office reveals a cluttered bulletin-board conspicuous in McQuarrie's scene description: "It is a breathtaking disaster of papers, wanted posters, rap-sheets, memos and post-its. This is in the neighborhood of decades. Rabin is a man with a system so cryptic, so far beyond the comprehension of others, he himself is most likely baffled by it" (23). More than a plot device, this collage suggests the broader textual fund from which Verbal "knits" (this anagram perhaps accounts for the unusual spelling of Verbal's surname) a story for Kujan. In its profusion, the bulletin board insinuates a universe consisting not of referentials, but rather a bricolage of overlapping texts—"practices, discourses, and textual play," as Jameson would have it. A master bricoleur, Verbal appropriates random signifiers lying about Rabin's office (we see him scan the room carefully upon entrance)—Skokie Quartet, Kobayashi, Redfoot, Guatemala—and writes them into his own story. Verbal's digression about the "Skokie Quartet" serves to illustrate the consequent reality effect. Kujan dismisses the obscure detail in Verbal's criminal past as "totally irrelevant"; but in its very triviality, the aside comprises part of the "concrete details" that certify the narrative.

The prominent character of Kobayashi is likewise drawn from the textual reservoir of Rabin's office; but he emerges as part of the representational tactic of Orientalism. As we have seen, hard-boiled fiction and film noir exemplify the ways in which western culture imagines for itself "a great Asiatic mystery" to be studied, judged, and disciplined. Said also points out that Orientalism is, like Barthes's reality effect, "a form of radical realism": "Anyone employing Orientalism, which is a habit for dealing with questions, objects, qualities, and regions deemed Oriental, will designate, name, point to, fix what he is talking or thinking about with a word or phrase, which then is considered either to have acquired, or more simply to be, reality."[35] Just as insignificant notation generates a "referential illusion," Orientalism exploits cultural memories of the East and, in turn, normalizes their reception. Not surprisingly, these two realist strategies work in tandem: the surrounding canvas of innocent detail camouflages the more properly allusive function of Orientalism. One reviewer notes that the character of Kobayashi recalls "Gielgud playing Chang the Deputy Lama in *Lost Horizon*."[36] Kobayashi's strange, theatrical appearance belies the authenticity of Verbal's account. And whether Verbal is cued by his notice of the word "Kobayashi" to embark upon a more dramatically Orientalist vein of narration or simply and opportunistically accommodates the name to a preconceived motif, this unlikely figure ushers in his rendition of the Oriental mastermind, Keyser Soze: "He is supposed to be Turkish. Some say his father was German. Nobody believed he was real. Nobody ever saw him or knew anybody that ever worked directly for him.

But to hear Kobayashi tell it, anybody could have worked for Soze. You never knew. That was his power." Adumbrating Verbal's own ruse, this last phrase interprets the figure of Keyser Soze as mysterious, ineffable, threatening, and altogether consistent with the workings of Orientalism. Verbal culls Soze not from Rabin's cluttered office, but from the archive of criminal lore. The wily con man capitalizes upon Soze's supposed Eastern origins to paint a character replete with Orientalist associations. The surreal flashback that accompanies his account of the Soze myth—the hazily shot interior of Soze's home, itself festooned with Persian rugs, is more reminiscent of a Eugène Delacroix painting (*The Death of Sardanapalus*, perhaps, given the circumstances) than a realist crime drama. This portion of the sequence may indeed recall the Orientalism that came to pervade European painting throughout the nineteenth century. Even as we are subjected to a shot of the Hungarian raping Soze's wife, the camera pans to a painting of a reclining odalisque—an image that underscores the Orientalism of Verbal's narrative and forces a juxtaposition of text and referent. Soze's murder of his own violated family, and the subsequent mass killings, recollect the extravagant violence historically ascribed to the Orient: "He kills their kids, he kills their wives, he kills their parents and their parents' friends. . . . He burns down the houses they live in and the stores they work in, he kills people that owe them money. And like that he was gone. Underground. No one has ever seen him again. He becomes a myth, a spook story that criminals tell their kids at night." Soze emerges from this hyperbolic history a composite of Ghengis Khan and Fu Manchu, a reification of the conventional Oriental criminal mastermind. Trusting his bed of insignificant notation, Verbal elaborates the Soze myth (Arkosh Kovash has introduced Soze outside Verbal's narrative frame), in itself perhaps too fantastic to persuade Kujan. But here again, we witness a transition from the irrational suggested in the exotic to the subtle processes by which the realist text appropriates, exploits, and naturalizes incumbent cultural mythologies.

The film's conclusion intensifies its challenge to the noir ethos. In heist films such as *The Asphalt Jungle*, the ringleader fails to pull off the caper, but remains coherent in his struggle against an indifferent universe. Throughout the course of the narrative, Verbal has appeared the antithesis of the noir protagonist. Given to talk rather than violent action, Verbal also physically departs from the tough, monadic body of hard-boiled antiheroes such as Sterling Hayden's Johnny Clay and, indeed, Gabriel Byrne's Dean Keaton. Kujan all but declares this opposition as he assures Verbal that Keaton has duped and exploited him: "He saved you because he wanted it that way. It was his will . . . Keaton was Keyser Soze. . . . The kind of guy who could wrangle the wills of men like Hockney and McManus. The kind of man who could engineer a police line-up from all his years of contacts in N.Y.P.D. He used all of you to get him on that boat. He couldn't get on alone and he had to pull the trigger himself to make sure he got his man." The final shots of the film see a radical reversal of these apparent certainties. Verbal leaves the station one of the doomed suspects; he refuses to believe that his hero Keaton has betrayed him and he remains at once terrified and defiant of the dual threat posed by establishment and underworld. But even as Kujan realizes his error, Verbal undergoes a dramatic transformation, shedding his limp and using his once paralyzed hand to deftly light a cigarette. The point here is neither a return to the "normal" body—one that aligns physical and psychic autonomy—nor the certain identification of Verbal as Keyser Soze. Against the spectacularly alienated protagonists of heist noir, Singer and McQuarrie leave us with a shape-shifting "pretzel man."

RELEASED ON THE HEELS of *The Usual Suspects* in 1995, David Fincher's *Seven* sees Kevin Spacey return to the screen as a serial killer who preaches a deadly sermon against his immoral society. John Doe patterns each of his murders upon one the seven deadly sins, ultimately inscribing his pursuer Detective Mills (Brad Pitt) and himself into the text of the grisly sermon. A self-avowed jeremiadist, Doe should also be understood a reiteration of the deconstructive confidence man inimical to noir's authenticating alienation. In its setting and three principal characters—Mills, Somerset (Morgan Freeman), and Doe—*Seven* presents a spectrum of figures that straddles the divide between modern and postmodern noir. *Seven*'s urban setting impresses many critics as an almost reflexive evocation of the noir dystopia. Hirsch, for example, describes this nameless metropolis as "the most richly rendered symbolic space to date in the history of neo-noir[,] . . . a stylized *re*-presentation of the crime-filled, studio-built, dark city of classic noir, a place of ramshackle, derelict buildings with murky brown hallways and cluttered warrenlike rooms into which light and air never penetrate" (281). Richard Dyer likewise notes the film's careful "oligochromatic" adherence to a narrow range of muted colors and its rain-soaked mise-en-scène, which at once symbolizes human sin and alludes to pretexts such as *Blade Runner* and *The Terminator* (62). For Steffen Hantke, the city of *Seven* "is simply a noir icon, stripped of all geographic and cultural specificity," which, in concert with the rural setting of the conclusion, "functions as a metatextual nod toward the noir tradition."[37] In short, just as John Doe exploits this infernal city as a perfect stage for his dramaturgical sermon,[38] Fincher and screenwriter Andrew Kevin Walker find in their setting a ready means of situating *Seven* within noir conventions and foreshadowing the way in which the film will undermine noir's concomitant realism and authenticating alienation. John Doe is therefore not only a serial killer and a preacher but also a confidence man whose homiletic murders become an all-consuming text.

As Dyer points out, *Seven* turns upon a biracial "buddy cop" formula that recalls *Deadly Pursuit* and the *Die Hard*, and *Lethal Weapon* films, all of which reverse the stereotypes of white rationality and black libidinality (Dyer 24). Fincher and Walker scramble the variables present in these films: while the white detective Mills is at once domestic and impulsively violent, Somerset emerges as a calm and reflective isolato. I would suggest that the most important distinction between Mills and Somerset is not simply a psychic duality between libido and superego (assignments that stretch back beyond the 1980s to buddy detective films such as *Private Hell 36* [Don Siegel, 1954], and *Stray Dog* [Akira Kurosawa, 1949]), but rather the varying degrees of semiotic perspicacity adopted by each of these policemen. If Mills has unreflectively constructed himself as an embattled noir hero, then Somerset exhibits a level of hermeneutic savvy that enables him to retain his subjectivity against John Doe's sophisticated assault. The first conversation between Mills and Somerset reveals that the ambitious detective has sought transfer from "a nice quiet town" to the urban force. Despite his altruistic professions ("maybe I thought I could do more good here than there"), this self-styled "Serpico" understands himself in terms of violent confrontation with a world of crime and corruption.[39] In a revealing anecdote, Mills confides to Somerset that he has remorselessly killed a suspect: "I expected it to be bad, you know. I took a human life . . . but I slept like a baby that night. I never gave it a second thought." As the film proceeds, we come to see Mills as abusive, insensitive, homophobic, and anti-intellectual.[40] In terms of discernible noir pretexts, Mills clearly derives from figures such as Carrol John Daly's Race Williams, Mickey Spillane's Mike Hammer, and Don Siegel's Dirty Harry Callahan (Clint Eastwood)—detectives who eschew cerebral activity in favor of brutal action. This opposition is clearly registered in the presentation of Mills's body; the more physically active of the duo, Mills is increasingly battered and bloodied. As with almost all noir protagonists, however, such contusions only serve to underscore a subject locked in combat with his environment.

No less alienated than Mills, Somerset recalls Chandler's Phillip Marlowe rather than Mike Hammer. At the beginning of the narrative, we find Somerset in his final week of police work, anticipating retirement to a home in the country. Methodical, reflective, and erudite, he appears all too sensitive to the human suffering engendered within the metropolis; like Marlowe, Somerset wages a lonely war against the absurd and retreats from the world's chaos into the sanctuary of his apartment, where he soothes himself with the regular cadence of a metronome. But even as he reiterates the "slumming angel"[41] of noir, Somerset also has one foot in the metafictional universe of postmodernism. His name, for example, obviously alludes to modernist writer M. Somerset Maugham, whose existential questers stand as distant pretexts for Freeman's character. When in the course of their investigation Somerset and Mills touch upon *Of Human Bondage* ("It's not what you think it is," Somerset assures his partner), the allusion becomes overwrought, broaching the ludic excess signification common to postmodernist parodies of noir minimalism. The very hermeneutic nature of Somerset's investigative tactics likewise elicits postmodernist concerns; as he delves into library records and reads in Doe's medieval pretexts, Somerset begins to resemble a detective from the pages of Pynchon and Borges rather than any noir detective. In one of the most lyrical moments in *Seven,* Somerset demonstrates his traverse of modern and postmodern literary modes: "We write everything down and note what time things happened. . . . We put it in a nice neat pile and file it away, on the slim chance it's ever needed in a courtroom. It's like collecting diamonds on a desert island. You keep them just in case you ever get rescued, but it's a pretty big ocean out there." When Mills pronounces this nuanced observation "Bullshit," Somerset concludes, "I'm, sorry, but even the most promising clues usually lead only to other clues. I've seen so many corpses rolled away unrevenged." With its images of isolation and futility, the remark most certainly conjures the task of the hard-boiled detective. But here is also an attention to interpretation and signification: the detectives' job is to assemble a text that will, as Somerset goes on to suggest, "play well in a courtroom." Like John Doe himself, Somerset recognizes the dependency of identity upon representation and this awareness renders him a fit adversary for the malevolent con man John Doe.

As evinced in texts such as *Nightmare Alley* and *The Grifters,* the confidence man is transformed within the noir imagination from rhetorician into neurotic. *Seven* reverses this dynamic, seizing upon the serial killer—a sign of psychological deviance—and translating that figure into the signfying con man. In the enigmatic character of John Doe, Fincher and Walker skirt psychology for a direct counterpoint to the worldview asserted by hard-boiled fiction and film noir. Even before the 1957 arrest of Ed Gein returned the serial killer to national prominence, films noirs such as *D.O.A., The Night of the Hunter,* and *Dark City* (William Dieterle, 1957), had foregrounded the "homicidal maniac" as a locus of irrational or libidinal forces that confront the protagonist. Other noirs, including *M* (Joseph Losey, 1951), *Without Warning!* (Arnold Laven, 1952), *The Sniper*

(Edward Dmytryk, 1960), and *Dirty Harry* would elaborate this gesture, elevating the serial killer proper into a representation of criminal pathology. As Eileen McGarry observes of the latter film, "Crime is not seen as a social phenomenon; rather all crimes and all criminals are equated with the psychotic Scorpio Killer" (92). From its first images, *Seven* undertakes a revision of this noir convention: the title sequence finds Doe pouring over his journal, an amalgam of handwritten scrawl, typewritten text, and photographs of mutilated bodies. While the introductory montage unquestionably suggests the killer's murderous obsession, here is also a foreshadowing of the way in which Doe generates a homiletic text that consumes his victims. As Mills realizes, "He's preaching," Somerset replies, "These murders are his masterwork. His sermon to all of us." Doe hereby constructs a homily that eradicates not only the life but also the identity of each victim, transcribing the unfortunate into an allegorical symbol of the sin in question. Doe is also repeatedly characterized as a performance artist who transforms bodies into sculptures; the crime-scenes themselves become discrete texts, legible spaces resembling art installations (Dyer 45–46). In one of the most telling moments of the film, Mills and Somerset discover this artist's "studio." While Mills charges about the apartment, Somerset wanders into Doe's archive where he finds two thousand notebooks. As he peruses the graphomaniac's hand, he realizes the implications of this evidence cache: "If we had fifty men, reading in 24 hour shifts, it would still take two months." As in postmodernist fictions such as *The Crying of Lot 49*, *Seven* inverts the modernist search for meaning; like Oedipa Maas, Mills faces the problem of delimiting a superabundance of textual material that threatens to subsume self and world.

Doe's role as an agent of excess signification becomes all too clear in the climactic sequence of the film. As Mills and Somerset drive John Doe into the desert, the killer explains the logic behind his jeremiad: "We see a deadly sin on every street corner, in every home. And we tolerate it. We tolerate it because it's common, it's trivial. We tolerate it morning, noon and night. Well, not anymore. I'm setting the example, and what I've done is going to be puzzled over and studied and followed, forever." Preeminently concerned with hermeneutics, Doe hopes not only to preach a sermon that defamiliarizes sin, but, perhaps more importantly, to create a self-perpetuating text that will ever absorb its readers. The short-term effect of the text is certainly the absorption of Mills and Doe himself. Doe writes himself into the sermon, murdering and decapitating the pregnant Tracy Mills (Gwyneth Paltrow) in a gesture of "Envy" for the detective's cozy domestic life. This master stroke also proves a mechanism for luring Mills into the text: shooting Doe, he abnegates himself to become the embodiment of "Wrath." Read against a film such as *Dirty Harry*, this stark development thoroughly subverts the noir protagonist; the vigilantism by which these figures stave off an entropic world becomes a means of destroying this alienated subjectivity. Although he does not physically perish, Mills, like Scottie in Hitchcock's *Vertigo,* has lost his psyche to the con man's machinations—dumb and devastated, he faces certain institutionalization. But what of Somerset, the detective who has all along exhibited dangerous affinities with Doe's hypertextual world? During the terrible ordeal in the desert, Somerset vainly admonishes Mills, "If you kill him, He wins." Yet more telling, however, is the film's final line, in which Somerset observes: "Ernest Hemingway once wrote, 'The world is a fine place and worth fighting for.' I agree with the second part." While Somerset's quotation of *For Whom the Bell Tolls* may have been a concession to producers' desires for a "crumb of Hollywoodian comfort,"[42] the line may indeed be read as an appropriate response to Doe's attack on noir worldview. Witnessing the absorption of Mills into Doe's sermon, Somerset invokes Hemingway as an almost talismanic guarantor of authenticating alienation. Somerset will now forgo retirement to his pastoral retreat; Mills's fate has reminded him that he owes his identity to the solitary crusade on behalf of this not so fine place.

CHRISTOPHER NOLAN's *Memento* posits a resolution to the crisis of films such as *The Usual Suspects* and *Seven.* While recognizing the way in which the conventional noir protagonist has been undone by the con man, *Memento* proceeds to dramatize the synthesis of these two antithetical figures. Nolan takes for his antihero a highly recognizable noir character: Leonard Shelby (Guy Pearce) is an insurance investigator stricken with anterograde amnesia. From what we can discern of this necessarily hazy back story, Leonard has suffered a violent attack that claimed the life of his wife and deprived him of short-term memory. While Leonard retains distant recollections of his former life, he cannot "make new memories." Faced with this terrifying dilemma, Leonard assembles a portable archive that enables him to pursue his sole purpose of revenge against the culprit known only as James or John G. Consisting of handwritten notes and Polaroid photographs, this archive is most dramatically "embodied" in a pastiche of tattoos that adorn Leonard's form: inscribed in contrasting styles by different tattooists, these messages variously remind Leonard to "Find him," advise him that "Memory is Treachery," and provide a record of "the facts" of his quest. Leornard also finds himself aided and/or obstructed by familiar noir figures such as ex-cop Teddy (Joe Pantoliano) and femme fatale Natalie (Carrie-Anne Moss), who at one point explains in excruciating detail her plot against Leonard, knowing that he will soon forget the admission.

The film's narrative tension arises from Leonard's persistent attempts to complete his mission in spite of sketchy information, his debilitating condition, and the threats posed by everyone he meets. In keeping with its generally reflexive tenor, *Memento* declares the self-constitutive function of Leonard's investigation: responding to Teddy's reminder "You're living," Leonard counters, "Just for revenge. That's what keeps me going. It's all I have." Through a deft manipulation of the amnesiac formula, Nolan steers *Memento* away from the possibilities of modernist self-realization and into the problematics of postmodernist self-construction. Whereas the earlier films posit some rupture of middle-class normality (most particularly amnesia) as an opportunity for authenticity and self discovery, *Memento* presents short-term memory loss as a means of dramatizing the fragility of the human subject.

Noting pretexts such as *Somewhere in the Night,* Richard Armstrong observes that "*Memento* is the logical end game of the amnesiac strain of film noir" (119); Nolan does aggressively pursue the implications of noir amnesia, but he does so in a way contrary to his modernist predecessors. *Memento* recalls not only *Somewhere in the Night, The Blue Dahlia,* and *Double Indemnity,* as Armstrong suggests, but also romans noirs such as David Goodis's *Nightfall* (1947) and Richard Neely's *Shattered* (1969). Such texts follow the pattern in which some disruption of normality proves strangely fortuitous, inaugurating a drama of self-realization. In Neely's novel, for example, narrative conflict emerges from the protagonist's struggle to rediscover identity: "A fragmented memory began to form. For a split instant the pieces darted together like metal fittings homing to a magnet. Then they fell apart."[43] As Žižek argues, "Classical . . . *noirs* abound with cases of amnesia in which the hero does not know who he is or what he did during his blackout. . . . [A] successful recollection means that, by way of organizing his life-experience into a consistent narrative, the hero exorcises the dark demons of the past. . . . "[44] Preservation of short-term memories, however, is precisely what enables noir amnesiacs to investigate themselves. Nolan inverts this scenario and in doing so propels *Memento* into the dilemma of the floating signifier. In a revealing conversation with Teddy, Leonard postulates that his notes on "the facts" transcend interpretation: "Facts, not memories: that's how you investigate. I know, it's what I used to do. Memory can change the shape of a room or the color of a car. It's an interpretation, not a record. Memories can be changed or distorted and they're irrelevant if you have the facts." This hermeneutic is belied, however, by his later recommendation, "You might catch a sign and attach the wrong meaning to it. . . . It's all about context"—an assertion against the objectivity of raw data. Leonard's struggle to maintain a stable collection of facts dramatizes the contextual nature of experience and the consequent instability of identity. Even the most immediate data assume new meanings as Leonard sloughs and replaces short-term memories; facts notwithstanding, Leonard must continually reinterpret his data with new interpretations derived from direct experience. One of the most telling subplots in this respect is Leonard's confrontation with Dodd (Callum Keith Rennie). When the drug-dealer accosts Leonard because he is wearing the clothes and driving the Jaguar belonging to rival pusher Jimmy Grantz (Larry Holden), the two engage in a running battle within which pursuer and pursued continually exchange places. As he finds himself inexplicably running through a trailer park, Leonard wonders, "What the fuck am I doing?" Glimpsing Dodd, he assumes "Chasing him!" The tables turn again, however, when Leonard sees Dodd approach with a gun: "FUCK! He's chasing me." The scenario will later repeat itself when Leonard attempts to ambush Dodd in his motel room, which proves the worst tactic for a man in Leonard's position. As we shall see, the central tension of *Memento* lies not in the conventional mystery formula of investigation and solution, but rather in the protagonist's contention for the right of self-fashioning. Nolan punctuates this thematic of contextualization by placing the viewer in Leonard's unfortunate predicament, for we too are deprived of the contexts by which we might make sense of the events paraded before us. William G. Little recommends that this narrative structure makes for a traumatic filmgoing ordeal: "The film's unusual formal construction certainly unsettles viewer expectations of temporal continuity and coherence, expectations shaped by mainstream Hollywood cinema's commitment to linear narrative" (67).

In this vertiginous film, Nolan conjures the penultimate noir phantasm, a nightmare registered on one hand by Leonard's conspicuous tattooing. For Little, the motley collection of ink is at odds with itself, representing at once Leonard's attempt to exoticize and distance himself from a mechanized world and yet "compulsively model" the very disciplinary practices from which he wishes to escape by inscribing himself with bits of typographical information (80–81). Robert Avery, on the other hand, argues that the tattoos suggests white masculinity rather than the exotic: "To look at Leonard's body, to see the tattoos, is to see his whiteness" (35). At the same time, however, Avery recognizes the tattooed form as an "abject body . . . permeable, blemished, without 'subject boundaries'" (11). These observations appear all the more persuasive when we take into account the significance of tattooing within the noir imagination. As we have seen, hard-boiled fiction and film noir locate the tattoo as a sign of abjection and excess signification. For Hammett's Continental Op, tattoos conjure the corporeal and psychic violence of the colonial periphery. In *Nightmare Alley*, William Lindsay Gresham likewise figures the heavily tattooed body as a dangerously abysmal text, a scapegoat for the disturbing implications of the confidence man. Postmodernist noir exploits these earlier associations; Martin Scorsese underscores his portrait of the terroristic con man Max Cady by memorably clothing this villain in allusive tattoos. More recently, K. W. Jeter literalizes the floating signifier and subjective dissolution by imagining autonomous, animated tattoos. Like the figure of the confidence man, tattoos posit for noir protagonists the twin horror of physical puncture—violation of the hard-boiled body—and the subjugation of that body to unstable significations. Nolan's portrait of Leonard Shelby therefore reads as a climactic example of "tattoo noir," for this figure sees the uninhibited inscription of the noir body. Leonard may intend his tattoo collection as an adjunct to his role as hard-boiled detective,[45] a hedge against short-term memory loss and anonymity, but this tactic only exacerbates his predicament. Leonard must not only negotiate a world of unstable signs; he *is himself* an unstable sign open to constant reinterpretation.[46]

Yet more unsettling than Leonard's pervasive tattooing is his vulnerability to manipulation. It is altogether appropriate that Leonard has formerly worked as an insurance investigator; as suggested in the complex digression about Sammy Jankis (Stephen Tobolowsky), Leonard was, like Barton Keyes in Cain's *Double Indemnity* (1936) or Jim Reardon (Edmond O'Brien) in *The Killers* (Robert Siodmak, 1946), devoted to discovering frauds and "arresting" the dynamic self of the confidence man. Whether or not Sammy was himself a con man faking anterograde memory dysfunction, as Teddy insists, Leonard has suffered a cruel reversal, for he is now a perpetual "mark" in a world of grifters. Teddy claims to have conned Leonard for his own benefit; he purports to be an ex-cop who provides Leonard an inexhaustible context for being and satisfaction:

> I was the cop assigned to your wife's case. . . . I thought you deserved a chance for revenge. I'm the one that helped you find the other guy in your bathroom that night. The guy that cracked your skull and fucked your wife. We found him, you killed him. But you didn't remember, so I helped you start looking again, looking for the guy you already killed. . . . I gave you a reason to live, and you were more than happy to help. You don't want the truth. You make up your own truth. . . . You, you wander around, you're playing detective. You're living in a dream kid. A dead wife to pine for. A sense of purpose to your life.

In this formulation, Leonard and Teddy collaborate toward a narrative of authenticating alienation which will cohere a damaged self. Like Pynchon,

Auster, and Jeter, Nolan recognizes the noir ethos as an intervention into identity crisis. But Teddy is not so altruistic as he claims, in that he conscripted this unfortunate as a personal hit-man. It turns out that Teddy travels about with his unwitting partner, encouraging him to murder "JG's" (like Natalie's drug-dealing boyfriend Jimmy Grantz) and then absconding with their ill-gotten gains. While Teddy is undoubtedly the most prominent con man in *Memento*, he is joined by opportunists such as Natalie: she sadistically abuses Leonard and hopes to exploit him as a weapon against her boyfriend's rival Dodd. "I'm gonna use you," she declares, "I'm telling you because I'll enjoy it more if I know that you could stop me if you weren't a freak." Although this plot fails, it reiterates Leonard's susceptibility to opportunists; he even falls prey to Burt (Mark Boone Junior), the motel clerk who charges him for two rooms. Incapable of forming new memories, Leonard reads as a noir hero degraded to renewable resource for the con man's operations. *Seven*'s John Doe successfully coopts the vengeful Detective Mills for his definitive jeremiad, but Teddy exploits Leonard in an open-ended series of cons.

Teddy assures Leonard that his search for John G. is a "romantic quest that you wouldn't end even if I wasn't in the picture." The line foreshadows the film's resolution of the conflict between noir protagonist and confidence man. It is fitting that these climactic scenes transpire amid the looming fuel tanks of an abandoned refinery, a setting reminiscent of pivotal moments in *White Heat* (Raoul Walsh, 1949), *D.O.A.*, and *Touch of Evil*; the industrial wasteland here again becomes an arena for the grim struggle between self and world. But Nolan rehearses the archetypal noir confrontation with a critical difference. Refusing the authenticating alienation of these earlier films, Nolan does return some measure of agency to a damaged subject. In the final sequence, Nolan provides a context for the opening scene in which Leonard kills Teddy. We now understand that Leonard, in a moment of lucidity, condemns Teddy as one of the John G's that he must eradicate. Following Teddy's revelatory speech, Leonard reflects "I'm not a killer. I'm just someone who wanted to make things right. . . . Do I lie to myself to be happy? In your case, Teddy, yes, I will." He burns the photo of Jimmy's corpse and captions Teddy's snapshot with the fatal warning "Don't believe his lies." The stage is now set for the hard-boiled hero's violent ejection of the con man and his reclamation of a fragile subjectivity. With this gesture, Nolan reworks the revenge plot that anchors noirs such as *D.O.A.* and *I, the Jury*. Unlike vigilantes Frank Bigelow and Mike Hammer, however, Leonard cannot simply and innocently assume the role of the dogged existential hero "who wanted to make things right" by meting out personal justice; this plot line has been exposed, along with noir ideology in general, as a "technology of the self." But while the execution of Teddy arises from his own nihilistic con game, this act holds dramatic meaning for Leonard in that he finally trumps the arch-enemy of noir. In order to accomplish this liberating gesture, Leonard must con himself; that is to say, he assumes the persona of both con man and mark. Driving away from his decisive encounter with Teddy (more pivotal, really, than the murder scene itself), Leonard engages in another of the film's more forthright philosophical reflections: "I have to believe in a world outside my own mind. I have to believe that my actions still have meaning even if I can't remember them. I have to believe that when my eyes are closed, the world's still here. Do I believe the world's still here? Is it still out there? Yeah. We all need mirrors to remind ourselves who we are. I'm no different." As Teddy recommends, the hunt for John G. provides an ongoing context within which Leonard's actions remain meaningful. Assured that he will forget this epiphany, Leonard may persist with his search for the elusive John G. In Baudrillard's terms, Leonard has "reaped the symbolic benefits of alienation, which is that the Other exists, and that otherness can fool you for the better or the worse."

"The self that has nothing to remember and nothing for which to hope," writes philosopher Calvin O. Schrag, "is a self whose identity stands in peril" (37). This utterance might serve as an epigraph for *Memento*, which recognizes in the noir ethos a story of human identity as it evolves under the contrapuntal worlds of modernism and postmodernism. To persist with Schrag's language, *Memento* exemplifies the ways in which the modernist subject of noir has "become a prime target for the protagonists of postmodernism." In films noirs of the 1990s, an arch-postmodernist protagonist, the signifying confidence man, takes for its central dupe the hard-boiled hero that represents "tendencies to construct a sovereign and monarchical self, at once sufficient and self-assured, finding metaphysical comfort in a doctrine of an immutable and indivisible self-identity." Just as Teddy harangues Leonard for maintaining a sense of purpose by "playing detective," the con man very generally exposes noir agonism as a self-constituitive strategy veiled in the tactics of realism. Literally embodying excess textuality, con artists such as Max Cady, Verbal Kint, and John Doe implicate the supposedly autonomous noir hero as "an accomplice in the utterances of speech acts and in the significations of language." If it weren't for *Memento*, we might assume that the existential hero of noir had been eclipsed and transformed by the confidence man into a nonsubject "simply dispersed into a panorama of radically diversified and changing language games." This threatening hermeneutic function explains the marked anxiety that attends the figure of the confidence man in noir fictions ranging from Hammett's Continental Op stories through Gresham's *Nightmare*

Alley and into Thompson's *The Grifters*. However tragic and destructive, Leonard Shelby ("Shall Be"?) sees the integration of the hard-boiled determination and rhetorical sophistication toward the end of subjective possibility; he represents a self that continually emerges from "stories in the making" (Schrag 26–27). Taken on its own, the ascendance of the confidence man in late-twentieth-century film noir may be interpreted as an aggressive strain of the nihilist postmodernism of cineastes such as David Lynch. I would suggest, however, that the constructivist vision of these films accompanies and illuminates a more redemptive vision of the noir hero as a "connected guy."

CONCLUSION

CONNECTED GUYS

THE RECONSTRUCTED SUBJECT OF 1990s FILM NOIR

> *When I introduce you, I'm gonna say, "This is a friend of mine." That means you're a "connected guy."*
> —Benjamin "Lefty" Ruggiero (Al Pacino), *Donnie Brasco* (Mike Newell, 1997)

Lefty's telling utterance in *Donnie Brasco* captures not only the peculiar relationship that develops between himself and Donnie (Johnny Depp), but also an important strand of postmodernist film noir. Even as many 1990s films foreground the dialectic between modernist noir quester and postmodernist con-man, another series "reconstructs" noir subjectivity, positing a self derived neither through authenticating alienation nor ludic signification, but rather through openly acknowledged networks of relationships. While the advent of the confidence man may be read as part of what Schrag terms "the continuing project of deconstructing the Cartesian doctrine of the sovereign subject," the crime films treated in this conclusive chapter reimagine identity so as to

> make possible the advential or supervenient presence of the other—the other not simply as other-for-me but as staking an ontological claim on my own subjectivity. The otherness of the other needs to be granted its intrinsic integrity, so that in seeing the face of the other and hearing the voice of the other I am *responding* to an exterior gaze and an exterior voice rather than carrying on a conversation with my alter ego. . . . I encounter the entwined discourse and action of the other and respond to it, and in this encounter and responding I effect a self-constitution, a constitution of myself, in the dynamic economy of being-with-others. (84)

Schrag acknowledges that this mode of identity has been "infected with the dehumanizing threats of racism and colonialism" (81). As we have seen, noir emerges from late-Victorian adventure to locate in others an adjunct to the subjectivity of the protagonist. Throughout the 1990s, however, noir has taken a different turn, evoking high-noir pretexts in order to celebrate "the dynamic economy of being-with-others." While Carl Franklin's *One False Move,* Quentin Tarantino's *Reservoir Dogs,* and Mike Newell's *Donnie Brasco* explore the inevitability of relational identity, *Bad Lieutenant, Things to Do in Denver When You're Dead,* and *Hard Eight* adopt diverse noir formulae in order to move away from authenticating alienation for a more frankly constructed human subjectivity: the hero migrates from hard-boiled alienation and insulation to open relationship with others.

HOWEVER EXCEPTIONAL, the "self in community" has occasionally shown itself throughout the alienated universe of film noir. "Buddy cop" noirs provide the most obvious break from noir isolation; while films such as *Private Hell 36* (as its title implies) and *Seven* dramatize the estrangement of two partners, the buddy cop formula generally distributes focalization between two protagonists who must cooperate toward a common goal. Under the direction of Akira Kurosawa and Sam Fuller, respectively, the detective pair moves beyond a celebration of teamwork to assume profound psychological and philosophical resonance. We might recall Kurosawa's *Stray Dog* (*Nora Inu,* 1946), a thriller set in post-WWII Tokyo. When eager rookie Det. Murakami (Toshiro Mifune) loses his Colt service automatic to a pickpocket, he must undertake a manhunt that will expunge his personal shame and save the public from a serial killer, a deranged war veteran named Yusa (Isao Kimura). The film could easily gravitate toward a conventional hard-boiled detective story in which Murakami pursues a lonely quest for the missing handgun. But even as *Stray Dog* evokes the anomie of postwar Japan, the film engages in a complex treatment of relational identity. As James Goodwin explains, Kurosawa adapted *Stray Dog* from his own unpublished novel inspired by Georges Simenon's police procedurals; but in contrast to the detached Maigret, Murakami experiences a deep identification with his quarry (63). He accomplishes this on one hand by exploiting the hard-boiled quest itself as a vehicle for exploration of subject-object relations. Harking back to the roots of the detective story, Murakami immerses himself in Yusa's psyche, reading his letters, interviewing his girlfriend, and in effect becoming a displaced veteran like the killer himself. Indeed, Murakami openly expresses his empathy for Yusa's alienation. The sense of relational subjectivity likewise emerges through Murakami's collaboration with a senior partner, Detective Sato

(Takashi Shimura). Patient and sympathetic, this seasoned policeman offers a counterpoint to Murakami's dangerous rashness and autonomy as well as his identification with the killer Yusa. In a tender sequence, Sato brings Murakami home to his family and we see here a vision of the world-weary detective as a figure derived from various coexistent networks and spheres. *Stray Dog* reaches its climax when Yusa wounds Sato, leaving Murakami to face the killer on his own. As the opponents struggle in a muddy field, their clothing becomes indistinguishable; affinities between the two are heightened by a crane-shot that aligns detective and criminal. With this film, Kurosawa offered the first buddy-cop film noir; the movie would be followed by productions such as *Dragnet*, which similarly integrated the conventions of hard-boiled detective fiction into the police procedural. *Stray Dog* is yet more distinctive, however, in its presentation of an alternative to the authenticating alienation of the noir ethos at large. Unlike his American counterparts, and indeed, unlike the hard-boiled ronin that Kurosawa himself adapted from Hammett in *Yojimbo* (1961), Murakami and Sato read as noir heroes who understand themselves not merely through agonistic confrontation, but rather in terms of relationships and communities.

Kurosawa would continue to contribute to the noir canon with *The Bad Sleep Well* (1960) and *High and Low* (1963); these pictures elaborate the auteur's vision of relational identity. He was joined in the 1950s, however, by another cineaste whose films challenged the alienated subjectivity of noir. As Grant Tracey argues, "Fuller's tabloid cinema" departs from noir existentialism by "providing a moral framework to his scenes. . . . Fuller often collides narrative modes and combines gritty story telling with a desire to move us beyond story . . . to larger discursive issues" (160, 173). Whether working within the Western genre in *Run of the Arrow* (1957), the war film in *The Steel Helmet* (1951) and *China Gate* (1957), or film noir in *House of Bamboo* (1955), Sam Fuller consistently elides heroic individualism in order to explore the complexities of relational identity. In these films, protagonists such as *China Gate*'s Sergeant Brock (Gene Barry) are tough, sometimes racist loners incapable of extricating themselves from involvement with comrades and lovers. This tendency is nowhere more clear than in the early buddy cop endeavor *The Crimson Kimono*. Like Murakami in *Stray Dog*, Joe Kojaku (James Shigeta) and Charlie Bancroft (Glenn Corbett) are veterans (this time of the Korean War) who continue their military camaraderie as Los Angeles police detectives. This picture of democratic amity is disrupted, however, when the buddies investigate the murder of stripper Sugar Torch (Gloria Pall). Enlisting artist Chris Downes (Victoria Shaw), both detectives fall for the young woman; to

Charlie's chagrin, Chris prefers Joe. In this interesting mystery, pursuit of the killer is compounded by the tensions of the interethnic love-triangle: despite Charlie's protestations, Joe presumes that his partner's resentment is motivated by racism rather than simple jealousy. He breaks off his courtship of Chris and plans to leave the force. Fuller resolves the film's multiple conflicts in a characteristically melodramatic climax—Joe and Charlie nab Sugar's murderer, herself a jealous lover, amidst a Nisei festival in Little Tokyo. Surrounded by juxtaposed images of Japanese-American assimilation and cultural difference, Joe overcomes his feelings of alienation and seals his relationship with Chris in the embrace of a classical Hollywood ending. As Tracey observes, "This is the larger theme in the film (Kojaku's liminality and his troubled relationship with Charlie) and perhaps suggests . . . the need for greater *real* integration in our society (separate is not equal)" (168). Fuller therefore rejects conventional hard-boiled alienation—the white detective's confrontation with an endo-colonial urban jungle—and its progressive counterpart: Kojaku's absolute marginalization within a racist American society. He instead establishes a narrative fraught with noir thematics of alienation and then dramatizes the protagonists' struggle to maintain a relationship against the anomic forces of the modern metropolis.

"Buddy noir" films persist throughout the ensuing decades as an occasional alternative to the authenticating alienation of conventional noir. In *Hickey and Boggs* (1972), for example, Robert Culp recasts his television partnership with Bill Cosby for a profound meditation on the hard-boiled detective formula. Hired as ignorant stalking-horses, the eponymous PI's become embroiled in a competition between militant Latinos and mobsters searching for a cache of stolen money. The plot becomes increasingly apocalyptic as Hickey and Boggs confront everything from bodybuilders to air assaults, an index into the manifold global threats of the Vietnam era. The action-packed plot is punctuated by the detectives' self-conscious commentaries on their calling: while Boggs maintains his existential heroism, Hickey remarks, "there's nothing left of this profession; it's all over. It's not about anything." Labeling the film an example of the "post-*noir*," Elizabeth Ward finds in these outgunned anti-heroes "a severe statement about the place of men in the world that is as dismal as any from the classic period of film noir. Both of these men are adrift, alienated from their environment and their families, clearly out of any mainstream lifestyle. They are superfluous figures wandering through the urban landscape" (239). But unlike contemporary neo-noir films, such as Arthur Penn's *Night Moves* (1975), which also intensify the alienated milieu of the classic period, *Hickey and Boggs* preserves a sense of dialogic engagement between subjects. The same may be said of Wayne Wang's avant-garde film *Chan Is Missing* (1982), in which two San Francisco cabbies—Jo (Wood Moy) and Steve (Marc Hayashi)—search Chinatown for Chan Hung, a Chinese immigrant who has apparently absconded with four thousand dollars. The black-and-white mystery on one hand reads as a homage to *The Lady From Shanghai* and other San Francisco noirs. With manifold allusions to detective fictions ranging from Earl Derr Biggers's Charlie Chan mysteries to *The Rockford Files* and *Magnum PI,* Wang alerts viewers to its revisionist program. As with Fuller's *The Crimson Kimono, Chan Is Missing* conjures and sidesteps the high-noir polarization of white isolato against urban jungle; its detective heroes are the Chinese-Americans objectified in Hammett and Welles. In the end, Jo and Steve end up with more questions than answers: "I've already given up on finding Chan Hung," Jo laments in his voice-over narrative, "But what bothers me is that I no longer know who Chan Hung really is." However concerned with the divisive potential of the American urban experience, *Chan Is Missing* also foregrounds the strong relationships between various characters. At the conclusion of the narrative, we have every indication that Jo and Steve will proceed with their joint venture of starting their cab company and will continue their good natured dialogues about issues ranging from the contradictions of Asian-American experience to which horse to bet on in the trifecta.

DURING THE 1990s, however, many filmmakers found in noir a vehicle for explorations of relational identity. Carl Franklin inaugurated his own career and this revisionist sequence of films with *One False Move,* a buddy cop picture that dramatizes the inevitability of the self-in-community. Reversing the Western trajectory of the road movie, Franklin presents an interracial trio of criminals fleeing Los Angeles into the deep South. After a shocking mass murder, ex-cons Wade "Pluto" Franklin (Michael Beach) and Ray Malcolm (Billy Bob Thornton) head for Houston in order to sell stolen drugs; Ray's mulatta girlfriend Lila "Fantasia" Walker (Cynda Williams) takes a bus for her hometown of Star City, Arkansas to visit her mother and son. Murdering a Texas trooper who recognizes them, Pluto and Ray likewise proceed to Star City. They are expected by another multiracial party—L.A. detectives Dud Cole (Jim Metzler) and John McFeely (Earl Billings) along with local Police Chief Dale "Hurricane" Dixon (Bill Paxton). As he eagerly assists with the investigation, Dale reveals his desire to move west and join the LAPD, much to the amusement of Cole and McFeely. The two plotlines are united not only by the crime and detection formula but also by Dale's hidden connection with Lila; years ago,

Hurricane raped and impregnated the seventeen-year-old girl, propelling her into a life of crime.

Roundly praised, Carl Franklin's debut film has received considerable scholarly attention. Proclaiming Franklin's crime films "postmodern noirs with a difference," Justus J. Nieland locates *One False Move* within the African American hard-boiled tradition inaugurated by Chester Himes. Charles Scruggs finds in the film a deconstruction of the opposition between urban hell and pastoral Eden. The initial polarization of L.A. and the "hortus conclusus" of Star City decays as we find that femme fatale Lila/Fantasia has been created in the "unweeded garden" of Southern racism and violence (327–30). Both critics broadly agree that the film's tandem multiracial trios present an impressive meditation upon relational identity. While Pluto is disturbed by Fantasia's liaison with his white partner, the unabashedly racist Dixon has fathered a child with a black woman. The L.A. detectives, on the other hand, interact with Hurricane through stereotypes about urban and rural life. If conventional noir protagonists often define themselves via confrontation with racial otherness (recall Phillip Marlowe's phantasm of black rape), then Chief Dixon must face his inextricable relationship with the Other. *One False Move* concludes with a shootout that leaves Pluto, Ray, and Fantasia dead and Dixon critically injured. But this physical and psychic debilitation renders him open to connection with his mixed-race son Byron (Roger Anthony Bell). In this respect, *One False Move* recalls the conclusion of Fuller's *China Gate*, the first American film about the Vietnam War, in which hard-boiled legionnaire Sgt. Brock must recognize his Amerasian son. However abbreviated and open-ended, Dixon's journey toward the self-in-community anticipates ensuing 1990s films noirs that would see authenticating alienation give way to "being with others."

More needs to be said about Franklin's revisions of noir ideology; his faithful adaptation of Walter Mosley's *Devil in a Blue Dress* (1995) not only explicitly responds to the racism of midcentury noir, but in doing so reimagines the oppositional subjectivity of the tough-guy private detective. Easy Rawlins (Denzel Washington) may experience the alienation of African Americans living in a racist society, but he also understands himself as a part of the larger mosaic of his South Central L.A. community (a thematic underscored by the film's poignant conclusive shot). While Franklin amplifies thematics inherent in the buddy cop film noir, Quentin Tarantino and Mike Newell respectively adopt the "undercover" formula, reversing the trajectory of this subgenre. High noir films such as *White Heat* and *Appointment with Danger* (Lewis Allen, 1951) turn upon the protagonist's struggle to preserve an impenetrable subjective core against the threats of discovery and/or corruption. Walsh, for example, presents in Cody Jarrett (James Cagney) a monstrous gangster with whom no "real" relationship is possible: infiltrator Vic Pardo/Hank Fallon (Edmond O'Brien) emerges as a heroic isolato capable of conserving an essential self against Jarrett's criminal milieu. In *Reservoir Dogs,* Tarantino deploys undercover noir toward very different ends. Police detective Freddy Newendyke (Tim Roth) infiltrates a gang of thieves planning a jewel heist. From its outset, however, *Reservoir Dogs* veers away from the alienation endemic to undercover work and focuses instead upon the deconstructive concerns associated with postmodernism. We find embedded within the film's opening sequence (breakfast at Uncle Billy's Pancake House) an extended colloquium about topics ranging from possible interpretations of Madonna's 1984 hit "Like A Virgin" to the ethics of tipping; its common denominator is a preoccupation with contextual meanings: "They're servin' ya food," declaims Mr. White, " you should tip 'em. But no, society says tip these guys over here, but not those guys over there. That's bullshit." Attention to hermeneutics persists into the criminal plot itself, centrally informing the film's vision of human identity. Aside from Joe Cabot (Lawrence Tierny) and his son Nice Guy Eddie (Chris Penn), each of the thieves is known by a color-coded name assigned by Joe. As with the opening sequence, the assignment of names becomes a disquisition on meaning: "You get four guys fighting over who's gonna be Mr. Black. Since nobody knows anybody else, nobody wants to back down. So forget it, I pick. Be thankful you're not Mr. Yellow." Tierney had of course played the heavy in *The Devil Thumbs a Ride* (Felix E. Feist, 1947) and *Born to Kill* (Robert Wise, 1947). Although he dedicates *Reservoir Dogs* to Tierney, among others, Tarantino here charges the archetypal noir tough with limiting the freeplay of language and identity, a task that will prove tragically futile as "intertextual" subjects develop beyond the boss's control.[1]

The most pressing of these threats is of course Freddy/Mr. Orange, the covert policeman whose cover represents a study in rhetorical manipulation. Under the tutelage of Holdaway (Randy Brooks), who insists, "An undercover cop has got to be Marlon Brando . . . naturalistic as hell," Freddy learns the value of realism in establishing a fictional self:

> It's the details that sell your story. Now this story takes place in this men's room. So you gotta know the details about this men's room. You gotta know they got a blower instead of a towel to dry your hands. You gotta know the stalls ain't got no doors. You gotta know whether they got liquid or powdered soap, whether they got hot water or not, 'cause if you do your job when you tell your story, everybody should believe it. And if you tell your

story to somebody who's actually taken a piss in this men's room, and you get one detail they remember right, they'll swear by you.

Written to authenticate Freddy's criminal credibility, the drug-sniffing dog anecdote relies upon concrete details (the insignificant notation of Barthes's reality effect) as a means of anchoring its verisimilitude. In *Reservoir Dogs,* fictive selves and realities eclipse the referential universe of classic noir. Given Tarantino's constructivist vision, we might be tempted to align his inaugural film with the confidence man noirs of the 1990s; like Singer's Verbal Kint, both Freddy and Joe operate primarily through textual manipulation rather than logistical brilliance or simple force of will. And yet Tarantino directs his undercover noir away from deconstruction and into a dramatization of the relational self. While Joe's "crew" consists of dynamic, unstable subjects, Mr. Orange and Mr. White (Harvey Keitel) establish a bond so deep that Mr. White ultimately turns against old friends in defense of his new buddy: "Joe, trust me on this, you've made a mistake. He's a good kid. I understand you're hot, you're super-fuckin pissed. We're all real emotional. But you're barking up the wrong tree. I know this man, and he wouldn't do that." Although the anguished White shoots Freddy at the end of the film, their relationship reads as a revision of both the autonomous self of high noir and the ludic subject that we discern in many postmodern noirs. The undercover cop Freddy is neither existential isolato nor protean confidence man but rather an entity dependent upon local contexts and relationships.

Mike Newell's *Donnie Brasco* pursues a course quite similar to that of *Reservoir Dogs.* The film begins with a straightforward reworking of the undercover formula: FBI agent Joe Pistone (Johnny Depp) assumes the character of aspiring wiseguy Donnie Brasco in order to infiltrate a Mafia crew. Increasingly immersed in the underworld, Joe grows anxious, violent, and estranged from his family. As in *Reservoir Dogs,* the cover persona threatens to subsume the hero's "real" self; "You're becoming like them," Maggie (Anne Heche) charges, as Joe begins to assume Donnie's intimidating affect with his family and his FBI superiors. After slapping her, he replies, "I'm not becoming like them, Maggie. I am them." Though more restrained than the loquacious *Reservoir Dogs, Donnie Brasco* does offer reflexive meditations that illuminate its treatment of identity. Perhaps most prominent of these is Joe's explication of the phrase "Forget about it":

> "Forget about it" is like, uh—if you agree with someone, you know, like "Raquel Welch is one great piece of ass forget about it." But then, if you

disagree, like "A Lincoln is better than a Cadillac? Forget about it!" you know? But then, it's also like if something's the greatest thing in the world, like Mingrio's Peppers, "forget about it." But it's also like saying "Go to hell!" too. Like, you know, like "Hey Paulie, you got a one inch pecker?" and Paulie says "Forget about it!" Sometimes it just means forget about it.

With subtle shifts in intonation, the same phrase might hold multiple contradictory meanings. Comparable to the "Like a Virgin" roundtable in *Reservoir Dogs*, this quiet reflection on polysemy suggests the unstable nature of all utterance; but it also points to the ways in which Joe himself mutates with changes in context. Here again, the film's deconstructive tendencies give way to an exploration of relational subjectivity. Just as Freddy and Larry develop a tragically close relationship in *Reservoir Dogs*, Donnie becomes inextricably bound to Lefty: "This job is eating me alive.... And if I come out, this guy, Lefty dies. They're gonna kill him, because he vouched for me, because he stood up for me.... That's the same thing as if I put the bullet in his head myself...." While Donnie hopes to give Lefty an "out" before the FBI sting, Lefty resolutely stakes and ultimately forfeits his life on the basis of Donnie's fidelity. The film leaves Donnie/Pistone dazed and traumatized by the undercover ordeal: "I spent all these years trying to be the good guy, the man in the white hat. For what? For nothing." Both Newell and Tarantino hereby deprive the noir undercover formula of its naturalizing power. Whereas classic noir camouflages subject/object construction within the polarization of infiltrator and criminal, *Reservoir Dogs* and *Donnie Brasco* reimagine the noir subject as a "connected guy," a figure derived through communities, whether legitimate or illicit.

One False Move, *Reservoir Dogs*, and *Donnie Brasco* sensitize us to a series of 1990s films noirs that reiterate the journey from alienated authenticity to "connected" subjectivity. A striking example of this movement occurs in Abel Ferrara's *Bad Lieutenant* (1992); despite its hyperbolic violence, this controversial film is surprisingly redemptive in its treatment of relational subjectivity. *Bad Lieutenant* evokes the recognizable formula of the corrupt policeman, a motif that begins with Hammett's first story, "The Road Home" (in which a New York City detective contemplates cultural and ethical defection), and flourishes in films such as *Where the Sidewalk Ends* (Otto Preminger, 1950), *Rogue Cop* (Roy Rowland, 1954), *Shield for Murder* (Edward Koch and Edmond O'Brien, 1954), and *Pushover* (Richard Quine, 1954). Like the adventurous renegades of Joseph Conrad and John Russell, the defector in these films manages some sense of regeneration by late return to honor and professionalism. But here again, subjectivity arises within a lonely drama of fall and redemption. The first movements of the film establish the excesses of the titular "bad lieutenant"—he steals drugs, smokes crack, shoots heroin, and indulges in orgies with prostitutes. What's more, he bets on the Dodgers against the Mets in the 1988 National League Championships, encouraging his colleagues to back the home-team (in order to drive up the odds). Keitel's lieutenant sees an unlikely opportunity when a nun is raped by two Puerto Rican youths who also desecrate the altar and steal a Communion chalice—he hopes to apprehend the miscreants and earn a $50,000 reward. This hopelessly perverse grail quest takes on a frankly spiritual dimension as the lieutenant, disturbed by the nun's forgiveness of her attackers, experiences visions of a bloody, crucified Christ. In the midst of a spiritual crisis, he apprehends the rapists, gives them $30,000 he has borrowed to pay his debts, and frees them. Moments later he is murdered by his mobster/creditors. Like Carl Franklin's *One False Move, Bad Lieutenant* concludes with a moment of reconciliation between the noir antihero and the racial Other so often objectified throughout noir. On one hand, we might be tempted to cynicism, as is Foster Hirsch, who finds *One False Move* "another tribute to a white male who finally grows up" (*Detours and Lost Highways* 302). But we should also recognize the ways in which these films contribute to a general revision of noir ideology.

THUS FAR, we have encountered films that evoke various noir police characters—buddy cops, undercover cops, and corrupt cops.[2] In each case, the alienated noir protagonist finds himself bound with some "Other" figure. Our final pair of texts must be recognized as revisions of specific films noirs. Though less explicitly Christian than *Bad Lieutenant*, Gary Fleder's *Things to Do in Denver When You're Dead* also turns upon religious themes. Jimmy the Saint (Andy Garcia) is a small businessman with underworld connections: he runs a legitimate business that enables the terminally ill to videotape advice for their loved ones. He finds his "normal" life interrupted by "The Man with the Plan" (Christopher Walken), a crime boss who recruits Jimmy for one last "action": the intimidation of a rival for his son's affections. When Jimmy's unstable crew murders both lovers, the Man orders their painful execution via a method known only as "Buckwheats." Jimmy is given forty-eight hours to either leave town or suffer an excruciating death. Forgoing escape, Jimmy uses his last hours attempting to rescue his crew. When this fails, he strives to protect his lover Dagney (Gabrielle Anwar) and his friend Lucinda (Fairuza Balk). Jimmy finally agrees to father Lucinda's child, hoping to persist through their progeny. In a sentimental concluding shot—an imagined scene or vision of the afterlife—we see the murdered men enjoying "boat drinks," a symbol of hard-won community. Jimmy at one point finds Dagney watching a black-

and-white movie on TV: Maté's *D.O.A.* On one hand a reflexive "generic" allusion, this quotation also underscores the "memorial" theme central to the film, for Fleder treats us to Maté's close-up of the epitaph for Raymond Rakubian, thereby underscoring Jimmy's desire to be remembered as "the Saint." Read as a central pretext for *Things to Do in Denver When You're Dead*, *D.O.A.* illuminates Fleder's reprise of film noir. As we have seen, Maté's Frank Bigelow falls into an irrational world of violent crime when he is poisoned and left with a few days to live. In an act of existential defiance, he penetrates an Armenian crime ring in Los Angeles, ultimately killing his own murderer. Fleder adopts a similar "last days" motif, but sidesteps the agonist drama of *D.O.A.* in order to project the noir hero as a "connected guy" who emerges from the intersection of spaces and communities.

Paul Thomas Anderson has remarked that his 1996 film *Hard Eight* was inspired in part by Jean-Pierre Melville's *Bob le Flambeur* (1955)[3]; but the film also recalls and revises another midcentury noir—William Dieterle's *Dark City* (1950). Dieterle casts Charlton Heston as bookie and professional gambler Danny Haley, who, with the help of his friends, fleeces Arthur Winnant (Dan Defore) in a card game. The distraught Winnant commits suicide and is avenged by his brother Sidney (Mike Mazurki). After his friend Barney (Ed Begley, Sr.) is murdered, Haley seeks out Winnant's widow, hoping to get a line on Sidney. He's so moved by the plight of Mrs. Winnant (Viveca Lindfors) that he heads for Las Vegas in order to win back the money that he had swindled from her husband. In Vegas, Haley meets his gambling chums and his torch-singer girlfriend Fran Garland (Lizabeth Scott). But he must also face the monomaniacal Sidney, who has followed the group to Sin City. This classic noir antihero tragically participates in his own isolation; embittered by a divorce, the Ivy Leaguer has adopted a lifestyle that objectifies others and refuses intimacy. This sense of alienation is particularly keen in the climactic sequence in which Sidney, registered only as a pair of murderous hands, stalks the gambler in a darkened room. Dieterle in a sense anticipates the "connected guy" of '90s noir in that he charts Haley's growth into redemptive relationships with Fran and his buddy Soldier (Harry Morgan); what is perhaps most memorable about the film, however, is its treatment of a self-alienated gambler whose sharp dealing has provoked the wrath of the maniacal Sidney.

Hard Eight reworks the basic elements of *Dark City*, amplifying its thematics of relational identity. Anderson makes clear his disposition toward noir as a whole in the opening sequence of the film, which distantly invokes Edward Hopper's 1942 painting *Nighthawks*. John Finnegan (John C. Reilly) huddles at the door of a roadside diner; the building's conspicuous midcentury architecture—featuring a severe downward sloping roof—underscores the drifter's declining prospects. A trenchcoated form emerges from the left as if to menace this unfortunate. While the looming presence is indeed a dangerous character, he has no such designs upon John. He introduces himself and brings the isolato into the warmth and light of the diner and the small but vital community suggested by Hopper's painting. During their short conversation, John reveals that he has in desperation gone to Las Vegas in order to win enough money to bury his mother. Over coffee and cigarettes, Sydney extends a helping hand: "John, we're sitting here. I bought you a cup of coffee, gave you a cigarette. Look at me. You wanna be a wise-ass, go outside and take a seat. If you wanna talk to me . . . well, then—Never ignore a man's courtesy. Let's talk about Vegas. Let's talk about what happened to you." The sequence closes with a tableau of coffee cups and an ashtray that assumes throughout the film a sacramental quality, suggesting the possibility of community within the alienated and tragic milieu of the Nevada casinos. It turns out that Sydney (Philip Baker Hall) is an "old hood" from Atlantic City; he murdered John's father and now seeks to undo the wrong. He shows John how to negotiate the casinos of Vegas and Reno; two years later, they're still together. Sydney ultimately engineers a romance between John and cocktail waitress-cum-prostitute Clementine (Gwyneth Paltrow). Clem emerges as a kind of accidental femme fatale—fearing commitment, she celebrates their quickie nuptials by hustling a vacationer in the casino bar. When the client won't pay, she and John hold him "hostage" in a motel room. Sydney of course intervenes to resolve the crisis and sends them on a honeymoon to Niagara Falls. At the conclusion of *Hard Eight,* Sydney reprises his murderous past, but only to protect his strange relationship with John. He ambushes John's sleazy friend Jimmy (Samuel L. Jackson), who threatens to reveal the dark secret of Atlantic City. Finally confessing to John, "I love you like you were my own son," Sydney represents a thoroughgoing transformation of the vengeful and anomic world of *Dark City.* Although Sydney cannot escape his violent past (he significantly notices and hides a spot of Jimmy's blood on his cuff), he is not, as D'Aries and Hirsch argue, "locked within a moral and existential prison . . . a prison without bars and without escape."[4] As in other late-twentieth-century films noirs, this antiheroic protagonist evolves from a condition of anomie toward a subjectivity founded in a community, however small and contingent.

D'Aries and Hirsch also suggest that *Hard Eight* skirts a nihilistic relativism evident in many contemporary films noirs.[5] And yet Anderson's Sydney, along with the other "connected guys" reviewed throughout this chapter, represents a model of identity that harbors quite as much ethical purchase as the existentialist hero of noir. In the wake of postmodernist noirs that in various ways destabilize the subject, these films encourage us to imagine oneself as "a being among others" whose actions hold profound social and philosophical implications. Throughout the 1990s, we find the existential hero of noir overtaken by its old adversary, the confidence man who bodes a subjectivity founded in open-ended narrative. But the dialectic between the radically different selves implied by the con man and the noir isolato yields a new hybrid figure. In *Memento*, the conventional noir antihero gives way to a protagonist quite obviously and even joyously derived from "stories in the making." While Nolan's Leonard Shelby gravitates toward a nihilist postmodernism, we may discern a counterpoint in the "connected guys" of '90s noir. However traumatized, figures such as Franklin's Hurricane Dixon, Newell's Donnie Brasco, and Anderson's Sydney remind us that we owe ourselves to others, to the networks within and by which we derive identity. These unlikely antiheroes demonstrate the way in which noir has moved beyond both authenticating alienation and ludic postmodernism to achieve a redemptive vision of community and interdependence.

NOTES

INTRODUCTION

1. See "First Brands reinvents the plastic bag; With patented Quick-Tie/TM Flaps, GLAD/R transforms the trash bag business by eliminating twist ties–An American Institution—."

2. For more on the commercialization of noir, see Foster Hirsch, *Detours and Lost Highways: A Map of Neo-Noir* (5).

3. Hutcheon introduced this term in her 1987 article "Beginning to Theorize Postmodernism."

4. For a response to this critical debate, see Suzanne Loza, "Orientalism and Film Noir: (Un)Mapping Textual Territories and (En)Countering the Narratives."

5. See also Raymond Durgnat, "Paint It Black: The Family Tree of the the Film Noir."

6. James Naremore finds the transgeneric account of noir inadequate because it elides the hybridity of supposedly "stable" genres (6).

7. Naremore hints at the imperial adventure context, but likewise retreats from this argument: " . . . noir offers mostly white audiences the pleasure of 'low' adventure, having little to do with the conquest of nature, the establishment of law and order, the march of empire" (220). See also Durgnat, "Paint It Black" 45; John Cawelti, *Adventure, Mystery, and Romance* 76.

8. See Jon Thompson, *Fiction, Crime, and Empire: Clues to Modernity and Postmodernism;* Cheryl Edelson, "The Heterotopias in the Rue Morgue"; and Stanley Orr, "'I think it was his eye!': Edgar Allan Poe, Crime Fiction, and Panopticism" (papers presented at the 11th Annual Conference on American Literature, Long Beach, CA, May, 2000).

9. See Nancy Harrowitz, "Criminality and Poe's Orangutan: The Question of Race in Detection"; John Carlos Rowe, *Literary Culture and U.S. Imperialism: From the Revolution to World War II.*

10. Alain Silver, "Son of *Noir*: Neo-*Film Noir* and the Neo-B Picture" 331.

11. Jean Baudrillard, *Simulations* 12–13.
12. See James Naremore, *More Than Night: Film Noir in Its Contexts* 211–19; 254–77.

CHAPTER ONE

1. See also Willett's discussion of Hammett (40–42).
2. In her 1992 article "Hard-Boiled Ideology," Bethany Ogdon observes that the hard-boiled detective's freedom from family and consociational ties is underscored by the imagination of an armored body that contrasts with the "soft-boiled," destroyed, and even dedifferentiated bodies of racial and sexual others (82). Following Ogdon, Jopi Nyman argues, "The body is secondary to mind in hard-boiled fiction, but has a major function as a signifier of power" (90).
3. See Edward Said, *Culture and Imperialism* 130.
4. Becke, "A Truly Great Man," 86. All citations of Louis Becke's stories refer to the following anthologies: *By Reef and Palm and The Ebbing of the Tide; South Sea Supercargo; Pacific Tales.*
5. Becke, "Deschard of Oneaka" 310.
6. Quoted in Slotkin 111.
7. Quoted in Slotkin 120.
8. Musser, *Emergence of the Cinema: The American Screen to 1907* 225.
9. In *The Lonely Crowd* (1950), David Riesman asserts that "many inner-directed individuals can remain stable even when the reinforcement of social approval is not available—as in the upright life of the stock Englishman isolated in the tropics" (24).
10. In *The Island of California: A History of the Myth,* Dora Beale Polk provides an overview of this tradition.
11. Leroy Lad Panek notes this context in *Reading Early Hammett: A Critical Study of the Fiction Prior to* The Maltese Falcon. He declares "Ber-Bulu" "an anti-adventure story . . . in which the action is . . . trivial and domestic and in which the hero is . . . a rogue who observes human silliness and sails off with an unmerited reward" (35).
12. Said, *Orientalism* 206.
13. Kaplan, *Looking for the Other* 93. See also Ogdon, "Hard-Boiled Ideology."
14. John Walker Lindh argues, "The absence of stable identity in Hammett's work corresponds to an epistemological uncertainty concerning the nature of being. The anthropomorphic character of objects suggests a capacity for mutability that undermines the potential for a fixed essence" (131).
15. See also Ralph Willett's *The Naked City* 1–15. I derive the term "endo-Orientalism" from Paul Virilio, who describes in *Critical Space* "a post-industrial ENDO-COLONIALISM succeeding the EXO-COLONIALISM of the central empires of the industrial era" (59).
16. Ogdon contends that "physical punishment rituals" reinforce the hard-boiled detective's sense of an armored physical person opposed to exoticized and "violently destroyed bodies" (79–80).
17. Fredric Jameson, *Postmodernism, or, The Cultural Logic of Late Capitalism* 11. For a thorough commentary on these modernist thematics in hard-boiled detective fiction, see chapter 6 of Cawelti's *Adventure, Mystery, and Romance.*

18. All citations of the Continental Op stories refer to *Dashiell Hammett: Crime Stories and Other Writings*.

19. For an authoritative treatment of race-politics and instrumentalism, see Martin Kevorkian's study *Color Monitors: The Black Face of Technology in America*.

20. See also Ogdon 76.

21. Spurr 78.

22. In *Adventure, Mystery, and Romance,* John Cawelti observes, "One might interpret Poe's invention of the detective as a means of bringing the terrifying potency of the gothic villain under the control of rationality and thereby directing it to beneficial ends" (95).

23. All citations of Sherlock Holmes stories refer to *The Complete Sherlock Holmes*.

24. Slotkin 222–23, 228.

CHAPTER TWO

1. See Paul Skenazy, *The New Wild West: The Urban Mysteries of Dashiell Hammett and Raymond Chandler*.

2. "The Simple Art of Murder" 20. Marlowe describes himself a "shop-soiled Galahad" (209) in chapter 28 of *The High Window* (1942).

3. See *Raymond Chandler*. Dir. David Thomas. RM Associates, 1988.

4. Quoted in Polk 125.

5. Boime 1–5.

6. Rowe 119.

7. See also Ogdon's reading of this moment in "Hard-boiled Ideology" 78.

8. Following Hamilton, Skenazy, Durham, and Grella, Rzepka writes, "Like a Streetwise Natty Bumpo, [the hard-boiled detective] patrols a violent frontier between civilization and savagery, with a foot in each world" (695). See also Abbott 89.

9. Recall Ogdon's contention that hard-boiled detective emerges "the sole normal person . . . constantly under siege." Abbott similarly contends "Chandler and Cain were forced to confront . . . ambiguous expressions of white male urban existence—visions of bodies out of control, conflicting and even transgressive desires, [and] complicated racial dread . . . " (18).

10. See Blake Allmendinger, "All About Eden."

11. McCann 169–70.

12. See Rzepka 700.

13. Rzepka 707.

14. See McClintock's *Imperial Leather: Race, Gender, and Sexuality in the Colonial Contest*.

15. In *Detective Fiction and the Rise of Forensic Science,* Ronald R. Thomas reads this moment as "an at least unconscious acknowledgment that in this cultural moment, the camera—and by implication, the detective—has been emptied of its potency . . . " (184).

16. McCann discusses Chandler's portrayal of Canino within the context of an important but incidental "symbolic power of racial definition" (163).

17. See Hiney 50–69.

18. See also McCann 167.

19. Rzepka 707; see also Skenazy 38–39.

20. With regard to the latter figure, McCann argues that "*The Lady in the Lake* suggests that Marlowe's body is not crushed, that he remains a man, because, rather than falling amid corrupt confederates and evil women, he became part of the fellowship of decent men" (141). See also Abbott, who suggests that the tough guy "must work to present his body as an unmarked one: raceless, transparent, universal" (89).

21. See *Where the Pavement Ends* 104–5.

22. In *The Gift: The Form and Reason for Exchange in Archaic Societies* (1925), Marcel Mauss contends that the anomic fate of modern man arises from capitalism's eclipse of ancient economies of gift exchange.

23. While Lennox's observations on the quiet bar recall the older waiter's celebration of the café in "A Clean, Well-Lighted Place," an emphasis upon gifts and communal drinking may also be found in the homosocial fishing sequences of *The Sun Also Rises*.

24. For Abbott, the "real threat" here is "the male femme fatale" who subverts "the hermetic gender binary by which Marlowe functions . . . " (121).

CHAPTER THREE

1. For more on this debate, see Krutnik, chap. 3; Marling, chap. 6.

2. I am thinking of Said's suggestion in *Orientalism* that the Orient expands in the western imagination to include everything "residing to the far east, west, south, and north of Europe" (117).

3. Borde and Chaumeton find *The Shanghai Gesture* redolent of "*film noir* qualities such as nightmarish, weird, erotic, ambivalent, and cruel" (18).

4. Krutnik 86.

5. See Kaplan, "The 'Dark Continent' of Film Noir" 193.

6. See Torgovnick 23–26.

7. See Kaplan, "The 'Dark Continent' of Film Noir" 196

8. See also Kaplan, "The 'Dark Continent' of Film Noir" 198.

9. Kaplan, "The 'Dark Continent' of Film Noir" 193.

10. Harry Lawton, *Willie Boy: A Desert Manhunt* x. See also James A. Sandos and Larry E. Burgess, *The Hunt for Willie Boy: Indian-Hating and Popular Culture*.

11. See Sandra M. Gilbert and Susan Gubar, *The Madwoman in the Attic: The Woman Writer and the 19th Century Literary Imagination*.

12. For a thorough treatment of noir misogyny, see Janey Place's "Women in Film Noir."

13. Meyers xiv.

14. See Starr 92, 266.

CHAPTER FOUR

1. See Borde and Chaumeton 21, 29, 54.

2. For a broad discussion of themes of paranoia in Himes's crime fiction, see chapter 2 of Woody Haut's study *Pulp Culture: Hardboiled Fiction and the Cold War*.

3. See also McCann 266.

4. For more on the gender-politics of *If He Hollers Let Him Go*, see Wheeler 41–46; Ikard 29–48.

5. The films in question are *The Fallen Sparrow* (Richard Wallace, 1943), *Ride the Pink Horse* (Robert Montgomery, 1947), and *In A Lonely Place*.

6. Woody Haut observes of *In A Lonely Place*, "Reading the author reading Dix, one enters the text by way of a voice twice removed" (130).

7. Haut suggests, "What is interesting is how Hughes has taken the pulp culture cliché of contrasting women—housewife and *femme fatale*—and turned their traditionally adversarial relationship into an alliance whose target is Dix" (128).

8. See Naremore 225; Biesen 77.

9. Quoted in Dower 63.

10. Quoted in Yogi 63.

11. With particular attention to this episode, Wheeler briefly glosses Ichiro's "noir mantle" (122, 132).

12. See Fotsch 102–3.

13. See Robin Wood, "Ideology, Genre, Auteur" 46–51.

14. See Yogi 67, 73.

15. For Stan Yogi, "Freddie's fragmented character follows him even in death"; his fate is a "physical reminder of his shattered life" (73).

16. See Sledge 31.

17. See Marc Vernet, "Film Noir on the Edge of Doom."

CHAPTER FIVE

1. Richardson 25.

2. See Richardson 13–21.

3. In "The Death of the Author," Barthes explains that this opposition between meaning and insignificance concurs with broader western notions of authorship and identity. Just as unsignifying notation limits meaning within the text, Barthes writes, "To assign an Author to a text is to impose a brake on it, to furnish it with a final signified to close writing" (53). The binary work/author in turn works to ensure the "prestige of the individual," the "human person" (49).

4. Oliver and Trigo argue, "[T]he alienating effect to which stereotypes are put in *The Lady From Shanghai* paradoxically produces a temporarily stable reality effect" (54).

5. Hutcheon, *Poetics* 57.

6. Bakhtin 6.

7. Bakhtin 12.

8. Bakhtin 39.

9. Bakhtin 33.

10. The Bradbury Building housed Marlowe's office in *Marlowe* (Paul Bogart, 1969) as well as the climactic scene of *D.O.A.*

11. See, for example, Naremore 265 and Shaviro 149.

12. With respect to *Gravity's Rainbow*, we might also recall Tyrone Slothrop's imagi-

nation of himself as "a hardboiled private eye" who is "gonna go out all alone and beat the odds, avenge my friend that They killed, get my ID back and find that piece of mystery hardware" (561).

13. Silver and Ward, *Film Noir* 2.
14. Hite 73.
15. For an overview of scholarship on "Oedipa Mass" and "Pierce Inverarity," see Grant 3–8.
16. Chatterjee and Nicholson 305.
17. Berresem 95.
18. Putz 378.
19. Hayles 121.
20. It may be helpful to compare Oedipa's dilemma at this point in the novel to that of Hugh Godolphin in *V.* Proliferation of clues about the elusive Vheissu call into question his investigation of this mysterious locale.
21. With respect to this passage, Watson observes, "In becoming the detective, she becomes part of the sinister force she is pursuing" (60).
22. Grant 120.
23. Hemingway 33.
24. Recall Laura Otis's characterization of Holmes as an "imperial immune system."
25. Auster, Interview 297.
26. Tysh 46.
27. Auster, Interview 303.
28. In her Derridean reading of the trilogy, Alison Russell cursorily notes the presence of "Film Noir signifiers" and argues that the novels of the trilogy "employ and deconstruct the conventional elements of the detective story, resulting in a recursive linguistic investigation of the nature, function and meaning of language" (71). These implications have been elaborated by Steven E. Alford, who suggests that Auster's "questions of identity flow into questions about textuality, and undermine the ontologically distinct categories of author, narrator, and reader." Citing Hutcheon, Alford concludes that Auster has "moved away from the modernist, alienated fiction of the other, exemplified in Hammett and others of the hard-boiled school, to a postmodern fiction of difference" (29). See also Oscar De Los Santos, "Auster vs. Chandler: Or, Cracking the Case of the Postmodern Mystery."
29. Alford concludes that the narrator of *The Locked Room* is "{Auster}, narrator of *City of Glass* and *Ghosts,* so long as we understand both the terms 'narrator' and 'author' as standing for what we might call a locus of textual space, one which nominally includes you, me, and Paul Auster author" (27).
30. Auster, *The Locked Room* 294.
31. See Alford.
32. Marlowe makes a similar admission in Chapter 30 of *The Big Sleep*.
33. Chandler, Introduction, viii.
34. For more on Woolrich as "a writer whose sensibility is most deeply noir," see Hirsch, *Dark Side of the Screen: Film Noir* 43–46.
35. Woolrich 1.
36. Barthes, *Writing Degree Zero* 37.

37. See Naremore 23.
38. Barthes, *S/Z* 10.
39. Kristeva 187.
40. The character is the titular figure in Melville's "Jimmy Rose" (1855); the allusion exemplifies the reflexive intertextuality of Auster's novels.
41. Incidentally, with the exception of *Fallen Angel* (1946), all of these films were released in 1947, the year of the "narrative present" in *Ghosts*.
42. Ottoson 132.
43. Chandler, "The Simple Art of Murder" 8.

CHAPTER SIX

1. Barthes, *S/Z* 10.
2. Rafferty 156.
3. Hoberman 10.
4. McRobbie 40.
5. Reading Fritz Lang's *The Woman in the Window* (1944) and *Scarlet Street* (1945) as "man's melodramas," Florence Jacobowitz argues that both melodrama and film noir "share the overriding principle of constriction and entrapment as a defining motif, whether it be in the family or within patriarchal social organizations and demands of gender ideals" (51).
6. See Goulart 229–30.
7. Haut 149–50.
8. Geherin 24–25.
9. Kelly 149–61.
10. Diski 12.
11. Leibman 168.
12. Place and Peterson 31.
13. Leibman 182.
14. Rafferty 156. See also Blake Lucas, who notes Mitchum's reptilian aspect in *Cape Fear*.
15. Diski 12.
16. Leibman 182.
17. Kolker 162.
18. Hoberman 11.
19. McRobbie 40.
20. For more on *Cape Fear*'s "intertextual homage," see Kristen Thompson's essay "*Cape Fear* and Trembling: Familial Dread."
21. Letts finds Scorsese's direction "distractingly showy": "We see . . . visual devices which have become de rigueur in psychopath films and which are supposed to be intrinsically frightening but aren't. Similarly there are too many references to Hitchcock—1950s technicolor skies, spooky film-noir close-ups and kitsch swiveling camera-work—none of which contributes anything at all to the forward momentum of the film." See also Simon 57.
22. Klawans 828.

23. Hoberman 10.
24. Simon 56. See also chapter 6 of Lesley Stern's *The Scorsese Connection*.
25. Simon 60.
26. Hoberman 10. See also Diski's piece, "The Shadow Within."
27. Hoberman 11.
28. McRobbie 40.
29. Letts 36.
30. Wood 152.
31. See Cawelti, *Adventure, Mystery, and Romance* 75.
32. Larsen describes the office-building as "a glossy paradigmatic site of the 90s booming economy" (40).
33. See Cawelti, "*Chinatown* and Generic Transformation" 310.
34. "When the bunch of criminals meet in the lineup," writes Larsen, "Singer encourages his actors to play for comic bravado. . . . They're like ham actors at an audition, which is more or less what a lineup amounts to, a tryout for the drama of a trial" (24).
35. Said, *Orientalism* 40, 72.
36. Kemp 61.
37. Steffen Hantke, "Boundary Crossing and the Construction of Cinematic Genre: Film Noir as 'Deferred Action.'"
38. See Hirsch 281; Dyer 46.
39. Pat Gill argues that "Mills reveals himself again and again to possess a 'mediated' understanding, to engage with the flattened glorified image, the visual representation, and the popular conception" (54).
40. See Dyer 24–25.
41. I am thinking here of Ross Macdonald's famous homage to Chandler.
42. Dyer 77.
43. Neely15.
44. Žižek, *Tarrying With the Negative* 11–12.
45. See Little 82.
46. For Amrohini Sahay, *Memento* "stages the new corporate dogma of identity under globalization": "a 'moment-to-moment,' contingent and pragmatic basis which needs to be revised and 're-done' based on new information."

CONCLUSION

1. For more on this aspect of the film, see Fred Botting and Scott Wilson, "By Accident: The Tarantinian Ethics"; Mark T. Conard, "*Reservoir Dogs*: Redemption in a Postmodern World."
2. We find this schema reiterated in other 1990s films noirs. Luc Besson's *The Professional* (1994), for example, sees the noir fixture of "the cleaner" or assassin undergo a shift from isolation to community.
3. D'Aries and Hirsch elaborate Anderson's debt to *Bob le Flambeur*.
4. D'Aries and Hirsch 94–99.
5. D'Aries and Hirsch 100.

WORKS CITED

Abbott, Megan E. *The Street Was Mine: White Masculinity in Hardboiled Fiction and Film Noir.* New York: Palgrave Macmillan, 2002.

Alford, Steven E. "Mirrors of Madness: Paul Auster's *The New York Trilogy.*" *Critique: Studies in Contemporary Fiction* 37.1 (Fall 1995): 17–33.

Allen, Lewis, dir. *Appointment With Danger.* Perfs. Alan Ladd. Phyllis Calvert, and Paul Stewart. Paramount Pictures, 1951.

Allmendinger, Blake. "All About Eden." *Reading California: Art, Image, and Identity, 1900–2000.* Eds. Stephanie Barron, Sheri Bernstein, and Ilene Susan Fort. Berkeley: University of California Press, 2000. 113–28.

Anderson, Paul Thomas, dir. *Hard Eight.* Perfs. Phillip Baker Hall, John C. Reilly, and Gwyneth Paltrow. Green Parrot Productions, 1996.

Aronowitz, Stanley, and Henry A. Giroux. *Postmodern Education: Politics, Culture, and Social Criticism.* Minneapolis: University of Minnesota Press, 1991.

Auer, John H., dir. *Hell's Half Acre.* Perfs. Wendell Corey and Evelyn Keyes. Republic Pictures, 1954.

Auster, Paul. Interview with Larry McCaffery and Sinda Gregory. 1989–90. *The Art of Hunger: Essays, Prefaces, Interviews, and* The Red Notebook. By Paul Auster. New York: Penguin Books, 1993. 277–320.

———. *The New York Trilogy.* New York: Penguin, 1990.

Bakhtin, M. M. "From Epic to Novel: Toward a Methodology for the Study of the Novel." *The Dialogic Imagination: Four Essays.* Ed. Michael Holquist. Trans. Caryl Emerson and Michael Holquist. Austin: University of Texas Press, 1981. 3–40.

Barthes, Roland. "The Death of the Author." *The Rustle of Language.* Trans. Richard Howard. Berkeley: University of California Press, 1986. 49–55.

———. "The Reality Effect." 1968. *The Rustle of Language.* Trans. Richard Howard. Berkeley and Los Angeles: University of California Press, 1986. 141–48.

———. *S/Z.* Trans. Richard Miller. 1970. New York: The Noonday Press, 1974.

———. *Writing Degree Zero.* 1953. Trans. Annette Lavers and Colin Smith. New York: Hill and Wang, 1968.
Baudrillard, Jean. "The Ecstasy of Communication." Trans. John Johnston. *The Anti-Aesthetic: Essays on Postmodern Culture.* Ed. Hal Foster. Seattle: Bay Press, 1983.
———. *Simulations.* Trans. Paul Floss, Paul Patton, and Philip Bleitchman. New York: Semiotext(e), 1983.
Becke, Louis. *By Reef and Palm and The Ebbing of the Tide.* 1894. Philadelphia: J. B. Lippincott Company, nd.
———. *Pacific Tales.* Pacific Basin books. London: KPI, 1987.
———. *The Pearl Divers of Roncador Reef, and Other Stories.* London: J. Clarke, 1908.
———. *South Sea Supercargo.* Honolulu: University of Hawaii Press, 1967.
———. *Under Tropic Skies.* Philadelphia: Lippincott, 1905.
———. *Yorke the Adventurer, and Other Stories.* London: T. Fisher Unwin, 1901.
Behdad, Ali. *Belated Travelers: Orientalism in the Age of Colonial Dissolution.* Post-contemporary interventions. Durham, NC: Duke University Press, 1994.
Benjamin, Walter. *One Way Street* (selection). 1928. *Reflections: Essays, Aphorisms, Autobiographical Writings.* Trans. Edmund Jephcott. Ed. Peter Demetz. New York: Shocken Books, 1978. 61–94.
Besson, Luc, dir. *The Professional.* Perfs. Jean Reno, Gary Oldman, and Natalie Portman. Gaumont, 1994.
Bernhardt, Curtis, dir. *The High Wall.* Perfs. Robert Taylor, Audrey Totter, and Herbert Marshall. MGM, 1947.
Berresem, Hanjo. *Pynchon's Poetics.* Urbana and Chicago: University of Illinois Press, 1993.
Biesen, Sheri Chinen. *Blackout: World War II and the Origins of Film Noir.* Baltimore: The Johns Hopkins University Press, 2005.
Blair, John G. *The Confidence Man in Modern Fiction: A Rogue's Gallery with Six Portraits.* New York: Barnes, 1979.
Bogart, Paul, dir. *Marlowe.* Perfs. James Garner, Gayle Hunnicutt, and Carroll O'Connor. MGM, 1969.
Boileau-Narcejac. *Le Roman Policier.* Press Universitaires de France, 1975.
Boime, Albert. *The Magisterial Gaze.* Washington: Smithsonian Institution, 1991.
Borde, Raymond, and Etienne Chaumeton. *A Panorama of American Film Noir, 1941–1953.* 1955. Trans. Paul Hammond. San Francisco: City Lights Books, 2002.
Botting, Fred, and Scott Wilson. "By Accident: The Tarantinian Ethics." *Theory, Culture and Society* 15.2 (1998): 89–113.
Brantlinger, Patrick. *Rule of Darkness: British Literature and Imperialism, 1830–1914.* Ithaca: Cornell University Press, 1988.
Brecht, Bertolt, and John Willett. *Brecht on Theatre: The Development of an Aesthetic.* New York: Hill and Wang, 1978.
Britton, Andrew. "The Lady From Shanghai: Betrayed by Rita Hayworth." *The Book of Film Noir.* Ed. Ian Cameron. New York: Continuum, 1992. 213–21.
Brown, Fredric. *The Fabulous Clipjoint.* 1948. Boston, MA: Gregg Press, 1979.
Burroughs, Edgar Rice. *Tarzan of the Apes.* 1912. Penguin twentieth-century classics. New York: Penguin Books, 1990.
Cameron, James, dir. *The Terminator.* Perfs. Arnold Schwarzenegger, Michael Biehn, and Linda Hamilton. Orion Pictures Corporation, 1984.

Camus, Albert. *The Myth of Sisyphus and Other Essays*. Trans. Justin O'Brien. New York: Vintage, 1955.

Castillo, Debra A. "Borges and Pynchon: The Tenuous Symmetries of Art." *New Essays on* The Crying of Lot 49. Ed. Patrick O'Donnell. Cambridge: Cambridge University Press, 1991. 21–46.

Cawelti, John G. "*Chinatown* and Generic Transformation in Recent American Films." *Film Theory and Criticism*. Eds. Gerald Mast, Marshall Cohen, and Leo Braudy. 4th ed. New York and Oxford: Oxford University Press, 1974. 498–511.

———. *Adventure, Mystery, and Romance: Formula Stories as Art and Popular Culture*. Chicago: University of Chicago Press, 1976.

Chandler, Raymond. *The Big Sleep*. 1939. New York: Vintage, 1988.

———. *The High Window*. 1942. New York: Vintage, 1992.

———. "Introduction to *The Simple Art of Murder*." *Raymond Chandler: Later Novels and Other Writings*. Ed. Frank MacShane. New York: Library of America, 1995.

———. *The Little Sister*. 1949. Harmondsworth, Middlesex: Penguin Books, 1961.

———. *The Long Goodbye*. New York: Ballantine Books, 1953.

———. "The Simple Art of Murder: An Essay." 1934. *The Simple Art of Murder*. New York: Ballantine Books, 1984. 1–21.

———. "The Tropical Romance." *Chandler Before Marlowe: The Early Prose and Poetry*. Ed. Matthew Bruccoli. Columbia: University of South Carolina Press, 1973. 68–70.

Chatterjee, Ranjit, and Colin Nicholson. *Tropic Crucible: Self and Theory in Language and Literature*. Singapore: Singapore University Press, National University of Singapore, 1984.

Christianson, Scott R. "'A Heap of Broken Images': Hardboiled Detective Fiction and the Discourse(s) of Modernity." *The Cunning Craft: Original Essays on Detective Fiction and Contemporary Literary Theory*. Eds. Ronald G. Walker and June M. Frazier. Macomb: Western Illinois University Press, 1976. 135–48.

Chung, Sue Fawn. "From Fu Manchu, Evil Genius, to James Lee Wong Popular Hero." *Journal of Popular Culture* 10.3 (Winter 1976): 534–47.

Conard, Mark T. "*Reservoir Dogs*: Redemption in a Postmodern World." *The Philosophy of Neo-Noir*. Ed. Mark T. Conrad. Lexington: University Press of Kentucky, 2007. 101–118.

Conrad, Joseph. *Heart of Darkness*. 1899. New York: Bedford St. Martin's, 1996.

———. *Lord Jim: A Tale*. Oxford: Oxford University Press, 2002.

———. "An Outpost of Progress." *The Complete Short Fiction of Joseph Conrad*. Ed. Samuel Hynes. New York: Eccho, 1991.

Coppola, Francis Ford, dir. *The Conversation*. Perfs. Gene Hackman, John Cazale, and Robert Duvall. Paramount, 1974.

Couturier, Maurice. "The Death of the Real in *The Crying of Lot 49*." *Pynchon Notes* 20–21 (1981): 5–29.

Culp, Robert, dir. *Hickey and Boggs*. Perfs. Robert Culp and Bill Cosby. United Artists, 1972.

Dahl, John, dir. *Red Rock West*. Perfs. Nicholas Cage, Lara Flynn Boyle, and Dennis Hopper. DeLuxe, 1992.

D'Aries, Donald R., and Foster Hirsch. "'Saint' Sydney: Atonement and Moral Inversion in *Hard Eight*. *The Philosophy of Neo-Noir*. Ed. Mark T. Conrad. Lexington: University Press of Kentucky, 2007. 91–100.

Das, Prasanta. "Oedipa's Night Journey in Pynchon's *The Crying of Lot 49*." *Notes on Contemporary Literature* 23.2 (1993): 4–5.

Dassin, Jules, dir. *The Naked City*. Perfs. Barry Fitzgerald, Howard Duff, and Dorothy Hart. Universal Pictures, 1948.

———, dir. *Night and the City*. Perfs. Richard Widmark, Gene Tierney, and Herbert Lom. Twentieth Century Fox, 1950.

De Los Santos, Oscar. "Auster vs. Chandler: Or, Cracking the Case of the Postmodern Mystery." *Connecticut Review* 16.1 (Spring 1994): 75–80.

Denby, David. "Boys Will Be Boys." Rev. of *The Usual Suspects*, dir. Bryan Singer. *New York* (August 28 1995): 118.

Denzin, Norman K. "*Blue Velvet*: Postmodern Contradictions." *Theory. Culture and Society* 5.2–3 (1987): 461–73.

Dick, Philip K. *Do Androids Dream of Electric Sheep?* New York: Signet, 1968.

———. *Flow My Tears, The Policeman Said*. 1974. New York: Vintage Books, 1993.

Dieterle, William, dir. *Dark City*. Perfs. Charlton Heston, Lizabeth Scott, and Mike Mazurki. Paramount Pictures, 1950.

———, dir. *The Turning Point*. Perfs. William Holden, Edmond O'Brien, and Alexis Smith. Paramount Pictures, 1952.

Diski, Jenny. "The Shadow Within." Rev. of *Cape Fear*, dir. Martin Scorsese. *Sight and Sound* (February 1992): 12.

Dixon, Robert. *Writing the Colonial Adventure: Race, Gender, and Nation in Anglo-Australian Popular Fiction, 1875–1914*. Cambridge: Cambridge University Press, 1995.

Dmytryk, Edward, dir. *Murder, My Sweet*. Perfs. Dick Powell, Claire Trevor, Anne Shirley, and Otto Kruger. RKO, 1945.

———, dir. *The Sniper*. Perfs. Adolphe Menjou, Arthur Franz, and Marie Windsor. Columbia Pictures, 1952.

———, dir. *Till The End of Time*. Perfs. Guy Madison, Dorothy Maguire, and Robert Mitchum. RKO, 1946.

Dower, John W. *War without Mercy: Race and Power in the Pacific War*. New York: Pantheon Books, 1986.

Doyle, Arthur Conan. *The Complete Sherlock Holmes*. Garden City: Garden City Publishing Company, Inc., 1938.

Dugan, Dennis, dir. *Problem Child*. Perfs. John Ritter, Jacke Warden, and Michael Oliver. Universal Pictures, 1990.

Durgnat, Raymond. "Paint It Black: The Family Tree of the Film Noir." *Film Noir Reader*. Ed. Alain Silver and James Ursini. New York: Limelight Editions, 1996. 46–47.

Dussere, Erik. "Out of the Past, Into the Supermarket: Consuming Film Noir." *Film Quarterly* 60, no. 1 (Fall 2006): 16–27.

Dyer, Richard. *Seven*. London: British Film Institute, 1999.

Eagleton, Terry. "Capitalism, Modernism and Postmodernism." *Against the Grain: Essays 1975–1985*. London: Verso, 1986. 131–47.

———. *Literary Theory: An Introduction*. Minneapolis: University of Minnesota Press, 1983.

Edelson, Cheryl. "Poe and Foucault: Heterotopias in the Rue Morgue." Paper presented at the American Literature Association 11th Annual Conference, Long Beach, CA. 26 May 2000.

Ellsaesser, Thomas. "Tales of Sound and Fury: Observations on the Family Melodrama." *Film Theory and Criticism: Introductory Readings*. Eds. Gerald Mast, Marshall Cohen, Leo Braudy. 4th ed. New York and Oxford: Oxford University Press, 1992. 512–35.

Erickson, Todd. "Kill Me Again: Movement Becomes Genre." *Film Noir Reader*. Eds. Alain Silver and James Ursini. New York: Limelight Editions, 1996. 307–329.

Ferrara, Abel, dir. *Bad Lieutenant*. Perfs. Harvey Keitel, Frankie Thorn, and Robin Burrows. Aries Films, 1992.

Feist, Felix, dir. *The Devil Thumbs a Ride*. Perfs. Ted North and Lawrence Tierney. RKO Pictures, 1947.

Figgis, Mike, dir. *Stormy Monday*. Perfs. Melanie Griffith, Tommy Lee Jones, and Sting. Atlantic Entertainment, 1988.

Fincher, David, dir. *Seven*. Perfs. Brad Pitt, Morgan Freeman, and Gwyneth Paltrow. New Line Cinema, 1995.

Fine, David M. *Los Angeles in Fiction: A Collection of Original Essays*. Albuquerque: University of New Mexico Press, 1984.

"First Brands reinvents the plastic bag; With patented Quick-Tie/TM Flaps, GLAD/R transforms the trash bag business by eliminating twist ties—An American Institution—." *Business Wire*. July 13, 1995. FindArticles.com. 22 Jun. 2008. http://findarticles.com/p/articles/mi_m0EIN/is_1995_July_13/ai_17237908

Fishburn, Katherine. *Richard Wright's Hero: The Faces of a Rebel-victim*. Metuchen, NJ: Scarecrow Press, 1977.

Fleder, Gary, dir. *Things To Do In Denver When You're Dead*. Perfs. Andy Garcia, Christopher Walken, and Gabrielle Anwar. Miramax Films, 1995.

Fleming, Victor. *A Guy Named Joe*. Perfs. Spencer Tracy, Irene Dunne, and Van Johnson. MGM, 1943.

Fontana, Ernest. "Chivalry and Modernity in Raymond Chandler's *The Big Sleep*." *Western American Literature* 19.3 (1984): 179–86.

Foster, Hal. "Postmodernism: A Preface." *The Anti-Aesthetic: Essays on Postmodern Culture*. Port Townsend, WA: Bay Press, 1983. ix–xvi.

Fotsch, Paul Mason. *Watching the Traffic Go by: Transportation and Isolation in Urban America*. Austin: University of Texas Press, 2007.

Foucault, Michel. *Technologies of the Self: A Seminar with Michel Foucault*. Eds. L. Martin, H. Gutman, and P. Hutton. Amherst: University of Massachusetts Press, 1988.

Franklin, Carl, dir. *Devil in a Blue Dress*. Perfs. Denzel Washington, Jennifer Beals, and Don Cheadle. TriStar Pictures, 1995.

———, dir. *One False Move*. Perfs. Billy Bob Thornton, Bill Paxton, Cynda Williams, and Michael Beach. Columbia Pictures, 1992.

Frears, Stephen, dir. *The Grifters*. Perfs. John Cusack, Angelica Huston, and Annette Bening. Cineplex-Odeon Films, 1990.

Fuller, Samuel, dir. *China Gate*. Perfs. Gene Barry, Angie Dickinson, and Nat "King" Cole. Twentieth Century Fox, 1957.

———, dir. *The Crimson Kimono*. Perfs. James Shigeta, Glenn Corbett, and Victoria Shaw. Globe Enterprises, 1959.

———, dir. *House of Bamboo*. Perfs. Robert Stack, Robert Ryan, and Shirley Yamaguchi. Twentieth Century-Fox, 1955.

Gates, Henry Louis. *The Signifying Monkey: A Theory of Afro-American Literary Criticism*. New York: Oxford University Press, 1988.
Gault, William Campbell. "Hibiscus and Homicide." Maxim Jakubowski, ed. *The Mammoth Book of Pulp Fiction*. New York: Carroll & Graf Publishers, 1996. 486–527.
Geherin, David. *John D. MacDonald*. New York: Frederic Ungar Publishing Co., 1982.
Gilbert, Sandra M., and Susan Gubar. *The Madwoman in the Attic: The Woman Writer and the Nineteenth-Century Literary Imagination*. New Haven: Yale University Press, 1984.
Gill, Pat. "Apprehending Criminals: Genre and Interpretation in *Seven*." *Cultural Studies ↔ Critical Methodologies* 2 (2002): 47–68.
Goodis, David. *Nightfall: A Novel*. Lakewood, CO: Millipede Press, 2007.
Goodwin, James. *Akira Kurosawa and Intertextual Cinema*. Baltimore: Johns Hopkins University Press, 1994.
Goulart, Ron. *The Dime Detectives: A Comprehensive History of the Detective Fiction Pulps.* New York: the Mysterious Press, 1988.
Goulding, Edmund, dir. *Nightmare Alley*. Tyrone Power, Joan Blondell, and Coleen Gray. Twentieth Century Fox, 1947.
Grant, J. Kerry. *A Companion to* The Crying of Lot 49. Athens and London: The University of Georgia Press, 1994.
Green, Martin. *Dreams of Adventure, Deeds of Empire*. New York: Basic Books, 1979.
Gresham, William Lindsay. *Nightmare Alley*. Ed. Robert Polito. *Crime Novels: American Noir of the 1930s and 40s*. New York: Library of America, 1997.
Griffith, D. W., dir. *The Musketeers of Pig Alley*. Perfs. Elmer Booth, Lillian Gish, and Clara T. Bracy. Biograph, 1912.
Grist, Leighton. "Out of the Past, a.k.a. Build My Gallows High." *The Book of* Film Noir." Ed. Ian Cameron. New York: The Continuum Publishing Company, 1992. 203–212.
Hammett, Dashiell. "Ber-Bulu." *Sunset Magazine* (March 1925): 17–20.
———. *Crime Stories and Other Writings*. New York: Library of America, 2001.
———. *The Maltese Falcon*. 1930. New York: Vintage, 1972.
———. *Nightmare Town*. New York: Knopf, 1999.
———. "The Road Home." 1922. *The Hard-Boiled Detective: Stories from* Black Mask Magazine *(1920–1951)*. Ed. Herbert Ruhm. New York: Vintage Books, 1977. 31–44.
Hantke, Steffen. "Boundary Crossing and the Construction of Cinematic Genre: Film Noir as 'Deferred Action.'" *Kinema: A Journal for Film and Audiovisual Media* (Fall, 2004) 9 January, 2006. 15 June 2006. http://www.kinema.uwaterloo.ca/hant042.htm.
Harrowitz, Nancy A. "Criminality and Poe's Orangutan: The Question of Race in Detection." *Agonistics: Arenas of Creative Contest*. Eds. Janet Lungstrum and Elizabeth Sauer. Albany: State University of New York Press, 1997. 177–95.
Haut, Woody. *Pulp Culture: Hardboiled Fiction and the Cold War*. London: Serpent's Tail, 1995.
Hayles, N. Katherine. "'A Metaphor of God Knew How Many Parts': The Engine that Drives *The Crying of Lot 49*." *New Essays on* The Crying of Lot 49. Ed. Patrick O'Donnell. Cambridge: Cambridge University Press, 1991. 97–126.
Hellman, Lillian. *Scoundrel Time*. Boston: Little, Brown, 2000.
Hemingway, Ernest. "A Clean, Well-Lighted Place." 1933. *The Snows of Kilimanjaro and Other Stories*. New York: Charles Scribner's Sons, 1961. 29–33.

Himes, Chester. *All Shot Up.* 1960. New York: Thunder's Mouth Press, 1996.

———. *If He Hollers Let Him Go.* 1945. Foreword by Graham Hodges. New York: Thunders Mouth Press, 1986.

Henry, O. *The Head-Hunter.* New York: The Ridgway Company, 1908.

Hiney, Tom. *Raymond Chandler. A Biography.* Chatto & Windus, London 1997.

Hirsch, Foster. *The Dark Side of the Screen: Film Noir.* San Diego: A. S. Barnes, 1981.

———. *Detours and Lost Highways: A Map of Neo-Noir.* New York : Limelight Editions, 1999.

Hitchcock, Alfred, dir. *Rear Window.* Perfs. James Stewart, Grace Kelly, and Thelma Ritter. Paramount, 1954.

———, dir. *Vertigo.* Perfs. James Stewart, Kim Novak, and Barbara Bel Geddes, Paramount Pictures, 1958.

———, dir. *The Wrong Man.* Perfs. Henry Fonda and Vera Miles. Warner, 1956.

Hite, Molly. *Ideas of Order in the Novels of Thomas Pynchon.* Columbus: Ohio State University Press, 1983.

Hively, Jack, dir. *Street of Chance.* Perfs. Burgess Meredith, Clare Trevor, and Louise Platt.

Hoberman, J. "Sacred and Profane." Rev. of *Cape Fear,* dir. Martin Scorsese. *Sight and Sound* 1.9 (February 1992): 8.

Hocker Rushing, Janice, and Thomas S. Frentz. *Projecting the Shadow: The Cyborg Hero in American Film.* Chicago and London: The University of Chicago Press, 1995.

Holden, Stephen. "Rev. of *Brick,* dir. Rian Johnson." *New York Times,* 31 Mar. 2006. Web. 10 June 2008. http://movies.nytimes.com/2006/03/31/movies/31bric.html.

Hopper, Dennis, dir. *The Hot Spot.* Perfs. Don Johnson, Virginia Madsen, and Jennifer Connelly. Orion Pictures, 1990.

Hopper, Edward. *Nighthawks.* 1942. The Art Institute of Chicago.

Hughes, Dorothy B. *In a Lonely Place.* 1947. New York: Bantam, 1979.

———. *Ride the Pink Horse.* 1946. New York: Penguin Books, 1988.

Huston, John, dir. *The Asphalt Jungle.* Perfs. Sterling Hayden, Louis Calhern, Jean Hagen, and James Whitmore. Warner Brothers, 1950.

———, dir. *Key Largo.* Perfs. Humphrey Bogart, Lauren Bacall, and Edward G. Robinson. Warner Bros., 1947.

Hutcheon, Linda."Beginning to Theorize Postmodernism." *Textual Practice* 1.1 (1987): 10–31.

———. *A Poetics of Postmodernism: History, Theory, Fiction.* London & New York: Routledge, 1988.

———. *The Politics of Postmodernism.* London and New York: Routledge, 1989.

Ikard, David. *Breaking the Silence: Toward a Black Male Feminist Criticism.* Louisiana State University, 2007.

Jacobowitz, Florence. "The Man's Melodrama: The Woman in the Window and Scarlet Street. *The Book of Film Noir.* Ed. Ian Cameron. New York: Continuum, 1992. 152–64.

Jameson, Fredric. "On Raymond Chandler." *Southern Review* 6.3 (Summer 1970): 624–50.

———. *Postmodernism, or, the Cultural Logic of Late Capitalism.* Durham: Duke University Press, 1991.

Jeter, K. W. *Noir*. New York: Bantam Books, 1998.
Johnson, Rian, dir. *Brick*. Perfs. Joseph Gordon-Levitt, Nora Zehetner, and Lukas Haas. Bergman Lustig Productions, 2005.
Kaplan, Amy. "The Birth of an Empire." *PMLA* 114, no. 5 (Oct. 1999): 1068–79.
Kaplan, E. Ann. "The 'Dark Continent' of Film Noir: Race, Displacement and Metaphor in Tourneur's *Cat People* (1942) and Welles' *The Lady from Shanghai* (1948). 1978. *Women in Film Noir*. Ed. E. Ann Kaplan. London: British Film Institute, 1998. 183–201.

———. *Looking for the Other: Feminism, Film, and the Imperial Gaze*. New York: Routledge, 1996.
Kasdan, Lawrence, dir. *Body Heat*. Perfs. William Hurt, Kathleen Turner, and Richard Crenna. Warner Brothers, 1981.
Kauffmann, Stanley. "Southern Discomfort." Rev. of *Cape Fear*, dir. Martin Scorsese. *New Republic* (December 9, 1991): 28.
Kazan, Elia, dir. *Panic in the Streets*. Perfs. Richard Widmark, Paul Douglas, and Jack Palance. 20th Century-Fox, 1950.
Keep, Christopher, and Don Randall. "Addiction, Empire, and Narrative in Arthur Conan Doyle's *The Sign of the Four*." *Novel: A Forum on Fiction* (Spring 1999): 207–221.
Kelly, R. G. "The Precarious World of John D. MacDonald." *Dimensions of Detective Fiction*. Eds. Larry N. Landrum, Pat Browne, and Ray B. Browne. Bowling Green, OH: Popular Press, 1976. 149–61.
Kemp, Phillip. Rev. of *The Usual Suspects*, dir. Bryan Singer. *Sight and Sound* 5.9 (September 1995): 61.
Kevorkian, Martin. *Color Monitors: The Black Face of Technology in America*. Ithaca: Cornell University Press, 2006.
Kipling, Rudyard. "Mandalay." *The Literature of England*. Eds. George K. Anderson and Karl J. Holzknecht. Chicago: Scott, Foresman, and Company, 1953. 1043.
Klawans, Stuart. Rev. of *Cape Fear*, dir. Martin Scorsese. *The Nation* (December 23, 1991): 826.
Koch, Howard W., and Edmond O'Brien, dirs. *Shield for Murder*. Perfs. Edmond O'Brien, Marla English, and John Agar. United Artists, 1954.
Kolker, Robert Phillip. *A Cinema of Loneliness: Penn, Kubrick, Scorsese, Spielberg, Altman*. 2nd ed. New York and Oxford: Oxford University Press, 1988.
Kristeva, Julia. *Strangers to Ourselves*. Trans. Leon S. Roudiez. New York: Columbia University Press, 1991.
Krutnik, Frank. *In A Lonely Street: Film Noir, Genre, and Masculinity*. 1991. London and New York: Routledge Press, 1993.
Kubrick, Stanley, dir. *The Killing*. Perfs. Sterling Hayden, Coleen Gray, and Val Cannon. United Artists, 1956.
Kurosawa, Akira, dir. *Nora Inu* [*Stray Dog*]. Perfs. Toshiro Mifune, Takashi Shimura, and Isao Kimura. Toho Company, 1949.
Larsen, Ernest. *The Usual Suspects*. London: British Film Institute, 2002.
Laughton, Charles, dir. *The Night of the Hunter*. Perfs. Robert Mitchum, Shelly Winters, and Lillian Gish. United Artists, 1955.
Lawton, Harry. *Willie Boy: A Desert Manhunt*. Balboa Island, CA: Paisano Press, 1960.

Lee, Rachel. "Journalistic Representations of Asian Americans and Literary Responses." In *An Interethnic Companion to Asian American Literature*. Ed. King-kok Cheung. Cambridge, MA: Harvard University Press, 1997. 249–73.

Leibman, Nina C. "The Family Spree of Film Noir." *Journal of Popular Film and Television* 16.4 (Winter 1989): 168–84.

Letts, Vanessa. "Dirty deeds." Rev. of *Cape Fear*, dir. Martin Scorsese. *The Spectator* (7 March 1992): 35.

Lewis, Barry. "The Strange Case of Paul Auster." *The Review of Contemporary Fiction* 14.1 (Spring 1994): 53–61.

Limerick, Patricia Nelson. "What Raymond Chandler Knew and Western Historians Forgot." *Old West–New West: Centennial Essays*. Ed. Barbara Howard Meldrum. Moscow, ID: University of Idaho Press, 1993. 28–39.

Lindh, John Walker. "City Jungles and Expressionist Reifications from Brecht to Hammett." *Twentieth Century Literature*. 44. 1 (1998): 119–34.

Little, William G. "Surviving *Memento*." *Narrative*. 13.1 (2005): 67–83.

Littlewood, Derek, and Peter Stockwell. *Impossibility Fiction: Alternativity, Extrapolation, Speculation*. Rodopi perspectives on modern literature, 17. Amsterdam: Rodopi, 1996.

Losey, Joseph, dir. *M*. Perfs. David Wayne, Howard Da Silva, and Martin Gabel. Columbia Pictures, 1951.

Lott, Eric. "The Whiteness of Film Noir." *Whiteness: A Critical Reader*. Ed. Mike Hill. New York and London: New York University Press, 1997. 81–101.

Loza, Susana. "Orientalism and Film Noir: (Un)Mapping Textual Territories and (En)Countering the Narratives." *The Southern Quarterly* 39(4): 161–74.

Lucas, Blake. "Cape Fear." *Film Noir: An Encyclopedic Reference to the American Style*. 3rd ed. Eds. Alain Silver and Elizabeth Ward. Woodstock, NY: Overlook Press, 1993. 51.

Lynch, David, dir. *Blue Velvet*. Perfs. Kyle Maclachlan and Isabella Rossellini. MGM/United Artists, 1986.

MacDonald, John D. *Cape Fear* (Formerly titled *The Executioners*). 1957. New York: Fawcett Gold Medal, 1991.

Macek, Carl. "D.O.A." *Film Noir: An Encyclopedic Reference to the American Style*. 3rd ed. Eds. Alain and Elizabeth Ward. Woodstock, NY: Overlook Press, 1993.

MacShane, Frank. *The Life of Raymond Chandler*. Boston: G. K. Hall & Co., 1986.

Mamet, David, dir. *House of Games*. Perfs. Michael Hausman, Jonathan Katz, Lindsay Crouse, Joe Mantegna, and Mike Nussbaum. Orion Pictures. 1987.

Mankiewicz, Joseph L., dir. *Somewhere in the Night*. Perfs. John Hodiak, Nancy Guild, and Lloyd Nolan. Twentieth Century-Fox, 1946.

Marling, William. *The American Roman Noir: Hammett, Cain, and Chandler*. Athens: University of Georgia Press, 1995.

Marshall, George, dir. *The Blue Dahlia*. Paramount Pictures, 1946.

Maté, Rudolf. dir. *D.O.A*. Perfs. Edmond O'Brien, Pamela Britton, and Luther Adler. United Artists, 1950.

Mauss, Marcel. *The Gift: The Form and Reason for Exchange in Archaic Societies*. 1925. Trans. W. D. Halls. London: Routledge, 1990.

McCann, Sean. *Gumshoe America: Hard-Boiled Crime Fiction and the Rise and Fall of New Deal Liberalism*. Durham, NC: Duke University Press, 2001.

McClintock, Anne. *Imperial Leather: Race, Gender, and Sexuality in the Colonial Contest.* New York and London: Routledge, 1995.

McGarry, Eileen. "Dirty Harry." *Film Noir: An Encyclopedic Reference to the American Style.* 3rd ed. Eds. Alain Silver and Elizabeth Ward. Woodstock, NY: Overlook Press, 1993. 92.

McLaughlin, Joseph. *Writing the Urban Jungle: Reading Empire in London from Doyle to Eliot.* Charlottesville: University Press of Virginia, 2000.

McQuarrie, Christopher. *The Usual Suspects* (original script). Culver City, CA: Blue Parrot, Inc. 1994.

McRobbie, Angela. Rev. of *Cape Fear,* dir. Martin Scorsese. *Sight and Sound* (March 1992): 39.

McTiernan, John, dir. *Die Hard.* Perfs. Bruce Willis, and Bonnie Bedelia, and Reginald VelJohnson. Twentieth Century-Fox, 1988.

Melville, Jean-Pierre, dir. *Bob le Flambeur.* Perfs. Roger Duchesne, Isabelle Corey, and Daniel Cauchy. O.G.C./Studio Jenner, 1955.

Mitsuda, Kristi. "'A Neo-Noir High School Tale: Rian Johnson's 'Brick.'" indieWire. February 25, 2007. http://www.indiewire.com/article/a_neo_noir_high_school_tale_rian_johnsons_brick/.

Meyers, Jeffrey. "Introduction to *Sunset Boulevard.*" *Sunset Boulevard.* By Billy Wilder. Berkeley: University of California Press, 1999.

Michaels, Lloyd. *The Phantom of the Cinema: Character in Modern Film.* Albany: State University of New York Press, 1998.

Miller, D. A. *The Novel and the Police.* Berkeley and Los Angeles: The University of California Press, 1988.

Montgomery, Robert, dir. *Rise the Pink Horse.* Perfs. Robert Montgomery, Wanda Hendrix, and Thomas Gomez. Universal International Pictures, 1947.

Morton, Marcus. "'Sin City' a sign of postmodern corruption." *Santa Cruz Sentinel.* 29 April 2005. 15 June 2005. http://www.scsextra.com/story.php?sid=25717.

Mosley, Walter. *Devil in a Blue Dress.* New York: Norton, 1990.

Murphet, Julian. "Film Noir and the Racial Unconscious." *Screen* 39 .1 (1998): 22–35.

Musser, Charles. *The Emergence of the Cinema: The American Screen to 1907.* New York: Scribner's, 1990.

Naremore, James. *More Than Night: Film Noir in its Contexts.* Berkeley: University of California Press, 1998.

Neely, Richard. *Shattered.* 1969. New York: Vintage Crime/Black Lizard, 1991.

Newell, Mike, dir. *Donnie Brasco.* Perfs. Johnny Depp, Al Pacino, and Anne Heche. TriStar Pictures, 1997.

Nieland, Justus J. "Race-ing Noir and Re-Placing History: The Mulatta and Memory in *One False Move* and *Devil in a Blue Dress.*" *Velvet Light Trap* 43 (Spring 1999): 63–77.

Nolan, Christopher, dir. *Memento.* Perfs. Guy Pearce, Carrie-Anne Moss, and Joe Pantoliano, Columbia/Tri-Star, 2000.

Nyman, Jopi. *Men Alone: Masculinity, Individualism, and Hard-Boiled Fiction.* Costerus, new ser., v. 111. Amsterdam: Rodopi, 1997.

O'Donnell, Patrick. Introduction. *New Essays on* The Crying of Lot 49. Ed. Patrick O'Donnell. Cambridge: Cambridge University Press, 1991. 1–20.

Ogdon, Bethany. "Hard-Boiled Ideology." *Critical Quarterly* 34.1 (Spring 1992): 71–87.
Okada, John. *No-No Boy.* Seattle: University of Washington Press, 1979.
Oliver, Kelly, and Benigno Trigo. *Noir Anxiety.* Minneapolis: University of Minnesota Press, 2003.
Olstein, Andrew. "'It's the end of the world . . .': smiling through the apocalypse with the noir generation." *Los Angeles* (October 1995): 53–59.
Otis, Laura. *Membranes: Metaphors of Invasion in Nineteenth-Century Literature, Science, and Politics.* Baltimore: Johns Hopkins University Press, 1999.
Ottoson, Robert. *A Reference Guide to the American Film Noir.* Metuchen, NJ: The Scarecrow Press, 1981.
Orr, Stanley. "'I think it was his eye!': Edgar Allan Poe, Crime Fiction, and Panopticism." Paper presented at the American Literature Association 11th Annual Conference, Long Beach, CA. 26 May 2000.
Panek, Leroy Lad. *An Introduction to the Detective Story.* Bowling Green: Popular, 1987.
———. *Probable Cause: Crime Fiction in America.* Bowling Green: Popular, 1990.
———. *Reading Early Hammett: A Critical Study of the Fiction Prior to the Maltese Falcon.* Jefferson, NC: McFarland & Company, 2004.
Paravisini, Lizabeth. "*Mumbo Jumbo* and the Uses of Parody." *Obsidian II: Black Literature in Review* 1.1–2 (1986): 113–25.
Patmore, Coventry. *The Angel in the House.* London: John W. Parker & Son, 1854.
Place, J. A., and L. S. Peterson. "Some Visual Motifs of Film Noir." *Film Comment* 10.1 (1974): 30–32.
———. "Women in Film Noir." *Women in Film Noir.* Ed. E. Ann Kaplan. London: BFI, 1980. 35–67.
Peckinpah, Sam, dir. *The Wild Bunch.* Perfs. William Holden, Robert Ryan, and Ernest Borgnine. Warner Brothers/Seven Arts, 1969.
Pichel, Irving, dir. *They Won't Believe Me.* Perfs. Susan Hayward, Robert Young, and Jane Greer. RKO, 1947.
Polan, Dana B. *In a Lonely Place.* BFI film classics. London: BFI Pub, 1993.
Polanski, Roman, dir. *Chinatown.* Perfs. Jack Nicholson, Faye Dunaway, and John Huston. Paramount, 1974.
Polk, Dora Beale. *The Island of California: A History of the Myth.* Lincoln and London: University of Nebraska Press, 1991.
Porfirio, Robert. "No Way Out: Existentialist Motifs in the *Film Noir.* 1976. Film Noir Reader.* Eds. Alain Silver and James Ursini. New York: Limelight Editions, 1996. 77–93.
Pratt, Mary Louise. *Imperial Eyes: Travel Writing and Transculturation.* London and New York: Routledge, 1992.
Preminger, Otto, dir. *Where the Sidewalk Ends.* Perfs. Dana Andrews, Gene Tierney, and Gary Merrill. Twentieth Century-Fox, 1950.
Putz, Manfred. "The Art of the Acronym in Thomas Pynchon." *Studies in the Novel* 23.3 (Fall 1991): 371–82.
Pynchon, Thomas. *The Crying of Lot 49.* 1966. New York: Harper and Row, 1986.
———. *Gravity's Rainbow.* New York: Viking, 1973.
———. *V.* 1961. New York: Harper & Row Publishers, 1990.
———. *Vineland.* Boston, Toronto, London: Little, Brown and Company, 1990.

Quine, Richard, dir. *Pushover.* Perfs. Fred MacMurray, Phillip Carey, and Kim Novak. Columbia Pictures Corporation, 1954.

Rabinowitz, Paula. *Black & White & Noir: America's Pulp Modernism.* New York: Columbia University Press, 2002.

Riesman, David, Nathan Glazer, and Reuel Denney. *The Lonely Crowd: A Study of the Changing American Character.* Yale Nota bene. New Haven, CT: Yale University Press, 2001.

Rafferty, Terrence. "Mud." Rev. of *Cape Fear,* dir. Martin Scorsese. *The New Yorker* (December 2, 1991): 156.

Ray, Nicholas, dir. *In a Lonely Place.* Perfs. Humphrey Bogart and Gloria Grahame. Columbia Pictures, 1950.

Reed, Ishmael. *Mumbo Jumbo.* New York: Atheneum/Macmillan, 1988.

Richardson, Carl. *Autopsy: An Element of Realism in* Film Noir. Metuchen, NJ and London: The Scarecrow Press, Inc., 1992.

Rodriguez, Robert, dir. *Desperado.* Perfs. Antonio Banderas, Selma Hayek, and Joaquim de Almeida. Columbia Pictures, 1995.

———, dir. *El Mariachi.* Perfs. Carlos Gallardo, Consuelo Gomez, and Jaime de Hoyos. Columbia Pictures, 1993.

Rodriguez, Robert, and Frank Miller, dirs. *Sin City.* Perfs. Bruce Willis, Jessica Alba, and Devon Aoki. Dimension Films, 2005.

Rowe, John Carlos. *Literary Culture and U.S. Imperialism: From the Revolution to World War II.* Oxford: Oxford University Press, 2000.

Rowland, Roy, dir. *Rogue Cop.* Perfs. Robert Taylor, Janet Leigh, and George Raft. MGM, 1954.

Royden Winchell, Mark. "Fantasy Seen: Hollywood Fiction Since West." *Los Angeles in Fiction: A Collection of Original Essays.* Ed. David Fine. Albuquerque: University of New Mexico Press, 1984. 165–86.

Russell, Alison. "Deconstructing The New York Trilogy: Paul Auster's Anti-Detective Fiction." *Critique* 31 (1990): 71–84.

Russell, John. *Far Wandering Men.* (Tauchnitz Edition, 4934). 1930.

———. *In Dark Places.* London: Thornton Butterworth Ltd., 1924.

———. *Where the Pavement Ends.* London: Thornton Butterworth Ltd., 1921.

Rzepka, Charles. "'I'm in the Business Too': Gothic Chivalry, Private Eyes, and Proxy Sex and Violence in Chandler's *The Big Sleep.*" *Modern Fiction Studies* 46.3 (2000): 695–724.

Sahay, Amrohini. "*Memento* and the Cultural Production of the New Corporate Worker." *The Red Critique* 3 (2002). 30 Oct. 2003. http://www.geocities.com/redtheory/redcritique/MarchApril02/memento.htm.

Said, Edward W. *Culture and Imperialism.* New York: Vintage Books, 1994.

———. *Orientalism.* New York: Vintage, 1978.

Sandos, James A., and Larry E. Burgess. *The Hunt for Willie Boy: Indian-Hating and Popular Culture.* Norman: University of Oklahoma Press, 1994.

Schlöndorff, Volker, dir. *Palmetto.* Perfs. Woody Harrelson, Elizabeth Shue, and Gina Gershon. Castle Rock Entertainment, 1998.

Schrader, Paul. "Notes on Film Noir." *Film Noir Reader.* Ed. Alain Silver and James Ursini. New York: Limelight Editions, 1996. 53–64.

Schrag, Calvin O. *The Self after Postmodernity.* New Haven: Yale University Press, 1997.
Schwab, Gabriele. "Cyborgs and Cybernetic Intertexts: On Postmodern Phantasms of the Body and Mind." *Intertextuality and Contemporary American Fiction.* Eds. Patrick O'Donnell and Robert Con Davis. Baltimore: Johns Hopkins University Press, 1989. 191–213.
Scorsese, Martin, dir. *Cape Fear.* Perfs. Robert DeNiro, Nick Nolte, and Jessica Lange. Universal, 1991.
———, dir. *Taxi Driver.* Perfs. Robert DeNiro and Jodie Foster. Columbia, 1976.
Scruggs, Charles. "The Pastoral and the City in Carl Franklin's *One False Move.*" *African American Review* 38.2 (Summer 2004): 323–34.
Shaviro, Steven. *Connected, or, What It Means to Live in the Network Society.* Electronic mediations, v. 9. Minneapolis: University of Minnesota Press, 2003.
Siegel, Don, dir. *Private Hell 36.* Perfs. Ida Lupino, Steve Cochran, and Howard Duff. The Filmmakers, 1954.
Silver, Alain, and Elizabeth Ward, eds. *Film Noir: An Encyclopedic Reference to the American Style.* 3rd ed. Woodstock, NY: Overlook Press, 1993.
———. "Son of *Noir:* Neo-*Film Noir* and the Neo-B Picture." *Film Noir Reader.* Eds. Alain Silver and James Ursini. New York: Limelight Editions, 1996. 331–338.
Simon, John. "Stick Figures in Depth." Rev. of *Cape Fear,* dir. Martin Scorsese. *National Review* (December 16, 1991): 56.
Simpson, Hassell A. "'So Long Beautiful Hunk': Ambiguous Gender and Songs of Parting in Raymond Chandler's Fictions." *Journal of Popular Culture* 28.2 (1995): 37–48.
Siodmak, Robert, dir. *The Killers.* Perfs. Burt Lancaster, Edmond O'Brien, and Ava Gardner. Universal, 1946.
Sirk, Douglas, dir. *All That Heaven Allows.* Perfs. Jane Wyman, Rock Hudson, and Agnes Moorhead. Universal-International, 1955.
Skenazy, Paul. *The New Wild West: The Urban Mysteries of Dashiell Hammett and Raymond Chandler.* Boise: Boise State University Press, 1982.
Sledge, E. B. *With the Old Breed, at Peleliu and Okinawa.* New York: Oxford University Press, 1990.
Slotkin, Richard. *Gunfighter Nation: The Myth of the Frontier in Twentieth-Century America.* New York: HarperCollins Publishing, Inc., 1992.
Sobchack, Vivian. *Screening Space: The American Science Fiction Film.* New York: Ungar, 1987.
Spanos, William V. "The Detective and the Boundary: Some Notes on the Postmodern Literary Imagination." *Boundary 2* I (Fall 1972): 147–68.
Spillane, Mickey. *I, the Jury.* New York: E.P. Dutton, 1947.
Springer, Claudia. *Electronic Eros: Bodies and Desire in the Postindustrial Age.* Austin: University of Texas Press, 1996.
Spurr, David. *The Rhetoric of Empire: Colonial Discourse in Journalism, Travel Writing, and Imperial Administration.* Durham: Duke University Press, 1993.
Starr, Kevin. *The Dream Endures: California Enters the 1940s.* New York: Oxford University Press, 1997.
Stern, Lesley. *The Scorsese Connection.* Bloomington: Indiana University Press, 1995.
Von Sternberg, Josef, dir. *Macao.* Perfs. Jane Russell, and Robert Mitchum. RKO, 1952.

———, dir. *The Shanghai Gesture.* Perfs. Walter Huston, Gene Tierney, and Victor Mature. United Artists, 1941.
Stevenson, Robert Louis. *The Beach of Falesá.* Ed. Barry Menikoff. Stanford, CA: Stanford University Press, 1987.
Swope, Richard. "Crossing Western Space, or the Hoodoo Detective on the Boundary in Ishmael Reed's *Mumbo Jumbo.*" *African American Review* 36.4 (Winter 2002): 611–29.
Tanner, Tony. *Thomas Pynchon.* London: Methuen, 1982.
Tarantino, Quentin, dir. *Pulp Fiction.* Perfs. John Travolta, Samuel L. Jackson, Uma Thurman, and Bruce Willis. Miramax Films, 1994.
———, dir. *Reservoir Dogs.* Perfs. Tim Roth, Harvey Keitel, and Michael Madsen. Miramax Films, 1992.
Telotte, J. P. "Fatal Capers: Strategy and Enigma in Film *Noir.*" *Journal of Popular Film and Television* 23.4 (Winter 1997): 163–70.
———. *Voices in the Dark: The Narrative Patterns of Film Noir.* Urbana and Chicago: The University of Illinois Press, 1989.
Tetzlaff, Ted, dir. *The Window.* Perfs. Bobby Driscoll, Barbara Hale, and Arthur Kennedy. RKO, 1949.
Thomas, David, dir. *Raymond Chandler.* RM Associates, 1988.
Thomas, Nicholas, and Richard Eves. *Bad Colonists: the South Seas Letters of Vernon Lee Walker and Louis Becke,* Durham, NC: Duke University Press, 1999.
Thomas, Ronald R. *Detective Fiction and the Rise of Forensic Science.* Cambridge: Cambridge University Press, 1999.
———. "Fingerprint of the Foreigner: Colonizing the Criminal Body in 1890s Detective Fiction and Criminal Anthropology." *English Literary History* 61 (1994): 655–83.
Thompson, Jim. "The Cellini Chalice." *Fireworks: The Lost Writings.* Eds. Robert Polito and Michael J. McCauley. New York: Mysterious Press, 1989. 58–101.
———. *The Grifters.* 1963. Berkeley: Black Lizard, 1985.
Thompson, Jon. *Fiction, Crime, and Empire: Clues to Modernity and Postmodernism.* Urbana and Chicago: University of Illinois Press, 1993.
Thompson, Kristen. "*Cape Fear* and Trembling: Familial Dread." *Literature and Film: A Guide to the Theory and Practice of Film Adaptation.* Eds. Robert Stam and Alessandra Raengo. Malden, MA: Blackwell, 2005. 126–47.
Thomspon, Lee J., dir. *Cape Fear.* Perfs. Robert Mitchum, Gregory Peck, and Polly Bergen. Universal Pictures, 1962.
Thorpe, Richard, dir. *Malaya.* Perfs. Spencer Tracy, James Stewart, and Sydney Greenstreet. MGM, 1949.
Torgovnick, Marianna. *Gone Primitive: Savage Intellects, Modern Lives.* Chicago: The University of Chicago Press, 1990.
Tourneur, Jacques, dir. *Out of the Past.* Perfs. Robert Mitchum, Kirk Douglass, and Jane Greer. RKO Pictures, 1947.
Tracey, Grant. "Film Noir and Samuel Fuller's Tabloid Cinema: Red (Action), White (Exposition), and Blue (Romance)." *Film Noir Reader 2.* Eds. Alain Silver and James Ursini. New York: Limelight Editions, 1999. 159–75.
Truman, Benjamin Cummings. *Semi-tropical California: its climate, healthfulness, productiveness, and scenery. . . .* San Francisco: A. L. Bancroft, 1874.

Tuttle, Frank, dir. *This Gun for Hire*. Perfs. Alan Ladd, Veronica Lake, Robert Preston, and Laird Cregar. Paramount-Universal, 1942.

Tysh, Chris. "From One Mirror to Another: The Rhetoric of Disaffiliation in *City of Glass*." *The Review of Contemporary Fiction* XIV.1 (Spring 1994): 46–52.

Ursini, James. "Angst at Sixty Fields per Second." Film Noir *Reader*. Eds. Alain Silver and James Ursini. New York: Limelight Editions, 1996. 275–88.

Vernet, Marc. "Film Noir on the Edge of Doom." *Shades of Noir: A Reader*. Ed. Joan Copjec. London/New York: Verso, 1993. 1–33.

Virilio, Paul. "Critical Space." *The Virilio Reader*. Ed. James Der Derian. Malden, MA: Blackwell Publishers, 1998. 58–72.

Wallace, Richard, dir. *The Fallen Sparrow*. Perfs. John Garfield and Maureen O'Hara. RKO, 1943.

Walsh, Raoul, dir. *White Heat*. Perfs. James Cagney, Virginia Mayo, and Edmond O'Brien. Warner Bros, 1949.

Wang, Wayne, dir. *Chan Is Missing*. Perfs. Wood Moy and Marc Hayashi. New Yorker Films. 1982.

Ward, Elizabeth, "The Post-Noir P.I.: *The Long Goodbye* and *Hickey and Boggs*." *Film Noir Reader*. Eds. Alain. Silver and James Ursini, 8th ed. 237–42.

Warrick, Patricia S. *Mind in Motion: The Fiction of Philip K. Dick*. Carbondale and Edwardsville: Southern Illinois University Press, 1987.

Watson, Robert N. "Who Bids for Tristero? The Conversion of Pynchon's Oedipa Maas." *Southern Humanities Review* 17 (Winter 1983): 59–75.

Welles, Orson, dir. *The Lady from Shanghai*. Perfs. Orson Welles, Rita Hayworth, and Everett, Sloane. Columbia Pictures, 1947.

———, dir. *Touch of Evil*. Perfs. Charlton Heston, Orson Welles, and Janet Leigh. RKO Pictures, 1958.

Whalen, Tom. "*Film Noir*: Killer Style." *Literature/Film Quarterly* 23.1 (1995): 2–4.

Wheeler, Elizabeth A. *Uncontained: Urban Fiction in Postwar America*. New Brunswick, NJ: Rutgers University Press, 2001.

Wilder, Billy. Interview with Cameron Crowe. *Conversations with Wilder*. By Cameron Crowe. New York: Alfred A. Knopf, 1999.

———, dir. *Double Indemnity*. Perfs. Fred MacMurray, Barbara Stanwyck, Porter Hall, and Edward G. Robinson. Universal, 1944.

———, dir. *Sunset Boulevard*. Perfs. William Holden, Gloria Swanson, and Nancy Olsen. Paramount, 1950.

Willett, Ralph. *The Naked City: Urban Crime Fiction in the USA*. Manchester and New York: Manchester University Press, 1997.

Williams, Raymond. *The Country and the City*. New York: Oxford University Press, 1973.

Wolfe, Peter. *Beams Falling: The Art of Dashiell Hammett*. Bowling Green: Popular, 1980.

Wood, Robin. *Hollywood from Vietnam to Reagan*. New York: Columbia University Press, 1986.

———. "Ideology, genre, auteur." *Film Comment* 13.1 (January/February 1977): 46–51.

Woolrich, Cornell. *"Rear Window" and Other Stories*. New York: Penguin Books, 1984.

Wright, Richard. *The Outsider*. New York: Harper and Brothers Publishing, 1953.

Wyler, William, dir. *The Best Years of Our Lives.* Perfs. Frederic March, Myrna Loy, Harold Russell, and Dana Andrews. Goldwyn, RKO, 1946.

Yogi, Stan. "You Had to Be One or the Other: Oppositions and Reconciliations in John Okada's *No-No Boy.*" *MELUS* 21.2 (1996): 63–77.

Yong Hall, Jasmine. "Jameson, Genre, and Gumshoes: *The Maltese Falcon* as Inverted Romance." *The Cunning Craft: Original Essays on Detective Fiction and Contemporary Literary Theory.* Eds. Ronald G. Walker and June M. Frazier. Macomb: Western Illinois University Press, 1976. 109–119.

Žižek, Slavoj. *Tarrying With the Negative: Kant, Hegel, and the Critique of Pure Ideology.* Durham: Duke University Press, 1993.

INDEX

Abbott, Megan 54, 213nn.8, 9, 214nn.20, 24
abjection 34, 35, 62, 72, 73, 193
Achebe, Chinua, 4
"Acquainted with the Night" (Frost), 51
adventure fiction: British imperial, 3–4, 24; late-Victorian colonial, 4–6, 14–19; American, 19–23; and hard-boiled fiction, 22–87, 133, 169–70; and film noir, 88–105, 171; and postmodern fiction, 161; and Victorian detective fiction, 5–7, 25, 26, 50, 146, 150, 216n.4
"The Adventure of the Empty House" (Doyle), 50
Adventures of Huckleberry Finn (Twain), 167
Africa, 4, 22, 55, 69, 78, 96, 104, 147
African-Americans, 20–21, 59, 84, 101, 111–17, 125, 146–52, 203
Ahn, Philip, 93
Alford, Steven, 216nn.28, 29, 31
alienation effect, 134–36, 145, 148, 164–65, 184. *See also* Brecht, Bertolt
All Shot Up (Himes), 111

All That Heaven Allows, 178
All the King's Men, 3
Allmendinger, Blake, 67, 213
American expansionism/Manifest Destiny, 19–22, 56–76, 100, 103
American Soldier in Love and War, 21
Amis, Suzy, 183
amnesia, 162, 192
Anderson, Paul Thomas, 13, 199, 208–10, 218n.3
Andrews, Dana, 108, 128
angst, 93, 111–12, 125, 145, 172, 175, 177
Anwar, Gabrielle, 207
Appointment With Danger, 203
D'Aries, Donald, R., 209, 218nn.3, 4, 5
"The Arm of Luno Capál" (Becke), 15, 19, 29
Armenian characters, 43, 63, 65, 101–2
Armstrong, Richard, 192
Aronowitz, Stanley, 107, 166
Arsenic and Old Lace, 3
"Arson Plus" (Hammett), 48
Asia, 19, 24, 26, 42, 47–48, 63, 71, 91, 93, 99, 123, 131, 185, 202, 203
Asphalt Jungle, The, 183, 186

235

Auster, Paul, 12, 1.07, 134, 137, 152–62, 165, 195, 216nn.25, 27, 28, 29, 30, 217n.40. See also *The Book of Illusions; Ghosts; Leviathan; The Locked Room; Mr. Vertigo; The New York Trilogy; Oracle Night*
authenticating alienation: and the confidence man, 166–97; and film noir, 88–105; and hard-boiled fiction, 14–87; and postmodernism, 133–65; and returning veteran's noir, 106–32. and the confidence man, 166–97; and community, 198–210; and theories of identity, 2, 7–8.
Ayotte, John, 22

Bad Lieutenant, 13, 199, 206–7
Bad Sleep Well, The, 200
Bakhtin, Mikhail, 137, 152, 154, 215nn.6, 7, 8, 9
Baldwin, Stephen, 182
Balk, Fairuza, 207
"Bar of Common Soap, A" (Becke), 17
Barry, Gene, 200
Barrymore, John, 63
Barthes, Roland, 11, 134–35, 156–57, 167, 179, 185, 205, 215–17nn.3, 36, 38, 216n.1. *See also* reality effect
Baudrillard, Jean, 7, 9, 51, 138, 164–65, 196, 212n.11
Beach, Michael, 202
"The Beach of Falesá, The" (Stevenson), 5
Beaumont, Hugh, 109
Becke, Louis, 4–5, 8, 15–19, 21–25, 27, 29, 37–38, 40, 49, 55, 62, 70, 78, 85, 133, 212. *See also* "The Arm of Luno Capál"; "A Bar of Common Soap"; "Bully Hayes: Pirate of the Pacific"; *By Reef and Palm and The Ebbing of the Tide;* "Chester's Cross"; "Collier: 'the 'Blackbirder'"; "A Dead Loss"; "Deschard of Oneaka"; *The Ebbing of the Tide;* "English Bob"; *His Native Wife;* "An Honor to the Service"; "In the Old Beach-Combing Days"; "Martin of Nitendi"; "The Methodical Mr. Burr of Maduro"; *Pacific Tales; The Pearl Divers of Roncador Reef;* "Prescott of Naura"; "Rangers of the Tia Kau"; "The Revenge of Macy O'Shea"; "Saunderson and the Dynamite"; *South Sea Supercargo;* "A Truly Great Man"; *Under Tropic Skies*
Beechey, Frederick William, 57
Begley, Ed, Sr., 208
Behdad, Ali, 61
Bell, General Franklin, 21
Bendix, William, 94, 109
Benjamin, Walter, 71–72
"Ber-Bulu" (Hammett), 15, 26–32, 36–38, 43, 45, 49, 212n.11
Berresem, Hanjo, 216n.17
Besson, Luc, 218n.2
Best Years of Our Lives, The, 108, 111, 123, 125, 128, 130
Better Homes and Gardens, 1
Biesen, Sheri Chinen, 108, 215n.8
"Big Knock-Over, The" (Hammett), 42, 43, 44, 49, 51, 116
Big Sleep, The (Chandler), 8, 53, 56, 61, 64–66, 68, 70–71, 73–77, 79, 82, 84, 102, 141, 216n.32
Big Sleep, The (Hawks, dir.), 71
Biggers, Earl Derr, 202
Bitzer, Billy, 21
Black Mask, 15, 22–24, 26, 32–33, 47–48, 55
Blade Runner, 162, 187
Blair, John G., 167
Blount, James, H., 21
"Blue, Carbuncle, The" (Doyle), 61
The Blue Dahlia (Chandler), 11, 108–11, 113, 115, 117–18, 123–25, 128, 130, 192
Blue Velvet, 10
Body Heat, 8–9
Bogart, Humphrey, 108, 112

Bogart, Paul, 215n.10
Boime, Albert, 58, 213n.5
The Book of Illusions (Auster), 152
Borde, Raymond, 88, 107–8, 214n.1
borders, 23, 34, 37, 43, 45–46, 48, 49, 51, 54, 64, 71, 87, 89, 92, 162
Bordwell, David, 88
Borges, Jorge Luis, 139, 189
Botting, Fred, 218n.1
boundaries, 16, 19, 25, 32–36, 41–44, 47, 50–51, 62, 64, 66–67, 72–73, 75, 83–84, 90, 131, 137, 146, 151, 153, 156, 159, 163–64, 193, 218n.37
Brackett, Charles, 102
Brackett, Leigh, 118
Brand, Neville, 101
Brando, Marlon, 204
Brantlinger, Patrick, 4–5, 72
Brecht, Bertolt, 134–37. *See also* alienation effect
bricoleur/bricolage, 12, 168, 172, 173, 185
Bridges at Toko Ri, The, 104
Britton, Andrew, 95, 96
Britton, Pamela, 101
Brooks, Phyllis, 90
Brown, Frederic, 87, 168, 172
Bruccoli, Matthew, 55
Bryant, Edwin, 57
Bubley, Esther, 118
"Bully Hayes: Pirate of the Pacific" (Becke), 16
Burroughs, Edgar Rice, 21, 22. *See also* *Tarzan of the Apes*
By Reef and Palm and *The Ebbing of the Tide* (Becke), 16, 212n.4
Byrne, Gabriel, 182, 186

California, 8, 26, 29, 47, 54, 56–58, 60–61, 65–66, 69–70, 72–76, 80, 82, 83, 89, 100, 103, 112–13, 138–40, 173, 212n.9
Cameron, James, 162
Camus, Albert, 19, 100, 147, 156. See also *Le Malentendu*; *The Outsider*; *The Stranger*
Cape Fear (Scorsese, dir.), 12, 166, 173, 174, 177–81, 217nn.20, 21
Cape Fear (Thompson, dir.), 174, 175–78, 217n.14
capitalism, 9, 14, 27, 74, 79, 110, 118, 127, 138, 163, 183
captivity narrative, 20, 24, 39, 41, 46, 68, 84, 94, 98
castaways, 17–18, 29, 69, 78, 170, 171
Cat People, 121
Cawelti, John, 7, 139, 182–83, 211n.7, 212n.17, 213n.22, 218nn.31, 33
"Cellini Chalice, The" (Thompson), 172
Chan, George, 94
Chan Is Missing, 202
Chandler, Raymond, 8, 11, 52–87, 99, 102–3, 109–11, 118, 121, 123–25, 128, 133–34, 138–42, 153–55, 157, 160, 167, 188, 213nn.1, 3, 9, 16, 216nn.28, 33, 216nn.28, 33, 217n.43, 218n.41. See also *The Big Sleep*; *The Blue Dahlia*; *Farewell, My Lovely*; *The High Window*; *The Lady in the Lake*; *The Long Goodbye*; "Red Wind"; "The Tropical Romance"
Charles, Lewis, 147
Chaumeton, Etienne, 88, 92, 107–8, 214n.3, 214n.1
China Gate, 13, 200, 203
Chinese/Chinese-American characters, 15, 43, 47, 49, 63, 71–72, 91, 94, 99, 200, 202, 203
City of Glass (Auster), 152, 216n.29
Claireborne, Walter, 152
"Clean, Well-Lighted Place, A" (Hemingway), 33, 78, 145, 148, 176, 214n.23
Coen, Ethan, 9
Cold War, 123, 214n.2
Collins, Wilkie, 6, 61
commodification, 2, 9, 10, 137–38, 163
community/networks, 2, 13, 23, 24, 70, 79, 80, 99, 122, 131, 165–66, 175,

198–99, 200, 202, 203, 206, 207–10, 214n.23, 218n.2
Conard, Mark T., 218n.1
confidence man/con man, 12, 40, 48, 50, 61, 77–87, 152, 172–74, 177, 179, 184, 166–98
Confidence-Man, His Masquerade, The, (Melville), 167–69
Conrad, Joseph, 4, 17–18, 21–22, 24–25, 27, 38, 55, 69–70, 75–76, 78, 88, 89, 96–97, 104. See also *Heart of Darkness; Lord Jim;* "An Outpost of Progress"
containment/continence, 6, 15, 23–52, 54, 60–87, 106, 133, 147–51
Corbett, Glenn, 200
Cornered, 108
corporeality/embodiment, 10, 18–22, 29, 31, 32, 34–35, 40–47, 48, 51, 62, 63, 64, 68–69, 70, 72, 73, 75–78, 87, 84–85, 102, 110, 116, 121, 133, 146, 162–65, 179, 184, 186–87, 190, 193–94, 212n.16, 213n.9, 214n.20
Cosby, Bill, 201
"Creeping, Siamese, The" (Hammett), 16, 48–49
Crimson Kimono, The, 13, 200–202
Crowe, Cameron, 104
Crying of Lot 49, The (Pynchon), 12, 134, 137–46, 156, 161, 190
Culp, Robert, 201
culture industries/mass culture, 2, 8–10, 20, 80, 81, 131, 138, 184
Custer, George Armstrong, 20
cyberpunk fiction, 12, 162–65

D.O.A., 89, 100–102, 115, 138, 142, 144, 189, 195, 207, 208, 215n.10
Dahl, John, 8
Daly, Carrol John, 23, 81, 188
Dana, Richard Henry, 57. See also *Two Years Before the Mast*
Das, Prasanta, 143
Dassin, Jules, 135, 168, 172
"Dead Loss, A" (Becke), 17

Dead Reckoning, 108, 112, 117, 123
"Dead Yellow Women" (Hammett), 15, 42, 43
Deadly Pursuit, 188
Death of Sardanapalus, The (Delacroix), 186
deconstruction, 13, 18, 107, 114, 137, 139, 143, 152, 170, 187, 198, 203, 204, 205, 206, 216n.28
Delacroix, Eugène, 186. See also *The Death of Sardanapalus.*
De los Santos, Oscar, 216n.28
Del Toro, Benecio, 183
democracy, 19, 110–13, 115–16, 127, 200
De Niro, Robert, 1, 179, 181
Denzin, Norman, 10
Defoe, Daniel, 4. See also *Robinson Crusoe.*
"Deschard of Oneaka" (Becke), 17–19, 21, 49, 85, 212n.5
Desperado, 11
detectives/detective fiction: hard-boiled, 2–3, 7–8, 10, 11, 13, 14–16, 22–52, 53–88, 90, 97, 99, 106–7, 110, 111; as police, 93, 95, 108, 119–22, 147–51, 188–207; and postmodernism, 138–65; Victorian, 5–7, 16, 25, 26, 35, 43, 44, 50, 54, 71, 87, 133, 138, 146, 150, 153, 155, 211n.9, 213nn.8, 9, 15, 22, 23, 216n.24
The Devil Thumbs a Ride, 204
Dick, Phillip K., 162
Dickens, Charles, 6
Die Hard, 188
Dieterle, William, 135, 189, 208
Dime Detective, 60, 64
Dirty Harry, 188–90
disease, 6, 54, 146–50
Diski, Jenny, 175–76, 217nn.10, 218n.26
Dixon, Robert, 4–5, 15, 38
Dmytryk, Edward, 93, 124, 125, 128
Do Androids Dream of Electric Sheep (Dick), 162

domesticity, 19, 32–37, 68, 69, 83, 87, 98, 101, 115, 116, 118, 120, 121, 122, 125, 127–28, 130, 171, 174, 177, 178, 180, 181, 190
Donnie Brasco, 13, 198–99, 205–6, 210
Double Indemnity (Cain), 194
Double Indemnity (Wilder, dir.), 9, 103, 108, 114, 192
Douglass, Paul, 147
Dower, John W., 123, 215n.9
Dowling, Doris, 109
Doyle, Arthur Conan, 6, 16, 35, 44, 50, 54, 61, 71, 87, 133, 146, 147. *See also* "The Adventure of the Empty House"; "The Blue Carbuncle"; "The Dying Detective"; *The Sign of Four*; *A Study in Scarlet*; "The Speckled Band"
"Dr. Ludwig Schwalbe, South Sea Savant" (Becke), 17
Dragnet, 200
Dugan, Dennis, 178
Durgnat, Raymond, 211nn.5, 7
Durham, Philip, 37, 213n.8
Dussere, Erik, 8
Dyer, Richard, 187, 188, 190, 218nn.38,40,42
"The Dying Detective" (Doyle), 50, 146

Eagleton, Terry, 7, 11, 145
Eastwood, Clint, 188
Ebbing of the Tide, The (Becke), 5, 16, 212n.4
Edelson, Cheryl, 211n.8
El Mariachi, 11
elegy/elegiac, 52, 54, 68, 75, 86, 95, 182, 184
Ellison, Ralph, 110
empire/imperialism, 3–7, 12–13, 16, 19–22, 24–25, 27–28, 30, 32, 36–38, 50, 54, 64, 66–68, 72–73, 77, 89–99, 102–5, 133, 211nn.7, 9, 212nn.3, 15, 213n.14, 216n.24
endo-colonial/endo-oriental spaces, 6, 37, 39, 42, 44, 64, 68–70, 89, 98, 101, 102, 139, 143, 201, 212n.15
Enlightenment, 5, 58, 90, 91, 110, 113, 127, 137, 150, 151, 170, 174
Europe/European, 4, 6, 16–22, 42, 47, 58, 89, 93, 97, 108, 116, 127, 129, 148
Evers, Richard, 16, 17
Executioners, The (MacDonald), 173–76
exotic/exoticism, 5, 6, 8, 15–16, 19, 21–23, 26, 29, 31–42, 44–47, 50, 51, 55, 60–64, 68, 69, 71–74, 76–78, 82, 87, 89, 90, 92, 94, 96, 98, 100–103, 115, 136, 146–48, 150, 161, 171, 186, 193, 212n.16
Expressionism, 87, 106, 134, 135, 143, 147

Fabulous Clipjoint, The (Brown), 168, 172
Fallen Angel, 159, 217
Fallen Sparrow, The (Hughes), 119, 215n.5
Far Wandering Men (Russell), 22
"Farewell Murder, The" (Hammett), 16, 47–48, 50
Farewell, My Lovely (Chandler), 62, 64, 142
femme fatale, 29, 32, 44, 46, 61, 71, 75, 77, 80, 82, 92, 94, 98, 99, 101, 102, 104, 115–18, 121–23, 126, 130, 162, 171, 172, 191, 203, 209, 214, 215. *See also* women
Ferrara, Abel, 13, 199, 206–7
Figgis, Mike, 8
film/radio adaptation, 71, 95–97, 122, 126, 171, 174, 177, 203
film noir: and adventure genre, 3, 8, 88–105, 171; community in, 198–210; confidence man in, 166–97; and genre theory, 2–3; and hard-boiled fiction, 8, 14–87; postmodernist parodies of, 133–65; and realism, 134–35; and WWII returning veterans, 106–32
Fincher, David, 12, 173, 187–89

Fine, David, 60
"Fire Walker, The" (Russell), 22, 37
Fisher, Phillip, 22
Fitzgerald, F. Scott, 102. See also *The Great Gatsby*
Fleder, Gary, 13, 199, 207–8
Fontana, Ernest, 54, 69, 74
For Whom the Bell Tolls (Hemingway), 191
Foster, Hal, 136
Fotsch, Paul Mason, 215n.12
Foucault, Michel, 5, 12, 133–34
"Fourth Man, The" (Russell), 22
Freeman, Morgan, 187
French New Wave, 10
frontier, 7, 8. 31, 39, 48, 51, 54, 61, 64, 100, 140, 161, 213n.8
Frost, Robert, 51
Fuller, Samuel, 13, 199–203

Gaddis, William, 170
gangsters, 108, 109, 152, 154, 179, 204, 205, 207
Garcia, Andy, 207
Gates, Henry Louis, Jr., 146, 148, 151
Gault, Campbell William, 43
Geherin, David, 174, 217n.8
Gein, Ed, 189
Ghosts (Auster), 12, 134, 152–53, 157, 161, 216–17nn.29, 41
gift exchange, 79, 80–82, 86, 214n.22. See also Mauss, Marcel
Gilbert, Sandra M., 214n.11
Gilda, 122
Gill, Pat, 218n.39
"Girl With the Silver Eyes, The" (Hammett), 45
Giroux, Henry, 107, 166
GLAD, 1, 211
"Gold Bug, The" (Poe), 6
Gomez, Thomas, 94
Goodis, David, 192
Goodwin, James, 199
Goulart, Ron, 217
Goulding, Edmund, 171

Gravity's Rainbow (Pynchon), 137–38, 215n.12
Great Gatsby, The (Fitzgerald), 102
Green, Martin, 3, 4
Greene, Graham, 96
Gresham, William Lindsay, 12, 79, 87, 168–71, 179, 194, 196. See also *Nightmare Alley*
Grifters, The (Thompson), 168, 172–73, 189, 197
Gubar, Susan, 214n.11
"Gun Metal" (Russell), 22
Guy Named Joe, A, 114
Gwyneth Paltrow, 190, 209

Hall, Phillip Baker, 209
Hammett, Dashiell, 14–52, 54–56, 60–63, 67, 69, 72, 75, 77, 79, 81, 87, 88, 90, 92, 99, 100, 115, 116, 123, 131, 133–34, 143, 151, 155, 193, 196, 200, 206, 212nn.1, 11, 213nn.18, 1, 216n.28. See also "Arson Plus"; "Ber-Bulu"; "The Big Knock-Over"; "The Creeping Siamese"; "Dead Yellow Women"; "The Farewell Murder"; "The Girl With the Silver Eyes"; "The House in Turk Street"; "The Man Who Killed Dan Odams"; *The Maltese Falcon*; "Nightmare Town"; "106,000 Blood Money"; "The Road Home"; *Red Harvest*; "Ruffian's Wife"; "Slippery Fingers"; "The Whosis Kid"
Hanson, Curtis, 9
Hantke, Steffen, 187, 218n.37
hard-boiled fiction. See adventure fiction; detectives/detection; film noir.
Hard Eight, 13, 199, 208–9
Harris, Joel Chandler, 59
Harrowitz, Nancy, 211
Haut, Woody, 11, 118, 174, 214n.2, 215nn.6, 7, 217n.7
Hawaiians, 43, 55
Hawthorne, Nathaniel, 143. See also "Young Goodman Brown"

Hayashi, Marc, 202
Hayden, Sterling, 183, 186
Hayes, Bully, 16
Hayles, N. Katherine, 142, 216n.19
Hayworth, Rita, 97
"Head-Hunter, The" (Henry), 21
Heart of Darkness (Conrad), 4, 15, 18, 22, 29, 54, 95–97
Heche, Anne, 205
Hedaya, Dan, 184
heist formula, 36, 166, 182, 184, 186–87, 204
Hellman, Lillian, 14
Hell's Half Acre, 122
Helmore, Tom, 173
Hemingway, Ernest, 55, 77–79, 105, 145, 191, 216n.23. *See also* "A Clean, Well-Lighted Place"; *For Whom the Bell Tolls*
Henty, G. A., 4, 24
Hermann, Bernard, 176
Heston, Charlton, 208
"Hibiscus and Homicide" (Gault), 43
Hickey and Boggs, 201
High Sierra, 164
High Window, The (Chandler), 213n.2
Himes, Chester, 11, 106–8, 111–18, 122–23, 129, 131, 133, 146, 203, 214n.2. *See also All Shot Up; If He Hollers Let Him Go*
Hirsch, Foster, 10, 106, 131, 136, 181–82, 187, 207, 209, 211n.2, 216n.34, 218nn.38, 3, 4, 5
His Native Wife (Becke), 17
Hitchcock, Alfred, 141, 155, 173, 191, 217n.21
Hitchens, Dolores, 118
Hite, Molly, 216n.14
Hoberman, J., 173, 177, 217nn.10, 18, 218nn.3, 18, 23, 26, 27
Holden, Stephen, 11
Holden, William, 102, 104, 105,
Hollywood, 2, 63, 64, 79, 88, 89, 95, 102, 103, 109–10, 117, 125, 127–29, 131, 135, 182, 191, 193, 201
Hopper, Dennis, 8

Hopper, Edward, 208. *See also Nighthawks*
"House in Turk Street, The" (Hammett), 15, 42, 45, 47, 63
House of Bamboo, 13, 200
House of Games, 8
Hudson, Rock, 178
Hughes, Dorothy, 11, 106, 107, 108, 111, 118–23, 123, 131, 133, 215n.7
Huston, John, 108, 123
Huston, Walter, 90–91
Hutcheon, Linda, 2, 11, 136–37, 182, 211n.3, 215n.5, 216n.28

identity/subjectivity: and colonial adventure fiction, 4–5, 14–22; in hard-boiled fiction, 22–87, 111–32, 166–76; in film noir, 88–105, 107–10, 166–97, 166–210; in postmodern fiction, 133–65; and postmodern theory, 8–10, 13, 173, 196–99. *See also* alienation; postmodernism
Idriess, Ion, 5
If He Hollers Let Him Go (Himes), 11, 107, 111–17, 132, 215n.4
In A Lonely Place, 11, 107, 119, 121, 122, 132, 215n.5
India/Indians, 6, 53, 54, 90, 104, 117
Indians (Native Americans), 15, 20, 45, 50–51, 63–64, 66, 100, 117, 214n.10
insignificance/insignificant notation, 135, 164, 179, 184, 185, 186, 205, 215n.3
Irish characters, 44, 46, 70, 99

Jackson, Samuel L., 209
Jacobowitz, Florence, 217n.5
Jameson, Fredric, 8, 9, 11, 41, 136, 185, 212
Japan, 124, 126, 128, 199
Japanese-Americans, 112–14, 123–31, 200–201

Jeter, K. W., 12, 133–34, 137, 162–66, 170, 194–95. See also *Noir*.
Johnson, Rian, 11
"Jungle Shadows" (Ivan Ignatieff), 22

Kaplan, Amy, 21
Kaplan, E. Ann, 29, 88, 96, 99, 212n.5, 7, 8, 9, 214n.9
Kasdan, Lawrence, 8, 9
Kazan, Elia, 12, 146–51
Keep, Christopher, 6
Keitel, Harvey, 205, 207
Kevorkian, Martin, 213n.19
Key Largo, 108, 112
Killers, The, 194
Killing, The, 135, 182–83
Kimura, Isao, 199
Kipling, Rudyard, 4, 17, 21, 24. See also "Mandalay"
Kiss of Death, 146
Klawans, Stuart, 179, 217n.22
"Knife, The" (Russell), 22
Koch, Edward, 206
Kolker, Robert Phillip, 177, 217n.17
Kristeva, Julia, 44, 159, 217n.39
Krutnik, Frank, 95, 214nn.1, 4
Kubrick, Stanley, 135, 178, 182
Kurosawa, Akira, 13, 188, 199–200

LA Confidential, 9
Ladd, Alan, 109
Lady in the Lake, The (Chandler), 53, 214n.20
Lady From Shanghai, The, 89, 95–97, 202, 215n.4, 5
Lake, Veronica, 110
Lang, Fritz, 136, 217
Las Sergas de Esplandián (Montalvo), 56
Las Vegas, 208–9
Laven, Arnold, 189
Lawton, Harry, 214n.10
Le Malentendu (Camus), 19
Le Samurai, 10

Lean, David, 105
Leave It To Beaver, 109
Lee, Rachel, 32
Leibman, Nina, 175–77, 217nn.11, 13, 16
Leibovitz, Annie, 1, 7
Letts, Vanessa, 179, 217n.21, 218n.29
Leviathan (Auster), 152
Lewis, Juliette, 177
Life and Adventures of Joaquin Murieta (Ridge), 60
Limerick, Patricia Nelson, 60, 67
Lindh, John Walker, 31, 212
Lindfors, Viveca, 208
Little, Frank, 14
Little, William G., 193
Locked Room, The (Auster), 152–53, 216nn.29, 30
London, 50, 85, 97, 172
Long Goodbye, The (Chandler) 56, 64, 77–86, 167, 170, 214n.23
Look Homeward Angel (Wolfe), 177
Lord Jim (Conrad), 22, 78, 104
Los Angeles, 57–61, 63–67, 69–70, 74, 77–78, 85, 101–2, 109–10, 112, 150, 165, 200, 202, 208
Losey, Joseph, 189
Lost Horizon, 185
Lott, Eric, 88
Loza, Suzanne, 211n.4
Lucas, Blake, 217n.14
Luez, Laurette, 101
Lummis, Charles Fletcher, 58
Lupino, Ida, 164
Lynch, David, 10, 11, 182, 197

M, 136
Macao, 89–90, 93–95, 98
MacDonald, John D., 87, 138, 141, 173–76, 180. See also *The Executioners*
Macdonald, Ross, 140, 141, 218n.41
MacMurray, Fred, 103
MacShane, Frank, 77
Magnum PI, 202
Maguire, Dorothy, 125
Malaya, 123

Maltese Falcon, The (Hammett), 15–16, 34, 37, 42, 47–48, 51, 61, 88, 136, 152, 212
Mamet, David, 8
"Man Who Killed Dan Odams, The" (Hammett), 37
"Mandalay" (Kipling), 24
"Mandarin's Jade" (Chandler), 56, 60–65, 68, 69, 71, 84, 102
Mankiewicz, Joseph L., 123, 192
"Martin of Nitendi" (Becke), 18, 49, 85
masculinity, 5, 22, 33, 38, 61, 71, 82, 97, 107, 126, 193, 130
Maté, Rudolph, 8, 89, 100–102, 142–43, 207–8
Mature, Victor, 91
Maugham, Somerset, 189. See also *Of Human Bondage*
Mauss, Marcel, 79, 214n.22
Mavity, Nancy Barr, 32
Mazurki, Mike, 91, 172, 208
McCann, Sean, 22–24, 26, 31, 49, 56, 67–68, 75, 81, 83–84, 86, 116, 213nn.11, 16, 18, 214n.20, 215n.3
McClintock, Anne, 32, 33, 34, 37, 42, 67, 147, 213n.14
McFeely, John, 202
McRobbie, Angela, 173, 177, 217nn.4, 19, 218n.28
Melville, Herman, 27, 38, 75, 159, 167–69, 217n.40
Melville, Jean-Pierre, 10, 208
Memento, 12, 173, 191–93, 195–96, 210, 218n.46
Metzler, Jim, 202
Mexico, 19, 46, 48, 59, 80, 82, 85, 119
Mexican/Mexican-American characters, 20, 57, 59, 66–67, 82–5, 113, 115, 117
Meyers, Jeffrey, 214n.13
Miller, D. A., 5
Miller, Frank, 11
Miller, Frank A., 58
Miller, Henry, 179
miscegenation 4, 16, 19, 22, 24, 27, 30, 92, 102

Mitchum, Robert, 1–2, 7, 93, 94, 108, 112, 125, 159–60, 166, 176, 179–80, 217n.14
Mitsuda, Kristi, 11
modernism, 7–8, 14, 23, 50, 54, 77–79, 86, 96–97, 102, 107, 136–37, 139, 153, 155–56, 159, 163, 166–68, 172–74, 189, 190, 192, 196, 198, 216n.28
Montalvo, Garci Rodríguez de, 56–57, 60, 65,
Montgomery, Robert, 215n.5
Morgan, Harry, 20
Moriel, Ayala, 8
Mosley, Walter, 203
Moss, Carrie-Anne, 191
Mostel, Zero, 147
Moy, Wood, 202
Mr. Vertigo (Auster), 152
Mumbo Jumbo (Reed), 12, 134, 146, 148–51
Munson, Ona, 91
Murder, My Sweet, 93
"Murders in the Rue Morgue, The" (Poe), 6, 35, 44, 211
Murphet, Julian, 89
Musketeers of Pig Alley, The, 179
Musser, Charles, 21, 212n.8

Naremore, James, 2, 9–10, 89, 96, 110, 136, 211–12, 215, 217
Native Son (Wright), 114
naturalism, 99, 119, 139, 167, 168, 172, 175, 180, 204
neo-noir, 8–11, 181, 187, 211nn.2, 10
Neely, Richard, 192, 218n.43. See also *Shattered*
New Orleans, 147–51
New York City, 15, 23–25, 93, 96–97, 99, 155, 168, 183, 206
New York Trilogy, The (Auster), 152–53, 159, 216n.28
Newell, Mike, 13, 198–99, 203, 205–6, 210
Nicholson, Colin, 140, 216n.16

Nicholson, Jack, 178
Nietzsche, Friedrich, 179. See also *Thus Spake Zarathustra; Will to Power*
Nightfall (Goodis), 192
Nighthawks (Hopper), 208
Nightmare Alley, 171
Nightmare Alley (Gresham), 12, 79, 168–72, 179, 189, 194, 197
"Nightmare Town" (Hammett), 14–15, 37–41, 51, 116
nihilism, 8, 10, 107, 130, 145, 163, 166–67, 173, 209. See also postmodernism
No-No Boy (Okada), 11, 106–7, 123, 125–32
Noir. See film noir
Nolan, Christopher, 12, 173, 191–95, 210
nostalgia, 8–12, 61, 67, 70, 136, 138, 167
Novak, Kim, 173
Nyman, Jopi, 212n.2

O'Brien, Edmond, 194, 204, 206
Oceania/the Pacific, 5, 14–19, 26, 27, 29, 30, 37, 39–40, 43, 55, 78, 93, 109–10, 123, 126, 131, 212n.4
Odets, Clifford, 102
The Odyssey, 98, 167
Of Human Bondage (Maugham), 189
Ogdon, Bethany, 62, 212nn.2, 13, 16, 213nn.20, 7, 9
Okada, John, 11, 106–8, 111, 123–31, 133. See also *No-No Boy*
"In the Old Beach-Combing Days" (Becke), 17
Oliver, Kelly, 90
One False Move, 13, 199, 202–3, 206, 207
"106,000 Blood Money" (Hammett), 46, 51
Oracle Night (Auster), 152
orientalism, 6, 12, 28, 32, 37, 45, 48, 54, 60–61, 63, 71, 74, 91–93, 98, 100, 101–2, 104, 123, 161, 184–86, 212n.12, 214n.2, 218n.35. See also Said, Edward
other/otherness, 7, 11–13, 16, 26, 34–35, 42–43, 49–51, 51, 57, 62–65, 68, 70, 81, 87–89, 96, 110, 117, 119–20, 133, 142–44, 149, 157, 163, 165, 178–79, 181, 196, 198–99, 203, 207, 208, 210, 212n.2, 216n.28
Otis, Laura, 6, 114, 216n.24
"Outpost of Progress, An" (Conrad), 38, 70
The Outsider (Camus), 156
The Outsider (Wright), 111

Pacific Tales (Becke), 212n.4
Pacino, Al, 198
Page, Thomas Nelson, 59
Palance, Walter Jack, 147
Pall, Gloria, 200
Palmetto, 8
Palminteri, Charles, 182
Panek, Leroy Lad, 212n.11
Panic in the Streets, 12, 146–52
panopticism, 5, 155
Pantoliano, Joe, 191
Paravisini Lizabeth, 146
parody. See postmodernism
Paxton, Bill, 202
Pearl Divers of Roncador Reef, The (Becke), 5, 16
Peck, Gregory, 180
Peckinpah, Sam, 105, 163, 183
Penn, Arthur, 201
Penn, Chris, 204
Peterson, Herman, 22
Philippines/Filipinos, 15, 16, 20–22, 26–27, 30, 43, 75, 91, 123
Phillip Baker Hall, 209
Place, Janey, 176, 214, 217n.12
Poe, Edgar Allan, 5, 16, 35, 44, 54, 71, 87, 133, 211n.8, 213n.22. See also "The Gold Bug"; "The Murders in the Rue Morgue"
Polan, Dana, 119, 121–22

INDEX / **245**

Polanski, Roman, 8
police/cops, 5, 6, 15, 16, 25–6, 82, 86, 90, 93, 95, 108–9, 117, 120, 144, 147–48, 150–51, 154, 156, 166, 169, 182–83, 186, 188, 194, 200, 204, 206–7; buddy cop formula, 120, 152, 180, 182–83, 187–88, 199–207
Polk, Dora Beale, 33, 212n.10, 213n.4
Porfirio, Robert, 100
Porter, Jean, 127
postmodernism: and alienation effect, 134–37, 145, 148, 164, 165, 184, 215n.4; and film noir, 9–11, 166–97; and parody, 11, 12, 137, 148, 149, 150, 162, 184; and the novel, 12, 133–65; and theories of identity, 2, 7–8, 86, 107, 166, 173, 196–99; and nihilism, 8, 11, 107, 145, 167, 173, 196, 197, 209, 210
Postlethwaite, Pete, 183, 185
Power, Tyrone, 171
Pratt, Mary Louise, 31, 110. *See also* contact zone
Preminger, Otto, 206
"Prescott of Naura" (Becke), 18
private detective/private eye, 118, 138, 144, 146, 150, 152, 153, 155, 160, 166, 178, 203, 216n.12. *See also* detectives
Private Hell 36, 188, 199
Problem Child, 178
The Professional, 218n.2
Psycho, 141
Pulp Fiction, 2, 10
pulps, 2, 10, 22, 24, 54, 74, 157, 160, 168, 174, 215n.7
Pursued, 3
Pushover, 206
Putz, Manfred, 216n.18
Pynchon, Thomas, 12, 107, 134, 137–41, 144–45, 156, 162, 165, 189, 194. *See also The Crying of Lot 49; Gravity's Rainbow; V.; Vineland*

Quine, Richard, 206

Rabinowitz, Paula, 11, 110, 111, 118
Rafferty, Terrence, 173, 179, 217nn.2, 14
"Rangers of the Tia Kau" (Becke), 25
Ray, Nicholas, 122
realism, 8, 9, 12–14, 63, 106, 132, 134–36, 147–48, 153, 156, 164–65, 166, 168–69, 172–73, 177, 179, 184–86, 188, 196, 204. *See also* film noir
reality effect, 134–36, 147–48, 164–65, 179, 184–85, 205, 215n.4. *See also* Barthes, Roland
Rear Window, 155
Rear Window (Woolrich), 155–56
Red Harvest (Hammett), 15, 37–38, 40, 90
Red Rock West, 8
"Red Wind" (Chandler), 60–61
Reed, Ishmael, 12, 134, 137, 146–51, 155, 162, 165
reflexivity, 31, 63, 68, 69, 78, 79, 82, 86, 106, 135–37, 146–49, 152–53, 164–65, 177–79, 182, 184, 187, 192, 205, 208, 217n.40. *See also* alienation effect; postmodernism
Reservoir Dogs, 13, 199, 204–6, 218n.1
Richardson, Carl, 134, 135, 215n1, 2
Ride the Pink Horse (Hughes), 108, 119, 159, 215n.5
Ridge, John Rollin, 60
Riesman, David, 212n.9
Ritter, John, 178
"Road Home, The" (Hammett), 15, 23–26, 28, 31–32, 36–38, 47–50, 206
Robinson, Edward G., 112
Robinson Crusoe (Defoe), 4
Robson, Mark, 104
The Rockford Files, 202
Rodriguez, Robert, 11
Roemheld, Heinz, 98
Rogue Cop, 206
Rohmer, Sax, 32
Roosevelt, Franklin Delano (FDR), 124
Roosevelt, Theodore, 20, 33, 77
Roth, Tim, 204

Rowe, John Carlos, 211n.9, 213n.6
Rowland, Roy, 206
"Ruffian's Wife" (Hammett), 15, 32–34, 36–38, 41, 47, 67, 72
Run of the Arrow, 200
Russell, Harold, 128
Russell, Jane, 94
Russell, John, 22, 37–38, 40, 55, 78, 94, 104, 206. See also *Far Wandering Men;* "The Fire Walker"; "The Fourth Man"; "Gun Metal"; *In Dark Places;* "The Knife"; "The Price of His Head"; *Where the Pavement Ends*
Rzepka, Charles J., 53, 71, 73, 213n.8, 12, 13, 214 n.19

Sahay, Amrohini, 218n.46
Said, Edward, 16, 91, 185, 212n.3, 12, 214n.2, 218n.35. See also orientalism
San Francisco, 8, 15, 42–44, 46, 49, 98–101, 139, 143–44, 202
"Saunderson and the Dynamite" (Becke), 17
savage/savagery, 4, 6, 7, 15–17, 19, 20–22, 28–32, 36, 38, 39, 42–47, 49, 47, 56, 57, 60, 61, 63, 64, 69, 72–77, 80, 82, 84, 97–99, 105, 110, 117, 123, 169, 213n.8
Scarlet Street, 217
Schrader, Paul, 108
Schrag, Calvin O., 13, 173, 196–99
Schwab, Gabriele, 164
Scott, Lizbeth, 208
Scorsese, Martin, 1, 12, 166, 173, 174, 177–81, 194, 217n.21, 218n.24
Scruggs, Charles, 203
Semi-tropical California (Truman), 8, 56–58, 65–66, 73–76, 83
serial killers, 119–22, 187–90, 199
Serpico, 188
Seven, 12, 173, 181, 187–91, 195, 199
sexuality, 10, 18, 26, 28–29, 35, 42, 45, 60, 114–18, 129, 174, 212n.3

Shakespeare, William, 4. See also *The Tempest*
Shattered (Neely), 192
Shaviro, Steven, 163–64, 215n.11
Shimura, Takashi, 200
Sign of Four, The (Doyle), 6, 44, 50
Silver, Alain, 8, 100, 138, 211n.10, 216n.13
Simon, Carly, 8
"Simple Art of Murder, The" (Chandler), 53–55, 68, 213n.2, 217n.43
Sin City, 11
Singer, Bryan, 12, 173, 182–84, 187, 205, 218n.34
Siodmak, Robert, 194
Sirk, Doulgass, 178
Skenazy, Paul, 42, 213n.1, 214n.19
Slade, Caroline, 118
Sledge, E. B., 123, 215n16. See also *With the Old Breed, at Peleliu and Okinawa*
"Slippery Fingers" (Hammett), 48, 51
Slotkin, Richard, 7, 15, 19–20, 22, 37, 50, 212n.6, 7, 213n.24
Smith, General Jacob, 20
Sniper, The, 189
"Snows of Kilimanjaro, The" (Hemingway), 78
Sobchack, Vivian, 129, 162
South Sea Supercargo (Becke), 212n.4
Spacey, Kevin, 182, 187
Spanos, William, 5
"Speckled Band, The" (Doyle), 35
Spillane, Mickey, 171, 188
Springer, Claudia, 162
Spurr, David, 44, 45, 213n.21
Stanley, Henry Morton, 69
The Steel Helmet, 200
Stern, Lesley, 218n.24
Sternberg, Joseph von, 8, 90, 93, 100, 123
Stevenson, Robert Louis, 4, 5, 17, 18, 21, 24, 27, 55, 70, 78. See also "The Beach of Falesá"; *The Strange Case of Dr. Jekyll and Mr. Hyde*
Stewart, James, 173

Stoddard, Charles Warren, 78
Stoddard, Theodore Lothrop, 21
Stoneman, General George, 65–67, 74
Stormy Monday, 8
The Strange Case of Dr. Jekyll and Mr. Hyde (Stevenson), 18
Stranger, The (Camus), 100
Stray Dog, 13, 188, 199–200
Street of Chance, 108
Strick, Wesley, 173, 177, 180
Study in Scarlet, A (Doyle), 6, 50
Sunset Boulevard, 89, 100, 102–5, 115
Sunset Magazine, 22, 32, 33
Swanson, Gloria, 103
Swope, Richard, 146, 151

Tanner, Tony, 138
Tarantino, Quentin, 10, 11, 13, 163, 199, 203–6, 218n.1
Tarzan of the Apes (Burroughs), 21–22, 33
tattooing, 6, 18, 19, 41, 44, 51, 76, 77, 163, 169, 170, 179, 191, 193, 194
Taxi Driver, 1
technology of the self, 12, 13, 133–34, 162, 164, 165, 195, 196. *See also* Foucault, Michel
Telotte, J. P., 99, 182
The Tempest (Shakespeare), 4
Tetzlaff, Ted, 155
Things to Do in Denver When You're Dead, 13, 199, 207–8
Third Man, The, 96
This Gun For Hire, 108
Thomas, David, 213n.3
Thomas, Nicholas, 16
Thompson, Jim, 172, 197. *See also* "The Cellini Chalice"; *The Grifters*
Thompson, Jon, 146, 211n.8
Thompson, Kristen, 217n.20
Thompson, Lee J., 173–78
Thornton, Billy Bob, 202
Thorpe, Richard, 123
Thus Spake Zarathustra (Nietzsche), 179

Tierney, Gene, 91, 172
Tierny, Lawrence, 204
Till the End of Time, 93, 108, 112, 123–28, 130
Tobolowsky, Stephen, 194
Todorov, Tvetzan, 146
Torgovnick, Marianna, 214
Touch of Evil, 195
Tourneur, Jacques, 12, 88, 121, 160
Tracey, Grant, 200, 201
Trigo, Benigno, 90, 99, 215n.4
"Tropical Romance, The" (Chandler), 52, 54–56, 61, 74–75, 84
"Truly Great Man, A" (Becke), 212n.4
Truman, Benjamin Cummings, 8, 56–61, 65–67, 69, 72–74, 77, 82–83. *See also Semi-tropical California.*
The Turning Point, 135
Tysh, Chris, 216n.26

Under Tropic Skies (Becke), 16
Usual Suspects, The, 12, 173, 181–84, 187, 191

V. (Pynchon), 140, 144, 216n.20
Vernet, Marc, 131, 215n.17,
Vertigo, 152, 173, 191
Victoria's Secret, 2
Vidor, King, 122
Vineland (Pynchon), 137–38
Virilio, Paul, 212n.15

Walken, Christopher, 207,
Walker, Andrew Kevin, 187–88
Walker, William, 20
Wallace, Edgar, 70
Wallace, Richard, 215n.5
Walsh, Raoul, 164, 195
Wang, Wayne 202
war: Civil War, 99, 168; Cold War, 123, 214n2; Korean, 200; Philippine-American, 20–22, 27, 30, 43, 123; Spanish American, 20–22; Spanish

Civil, 99, 168; U.S./Mexican, 20, 57, 65–67; Vietnam, 201, 203; WWII, 21, 43, 77–86, 106–132, 136, 199
Ward, Elizabeth, 201
Watson, Robert M., 142, 216n.21
Webster, Daniel, 38
Weekend's End, 3
Welles, Orson, 8, 88–89, 95–100, 133, 202
West, Nathanael, 102
Whalen, Tom, 10
Where the Pavement Ends (Russell), 22, 214n.21
Where the Sidewalk Ends, 206
White Heat, 195, 203
"White Tents" (Ayotte), 22
Whitman, Walt, 159
"Whosis Kid, The" (Hammett), 15, 42, 44–45, 51
Widmark, Richard, 146–47, 172
The Wild Bunch, 105, 183
Wilder, Billy, 8–9, 89, 100, 102–5, 133
Willett, Ralph, 212nn.1,15
Williams, Bill, 125
Williams, Cynda, 202
Willie Boy A Desert Manhunt (Lawton), 214n.10
Wilson, Scott, 218
The Window, 155

With the Old Breed, at Peleliu and Okinawa (Sledge), 81
women: as femme fatale, 29, 32, 44, 46, 61, 71, 75, 77, 80, 82, 92, 94, 98–99, 101–2, 104, 115–18, 121–23, 126, 130, 162, 171, 172, 191, 203, 209, 214, 215; as domestic angel; 29, 32, 33, 36, 45, 46, 67, 68, 72, 84, 97, 101, 115–17, 121, 122, 123, 171; as hard-boiled/noir protagonists, 32–38, 118–123
Wood, Robin, 181, 215
Woolrich, Cornell, 155–56, 216nn.34, 35
Wright, Richard, 110–11, 114
Wyler, William, 108
Wyman, Jane, 178

Yogi, Stan, 124, 131, 215
Yojimbo, 200
"Young Goodman Brown" (Hawthorne), 143

Zbysko, Stanislaus, 172
Žižek, Slavoj, 3, 162, 174, 181, 192, 218n.44